The Cruise

Cici Farmer

PARKER
HAYDEN
MEDIA

eBook ISBN: 978-1-950349-65-4
Print ISBN: 978-1-950349-66-1

Parker Hayden Media
5740 N. Carefree Circle, Ste 120-1
Colorado Springs, CO 80917

This is a work of fiction. Names, characters, places and incidents are either the products of the author's imagination or are used fictitiously. Any resemblance to actual persons (living or dead), events or locations is entirely coincidental.

Cover: LB Hayden
Art credits:
Woman on beach: netfalls/DepositPhotos
Dog on beach: pavlo.baliukh@gmail.com/DepositPhotos
Beach: wing-wing/DepositPhotos
Ship: db-rus/DepositPhotos

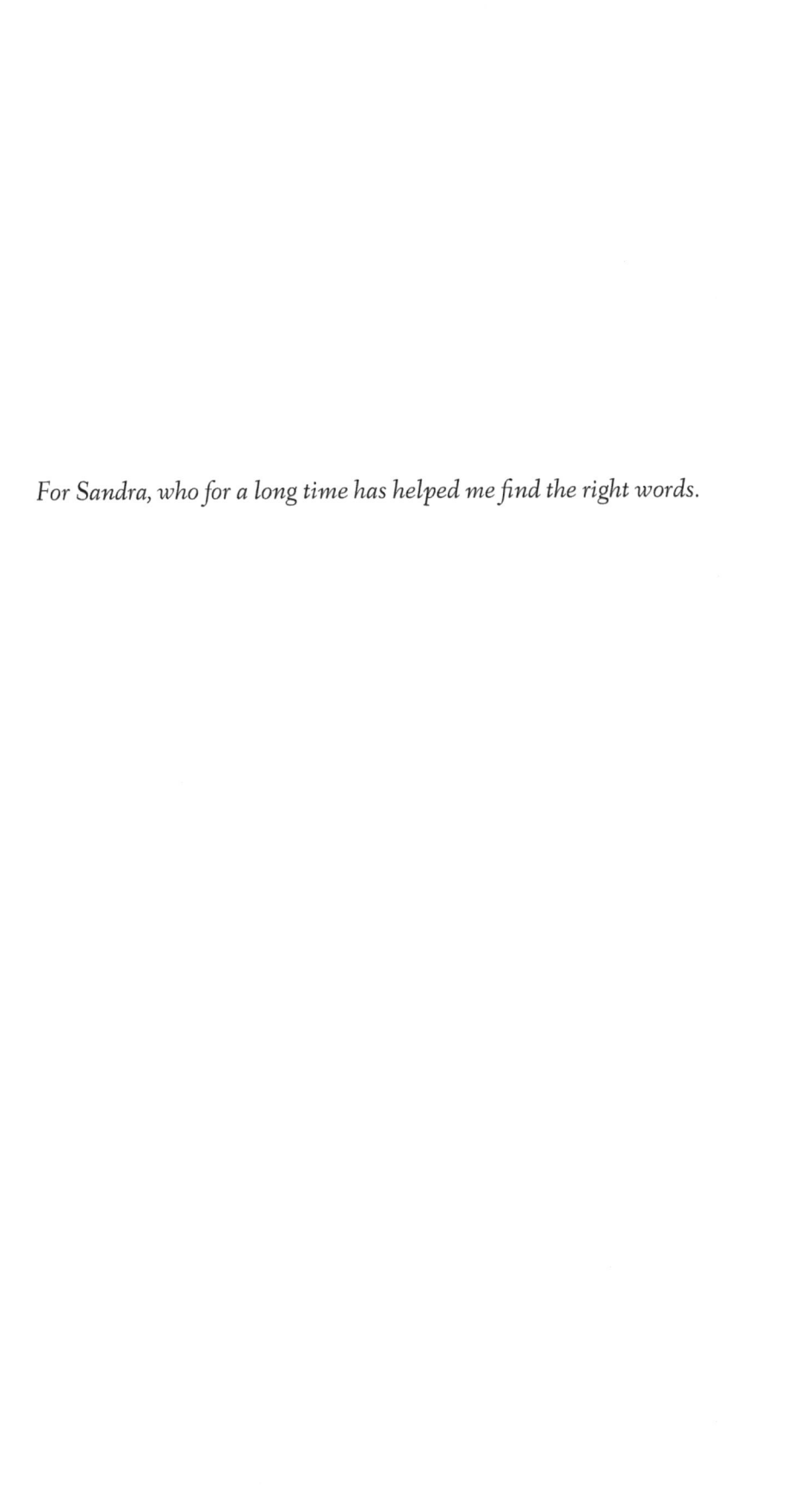

For Sandra, who for a long time has helped me find the right words.

Chapter One

I woke, like most every day, when I heard the old pipes thump as Joe turned the water off and the rattle as he slid the shower curtain back.

I cracked one eye and could just see him across the lump of my knees and my feet under the covers, through the open doorway to our bathroom, and I watched as he pulled his towel off the rack and started to dry himself roughly. I felt a little like a voyeur, which I supposed I was, watching him. Steam spilled out into the still dim bedroom.

He scrubbed himself with the towel as if he were attempting to remove barnacles. Men were so different from women; I dried myself as gently and carefully as if I were handling a piece of ripe fruit. I thought Joe might take off a layer of skin before he wrapped the towel around his hips. I could hear bits of some song. "King of the Road," I thought. Only Joe would sing Roger Miller at the butt crack of dawn.

I saw him glance in the full-length mirror hanging in the bathroom and bit back a smile as he stopped humming, then suck in the spare tire he was starting to carry around his waist, watched him rub a hand through the sparse hair on his chest, most of it graying, and pull back his shoulders. He really didn't look bad for fifty-three. Oh, not like the hard-bodied twenty-something he'd been in college, but still, not bad. Good genes apparently. Thank God, since Joe liked to eat. Also a good thing, since I liked to cook.

Still checking himself in the big mirror, he twisted sideways a little and curled an arm around like he was holding a football against his chest, held the other one up, palm out, imitating the guy on the Heisman trophy. I pushed the corner of my pillow into my mouth.

My husband. Even after almost thirty years, I felt a warm mellowing inside my chest. It wasn't the same as the almost jagged, urgent desire I'd once felt, but it was comfortable and familiar. *He* was comfortable and familiar.

I had loved Joe Daley since the first time I'd seen him, when I was a month shy of eighteen and he'd sat beside me in Sociology 101 my freshman year at Penn State. Shocking when I thought about it now. I'd been so young; he'd been a little more than a year older, a sophomore. I would not have wanted our kids to fall in love at such a young age. Of course, Joe and I hadn't married until I had finished school, when I was twenty-two. Twenty-two whole years. Still too young.

There was a slap as he snapped the towel before plopping it on the rack. In thirty years, he hadn't learned to hang up his towel so it could dry. There were times that made me want to scream, but this morning, I was feeling charitable and warm with love polished by three decades of shared living. There was a lot of water under our bridge.

I felt loving. Not horny, particularly. *Loving.* I weighed the thought of slipping the comforter and sheet off my shoulders, my hip, of letting my breast peek out of the nightgown I wore. Of offering my fading, spreading, but loyal body to Joe this morning. But I had never been big on morning sex. I hadn't brushed my teeth or washed the sleep out of my eyes. I needed to pee. My hair likely looked as if it had been run though a blender. Though I doubted Joe would mind my bedhead. I had no doubt that with just the least encouragement, he would be ready for some early morning delight and he'd probably not even notice that I *had* hair.

I kept my eyes closed, faking sleep, as Joe came into the bedroom to get dressed. I don't know why, exactly. Contrariness maybe. But that's what I did. Faked sleep. Like I faked other things sometimes. It was just easier. It made life run smoother. And after more than thirty years and three kids, we'd honed smooth, Joe and me.

Sometimes I missed the sharp, nearly desperate passion, the keen awareness of each other, the *romance*, of our early years together. When just looking at Joe made my panties wet and my nipples tight and pointy. When we could hardly wait to get naked together. We never had naked sex now. Partly because we'd gotten out of the habit; it was imprudent to have naked sex when you had kids who might pop in on you at any moment, looking for Legos, the dictionary, or lunch money. Now that our kids were grown and gone, we had more time. We had privacy. I thought we might slowly, gradually find our way back to the place where we could focus on each other, without the distractions of kids and kid activities and find the passion that was likely not so sharp and jagged and impatient anymore, but that might be sweet and delicious in a different way.

I was looking forward to finding out. Our kids all had jobs and their own apartments, had for a couple of years now: Jamie was an architect with a firm in Minneapolis. Doug worked in sales for an engineering supply company in Kansas City. And Annie was a nurse, in Pittsburgh, not so far away, thank God, because I would miss my baby, my only daughter, too much if she was in another time zone, another state.

I had been thinking a little about what it would be like to travel. Maybe take a road trip, drive across country to visit Jamie and Doug. Maybe to Charleston. I'd never been there but I had an old copy of the *Charleston Receipts* cookbook and, for whatever reason, it had stirred up a longing to see that city. I was thinking a romantic trip. Just the two of us. Sometimes, we were in a convertible on this trip, in my head.

I heard Joe open the dresser drawer where his underwear was, felt him sit on the end of the bed to pull on his jeans, then stand again, heard the closet door open, the sound of hangers being slid along the metal rod, the rustle as he put on a shirt and buttoned it. LL Bean plaid flannel. Joe was nothing if not predictable. Unless he had a meeting, he'd wear the same "uniform" every day: jeans, button-down shirt. A flannel or chamois shirt in the winter.

I listened to him take a deep breath and could picture him sucking in his stomach, pushing the shirttails down. He fumbled a little bit with the buckle and I heard him swear under his breath. My heart swelled suddenly with love. I knew him so well. He wasn't perfect, he drove me to the edge of annoyance sometimes. He was simple and uncomplicated and I knew some would think—thought—boring. But we'd made a pretty good life together.

He sat on the end of the bed again, next to my feet, to put on his socks and shoes. The jangle of Trouble's collar and her footsteps, always so soft and careful, came down the hallway. Breakfast time. If no one came to her when it was time, she came to them. I felt more than heard the dog's presence beside the bed.

"Hey, girl," Joe said and I could tell by the way his voice sounded that he was moving around the bed, heading out of the room.

What would I do, I wondered, if Joe looked at me here, still dozing, and just took off his clothes and climbed back into bed beside me? What if he wanted to stay in bed talking and *not* having sex? What if he came back upstairs in ten minutes with a cup of tea and one of the leaves from the ginkgo tree out back, that were at this time of year as golden and perfect as a piece of jewelry? What if he came home this afternoon with a bouquet of my favorite yellow roses, for no reason, just because? I snorted indelicately into my pillow.

A fleeting physical sensation struck me then, almost strong enough to cause me to catch my breath. Scalding heat followed at once, swept across every inch of me as if I'd spontaneously combusted. Sweat beaded above my lip, gathered at the nape of my neck, beneath the flannel sheets and under my nightgown, ran between my breasts and down the small of my back to soak the waist-band of my panties. *Holy three alarm fire!*

Life was speeding past, old age was knocking at my door, breathing down my neck, leaving me flushed and wet with sweat. Hot flashes sucked.

The kitchen was empty when I got out there, Joe already off to his office at the warehouse, Daley-Hallowell Trucking, leaving the coffee maker on, even though I didn't drink it, the carafe on the brewer half-full, a dried coffee stain on the counter where he'd filled a travel mug.

Trouble lay on her rug by the kitchen dresser, looking content, so apparently Joe had fed her, and let her out to pee. It wasn't unusual for Joe to head off to work without waiting to see me in the morning, but I felt a little flash of disappointment as I realized he was already gone. The kitchen smelled comfortingly of coffee and old house. It had been almost sunny when I got up; now the sky was dark, and a cold, relentless rain pinged against the wavy glass of the windows. Typical November in Pennsylvania.

Thanksgiving was just around the corner, and I was looking forward to it. Both boys would be home for the holiday and Annie for some part of the weekend, at least, depending on her work schedule. I missed them all. Missed being a full-time mom, having my children as the center of my life. In another corner of my brain, I started thinking about what food I would have that weekend. Their favorites, peanut butter pie for Jamie, blue cheeseburgers for Doug, veggie lasagna for Annie. I'd seen a recipe for hummus using white beans and roasted eggplant that I thought Annie would like. I'd make cookies: chocolate chip, peanut butter, and gingersnaps, and freeze them so the boys could each take some. I'd stock the fridge to overflowing because, if I had to guess, I'd say their own were filled with beer and, in Annie's case, yogurt, but not much else.

I showed my love with food. I needed to start a list. I loved food; I liked lists.

Holidays for the extended Daley family, at least The Big Two,

Thanksgiving and Christmas, were chaotic, loud and, generally speaking, celebrated here at our house. Langston is where Joe and his siblings all grew up, and our kids, too. This small town was where Joe's mother, Lillian, still lived. Since she was in a small condo now, no longer the home where Joe had grown up, holidays, and the associated chaos, landed here.

My mother-in-law would offer to "help with food" which was a nice way of saying she would bring hot, spiced cider and rolls and maybe a "salad" she'd make with canned pineapple and shredded coconut and Cool Whip. Cooking was not Lillian's forte. Another reason holidays were celebrated here. Not that I minded, really. Or even ever thought about it. Perpetually hosting family holidays was one of those things that had just evolved over the years.

I wiped the counter and made myself a cup of tea and headed into the den, the room where all the odds and ends of Daley living seemed to accumulate and where I had my "office." This morning, I was going to start editing my second cookbook. Later, this afternoon, I would go over to Father Julian's to cook. I'd been grocery shopping and preparing meals for Father Julian, and before him, Father Cecil, for sixteen years. At first, it had been the perfect job because it took a few hours a couple of afternoons a week, allowing me to be home for the kids when they got off the school bus. I had always liked to cook and bake, and the priests, both of them in turn, were always very appreciative, and always gracious, diners. But later, it grew into something much more.

I had started out making the same dishes, generally, for the priests that I made for my own family: stuffed pork chops, barbeque chicken, scalloped potatoes, vegetable soup, double chocolate cake. But in short order, I'd begun experimenting, pushing the culinary envelope, at least for me, because I had no formal training as a chef, or even as a cook. I just loved taking raw ingredients and turning them into food that made people close their eyes with pleasure, made them oooh and ahh with satisfaction. I enjoyed how cooking inspired me, brought out my creative side. That gave *me* satisfaction. Eventually, I'd put in a big garden, so that I could have easy access to fresh produce and herbs. I'd sourced local Angus beef and pork and chicken, because it was fresh, and I could have it custom cut. What could have been a relatively routine and mundane part-time job became something I loved.

After I'd been cooking for Father Cecil for a number of years, he had raved about my chocolate cake and mentioned what he considered my extraordinary culinary skills, my garden, the way I bought his beef and his chicken from local farms to his sister who happened to have a roommate who worked for a book publisher in New York City.

Cooking for Father was conceived from a phone call the sister's roommate made to me three years ago. The cookbook, about food and gardening, my family, and conversations and time spent with the priests I cooked for, as much as just recipes, had been surprisingly well-received. Now I was working on a second book, *Holidays in Father's Kitchen*.

The phone rang. As I picked it up, I noticed the caller ID. Jamie.

Uh, oh, what's wrong? It's a weekday morning, only a little past, I glanced at my watch, *six a.m. in Minneapolis.* Jamie was not a morning person. And although he wasn't technically a first born, he was the oldest and was subsequently endowed with all those particular traits: perfectionist, demanding, accomplished, self-absorbed, bossy, high maintenance. A little bit OCD. He was also exceedingly driven, and the guy you wanted on your team in crunch time. A call from him at this hour was not normal.

"Hey," I said, trying to keep the concern from my voice. With kids, especially boys, no news was generally good news. "What's up?"

"You don't have to sound worried, Mom, it's nothing bad."

"Okay, okay. I can't help it. Worry comes with the territory. One of the side effects of birthing children. How's work?"

"Work's good. Great. I'm slammed." The architectural firm where Jamie had worked since college did a lot of commercial buildings and an occasional resort.

I remained silent, still waiting. Jamie had not called to tell me he was busy.

Trouble wandered into the den. She looked at me, her dark eyes hiding nothing of what she thought or felt. Her tail wagged before she settled next to my feet and then sighed, a great Labrador sigh, before putting her head down on her legs and prepared to sleep, or wait, for me, with the patience of a long-suffering saint.

"I'm just calling about Thanksgiving."

Please don't tell me you're not coming home. I haven't seen you since last Christmas!

"I wondered if it would be okay if I brought a friend home? For the holiday."

A friend. What friend? If I had ears like Trouble, they'd be upright, alert.

"Of course," I said. "You don't have to ask that. Your friends are always welcome."

"I thought I'd better give you a heads up, so we don't run out of food or anything."

"Ha, ha, wise guy. I've ordered a twenty-three pound turkey. Who's the friend?" I finally asked, curiosity getting the better of me.

"This girl I've been seeing. Her name's Molly. Molly MacDonald. I met her at Cornell in the athletes' dining hall my first summer at college. I told you about her. She played hockey. She's from Minneapolis. We've been hanging out."

"Sure, I remember." I didn't remember a thing about a girl named Molly. And I would have, if Jamie had ever told me, which he hadn't, despite what he said, because boys, my boys anyway, practiced devoutly the adage "what happens at school, stays at school."

"What does she do?" I had a thousand questions about this girl, Molly, who was *hanging out* with Jamie and now coming to Pennsylvania for Thanksgiving, but I bit my tongue. Jamie had never had a serious girlfriend. Doug said he had his bar set too high. Annie concurred.

"She goes to law school here at the U." The University of Minnesota.

"Wow. Law school."

"Yeah, she's pretty cool."

Jamie is bringing a girl home! And they're flying home, too, so the girl, Molly, is either buying a plane ticket, or Jamie is buying it for her. That is not just casual hanging out. Is it? "It'll be lovely to have her."

"Awesome. We'll get our tickets today. I'll email our itinerary."

"I miss you, honey! Can't wait to get you home. And it'll be fun to have Molly, too."

I tried to strike just the right balance of hip mom and gracious host without sounding too excited, the kiss of death and every mother's surefire way of putting the kibosh on any budding relationship.

———

BEFORE I SETTLED in to my computer and the new cookbook, I opened my purse to make sure I had Father J's shopping list. I needed to grocery shop before I went over to the rectory today. I remembered starting a list for him last week, but it wasn't in my purse or the red leather organizer Annie gave me for Christmas last year. The mail from Saturday lay in a sloppy pile on the old cupboard against the wall. Joe must have brought it in. His idea of helping out was to dump it all here. He never bothered to sort it, or even to toss out the obvious junk. Did my shopping list get swept up in that pile? I picked it up and sat down at the desk, pulling the garbage can closer while flipping through the stack. Junk. Junk. Junk. Bill. Bill. Catalog.

There, near the bottom of the pile, was a glossy brochure showing an obviously tropical locale: blue ocean, even bluer sky, pale sand beach, a couple looking tenderly at each other.

I turned it over to see the back. More blue ocean, almost startlingly blue, with a large, gleaming white sailboat, another couple sunbathing on the deck. In the background were some rocky cliffs, more beach, palm trees, what was clearly an island. I could almost smell the suntan lotion, the salt water, the rum. The text said *Capture Your Dreams Charters. Chartered Sailing Yachts with Every Amenity. Our luxurious yachts, our experienced captains, and gourmet chefs will make your vacation one to remember.* Inside, there were descriptions of various options and amenities and names of different boats and one of them was circled in black, the ink smudged a bit.

What? I felt a small tickle of something approaching delight. I turned the brochure over and looked at the front again. *What is this? Where did it come from?* Was this Joe's? It had been buried in the pile of mail; clearly, Joe had brought it into the house with everything else.

An emotion pushed at the back of my throat, from a place inside I'd forgotten existed. I realized just then, right at that moment, I had not felt that kind of airiness—a joy that was light-hearted and carefree, full of *promise*—for so long I'd forgotten it existed. Not that I wasn't, hadn't, been happy. But there were lots of different kinds of happiness and it was this particular *variety* I'd forgotten about.

Was Joe planning something? Planning on taking me on a sailing yacht? Whoa. *I take back everything I ever thought about him being clueless. About him not being romantic.*

In the spring, we'd celebrate our thirtieth wedding anniversary. Was he thinking about something like this to celebrate? Like a second honeymoon?

Some couples celebrated milestone anniversaries with trips like this at ten years, or twenty-five. Joe and I never had. At ten years, we were trying to get Daley-Hallowell Trucking up and running and we had three young kids, and all the requisite expenses that went with them. A home and a business. Two mortgages. At twenty-five years, I'd made reservations at the nicest restaurant in town, and I'd been happy to celebrate with the kids. I'd thought who better to celebrate our accomplishment that surely a twenty-five year anniversary marked, than the three individuals who at once were a consequence and a blessing resulting from that commitment. As I recalled, Joe's mother had also joined us for that dinner.

I opened up the brochure and really studied the pictures. *A sailing yacht? Seriously?* I had no idea that Joe would be thinking about something like this. We didn't know anything about sailing or sailboats. *Your own captain. A personal, gourmet chef. Oh. My. Gosh.*

I smiled and it was a smile that reached inside me and made my chest feel warm. A distant part of my mind was thinking *bathing suit. Bathing suits, plural! Pedicure! Diet!* It wasn't a cross-country trip to visit the kids, but I'd take it.

I thought of watching Joe this morning, of how he'd flexed his muscles and sucked in his gut. It made me smile again. Had he been thinking about this, about bathing-suit weather and the Caribbean? I didn't know if I was most tickled because of the specifics of the vacation or simply because Joe had taken the initiative and thought of it. That was *so* unlike him. He'd never so much as suggested we take a picnic to the park at the Langston town dam on a summer Sunday. He was much more inclined to think, *Hey, I could get the weed whacking done before dark if I get started now.*

As well, vacations in general were not his thing. I couldn't say when we'd last gone on a real vacation, even a long weekend somewhere. Joe was more likely to spend weekends or holidays working in his office catching up on paperwork, or cleaning trucks, or moving freight around or working in the yard or painting the fence. Life, the business, had just seemed to get in the way of vacations somehow. I teased him that he didn't know how to "vacate," although in all honesty, I knew that had as much to do with his frugal nature as much as an inability to relax. I glanced again at the brochure in my hand. "This is *so* not Joe." I actually said the words out loud. I was stunned, and touched, by the idea of such luxury, such extravagance.

Joe hadn't said anything, so I guessed it was to be a surprise. I'd have a hard time pretending to be shocked at the idea. I shook my head, still looking at the pictures on the brochure, and couldn't keep from grinning.

—————

"Hey, hon. How was your day?" I asked when Joe came into the kitchen. Trouble lay on the rug by the antique sideboard and her tail thumped twice at Joe's appearance, though she didn't so much as lift her head. It was Friday, five days after I had found the brochure and still, Joe hadn't said anything.

I'd spent almost as much time wondering how he was going to tell me about the trip and trying to prepare myself to look surprised as I did browsing for bathing suits online. I'd been in high spirits all week and I looked at Joe now, the wooden spoon held mid-stir over a pot of sauce. The kitchen smelled of oregano and basil and garlic and tomatoes, and he sniffed as he came through.

"Okay. Yours?" He walked past me, peeling off his coat, stopping to peck my cheek. Joe's skin was cold and damp with rain and I caught the scent of diesel fuel and outdoors. "Smells good in here," he said, not waiting to hear my reply. "What's for supper? I'm starvin', Marvin."

"Spaghetti. I got caught up working on the book, so I made a big pot. Enough for us and Father J. He's having the same thing. Not that he minds."

"Rumph," Joe said from the mudroom where he'd gone to hang up his coat. Coming back into the kitchen, rolling up his sleeves, he nodded to the bottle of Tito's on the counter. "You hitting the sauce?" Acknowledging the wooden spoon in my hand, he added, "In more ways than one."

"Ha ha," I said, rolling my eyes.

There were times Joe's dopey, and occasional ill-timed, sense of humor, his dad jokes, rubbed me the wrong way. It made the kids absolutely crazy. They called him Mr. Doofus. But this week, I was seeing my husband through different eyes and my heart squeezed a little.

"It's for the sauce," I said, tipping my head toward the big pot. "Sausage and spinach. Laura's in town. She and your mom are coming for dinner."

"Great," he said with that tone that said it was anything but. "How was his Holiness today?"

"He's fine. Busy with the coat drive and the finance committee. Go watch the news or read the paper until your mom and sister get here."

"I forgot Laura was coming. She mentioned it the other day."

"When did you talk to her? Any news on The Mystery Man?" Laura rarely talked about her significant other, Michael—at least we thought he was the significant other—and only then if she was pressed. He'd never been to Langston or to a family gathering; we'd never met him. It was odd, really. He and Laura had been together for years. Like ten? Though how would we know? Joe and I called him The Mystery Man to each other.

"Didn't ask. She didn't say." Joe picked up the paper where I'd left it on the counter. "She called to see what I thought of doing something special for Mom for her birthday."

"Your mother's birthday is not 'til March."

"I know. But apparently she was talking to the other kids—" *Other kids* would be Joe's siblings: his brother Mark (Atlanta), his sister Diana (Pittsburgh), and youngest brother David (Akron) "—they all think Mom's getting up there, she might not be around for a lot more birthdays and we should do something really special."

"Hmm," I said, lifting the lid on the pot of salted water to see if it was boiling yet. Lillian would be eighty-two on her birthday and while she was definitely aging, she showed no signs of slowing down any time soon. "I don't think I'd tell her that you're planning something special for her before she kicks the bucket." I put the lid back on the pot and turned up the heat. "Like what are they thinking? A party?"

Joe disappeared into the family room with the paper. Trouble opened one eye to watch, to see if I was going somewhere. "Nah. Mark thinks we should get everyone together." I heard the sounds of Joe settling into the recliner, then the TV click on, heard the voice of the news lady on the local channel.

"You mean like *everyone*?" I called, louder, to be heard over the TV. "All of us, her grandchildren? Her sister and Uncle Gabe? Her nieces and nephews? Like that kind of get-everyone-together?" I held the wooden spoon over the pot of sauce and looked warily into the family room.

"No, they're just thinking all us kids."

"Who's thinking that? What kids?"

"The five of us and Mom of course. They thought she'd really enjoy spending some quality time with just her family. I mean—" there was a pause and I practically heard his mental head slap, "—her kids. No offense."

"Oh, none taken," I said, rolling my eyes and shaking my head. "Who's thinking this?" I asked again.

"Laura and Mark are in charge. They're the planners. You know that."

I did know that. I could have guessed. "Is it a surprise?" I asked, turning the sauce down and laying the wooden spoon on the cutting board. "This *something special* for your mother and just her kids?"

"I don't think so. I mean, Mom mentioned to David that she really liked sailing. She hasn't been on a sailboat since she was a teenager. So I guess it's kinda her idea."

A sudden leaden weight filled my chest. "What?" I asked, though my voice caught, couldn't seem to get past my chest. I cleared my throat.

"They want to take Mom sailing. Some cruise. Mark got the information. He sent a brochure. I stuck it someplace."

The sense that the bottom of my stomach had dropped away, that there was a great, yawing emptiness, was familiar, and even expected.

I knew it.

Somewhere, somehow, I had known all along.

What I felt wasn't surprise so much as the blossoming of the teeny-tiny seed of disbelief deep inside me. Not disappointment. It was bigger than disappointment, so much bigger as to be a different emotion altogether.

Without thinking, I picked up the bottle of vodka on the counter, the vodka I'd used in the sauce, unscrewed the lid, and put the bottle to my lips. I took three good, healthy slugs before I even felt the burn, the scalding catch-my-breath fire leap down my throat. I gasped. I didn't like vodka, any hard liquor, really. Certainly not straight. Drinking straight unadorned vodka was like drinking rubbing alcohol. *What the hell!* I took another deep breath, another gulp, barely noticing the smell, the awful taste, and how easy it went down when my mind was filled with something else.

My mouth open, I drew a breath. The emptiness was still there, but now it was covered with a warm alcoholic glow. I turned around when I heard the sound of footsteps on the porch and stared unseeing at the sink. There were no tears in my eyes, not even the threat of tears, surprisingly. What I felt was just a big dark hole inside.

The door opened and my mother-in-law called out, "Hello! Oh, it smells good in here! Brr! It's cold out! They're calling for snow flurries tonight."

"Hey!" Laura said.

I took a deep breath, still feeling the sharp, liquid heat of the vodka, and turned around. Pasted a smile on my face, moved around the island to be greeted by my mother-in-law, my sister-in-law.

"Thanks for having us," Laura said, pushing a gift bag into my hands.

Disillusionment, and something else, another emotion, something raw and inevitable I didn't want to explore, pushed at my throat. But I had no one to blame for that but myself. That stupid brochure. Those pictures, the scenes my imagination had been playing in my head all week. The order I had placed at Land's End. One-piece bathing suits with tummy control panels "designed to flatter."

"What's this?" I said, my voice sounding leaden to my own ears. "You didn't have to bring a gift."

Laura waved away my words. "It's nothing, just a little something for the season."

I opened the bag, pushed aside the tissue paper to reveal a big candle, obviously handmade and expensive looking. Something Joe would call "artsy." It smelled like spice and maybe sandalwood or something musky I didn't recognize. I could catch a whiff of it, even over the smell of garlic and onion.

"Oh, thanks." I brought it to my nose, sniffed. "It's beautiful. It smells like fall. Thank you. You didn't have to do that." *Is this the consolation prize? You all go on that unbelievable cruise. I'll stay here and keep the home candle burning.*

Briefly, I glanced at my sister-in-law. Joe's youngest sister was built like Joe's dad's side of the family, more like a wrestler than a ballerina. Unfortunately for her. But she always had a super-stylish haircut, one that made the most of her thick, wheat-colored hair and tonight was still dressed in work clothes, a very chic pant suit. Laura was the CFO for a reinsurance company, which had something to do with insuring insurance companies, a job I didn't understand exactly, but which obviously paid well. Plus, she had no kids, no family, no husband, ex or otherwise. Just Michael, The Mystery Man.

He also worked in some kind of finance that was beyond my understanding, but was clearly lucrative. Rumor had it that he maintained his own DC-area condo, that he didn't live in, because he lived with Laura at her place. It was a scenario about which neither Joe or I had ever been enlightened. I wondered how he felt about the cruise. Maybe he went on trips like that with his siblings and mother all the time. How would I know? I didn't even know if Michael had siblings. Up until tonight, I'd felt fairly *laissez faire* about Michael The Mystery Man, had adopted a *whatever floats your boat* sort of attitude. Now I felt downright snarky. Fuck Laura and Michael and their boat, too.

Laura was smiling at me, her face open and warm, and I felt a different sort of kick, wondering how she could help to plan and facilitate this absurd notion of a beyond-extravagant cruise for Lillian and Lillian's children *only*.

"Come on in," I said. "You can put your coats in the den. What would you like to drink?"

"I'll have my usual," Lillian said. "But I can get it." She walked into the dining room where I kept the liquor in an old cupboard I'd years ago painted with horizontal black and white stripes. I heard the sound of bottles clinking as Lillian found the bottle of scotch.

I knew I should be glad Joe's mom didn't expect to be waited on— I had no doubt that's how Lillian saw her actions, her helping herself. But today it pissed me off instead.

"Laura?" Lillian asked. "Do you want something? Joe?" she called into the family room where Joe was planted in his recliner, the nightly news anchor muted in the background.

"Maybe just a beer, if you have one," Laura said.

"I'll have one of those," Joe called back. "A Yuengling if we have it."

I glanced into the family room where I could just glimpse the top of my oblivious husband's head over the back of the recliner, his bald spot actually gleaming in the lamp light, and could feel emotion expanding in my chest, hardening. Why was I annoyed at my mother-in-law taking charge of getting everyone a drink or a cocktail? Why hadn't Joe asked me for a beer, or why didn't he get one out of the fridge himself? Why didn't Joe get off his damn chair and act like a host?

Why was he always happy to have his mother wait on him? Why did my mother-in-law's attempt to be polite and helpful all of a sudden grate. So. Much? Lillian was a *guest* here. She did not live here; it was not her house, despite the amount of time she spent with us. Tonight I wanted to smash something, listening to Lillian taking drink orders, getting into our liquor cupboard, after which she came back out to the kitchen and opened the freezer to put a couple of ice cubes in her glass.

A glass she'd taken out of the cupboard in the dining room no matter how many times I had tried politely to tell her those glasses were not for everyday use. They were one of the few things I had from Nana Hollis. They weren't terribly valuable, only sentimentally, but they were something I wanted to be able to hand down to Jamie or Doug or Annie someday.

They're not for everyday use, damn it!

It was actually hard for me to understand how my mother-in-law could not remember. The woman wasn't stupid.

In one part of my mind, I knew it was silly to be so concerned about the glasses, to be annoyed, suddenly, that my mother-in-law made herself so at home here. I wouldn't feel this keenly aggravated if it had been one of my friends who had done the same thing.

But a friend was not a mother-in-law. A friend was not planning a fucking cruise with my husband. Without me. I bit down on my nearly overwhelming desire to march into the family room, yank the fucking glass from Lillian's hand, and replace it with one of the everyday glasses.

If I ever did something so outrageous, I knew Lillian would be contrite and apologetic and it would be me who looked like a jerk. I would *feel* small and petty. I would have my precious glass, but Lillian would have won a battle that no one else knew had been waged. Certainly Joe would be clueless, and even if clued-in, would think that I was imagining a rivalry or enmity where none existed.

I could just hear his patronizing words. *Mom loves you. She respects you. She just didn't remember about the glasses. C'mon.* The look on his face that said it was stupid of me to care about something so trivial as old glasses. I opened the oven, feeling the heat, the aroma of melted butter and garlic and toasting bread washing over me. I closed my eyes and took a deep breath.

"Can I do anything to help?" my sister-in-law called from the family room.

There had been times I had enjoyed the camaraderie of having Laura in the kitchen with me. Joe's youngest sister was the fun, outgoing aunt, who bought awesome, thoughtful gifts and kept up with what was hip and trendy, who visited her nieces and nephews when her travels for her job brought her close. She'd been known to go barhopping with them—paying any cover charges and picking up the tab, which made her the coolest aunt on the planet.

Even tonight, I could practically see Joe perking up now that his sister was here. Lillian nearly sparkled in Laura's presence. Joe's brother Mark elicited the same reaction, when he was around. It was no surprise, really, that it was those two who were the brain trust responsible for dreaming up and planning Lillian's cruise.

I did not want to contend with Laura in the kitchen now. I couldn't reconcile fun, generous Aunt Laura and an extraordinarily extravagant family vacation for only select members of the family. How much would Lillian's cruise cost? What did a private on-board chef run these days? A sailing yacht captain at your beck and call?

"Just waiting for the pasta. Thanks, though," and I stuck out a finger and wrote "fuck you" in the steam on the window over the sink. I took another swig from the vodka bottle and this one made me cough.

"My goodness! Are you okay out there?" Lillian called.

Hell no, I'm not okay, I thought, but what I said was, "just swallowed down the wrong pipe."

The evening was a blur, the cruise did not come up, even though it never left my mind. It occurred to me suddenly that if Joe and his siblings and Lillian went on this trip, the sleeping arrangements would be weird. How would they divide up to fit into staterooms with queen-sized beds—three women and three men? The math didn't work out for six guests—three men, three women who were *not* couples. And that's what the brochure showed. Staterooms with queen-sized beds. No twins. No bunk beds.

Or were there six staterooms, one for each of them? My God! How much would *that* cost?

Joe would need a passport. We didn't have passports. Wasn't it fucked up that he would need one for a trip he was taking without his wife?

What would it all cost?

I stared at Lillian as she was telling Joe how the icemaker on her refrigerator was not working right. Her short silver hair was cut and styled, her nails filed into perfect half-moons. I knew as well as I knew my own name, that if I looked under the table, Lillian's legs would be crossed at the ankle.

Undoubtedly, Joe would be over at his mother's house tomorrow to fix the damn icemaker. Lillian would make him lunch, or dinner, and he would share the meal with her because he would *not want to hurt her feelings, because it made her happy*, because as the oldest child, *she leaned on him*.

Yada yada, I thought. It wouldn't matter if we had plans, which we never did, because Joe would rather be working. It would not matter if I had made lunch or dinner, or if I was home waiting. I could just hear him. "I just fixed Mom's icemaker. She invited me to dinner. She went to the trouble... C'mon, Cath. If you'd told me you'd fixed something, I could have come home. She wouldn't have cared. She could have come over here, too. Be reasonable."

Oh, I knew that song and dance well. Sooo well.

Reasonable had become my middle name.

I was damn sick of reasonable.

I had long ago forgiven Lillian for being unable to let go of her oldest son, had forgiven Joe for not being able to stand up to his mother on my behalf, as his wife, the woman he had vowed to put before all others. I had simply adjusted, accepted the fact that being a daughter-in-law was a delicate balancing act, without ever speaking of the unspoken rivalry between myself and my mother-in-law. I thought we both had come to terms with our roles in Joe's life, Lillian and me.

Apparently not, because the outrage, the resentment, was hot and sour in my chest now, as if it had simply lain dormant there for however many years.

This cruise was her—Lillian's, my mother-in-law's—idea. *She loved sailing. Since freaking when?* We lived almost four hundred miles from the nearest ocean, more than a hundred and fifty miles to a big lake, and I had never known Lillian to go there, not once, *ever*, in the thirty years I'd been married to Joe. The bitterness pushing up in the back of my throat was familiar and heavy. Apparently forgiven but *not forgotten.*

I sat at the table serving salad and garlic bread and it was like my brain had split into two. Listening to talk about icemakers while the image of blue sea and white sails would not leave my mind. I had stopped caring entirely—at some point between draining the pasta and taking my seat—that I had brought what I was feeling on myself.

"How is Michael?" I asked Laura out of the blue, perversely, because he certainly had not been part of the conversation. I smiled at my sister-in-law. "Any chance he'll join us for Thanksgiving this year? You two have been together, what? Ten years? It's just *silly,*" I knew my tone said it was anything but, "that we've never met. That he's never been here for a family holiday."

Fleetingly, there was something in her eyes at my question. Surprise for sure. Guilt? Defiance? Laura was the stubborn one, the family hardhead as Joe would say. She was definitely annoyed that I had asked. Well, good. I could feel Joe and Lillian looking at me, as surprised as Laura.

"No," Laura answered. "I don't think so. He'll spend it with his family."

Joe, being Joe, then asked, "Who's his family?"

Laura did look annoyed now, defensive, though she was trying not to. "His kids. He has two kids."

"Oh!" I said. After ten plus or minus years, we were just learning that? "Boys? Girls? How old?"

"They're welcome to come, too," Lillian said. Of course she did. Invite more people to my house for the holiday, something I wouldn't have even batted an eye about a week ago. Now, all I could think was clearly there were different rules for holidays here than for chartered sailing yacht cruises.

"Hell, yes," Joe said.

"If his plans change, he's welcome to come." I smiled at my sister-in-law and felt a petty satisfaction at the direction the conversation had taken. "The more the merrier, right?"

Laura smiled back but it was a smile that didn't quite reach her eyes. "I'll tell him." But I could tell that she would do no such thing.

I was perverse enough to stir the pot about Michael the Mystery Man, but I did not mention the cruise. Would not. I knew that to say the words was to legitimize the whole idea. And no one else mentioned it either. A super extravagant trip like that, and neither Laura nor Lillian nor Joe brought it up. And that felt deliberate. Like a conspiracy.

Chapter Two

"What's the deal on the trip?" I asked as I came into the bedroom later, rubbing lotion into my hands. I kept my voice level, calm, as if I were asking if my husband preferred sweet potatoes or squash for Thanksgiving dinner.

The bedside lights were still on, but Joe was flat on his back, snoring softly. I stared at him, his mouth open unattractively, the comforter down around his waist where I could see how his stomach was flabby, the sparse hair on his chest was white. I remembered the other day—was it only five days ago?—when I had watched him surreptitiously as he'd shaved and gotten dressed in the morning. I had felt loving, my feelings gentle and filling. Now, as I looked at him, it was as if he had changed, like Jekyll and Hyde, or I had. What I felt was no longer warm and soft, it was sour and mean and angry. I hummed inside, my feelings like a hornet's nest.

"Hey!" I said, pretending I hadn't noticed he was sleeping.

"Huuh, ache uum," Joe shook himself awake, cleared his throat. He brought his arm down from where it had laid across my pillow. Joe generally slept like he was the only occupant of a bed. He was actually an obnoxious bedmate. "What?"

"I said, what's the deal on this trip for your mom? The birthday trip with just *family*. I mean, just *her kids*?" I felt quarrelsome, but I couldn't help it. The rage was there, fueling me. I wanted a fight.

"What? Huh?" he said, trying to look alert. I didn't even feel bad for waking him.

"The birthday cruise. For your mom." I spoke slowly, as if to a child.

"I told you. I don't know. Just what's on that brochure Mark sent. He and Laura are planning it."

"How much is it going to cost? Do they have any idea how expensive something like that is? Seriously. A private chef? Your own private captain?"

"All I know is Mark said not to worry about the cost. He said he had a couple of good years and he can pick up the tab. Or most of it."

"Are you kidding me?"

"No. Why?" He looked at me perplexed, pulling the comforter up a little bit, like he was getting ready to turn on his side and go back to sleep. "What's wrong with that?"

"What's wrong with that?" I repeated. "Are you serious? There is so much wrong with that I don't know where to start. Like we're some charity case?"

"Shhh. Don't yell at me," Joe said, wincing. And like it always did, that wince, the condescending tone of his voice, made my blood pressure spike.

"I'm not yelling!"

"Yes, you are." He adjusted his pillow. "Do we have to do this tonight? I'm whipped."

I ignored the question. "Doesn't that make you feel kind of shitty?"

"What?" Joe sighed and rolled his eyes. The sigh and eye roll that said, *Okay, I guess we have to talk about this tonight.* "That Mark wants to pick up the tab? It was his idea. If he thinks it's so important, why shouldn't he?"

The contempt that lived deep inside me, the derision I sometimes

24

felt for Joe, when I knew he was calculating the cost of something, something that shouldn't matter, raised its ugly head. This was so like him. Joe was the guy who was conveniently absent when the waiter brought the bill, who was never the one to say, "Hey, this one's on me." He was always content to let someone else pay.

"Any other time, you're the first one to comment on the price of something. Even when you don't use words, it's always perfectly clear that you're noticing the price. Your mouth, your face, gets tight. But not this time. This time, you're not even asking?"

"Hey. I didn't have anything to do with planning this trip. I don't care if we go. In fact, I can't imagine spending seven days on a boat with just Mom and my brothers and sisters. Seriously, honey? What in the hell am I gonna do for that much time on a boat for chrissakes?"

Seven days? Just hearing him say that, I felt like someone had pulled the floor out from under me. I wanted to cry, felt the sadness, a kind of rejection, deep inside, but for some reason, the tears didn't come. *Seven days?*

We hadn't even spent seven days on our honeymoon. Didn't Joe see how wrong this was? To spend an extravagant vacation like this with his mother? His brothers and sisters? When he'd never done anything as remotely special as this with his own wife or kids? I didn't know what to say, how to start to tell him how fucked up I thought this was, and *he* was, because he wasn't thinking the same thing.

Joe seemed to conclude my silence was a sign that I'd been placated. "Thanks for having Mom and Laura for dinner. It was great. Your spaghetti is the best. I love that sauce." He smiled at me, the lopsided smile that I once thought was cute—days ago!—and tender. Then he turned on his side and punched his pillow again. "I'm bushed."

I stared at him, his back, stunned to my toes that he was taking this whole cruise brainchild in his stride. That he wasn't appalled by however the trip was conceived. "I need to check something in the kitchen," I said, still staring at the back of my husband's head.

———

In the kitchen, I scrolled through my laptop's address book, clicking on every female friend. They came from all aspects of my life, an assortment of women I knew, some for years, some for not so long, all of whom I considered friends. Some were older than me, some younger, but I considered all of them contemporaries in some way. A test group.

I didn't pre-select only women who I knew would agree with me, at least not intentionally. Most of them had a mother-in-law, or at least had had at one time. A couple were so *blessed* they had more than one: divorced, remarried.

Mother-in-law, I thought, taking another sip of vodka. I'd never put the bottle away after dinner. Good thing. It was coming in handy. It still didn't taste great, but it made for a very pleasant glow, that somehow seemed to make the roiling emotions inside me distill and separate so that I could identify them, what made up that *you're-fucking-kidding-me* feeling: Anger. Disappointment. Disbelief. Betrayal. Resentment. R.E.S.E.N.T.M.E.N.T.

MIL. *Monster-in-Law.* That was a movie. We'd seen it. Joe had thought it was dumb, and not very realistic. I had thought it was hilarious and right on the money.

Money. Oh, my God! This trip had to cost a fortune. I opened up a new tab and did a Google search. Took another sip. The site came up on my screen and I read the entire website, every page, looked at every option, every package, every boat.

Holy shit! Are you kidding me? Chartered, crewed trips starting at $19,990. And that was just the yacht charter cost. Not airfare. Not meals or incidentals on either end of the cruise. Tips? Who knew what else. It wasn't like I had experience with this kind of travel to know what was involved. Mark was paying for it? *He had a couple of good years? Clearly an understatement.*

I had never felt envious of Mark and Elaine, my brother- and sister-in-law. Joe's middle brother and his wife made no secret of the fact that they seemed to have plenty of disposable income though it had never before felt like flaunting. This felt like flaunting. Rubbing the noses of the rest of the family in it, more like.

This vodka was actually really nice. I took another sip. I felt determined. This idea, *my* brainchild, was making me feel stronger. I went back to the tab with my email. Typed.

SUBJECT: Poll.

I am conducting an obviously non-scientific survey.

What would you think if your husband and his siblings wanted to take their mother, your mother-in-law, on a "once-in-a-lifetime" trip for her birthday: a private, chartered sailing yacht cruise in the British Virgin Islands, the kind with a private gourmet chef and captain included? For seven days.

You, and any other spouses, are not invited.

Be honest.

I read over what I'd written. Took another drink.

It was amazing. After a while, my lips and tongue, my taste buds, no longer noticed the yucky taste. After a while, I didn't even feel the burn. I didn't think I could actually feel my teeth. I didn't know why I'd ever thought vodka tasted like rubbing alcohol. It didn't taste like anything. It was like water, like really expensive water that made everything *slow*. And a little blurred.

I hit send.

I felt amazingly light. My fingertips tingled. I really wanted to know what my friends thought. If they all thought this trip was a good idea, I would find a way to tamp down my own feelings, my resentment, my bitterness. My jealousy.

Was it jealousy? I glanced at the brochure.

Hell, yes!

But it was more than that. I was hurt that Joe would even think about going along on this cruise and not consider me, how I would feel. That it would send a message to me. About my value, my worth.

Our relationship. And my place in the family, *his family*, as well. Because from where I sat at the moment—if I was still sitting, I couldn't feel my ass anymore, either—it did not feel like *my family* at all.

How fucked-up was my mother-in-law that she wouldn't decline a shockingly extravagant offer that excluded family members, at least the ones she didn't give birth to? What kind of mother didn't want to include her grandchildren in a special birthday get-together? Was my mother-in-law truly so oblivious that it would not occur to her that a trip like this might cause a rift between her children and their spouses? Seriously? Was my mother-in-law somehow as clueless about this as she was about my great-grandmother Hollis's glasses? Could someone be that clueless? Twenty thousand dollars! I felt like the number was stamped on the inside of my eyelids, along with the images of blue sea and blue lounge chairs and white sails. I couldn't get over the extravagance! The one year we had taken the kids and gone to Bethany Beach in Delaware for a long weekend, Joe hadn't stopped bitching about the jacked-up tourist prices on everything from hotel rooms to ice cream cones. My stomach twisted itself into a knot again; bile pushed up the back of my throat and the loose, whoa-the-world-is-spinning feeling hit me. Oh, God. I hated being hungover, and there was no doubt hungover was in my future. I caught a whiff of vodka from the open bottle and knew I was going to be sick.

There was a ping, a text. Who was texting at this hour? I tapped on the message app.

Helene: Whose bright idea is this?

Even though it was just words, on a phone screen, I felt suddenly like I'd been hugged, pulled into the warm embrace of a friend. Helene's response, tendered so promptly and spontaneously, so closely echoed my own, I wanted to cry. And this time, tears burned against the back of my eyes.

> Me: Who do you think? Joe's family. Can you believe it?

Helene had been my friend since college. We had been random roommates our freshman year, the year I met Joe in that Sociology class. We'd chosen to room together the rest of our time at Penn State and had been friends ever since. Now, Helene was divorced and lived outside DC, actually not far from Joe's sister, Laura.

What was Helene doing up at 2:00 a.m.? I wondered fleetingly if something was wrong. But Helene had always been a night owl. She worked for some company doing highly classified computer stuff for the government, or some company who worked for the government. Helene and I didn't see each other often, but we still kept in touch via email and text messages. We might not connect for weeks or even months, but when we did, we picked right up where we left off. I supposed it had to do with coming-of-age together, sharing the things young women living in the same 20' x 20' room for four years inevitably share. Everything.

> Helene: You're kidding.

> Me: No I'm not. Doesn't it sound like something they'd talk about on an afternoon talk show? Maury. Or Dr. Phil.

> Helene: Sounds like something that would break up a marriage to me.

————

I FELT like shit the next morning.

I cracked one eye, nearly reeling from the pain that ricocheted through my head at the speed of light. I was on the family room couch; I sort of remembered crashing here last night, madly writing emails, madly drinking vodka. Madly, madly.

I was *mad*. Crazy. I should have my head examined. I would, except it had detached from my neck.

The two afghans that were generally folded on one end or other of the couch were piled over my upper body, but I was slowly becoming aware that my feet were not covered. They were cold. I wanted to cover them, but wasn't sure my hands were attached to my arms, either. I moved as slowly as I could manage, trying not to disturb it, my head, so I could push the blankets down over my feet. My brain screamed in protest though the sound coming from my mouth was more of a moan.

"Hey, hon," Joe called from the kitchen. I closed my eyes, trying to mute the pounding that seemed to be connected somehow to the nails in my eyeballs.

"You sick? Want me to get you something?"

I didn't know whether to shake my head or to voice denial; both options seemed to promise equal opportunity for misery.

"Jeri got sick yesterday." His voice was closer and I realized he had come to the doorway of the family room. I opened my eyes the tiniest fraction, tried to screen out the light; wondered, distantly, what time it was. What day was it? I closed my eyes again. "I sent her home," he said. "She said she felt like she was run over by a truck and she pretty much looked like it. Hope you're not getting what she had."

"Unnhmh," was all I could manage.

"Want me to bring you something?" He'd moved closer yet. His voice was coming from somewhere right over me. "Some Tylenol? Nyquil Cold and Flu?"

I found one of my hands under the blankets and was somehow able to hold it out, like a traffic cop, to stop Joe from sticking the nails farther into my eyeballs.

"Okay. Well, yell if you want something. Sorry you're feeling bad. I was bushed last night. I never even heard you come out here. You didn't have to worry about waking me up."

"Unnhmh," I said again. Men are so fucking clueless. I would have shaken my head and rolled my eyes if it wouldn't have meant I might vomit.

Joe gave my hip a pat as he went off, back to the kitchen. I heard him say "Hey, girl," to Trouble, heard the back door open and close.

I didn't hear anything else until the phone rang. Mercifully, my brain seemed to have found its moorings inside my skull, though there was still a dull pounding behind my eyes, between my temples. I was never drinking again. Ever. The phone rang another time. I debated pushing the blanket back and rising, to answer it myself.

I felt like shit, and the hurt and betrayal were still there. The feelings I'd been nursing while I'd been nursing that bottle of vodka. I was struck with a certainty. *I cannot do this.*

I could not swallow down all this *angst*—I didn't know a better word—about this fucking cruise, *Lillian's Cruise.* Even now, when my head throbbed and my mouth was so dry I could hardly work up a swallow, Lillian's Cruise was the first thing I thought of. The distress I felt was a kind of sorrow, because of something lost. It did not matter that I was apparently the only one who recognized that. Or perhaps it did matter, and *that* was the reason for the sorrow.

Mom mentioned that she really liked sailing. So if I mentioned I like 10-karat diamond rings, are you going to run out and buy one? Or how about a convertible? A fucking convertible! I'd been suggesting we get a convertible for years. A "fun" car. An empty-nester car. I had no idea why such an unpractical thing had settled in my head. It just had. I'd taken to joking about it. "When we get the convertible... "Or "We could take the convertible...." Needless to say, no convertible had as yet appeared in the driveway.

I will tell him no. No, that cruise will not happen, not for Joe. I will draw the line in the sand. I knew without a doubt that if Joe went on this trip, it would tear something vital and irreparable between us. If he didn't go, the vital something might already be torn.

Can't unring that bell, put that Genie back in her bottle.

The phone rang again, but before I could decide to get up to answer it, Joe did. I closed my eyes again and curled my legs higher, pulled the afghans up to my chin.

"Hey, Mom," Joe said.

I sighed against my palm. No matter what happened with this cruise, the *fucking cruise*, I knew I would never see my mother-in-law in the same way again. My mother-in-law, or Joe's siblings, Mark and Laura, in particular.

For the first time since learning about *Lillian's Cruise*, I wondered what the others, the other in-laws, thought about it. What would our kids think? There was the briefest, teeny, tiny flare of something in my chest. There was the chance that one or all might not be supportive of the cruise. Maybe I had allies.

"Ahh, that sounds nice," Joe was saying. "But Cath isn't feeling well. Jeri went home with some kind of bug yesterday. Must be going around."

The conversation was one-sided, but I could easily imagine my mother-in-law's side of it.

"That sounds good, but I think I should pass. We've got leftovers here. And Cath might need something. She looks like death warmed over now—" *Nice.* "—but she might feel up to eating something later."

Silence again as my mother-in-law said something. "Yep. You, too." He sounded normal, the way he always sounded. Happy, mostly, untroubled by life or anything happening in it.

"Hey, I'm going to run over to the hardware store and then stop at the office for a minute." He was standing over me again. Joe's "minutes" were never that. He likely wouldn't be back for a couple of hours. "You okay?"

Am I okay? I shrugged in way that didn't commit to anything but didn't open my eyes and, after a few moments, heard the door in the kitchen.

What's okay?

———

OVER THE NEXT FEW DAYS, while hurt and anger hardened and took shape inside me, Joe was—typically, obliviously—busy at work.

He got a business degree from Penn State. Back then, he hadn't really known what he wanted to do other than that he hoped to own his own business *someday*. After graduation, he took a sales job with Federated Logistics that required him to visit potential customers across Pennsylvania and the northeast. Joe was a natural salesman. He threw himself into his work in a way that didn't surprise me, but that did leave me feeling a little...extraneous. But soon enough I was a new mother with a baby girl, Nora, and I didn't notice, or miss honestly, Joe's less than 100 percent focus on life outside his job.

Then a local furniture store in town closed and the furniture people also owned a big, dusty warehouse which happened to be sited less than a mile from Interstate 80, right beside a petroleum terminal owned by Lloyd Hallowell, a cranky sixty-year-old who had no wife, no kids, but a lot of entrepreneurial spirit.

We had just scraped up enough money for a down payment on the house but Joe and Lloyd found a banker who would finance another mortgage on a business that didn't yet exist—the beauty of small towns and rock-solid family names. We must have been crazy!

Joe , because of his—albeit brief—experience with Federated Logistics, knew a little about the business of moving smaller quantities of freight, LTL, "less than a truckload." Lloyd Hallowell understood the petroleum business and had contacts and resources of his own. So Joe quit his job, and he and Lloyd converted the old warehouse into a cross-dock facility, bought a couple more trucks, and Daley-Hallowell Trucking was born. Four months before Nora died.

After last weekend when I'd learned about *Lillian's Cruise*, Joe went about his business, his life, like there was no issue, no problem, like everything was hunky dory. He did not notice I was upset, or if he did, he, in typical Joe-fashion, ignored it and waited for his world to right itself on its axis again without acknowledgement or accommodation from him. The bitterness percolated inside me like so much overcooked coffee.

At night, he rubbed my back while I lay facing away from him, reading, his hand straying around my rib cage to my breasts, or slipping beneath the edge of my panties to stroke my buttocks. He wanted sex! But I pressed my arm to my side, shifted in the bed, rolled onto my back to dislodge his hand. I didn't want to make love! I didn't feel loving. I didn't want sex.

The hurt and the anger were too big; there was no room for desire.

Joe would eventually get the hint and roll on his other side or his back, his breathing would slow, and he would fall asleep. At breakfast, at dinner, I waited. Waited for Joe to bring it up. I refused to ask, to be the one addressing the huge elephant—sailing yacht—in the room. The fact that Joe didn't know a problem existed was *part of the problem*. Asking him about it, yanking his head up out of the sand where it was buried (or from high and deep inside his ass), put the onus *on me*. It was akin to having to ask him if he loved me, instead of him just saying it of his own free will.

Not once did he mention the cruise. It was the only thing I could think about.

———

ON WEDNESDAY AFTERNOON, one of those perfect autumn days where the light was pure and golden and unhazed with summer's humidity, Father J came into the rectory kitchen where I was in the middle of making an old-fashioned Swiss steak for his dinner. It was one of the dishes that I'd included in my cookbook. The first one. It was comfort food and one of Father J's favorites. I had shallots and garlic sautéing in a pan on the stove and was chopping other vegetables for the tomato-based sauce.

Father J, short for Julius Joseph, could eat anything and everything without having to worry about his weight or his health—unlike poor Father Cecil, who had been the first priest I'd cooked for, who had had to watch his weight and his cholesterol. Father J was fair and blue-eyed, like a Viking, his hair still mostly blond. He was sixty-three, built like a lumberjack or a linebacker, what my mother called "raw boned," though he apparently had a metabolism like a distance runner. And he had an enormous sweet tooth. Despite his job—his calling—which had to expose him to the worst of human failings, he had the seemingly perpetual ability to make people feel like the best version of themselves. I thought it was a rare gift, and a bonus for a priest. He was one of the few people I counted on my list of Truly Good People.

"Hi there, Cathleen," he said as he came into the kitchen, his eyes lighting on my latest creation. He liked all sweets, although he loved pie, and I had made him shoo fly this afternoon, a recipe that had been my grandmother's. "My favorite," he said.

I snorted indelicately. "They're all your favorites, Father. I think I could bake up old gym socks in pastry and you'd love it."

"You probably could at that." He smiled.

And then I felt the sudden, nearly palpable thrum, as if the blood in my veins and arteries had just accelerated, the fleeting prelude to the wash of heat that almost immediately overcame me. Sweat popped out on my neck, under my hair. I felt it gather between my breasts, under the turtleneck I wore, and all of a sudden I had the nearly irresistible urge to rip off the sweater, to fan myself with the plastic cutting board I was using.

The physical reaction left a depression so heavy sometimes I thought it could be set on a scale and weighed.

Father J seated himself at the round table in the bay window and watched me work, seemingly unaware of my state. Maybe—hopefully—if he did notice, he just thought it was from standing over the stove and sautéing vegetables. Father had pulled a familiar bright blue cardigan over his black shirt and collar. I knew he would change into a sport coat if and when he left the house. I thought it was too bad that he couldn't just wear the cardigan; it suited him. Like Mr. Rogers, if Mr. Rogers had played defensive end.

"How about a piece of pie? And a glass of milk? If you have time?" I asked.

"There's always time for pie."

I went about the business of getting a plate and a glass, the milk from the fridge. While he ate, I went back to chopping and stirring.

"You okay? You seem quiet," Father said after a while, and I noticed he'd finished the pie and the milk.

"Oh, yeah. I'm fine. Just thinking. This time of year, this kind of weather always makes me feel melancholy."

I could tell he didn't quite believe me. I chopped some more. Father sat and watched patiently. "It's a gorgeous day. We won't get many more like this before spring. How are the kids?"

I smiled. "They're good. They'll all be home in a month for Thanksgiving."

"Joe?"

"He's fine. Busy with work. You know Joe. He's always busy."

Father's expression didn't change but I could feel his interest perk up: priestly radar, very similar to maternal radar. Had I sounded sarcastic? I gathered my dirty dishes and utensils and put them in the sink. Returned the canister of flour to the pantry. Did I slam the door a little? I glanced at Father J to see if he'd noticed. He was still sitting with his legs crossed, his hands behind his head, lounging in the kitchen chair, as much as anyone can lounge in a kitchen chair. I recognized the look on his face. Caring. Accepting. Patient. Oh, so patient. That, too, was a gift.

I didn't really want to talk about The Cruise to Father J. More accurately, I didn't want to be talked down off the ledge of my hurt and anger. I wasn't done being pissed off. He was a priest; he would remind me about true charitable giving, about taking the high road. I wasn't ready to hear that, wasn't sure I ever would be. Lillian's Cruise was bigger, with consequences that were, I could somehow sense, greater than bruised feelings.

Father J looked like he was prepared to sit on that kitchen chair 'til the cows came home.

36

"Joe's family is planning a cruise for Lillian. To celebrate her birthday. Chartered. On a yacht."

"Wow."

"Oh, yeah," I said. "For just the family. I mean, just *their family*. The five siblings, and Lillian of course."

"I see." Father nodded, but didn't take his hands from behind his head, didn't move from the lounging position, though his blue eyes watched me closely.

"I know. I should take the high road. I should be happy for Joe, for his brothers and sisters, for Lillian. But I just can't find that much goodness in my heart. I'm sorry—"

"For what? You don't have anything to be sorry for."

I stared at him.

"Who said that's how you should feel? I'd be hurt. I imagine you are."

"Ohhh, yeah," I said again, realizing that I was wringing the dishcloth between my hands. "I am hurt. And angry and bitterly disappointed—"

"I can talk to Joe," Father said. "And Lillian—"

"No!" I interrupted. "I appreciate that, Father, but no. And besides, if the plans got changed because of your intervention, it wouldn't change the fact that they got made in the first place." I studied his face. "I know you understand what I mean."

He uncrossed his legs and sat up in the chair, parked his elbows on the table, rested his chin on his clasped hands, his expression pained, and I knew that he shared my hurt. That, too, was his gift, the ability he had to empathize with people, put himself in their shoes. Sometimes I didn't know how he could bear the hurts and ills of an entire parish. "You have to talk to Joe. You need for him to understand how you feel."

"How can he not know how I feel? We've been married for thirty years." Almost.

"I get that. But it's where you have to start."

"Just thinking that I have to tell him the very idea is stupid and hurtful is...*wrong*."

"I'm sure no one intended for you to be so hurt."

"I don't think intention should enter into it. It's not like he accidently stepped on my toe. It makes a statement. About how his family sees me, about how Joe sees us, our marriage. Our life."

"But maybe he didn't mean to make that statement."

I cocked my head at him, raised one eyebrow ."That's like the bank robber saying he didn't *intend* to take people's money."

Father J smiled. "Well, not exactly like that."

"You get what I'm saying, Father."

"I do. But you have a lot of years of marriage behind you. It's a significant investment."

"That's what makes the whole thing wrong. I can talk 'til I'm blue in the face, but it won't change the fact that this trip was even conceived."

"You've been through a lot, you two. You know Joe loves you."

Blah blah, I thought irreverently. I suspected Father J knew I was thinking it, too. He had that knack. And he knew I struggled with the whole priest thing. No doubt a holdover from my United Methodist upbringing. In my heart of hearts, I was cynical about a lot of the Catholic church. Sometimes I was cynical about God. Losing a child will do that.

I looked down at the dishcloth in my hand. "Oh, we'll talk." After Joe brings it up. "But I don't know if that will fix things. If that will be enough."

"Enough?"

I shrugged, slapped the dishcloth on the counter a couple of times. "I don't know. Forget I said that." *You can glue the teapot back together but that doesn't mean it will hold water* is what I thought.

———

IT WAS AMAZING, I thought after another week had passed, how things in my life, and Joe's, went on like normal. Normal being the same as the past umpteen years. Joe woke up in the mornings, went off to the warehouse. Came home, read the paper, fell asleep in his chair. Slid his hand beneath my nightshirt when he wanted to initiate sex. Didn't notice when I faked it, and not even very enthusiastically. The fact that Joe got his rocks off and then fell easily asleep only fueled my rage.

What is wrong with Joe?

What is wrong with me?

———

I GOT a text from Joe's sister.

> Diana: Hey. Mom says you've invited everyone to Thanksgiving at your house. Sounds great as usual. Just wanted to check what time you were planning to eat and what we can bring?

News to me. I shook my head, rolled my eyes. Typical. My mother-in-law was a master at working the ends against the middle.

I made a bet with myself that Lillian would call and "mention" that Diana said I *offered* to host Thanksgiving. In any case, it appeared that I would be cooking turkey on Thanksgiving, which was also the norm, and ordinarily I wouldn't mind. It was being manipulated I was resenting. That and the assumption, *Lillian's assumption*, that the entire Daley clan, minus the Georgia Daleys, of course, would be together for the holiday. And there was the implicit message: for Thanksgiving purposes, apparently, the Daley family was my family.

In response to Diana's email, I started to type: *Oh, I did?*

Before The Cruise—BC—being pulled into Lillian's maneuvering would have made me feel like one of the family. I would have taken it in stride, laughed with Joe and Laura and Diana about it. I thought that kind of taking advantage, that kind of assumption, was a function of comfort, of ease, of years of shared history, of family, of friendship, even. But that was BC.

I recalled the hot flashes, and wondered fleetingly if what I felt about Lillian's Cruise was simply a result of too much estrogen or too little. I was not above or beyond doubting myself but then my eye caught the little number beside my inbox: 21, indicating how many new emails I had waiting, and I thought of the notes I'd had from friends, the results of my "poll," the emails that were still coming, some from women I didn't even know.

I stared at what I'd written to Joe's sister, Diana, and decided pissed off was better than any five-hour energy drink. It was energizing. I felt like pure, thick, hot adrenaline flowed through my veins. I took a deep breath, hit backspace. It looked like I would be hosting Daley Thanksgiving. The cruise would come up in conversation. How could it not? A once-in-a-lifetime trip like that? I changed my text.

> Me: Yes, Thanksgiving dinner will be here again. All of our kids will be home. I need to thank your mother for inviting everyone.

Diana would miss the sarcasm. She was a genius, a PhD chemist, very "book smart" but generally clueless about things outside her job. Actually, she was a lot like Joe. I ran through the things I could reasonably ask Diana to bring to Thanksgiving dinner. She didn't cook, or bake. Whatever she brought would be something she'd purchase at a store, restaurant, or bakery.

> Me: Do you want to bring some apple cider? A couple of bottles of white wine? We'll plan to eat around 4 or 4:30.

At least that was something I could cross off my shopping list.

Chapter Three

At seven thirty that night, while I was in the kitchen looking through a cookbook, and Joe was snoring in his recliner, the phone rang. I glanced at the handset on the counter beside me, and caller ID confirmed. Lillian. The phone rang again and a third time while I ignored it, until Joe finally roused himself and reached across to the small table by his chair to the extension and picked it up.

"Hey, Mom." He cleared his throat. "No, no, that's okay."

I pursed my lips, waiting.

"I don't know where she is. I thought she was here. Just a minute. Cath?" he called. "Hey, Cathleen?"

I sat silently, *Charleston Receipts* open before me to recipes for Cabbage au Gratin and Hot Slaw. I stared at the words, not really registering them. Joe couldn't see me from his chair, and I didn't move or make a sound. I'd bet $50 and a whole fucking bag of Hershey's Nuggets that he would not get out of the chair to see where I was.

"I don't know where she went." He settled back in the recliner. I was going to have to stop betting chocolate, but what was the fun of betting carrots and celery? It wasn't like I needed to fit into a new bathing suit.

"What's up?"

Silence while he listened. I knew what my husband would say, what my mother-in-law would say, without even being privy to the conversation.

"Okay. I'll tell her," Joe said. "Did Diana say what time?"

I shook my head, snorted.

"I don't know what she's thinking, but I'm sure that will be fine. Yeah, they'll all be here—" *Jamie, Doug and Annie,* "—and Jamie's bringing a friend. Cath can give you a call, okay? They are?"

Who? Are what?

Joe made some noise in his throat. "The city will be a frickin' zoo. Hope they have a great time. I'll watch on the TV."

New York. The Macy's parade. The Atlanta Daleys.

Yep. A million dollars wouldn't entice Joe to spend the Thanksgiving weekend in Manhattan.

"Did you talk to David?" he asked.

Joe's youngest brother David. The Ohio Daleys. More silence from the family room.

"Oh, yeah? What kind? I cocked my head, tapped the page of *Charleston Receipts. What kind of* what?

"They bringing it? Trouble will love that."

A dog, I guessed. Great. Likely an unhousebroken and untrained puppy which would be cute and adorable and would dig in my flower beds, track mud all over the house, and pee on my rugs. One more thing to deal with when the house would be full of people and I would be trying to create a feast for fourteen people. Just fucking great. Why didn't Joe suggest they leave their new puppy at home?

"Well, I'll tell her. She'll call you. Love you, too. Bye." There was the rattle of Joe trying to put the extension on the base. The creak of his recliner. "Hey, Cath?" he called.

I picked up the stack of folded laundry I'd put on the other stool. Walked into the family room. "Did you yell?"

I saw Joe notice the laundry in my arms. I let him assume I'd been in the laundry room and unable to hear the phone. "Hey, Mom called. She talked to Di. Wanted to know what you want her to bring for Thanksgiving. Di told her you offered to have it here, I guess."

Bingo. *Had I called that one or had I called that one?* "You do know that I didn't 'offer' to host the family Thanksgiving dinner? That this is your mother being your mother?"

Joe sighed, shifted in his chair. I could almost see him thinking, *Don't pick a fight.*

"I suppose," he said. "But is it that a big deal? I mean, the alternative is that we go to Mom's condo. Sit in each other's pockets. But if you want to eat at Mom's, I'm sure she won't care."

"Actually, that's not the only alternative," I said.

"What else is there?" My husband looked genuinely at a loss.

"Well, gee, let's see," I started. I knew I sounded smarmy and wise-ass, but I couldn't help it. "We could go to Maine to a B&B along the coast, we could pack up and go to see my Great Aunt Marie and Uncle Ben in Virginia, we could go to Arizona and visit my parents. We could just stay here, alone."

Joe looked at me and I could see him weighing my attitude, making a conscious effort to not react to it. "Do you want to go to visit your Aunt and Uncle? Do you want to go to Arizona?"

What I wanted was to smack him. "Maybe I do. Maybe we should. Maybe it would be good for your mother."

"To go to Arizona for Thanksgiving?"

"Arizona. Virginia. Anywhere. Nowhere even. It might be nice to make our own plans for once. Your mother is making them for us, without asking. Again."

"She's just trying to help out."

"Bull. Shit. Stop defending her."

"I'm not defending her—"

I glared at him, raised my eyebrows. Of course Joe was confused. There was nothing different about this holiday than any of the dozens that preceded it.

"Well, okay, maybe I am," he finally conceded. "But c'mon, Cath. She's just trying to help."

"Help? By inviting everyone here without talking to me first?"

"Hey. If it'll make you feel better, we can go to her place."

It's not that I care about having dinner here, I wanted to scream.

"C'mon, Cath. It'll be nice, everyone here. You love Thanksgiving. You like to cook, remember?"

"That's not the point."

"I know. But think of the good stuff. The kids will all be home." Joe looked at me. Smiled a smile I knew was intended to disarm my annoyance, my anger.

I made a mental note to stop at the liquor store and pick up some Bailey's. Maybe some brandy. A bottle of bourbon and another of vodka, even though the thought of that made my stomach roil.

———

"Hey, Mom!"

"Doug, honey! Hey, this is a nice surprise!"

"It's a phone call, Mom."

"Yeah, I actually get to hear your voice."

"Ahh. Now you're making me feel bad. I text because I know you're super busy. I don't want to interrupt something important."

"That's a mother's job. Number one in her job description. They teach it in Mom School. How to make your children feel bad."

"Ha. Well, you generally suck at that."

Ridiculously, my heart swelled. This kid had always had the ability to sweet-talk me, to say the right thing, to charm. "Too smart for his own good," Joe used to say. Secretly, I always thought it was Doug's way of competing with his older brother, the super achiever Golden Child. Which, in typical maternal fashion, made me feel guilty, as if I'd fallen short somehow in the mother department when it came to my second son. "I'm never so busy I don't want to talk to you. What's up?"

"Why does something have to be up? Can't I just call to tell the best mom in the world I love her?"

"Absolutely. What's up?" I asked again, smiling. My maternal radar was still beeping steadily in the normal range. Doug's voice was upbeat, happy. In the Grown-Up Life department, he seemed to have found his stride. He'd lucked out with his job. So often, Doug managed to luck out. Just when you thought he was screwing up, or goofing off, something good would happen to him, or for him. From the time he was a little kid, it had been like that. As a parent, I had waited with dread—still waited with dread if I was honest—for the other shoe to drop when it came to Doug. That luck was bound to run out.

"Hey, Greg invited me to a Chief's game."

"Greg, your boss?"

"Yeah. We have season tickets. The company. Most of the big wigs use them, they take customers and stuff. But Greg invited me. The game is on Thanksgiving."

"Oh," I said, the reason for the call clear now.

"It's only like a month until I'll be home for Christmas. And Kristine, that's Greg's wife, she's going to do the whole Thanksgiving dinner on Friday, and they invited me, so I'll still get turkey and stuff. I'll get the whole holiday experience, a big family dinner, and everything."

"Oh," I said, feeling the weight of disappointment, but offset with the pleasure, and pride, I felt for my baby boy. This is what parents were supposed to do, right? Raise them up and let them go. Give them wings.

"That sounds great," I said. "Of course we'll miss you. *I'll* miss you like crazy. But it sounds like you'll be having a fun time."

Joe mentioned it at dinner. He already knew. Doug had called him as well. What did surprise me was how disappointed Joe seemed to be that Doug would not be home.

"I miss 'em." His eyes, when he glanced at me, seemed to be extra glassy. Our children, I knew he meant.

Now that the kids were gone, Joe seemed to have so easily filled the emptiness of their leaving with the business—work—that I felt alone with the sense of loss. It surprised me, seeing that look in his eyes, on his face, to think that Joe missed our children, too. For a fleeting moment, I felt that old sense of connection, of shared communion that had once been the language we spoke, me and Joe, without ever opening our mouths.

———

EMAIL RESPONSES TO MY "POLL" continued to fill my in-box.

A few of the first respondents replied to all, so that more of the women, my friends, were privy to others' comments and that inspired more commenting. And there were the emails from women I didn't know, after some forwarded my poll to their friends. I could hardly get any work done on the cookbook for all the time I spent emailing. But given the way thoughts of The Cruise still made me feel, the emailing was therapeutic.

It was safe to say that the group thought the idea of a cruise, of the type planned by Lillian's children for Lillian and themselves, was outrageous. Comments ranged from "over my dead body," to "If Joe goes on that cruise, you should go on a trip that costs as much!"

That last one brought me up short. I appreciated the idea, but I also thought the woman had missed the point. Sure, in theory, if it was just about keeping score, I would plan some kind of vacation that cost whatever Joe would spend on The Cruise. If money was no object, and it was simply a matter of scorekeeping.

But money *was* an object, and so was *time*. And I didn't want to go on a trip, extravagant or otherwise, without Joe. Could not really imagine such an event. It was crazy. That was my point.

———

I CONTINUED GIVING Joe the cold shoulder. Partly because pretending everything was fine when it wasn't was not how I was wired, and partly because I wasn't done talking about the fucking cruise but I didn't want to be the one to bring it up. At first, he didn't seem to notice the cold shoulder, and that pissed me off even more. Damn it, Joe should bring it up.

Finally, on Thursday evening, he did, but only because his sister Laura called. "Hey, what's up?" I could hear the faint tinny sound of Laura's voice, but not the words.

Then Joe. "I'm at home. I don't have my calendar here. I'll have to call you tomorrow."

I was in the middle of putting a plate in the dishwasher and I paused there, bent over, staring at the plastic basket of dirty silverware, not wanting Joe to see me listening intently.

"What are you thinking?" he said next.

That's a question I'd like to ask them all: *What the hell are you thinking?* Maybe he was finally going to stand up to them, to Lillian? Put a stop to this ridiculous event? Something inside me lifted, fluttered; the vise that had been crushing my heart for the past three weeks loosened its hold.

"I mean, February's a crazy month for me. And the weather is always an issue—" I straightened. Turned. Stared at Joe. He was sitting at the counter, a magazine open in front of him. He didn't seem to be aware of me. "Okay. Well, I'll check. What dates again?" He reached for a pen and a Post-it, jotted something down. "Okay. I'll let you know tomorrow. What's wrong with April?"

The month we'd celebrate our thirtieth anniversary. Really?

He nodded. Doodled on the Post-it. I waited, the open dishwasher door pressing into the back of my calf. The vise had returned. My hands had inexplicably begun to tremble. I squeezed them into fists.

"Who was that?" I said when he disconnected. I was surprised at the way my voice sounded perfectly normal. *What is wrong with me? Why am I so upset about this stupid cruise?*

Some small part of me, buried deep inside, still wondered if I was being petty and small-minded. Had it just been bad timing? That I had learned about Lillian's cruise when I had thought it was *my* cruise and that's why I was so upset? Nothing as simple or easily tracked as PMS, not like that. Given my recent hot flashes and night sweats, the dry girl-parts, that ship—in honor of the nautical theme— had sailed. Some tiny part of me deep inside wondered: Was I being unreasonable?

Then once again I thought of all those blessed emails, the talk show's worth of emails: the venting, and the outrage and the commiserated resentment and hurt I'd had in response to my poll.

"Laura." Joe glanced back to his magazine, turned a page.

I mentally counted to ten, slowly. "What'd she want?"

"They need to book the boat for Mom's cruise. Wanted to check what dates worked best for me."

"So it's official?"

Joe must have heard something in my voice because he looked up again, and his expression was wary.

"I mean, that you're going?"

Joe didn't answer, but his mouth closed and I saw the muscles in his jaw work.

"Oh," I said and my fingernails cut into the palms of my hands.

"I don't know what you want me to say. I don't think it's a good idea. But they didn't ask me."

"It's a shitty idea." I didn't know if I'd ever felt as much antagonism, as much pure *hostility*, toward my mother-in-law, and my husband, as I did at that moment.

"Laura asked if you wanted to come."

"When did she ask that?"

"The other day."

Breath caught and held in my lungs. Burned almost, like some kind of toxic gas. "Why'd she ask that?"

"Why'd she ask?" he repeated and I knew my husband so well that I knew it was his way of buying time, that the wheels in his brain were spinning at a furious clip, like a fucking fan, while he thought about how best to answer that wouldn't get him in deeper hot water.

"Yeah. Why'd she ask that?"

"I told her I thought it wasn't right, maybe, not to take the spouses."

Wasn't right. Maybe. "You told her I was pissed." I knew it with a certainty that was as hard and cold and unforgiving as my granite countertop.

"No! No, I did not tell her that. I just said I thought we should do something that the spouses could do, too. Then she asked if you wanted to come."

"What other spouses are going? Patrick? Elaine? Hope?"

"Patrick has work, can't get away. David said boats make Hope green around the gills. Elaine's not going. I don't know why."

"Don't you think the fact that Hope gets seasick should have been taken into consideration when the idea was conceived? If they really want Hope—spouses—to go?"

Joe sighed, exasperated. "It's Mark's trip. If he wants to plan a cruise, that's his prerogative. If Hope barfs at the idea of a boat ride, I don't think that should matter to Mark, if he's footing the bill."

"Does this sound like a fun trip for spouses to you?" I asked finally.

"No! I don't think it sounds like a fun trip for me, either. But, shit, Cath, what am I supposed to do?"

"What are you supposed to *do*? What are *you* supposed to do?" I stared at him. *Grow a pair!* I thought spitefully.

He looked at me like he was seeing me for the first time, then shook his head, spoke almost as if he was talking to himself. "I knew it. When Laura first brought it up, I *knew* it was going to be a problem."

I couldn't have been more stunned if Joe had struck me. He knew it would be a problem? Because of me? Because I would be mad? Hurt? Because I would raise a stink? I stared at him and felt like the world as I knew it had somehow been an illusion.

"I mean, I knew it was a lose-lose from the get-go."

"Lose-lose?" I almost couldn't get the air from my lungs to pass through my vocal cords, wasn't sure if I could find the breath to speak.

"Yeah. You know what I mean."

"I don't have the foggiest notion what you mean."

"I'm damned if I do, damned if I don't."

Of course it was all about him. Poor Joe. "You mean there's no way you can make the right decision," I wanted to clarify.

"Yes! If I go, you'll be pissed. If I don't, they'll be pissed."

"You think your brothers and sisters will be pissed if you don't go on this cruise? Your mother?" I used his word. Pissed.

"No. Not *pissed.* But I'll feel like I let them down somehow."

Joe's lips were moving, but I couldn't really focus on the words. I couldn't get the comment out of my head: *I knew it was going to be a problem.*

Heard what he didn't say: *I knew you were going to be a problem.*

It was my shortcoming, one of them, the thing I disliked about myself, was even ashamed of: I was too fiery, too impassioned, quick-tempered. I got mad about stuff. I cared. I worked at trying to be more accepting, less *emotional.* A long time ago, I had admitted that to Joe. Back then, all those years ago, he had told me that we complemented one another in that way. I had passion where he was laid-back.

Now he was looking at me in a way that made me feel exposed and vulnerable and ashamed. I felt a whole different flavor of betrayal. Tears burned my eyes and filled my lids and overflowed down my cheeks. The ache, the emptiness inside me was so *much.* Joe still looked annoyed, put upon, that he *could not win,* that he *could only lose.*

"I can't believe you. I can't believe you said that," I finally got out.

"Relax, already. You're making it into a bigger deal than it is. It's just a trip," he said. "It's not like I committed adultery, for Christ's sake."

"No, it's not like *that,*" I said.

I somehow managed to leave the room, Joe flipping the pages of his magazine with aggrieved indifference.

Sure enough, in typical Joe fashion, his annoyance passed with amazing speed. Not two hours later, I was in the bathroom, rubbing Jergens into my hands and staring at my face in the mirror when he came in to brush his teeth. My skin looked thin and pale, as if all the blood had been drained from it; my eyes were red and sore-looking. Puffy.

"Hey, babe," he said as he passed behind me to his sink. "I love you. You know that."

"I know that," I said and heard the flatness in my voice. Joe didn't seem to notice. Whether or not he loved me had never been in doubt. But it didn't matter.

"I think you're just getting a little too wrapped up in this cruise thing. It's not a big deal. Really."

"Is that what you think?" I tried, desperately, to be calm, to sound rational and reasonable.

"Well, sure."

"How do you really feel about it? About taking your mom on an exotic, once-in-a-lifetime, extravagant—because let's face it, this cruise is *extravagantly extravagant*—kind of *vacation*. For lack of a better word."

"Well," he paused a little, studying me to see if I really was as calm, now, as I sounded. The defensive note crept back into his voice. "I think it's nice. A nice thing to do. I think it's fine. I think she deserves it."

I thought I actually felt each of those words as if they were blows. He thought Lillian *deserved* it? He'd never in all the years we'd been married expressed any sort of similar sentiment about his mother. Had never mentioned his mom and luxury like this in the same sentence. Ever. Joe couldn't be bothered to buy his mother a card, or a gift. Not once in thirty years. He depended on me to pick up a Mother's Day card, to order Easter flowers, to buy and wrap Christmas and birthday gifts. But he thought his mother deserved a cruise?

I knew Joe didn't even really comprehend or appreciate the complicated relationship he had with his mom, because he was a son,

Lillian's first born, because his father had died in a car accident and left Lillian a widow when Joe was only fifteen. The other kids, Mark, Laura, Diana and David, had been younger; David had only been seven when his dad had died. The dynamic between Joe and his mom was different than that between most mothers and sons, by virtue of Steve Daley's unexpected and tragic death.

Lillian had been forced to depend on Joe, and Joe had been forced to step up and be a man, before he'd ever really gotten to be a kid, a teenager. Joe even remembered people at his father's funeral telling him he would have to be the "man of the family." He'd had to be strong and dependable, and when I had first met Joe in that sociology class, his maturity, had set him apart from other college guys. And it was one of the things I'd been attracted to.

Though sometimes I didn't feel quite so understanding of the way Lillian still depended on Joe. It seemed to me as if Lillian took advantage of the situation.

He thought his mother *deserved* this cruise. There was no doubt in my mind that Joe was thinking about his father, about his mother losing her husband, that his sense of duty, for lack of a better word, his role as "man of the family" had a great deal to do with *what he thought*.

"I mean it's Mark's money," Joe went on. "If he wants to do something like this for Mom, it's not my place to tell him he can't."

"Do you think if your dad was alive, this kind of event would even be on anyone's radar screen?" I couldn't imagine it, not either way: Lillian and her five children without Steve. Lillian and her five children with Steve, but no other spouses. Wasn't Lillian Steve's spouse?

"Huh?" Joe asked.

"Would you all feel this need to do this *nice thing* for your mom if your dad was still living?"

Joe bent over and scooped water into his mouth with his palm. Splashed water over his face.

I went on, "I think this cruise is all about guilt. Mark feels guilty because he lives in Georgia and doesn't see your mom more, doesn't get to do stuff for her like you do. All of them feel guilty for not being there for your mom like they think they should be. You all feel guilty because your mom was tragically widowed."

Joe shrugged, wiped his hands and his face on his towel and passed behind me to the bedroom, unbuttoning his shirt as he went.

"Maybe. Some. But I don't think it's all about that," he said from the end of the bed where he sat to pull off his socks.

"More than some. I think there's a direct correlation between the extravagance of the gift and the degree of the guilt. I resent them dragging you, us, into their pathetic efforts to appease their own guilty consciences. Just because they feel guilty and inadequate, doesn't mean that you do. We do. We're there for your mom every day, any time. She's in our lives on a daily basis."

"I don't know," Joe hedged. He knew I was right, that I had raised a valid point, but he wouldn't concede it.

He glanced at me briefly, then stood up and unbuttoned his pants, unzipped them, pulled them off. Tossed them toward the hamper the way he did with his pants every night. I didn't think he had ever once put his dirty pants in the clothes hamper. I wanted to march over, grab the jeans and shove them in his face.

Pulling back the covers, he slid into bed. He lay on his side, his head propped up on one hand. His face looked tired and old, suddenly. "You're probably right."

His tactic for derailing any discussion that promised to become contentious. It infuriated me when he did that. It was so obvious. He'd once attended an HR workshop at a conference that presented strategies for handling irate people—customers or clients or employees—and rule number one was "the customer is always right." I knew when I was "being handled" and it drove me mad. Mad that Joe could follow fucking "strategies" and maneuvering and be so removed from his feelings, his emotions, even when it was *me* he was talking to. Not some irate client.

"Let's not talk about it anymore tonight." He patted my pillow, an invitation, smiled at me, a smile full of conciliation, meant to soothe, to mollify, like he was offering a fucking olive branch. Smiled the little smile that I knew. So. Well.

Rule number two. Postpone the dispute. I didn't think that was officially part of the irate customer policy but it was certainly Joe's.

Like that's gonna happen, I wanted to yell at him. *You're such an asshole.* Did he really not know me at all?

I went into the bathroom to pull on my nightgown. Be damned I would let him watch me undress. That would be sending him a message I had no intention of delivering on.

When I went back into the bedroom, the light from my bedside table was still on. Joe's eyes were closed, though I couldn't tell if he was actually asleep. As I pulled the covers down on my side of the bed, he opened his eyes.

"God, I'm tired," he said. But as I slid onto the bed, he reached for me. "But not too tired," he said with a wink.

"Not tonight."

"Ahh. You sure? You smell so good," he said taking a deep whiff. "I love that smell. That stuff you use at night. That lotion or cream or whatever. It really gets me."

Tough shit! "Yeah, well, I think I'm getting my period." I turned, facing away from Joe.

There was a weighty and telling silence. I could not see his face, but I could practically hear the rhythmic taps, like calculator keys, the *click click clicking* as he computed in his head, a kind of mental math: Irritable + Moody + Difficult + Emotional...

Then a riffling *cha-cha-cha-ching* as the calculator did its calculating thing and the final sum was tallied. The answer: = PMS.

"Ahhh," he said. "I thought you were done with that."

I pinched my eyes closed. Counted to ten, then fifteen, feeling my breath pressing against my lungs, as if my chest was being squeezed. "I guess not," I said, surprised I could say the words in an almost normal voice.

"Ah, that sucks."

Yeah, doesn't it?

———

"WHERE IS EVERYONE?"

I looked up from the cracker crumbs I was making for the scalloped oysters, pushing a rolling pin over a Ziploc bag of Ritz. It was one of the recipes that would be featured in the new cookbook, the one I was editing now, *Holidays with Father*. I'd grown up having oysters and other fish and seafood at holidays because on the eastern shore of the Chesapeake, fish was fresh and abundant. Making scalloped oysters was my way of tying my family heritage to Daley traditions. I glanced at my watch. 9:38, Thanksgiving morning. T-day kick-off.

The kitchen smelled of onion and sage and turkey and faintly of cinnamon and bacon and of the balsam candle I had burning. The windows were dewy with condensation. I'd found an oldies station on the internet and the sounds of Rosemary Clooney and Dean Martin and Frank Sinatra came from the computer in the den. Trouble lay on her rug sleeping, occasionally opening her eyes to take in what I was doing. Now she had lifted her head, looking at Joe, her tail thumping gently.

I had been so distracted, and over the music and the thoughts in my head, I hadn't heard Joe come in. He'd gotten up and gone to the office early. Thanksgiving was not a holiday in the trucking business. There were no holidays in the trucking business, really.

Things had drifted into a kind of holding pattern with us since the night a week ago. I had not mentioned Lillian's Cruise again and Joe certainly had not brought it up. Things were not settled; The Cruise, and the can of worms it had opened, was still out there, hanging over us.

The big room was warm and steamy, full of good smells and soft music and a thick sort of coziness. I did like to cook, it made me happy to plan and prepare; I took a great deal of personal satisfaction in the whole process. Part of the pleasure I felt was because of my kids, and Joe, too. I did it for them. Like a gift. Still, I would like to be asked. I had not gotten over my pique at Lillian for just assuming I could and would plan and prepare the Thanksgiving meal, but I had not said anything to my mother-in-law, or anyone else, except Joe. Force of habit based on almost thirty years of marriage, I supposed.

Marriage and habit, were they the same?

"Earth to Cath," Joe teased. "Where is everyone?" he asked again.

I gave myself a mental shake. "Still sleeping. Sorry, my mind was on something else."

"Nice, having them here." He smiled at me, and I recalled the way he had said he missed our kids.

I smiled back, feeling something light, joyful inside. "Really nice. I wish Doug was here, too. But it sounded like his day was going to be pretty fun." He'd called the night before and talked to everyone.

"A private suite at a Chief's game? He'll have a blast. That boy is livin' the dream."

Joe walked behind me to get to the cupboard for a mug, looking over my shoulder to see what I was doing. I caught a whiff of him, cold air and that pleasant combination of laundry detergent and fabric softener and deep dresser drawer. He was wearing an old green Daley-Hallowell Trucking sweatshirt, from ten or more Christmases ago. We'd had them printed for everyone in the family that year. He looked young, somehow, vulnerable, in the old shirt. He poured himself a cup of coffee from the pot I'd made earlier. "What do you think of Molly?" he asked. Jamie's *friend*.

"She seems like a really nice girl. Fun. Jamie's so intense, you know. She might be good for him."

"You think she's *the one*?"

I felt a brief uncalled-for stab of annoyance. Joe saw things so simply, so obviously in black and white only. He was so *literal*. He needed to have things spelled out for him; he was oblivious to subtlety and nuance.

"He's never brought a girl home for Thanksgiving before."

"I don't know," I said. "And I don't think I'd assume that, or he'll never bring a girl home again."

There was something delicate and precarious in the air, a tantalizing hint of peace, of accord so I determinedly squelched the annoyance stirred up by Joe's question. I glanced up at him, trying to latch on to whatever it was that was between us at this moment and that felt right, long-lost. "There's a plate of bacon and sausages in the oven keeping warm. If you wait a minute, I can make you a couple of eggs."

"Okay," he said, moving around to the other side of the island and pulling out one of the stools. That surprised me. Given how much we'd been arguing of late, I thought it was more likely he would disappear into the family room and his recliner and read the paper or something.

"Jamie said he wanted to take Molly into town, show her around. The high school, the warehouse. The dam."

"Sounds romantic."

I stopped rolling and looked at him. "Will you cut it out?"

"What? Romance is good."

"And you're an expert?" I was kind of teasing, kind of not. That annoyance was begging for attention. I ignored it.

"Of course. Where do you think Jamie got it? It's genetic."

"Oh, you're Mr. Hilarious."

"Remember the time we hiked up to the fire tower at school?" He meant when we were at Penn State. "We spent the afternoon there. If I remember correctly, you were missing your panties when we got home." He waggled his eyebrows at me.

Despite myself, I blushed. "I don't remember that."

"Well, I do." He popped a grape from the bowl on the counter into his mouth. "Pretty darn romantic if I do say so myself."

I picked up the Ziploc bag of crumbs, shook it, decided the crumbs were small enough. Avoided Joe's eyes which I could feel following me.

"You want two or three eggs?"

"Two's good." I could tell he was still watching me, knew he would have that little smile on his mouth, that his gray—not quite blue, not quite green—eyes would be bright and full of teasing and knowing. He was trying to pull me into his own good humor, something he once had done so effortlessly. He hadn't even had to pull, I had followed him willingly, gladly.

"Scrambled or over easy?"

"Over easy. Can I have toast, too?"

"Of course." I glanced at him and saw his attention had been caught by the newspaper on the counter. I got out the eggs, a spatula, stuck two slices of my homemade whole wheat bread in the toaster. Got a plate down from the stack of multi-colored Fiestaware that we used every day.

As I cracked the eggs, watching as the transparent whites immediately started to cook there was a brief moment of silence as one song ended and the next began to play, a slow, graceful melody and I hummed along softly before I even really recognized the song. "The Tennessee Waltz." Who sang this?

I loved this kind of music, knew the kids would tease me if, when, they heard, change the station as soon as they came down. There was something evocative about music from this era, something that tugged at me. I hummed the melody quietly, carefully, almost coasting on the sound of the singer's voice. Patti Page. It came to me. The whites were almost completely opaque and I poked at them with the spatula before flipping them, clapping the little aluminum lid over them, then turning the burner off. Hands gripped my shoulders. I gasped, startled, the hum catching in my throat in a hiccup.

Joe gripped me firmly. I turned my head to look at him. He was smiling, his eyes, those not blue, not green eyes were smiling, too, though I thought fleetingly the smile in his eyes lacked something. He pulled me around, into his arms, his left hand moving to my waist, his right sliding to mine, to the hand that still held the spatula and he gripped my hand around it, so that it waved from our joined hands like a band leader's baton. Whisking me around, we circled the island, leaving the pan of over-easy eggs which I tried to tell him were going to be over not-so-easy if I didn't take them off the heat and put them on a plate. His feet moved in the steps of the waltz.

"Shhh," he said against my forehead. "Forget the eggs. How 'bout we finish this dance in the bedroom and I can show you romantic." He waggled his eyebrows. Mr. Doofus. His cheerfulness felt forced. Mr. Doofus with a gun to his head.

There was a great, pregnant pause while I looked at him, close enough to see the stubble on his jaw; he hadn't shaved yet today. He was looking at me, his eyes intent on my face.Wasn't this what I wanted? Wasn't this kind of spontaneous intimacy like we'd once known the very thing I'd been missing, lamenting its loss?

"Hmmm," I said. If I acted desirous, maybe, hopefully, desire would follow?

I slid my hand down from his shoulder to his chest, lower, slipped it under the waistband of the sweatshirt and his T-shirt, felt the warmth of his skin, the faint sprinkling of hair on his abdomen. Deep inside myself, I scurried around, trying to rally the edges of my libido, my hormones, attempted to fan the flames of lust. Of physical love.

An image popped into my head: myself as a perky cheerleader, in a green flared miniskirt, with a big, white letter "D" for Daley on a matching green sweater, running back and forth before gymnasium bleachers, waving pompoms in a frenzied effort to get the crowd, a mob of disinterested and lethargic raindrop-shaped hormones to *sit up! Pay attention!* Let's *go!* Horny! Horny! Horny! Sex! Sex! Sex! When that didn't work, I tried to envision a hot love scene from a book, from a movie. What had I seen lately that was sexy? The scene from the movie *Country Strong*, when the hot, young male singer says to the hot, young female singer, "Tell me what you want," his voice husky and knowing. And she responds, "Don't make me say it." There was a responding flutter of need, a tiny puff of smoke from the spark. Like a Girl Scout using sticks to start a fire, I rubbed them harder, faster. Saw the cheerleader me stooped over, blowing frantically on the ember.

"Hmmm. You better be ready to put your money where your

mouth is," Joe said, and I thought there was a warmth in his eyes, a new interest. I moved my hand up under his shirt, higher, until I brushed his nipple, then I pinched it, lightly, then again, a little harder.

"Whoa, there, babe," Joe said and this time there was definitely interest, heat, desire.

He stopped the pretense of dancing and slipped both hands beneath my bottom, hefted me up, until he was holding me, my legs wrapped around his hips.

I felt ridiculous, fat, thought fleetingly about the kids, worried they'd appear any moment in the kitchen doorway. Children, no matter their age, did not want to be reminded that their parents had S.E.X. Joe? Joe would make a Mr. Doofus comment.

He nuzzled my neck. I felt his forefingers pressing against the seam of my pants, along my buttocks. A faint buzzing started in my ears, so faint I wasn't sure if I was really hearing it, or if it was my imagination. Maybe the dryer. Did I have clothes in the dryer?

"You mean it?" he said.

And I felt remorse, shame, regret, bloom inside me at the question. It jarred me. My husband had to ask that?

His voice was laced with fragile hope. We had not had sex for... How long? Days. A couple of weeks. Longer?

He had pulled back, was looking at my face, studying me, and I knew I could not say no. No matter how lethargic, how disinterested that bleacher full of hormones, my libido.

What is wrong with me? Isn't this what I wanted? Joe's interest? Joe's attention? The intimacy we'd once known? "Is that more talk? Where *is* that action?" I answered, wriggling my hips against the hard bulge in his jeans, so that there could be no mistake.

But then Trouble lifted her head and looked toward the porch, got to her feet, and moved to look out the small glass panes in the door. There was a squeal and yelling from the front yard, and I saw a tiny brown blur streak past. Trouble's tail started to wag. Joe slowly lowered me to the floor, though he kept me pressed close. The Ohio Daleys had arrived.

"Oh, my God!" I said, glancing over Joe's shoulder at the clock on the dresser. "Five hours early! I just put the turkey in the oven." Joe's arms still held me.

"Well, shit," he said. "Talk about timing."

Despite myself, I felt a wash of relief followed at the speed of light by guilt that tasted metallic on the back of my tongue. There would be no hanky-panky this morning. I would not have to stir up desire. I would not have to fake it.

"Happy Thanksgiving," he said finally, and I steeled my expression to show nothing of that relief, of the guilt. Joe wore the Mr. Doofus frown, his bottom lip pushed out like he was a pouting two-year-old.

Little footsteps thumped across the porch; the youngest Ohio Daley, our niece, Clara, pushed open the kitchen door. "Hey, Aunt Cath! Hey, Uncle Joe! WegotanewpuppyhernameisAnnie!" she yelled before slamming the door closed, making the picture hanging beside the door bounce against the wall, the brown blur of a puppy on her heels, yapping nonstop.

I flinched. Trouble looked back at me, her soft, caramel eyes wide and soulful.

"Hey. Morning," Jamie said coming from the family room, rubbing a hand through his hair, glancing toward the porch. "Guess the cousins are here."

Suddenly, I wanted to sit down and put my head on the counter, close my eyes. Five hours early. I'd peeled twenty potatoes. Was that enough?

Chapter Four

A clusterfuck. That was Joe's term for the kind of chaos into which Thanksgiving, all holidays with the Daleys, really, inevitably evolved. Devolved.

Shortly after the Ohio Daleys' arrival, Diana and Patrick came, then before long, Lillian. And while I understood that my mother-in-law did not want to miss any opportunity to spend time with her children, she did not begin to grasp the fact that she changed the dynamic of the family. Or more accurately, Lillian kept the family dynamic *from* changing. Which was irritating and wearying, sometimes more than others. Today, a lot.

The roles the Daley siblings had grown up with from birth could never be shed, not while the force that was their mother pulled on them all, like a powerful magnet. When Lillian was present, Joe would always be the oldest, the mature, responsible one, the one Lillian leaned on. Steady, dependable, reliable Joe.

Mark, CEO of a small tech company (one of those aggressively high energy places with no time clock and likely an espresso machine and a Vitamix in the break room) would always be the cool, fun brother, the brother who had no time for drama or dissention or anything that might cramp his fun-seeking style, the one who looked out for himself first, who managed to get what he wanted while keeping everyone else basking in the glow of his charm and charisma and coolness.

Diana, the scientist, a white lab coat-wearing chemist specifically, was hard-working and diligent and very bright. She'd always been the best student, the scholarship winner, the brainiac. She was very capable professionally, but in some ways, she was still such a naïve and inexperienced small town girl.

Laura was like Mark, fun-loving and always up for an adventure. The cool aunt with no children of her own. And no husband, just Michael the Mystery Man.

David, a high school gym teacher, the baby, the one who had struggled to find a niche, who had never had a chance to shine brightly in the eyes of the family because they had all gone off to their own adult lives by the time he was old enough to even try to shine. David still seemed like he was trying to catch up. Keep up.

What was my role in this family?

While the holiday picked up steam in the house behind me, I sat here on the old bench on the little side porch, hidden from the view of anyone passing through the pantry, a water glass full to the rim of chardonnay beside me, the bottle on the floor. At any other time, with any other gathering, I would never think of deserting my guests and disappearing for any length of time. But today, I didn't feel any remorse whatsoever at giving myself these few minutes of quiet time. Besides, what did people expect when they arrived five hours before the meal?

They did not consider themselves guests; they considered themselves family. Which, up until The Fucking Cruise, I did, too. With Lillian assuming the role of hostess as soon as she walked in the door, I didn't think anyone would even miss me. I took another drink.

I could still hear Clara's squeals and Annie's barking—Annie the puppy, not Annie the girl. Someone had turned on the television in the family room, loud. No doubt Lillian, so she could be watching for a glimpse of the Georgia Daleys at the Macy's parade. The kitchen door banged, open or shut, there was the distant thudding of footsteps running, the powder room door slammed, someone talking approached—Lillian—a cupboard in the pantry opened, closed, Lillian's voice faded.

"Hey," Patrick said, coming out on the porch. My brother-in-law was wearing a pair of sunglasses and a black leather jacket, the leather so soft it looked like something you could eat.

"Hey," I answered.

"Don't mean to interrupt—"

"You're not. I'm just sneaking in a little breather."

He nodded. I always had the feeling that Patrick saw things, read me in a way that no one else did. Not even Joe—especially not Joe. It was unsettling, and Patrick seemed to know that, too. Today, there was about Pat, as there always seemed to be, that almost electric awareness and a sense of waiting. An extraordinary kind of patience.

"Hiding from the masses?" he asked.

"Guilty." I picked up the glass and what was left of the white wine. Took a sip. Could not to save my life have explained why part of me wanted this interruption and part of me did not.

"Don't blame you." He sat down beside me. It was a short bench, so we were close enough that our legs touched. He was wearing khakis, crisp and pressed, and some kind of black leather slip-on shoes that looked expensive.

"What've you got there?" He looked pointedly at my glass.

"White wine. Want some?" I picked up the bottle.

He grinned and I felt it somewhere in the middle of my chest. Patrick looked so intense most of the time, so serious, that when he smiled, it was such a transformation. He wasn't good-looking in the traditional sense. His face was a little long, his forehead a little high, he had a beard and a mustache, the kind that was kept trimmed close, and it was showing some gray now. I couldn't see his eyes behind the sunglasses, but I knew they were dark. He was confident. Competent. He inspired trust, he was the guy, the attorney, you wanted on your side in a fight. "Planning on being here awhile?"

"Not necessarily. But I wanted to be prepared just in case."

He nodded, not quite smiling. "Preparedness is good."

"That sounds like something a Boy Scout would say. Or a lawyer."

"I am a lawyer. Never was a Boy Scout." And now he was barely smiling and looking at me. At some point, he'd taken off the sunglasses and stuck them in his shirt pocket.

"You want some?" I asked again.

"Sure," he said. "It would be impolite to let you drink alone."

I handed him the bottle, then my glass, unsure which he preferred, comfortable with him. Pat was good company. He was really smart, well read, and knowledgeable; his work, his clients, were interesting; he traveled a lot for his job so he had a different perspective on things in the world, current events and religion and politics. A conversation with Pat was generally thought-provoking and stimulating in a way I was unaccustomed to.

Pat grinned and reached for the bottle. Put it to his lips and took a drink, a move that was at odds with his smooth and polished professional look, but confirmed on some level my sense that there was a completely different man inside. He handed the bottle back to me. I topped off what was in my glass and set it on the porch floor between us.

"The holiday somehow takes on a more pleasant glow with a little alcohol on board," he said.

"Ha. That it does."

The old summer kitchen sat at the end of the narrow sidewalk leading from this little porch, its foundation hidden by a forest of daylily foliage that was just starting to wither and brown. "I love the summer kitchen," I said, not looking at Patrick. "Think of all the hours, all the work that took place in there."

"You're a romantic," Pat said, watching me and not even glancing at the summer kitchen.

"It tells stories. I can imagine women putting up food for the winter. Making jam and jelly, canning stuff. Making dozens of loaves of bread. Hundreds. Thousands. All the gallons and gallons of hot water that was heated to wash clothes. The smell of lye and lard simmering for soap. Can you imagine?" I liked thinking about the industriousness the old building once harbored. Taking care of it now felt like honoring that work and those unknown women.

My gardens, I had two, lay beyond the summer kitchen. From here, I could just see the edge of one.

"Nice shoes," Pat teased, jarring me from my thoughts.

I stretched out my legs to admire the pink Crocs that I liked to wear when I was on my feet cooking for a long stretch, that Annie had given to me a couple of years ago for Christmas. The ugliest shoes on the planet, like something one of the seven dwarves would wear. Pink because Annie and I loved pink. Like peonies, Annie had said in the little note with the gift. Like Pepto Bismol, Joe had said.

"I know," I said now with a smile. "But they're comfortable on days like today when I'm standing a lot. I'm too old for vanity."

"You're not too old. Not for vanity or anything else."

Beyond the little flicker of a thrill that I felt, there was something else, something that made me uncomfortable, that kept me from meeting his eyes, afraid of what I would see there.

"Who are you hiding from out here on the porch, with your wine bottle?" Pat asked.

"No one. Nothing. Really, not hiding."

"Okay," he said, taking another drink. I knew he didn't believe me. "How's work?"

Pat was a corporate attorney in a big firm in Pittsburgh. Also a Penn Stater, I'd met him in the dining hall our freshman year, the day before classes had started. Later, he'd end up joining Joe's fraternity and become a friend not just a fraternity brother. He'd been a business major, but after graduation, he had packed up and gone to Europe, drinking a lot of wine, he'd told me once. *A lot* of wine. The experience changed him, in some indefinable, hard-to-pin-down ways. In college, he had been a sweet, polite, earnest boy-next-door. Like Kevin on *The Wonder Years*. After, he was a little harder, there was an edge to him, a *worldliness*. He returned to the States more Sean Penn and went off to law school in Virginia.

At our wedding reception, I could remember watching him dance with Joe's little sister, Diana. Di had been in high school. After that, she went off to college, finished her undergrad in record time, then moved to Pittsburgh and spent a few years getting a PhD in applied chemical engineering. No one was more surprised than me when Diana announced that she and Pat were getting married. I hadn't even been aware they were dating. Neither had Joe. Pat and Di seemed not quite ill-suited, but just not two people you'd ever match up together.

"Work is good." Pat said. "Time-consuming. A lot of travel, which I like." There seemed to be some hidden meaning in that statement. I nodded. Took another drink of my chardonnay. "You ever want to travel? Get out of Langston?"

I glanced at him. "Actually, just a few weeks ago, I was thinking about traveling." I didn't say I was thinking about doing that with Joe, a convertible, visiting the kids. Somehow, when Pat asked, when he looked at me the way he was looking at me, I understood he meant something different, something maybe more sophisticated or cultured than a road trip to Kansas City.

Pat took another drink of the wine. He wore a crisply pressed button-down oxford in a mint green color under the leather jacket. He was lean, with a runner's body. Very different from Joe.

It made me smile to watch him drinking from a bottle, at least dressed as he was now, as Successful Attorney on Thanksgiving.

He said, "What's so funny?"

"You don't look like the kind of guy who guzzles from wine bottles."

"Looks can be deceiving."

He didn't smile when he said that. Once again, I ignored the sudden, silent invitation that was in his eyes and in his voice, to speak of things that were unspeakable. "Hey, I wanted to ask you something, was hoping I'd get a chance to today," I said, wanting to change the subject, even to one that was upsetting. "What do you know about the cruise? *The Cruise.*"

"Ahhh," he said, and I knew that I was not going to have to explain how the idea of Lillian's cruise made me feel, how hurtful it was, how *wrong*.

"Lillian's birthday gift."

"Yeah. Some gift, huh?"

Surprising me, Pat laughed.

"Seriously," I said, looking at him. "What do you think about it? Do you care?"

He looked at me, his brown eyes so dark I couldn't distinguish the pupil inside them. He'd stopped laughing, but I could tell he was fighting a smile.

"What do *you* think about it?" he answered. Answer a question with a question. Typical lawyer.

"I think it's fucked up."

He was smiling outright now. Indulgent. "It *is* fucked up."

"I can't decide if you're laughing with me or at me."

The smile left his face and it was as if it had never been there. Those brown eyes met mine unflinchingly. "Always with you."

There they were again, those unspoken words, and again, I ignored them, didn't touch them, went on as if I didn't recognize them. As if they were radioactive. "I can't imagine doing something like that without Joe." I gripped the glass, feeling the chill of the wine against my palms and fingers, the cold November air on the backs of my hands. "Did you say anything?"

"You mean, did I protest or say that Di couldn't go?"

"Well, yeah."

"Hell, no. If Di is on a boat somewhere for a week, that's a whole week I won't have to hear about invitro fertilization or embryo transfer or whatever damn scientific breakthrough they've come up with lately."

"What?" And then I realized Pat was talking about them, not about Di's work. About them having a baby. And then I thought *now?* Di is...forty-one? Forty-two? Pat was older than that. He was my age. Fifty-one. "*Really?*" I stared at him.

He sighed. "Why couldn't you bring out a bottle of something stronger than this? I'll go get—"

"No," I said. "No. Wait. You're trying to have a baby?"

"Diana is. I'm okay with no children. I am," he looked at me, "totally okay with it."

"I always just thought you two didn't want kids," I said. "I mean... You've been married what? Almost twenty years?"

"I want one thing. And it's not children. Not with Di." And what he did want, what he was saying without saying, was that he wanted me. I knew it as sure as I knew I'd be making casseroles and dishes with leftover turkey for the next three days. There was...an awareness, a sort of *electricity* between us...something I had never acknowledged to Pat or to anyone else.

"Don't say that."

I was afraid to look at him, though I was acutely conscious of the heat of him beside me on the bench. Finally, he took mercy on me and laughed, a little ruefully, then leaned back against the side of the porch and stretched his legs out. I could see the herringbone pattern of the socks he wore.

Just then, the door to the house opened, and Joe stuck his head out. "There you are. Hey, are we having anything to eat before The Big Meal? We're kinda hungry."

I glanced at Pat, whose eyes were dark, his mouth pulled up in a smile that was just his mouth. None of the rest of his face was engaged.

"Cath tell you Doug's going to the Chief's game?" Joe said to Pat. "Lucky bastard. His company's got a box and everything. Open bar, all the wings you can eat."

"She was just telling me," Pat said, and I stared at him, at his easy lie. "Sounds like a good time."

"What are you doing out here?" Joe didn't wait for an answer. "Mom and Laura are here."

"We're planning a trip," Pat said, teasing, "for in-laws only."

"Whatever," my clueless husband said, totally missing, or ignoring, the potential bomb Pat had lobbed at him. "But if she could make the gravy before she goes," Joe said, disappearing back into the pantry, "that'd be great. Mom can't make good gravy to save her life."

Ha ha. I glanced at Pat, smiled ruefully. Mr. Doofus. "It's good to be needed, I guess," I finally said. And felt the sudden, instantaneous, uncontrollable flood of heat burst from somewhere inside me to the top of my skull to the tips of my toes. Perspiration followed immediately. It was a sauna inside my sweater. I could feel beads of moisture under my nose. My hairline was damp. Were the words *hot flash* blazing across my forehead? *Just fucking lovely.* Sweat trickled between my breasts and down my back, into the waistband of my jeans.

"You are needed," Pat said. And again, I knew he was not talking about gravy or even Joe.

———

"—AND bless us Our Lord and these Thy gifts which we are about to receive—"

I looked around the table, seeing the assortment of bowed heads, the string of clasped hands. My mind wandered, Joe's voice like white noise accompanying my thoughts. My husband always asked the blessing anytime there was a Daley family gathering. His due, as the oldest of Lillian's children.

Maybe I should not have had that last glass of wine.

Maybe I should have had more.

When Pat and I had come in from the pantry porch, Lillian had already put out a spread of "snacks," pushing aside all "The Big Meal" preparations I had on the kitchen counter. *Make yourself at home,* I had wanted to say to my mother-in-law. *Let me get out of your way.*

I hadn't said anything, though, because just then I felt Pat touch the small of my (no doubt damp) back, lightly, briefly, and it was like all the pissed off-ness inside me drained out, and then Jamie and Molly had come in, and there were introductions to make and butternut squash casserole to mix up and whatever. The day chugged along, the minutes and hours passing in a blur of food preparation and hostessing, of being gracious and feigning polite interest in whatever or whoever was speaking to me, of sensory overload. I had another glass of wine.

All the while, my brain was thinking of the way that momentary touch of Pat's hand had felt, the way my anger, my resentment had just...gone. I found myself resenting the distraction of people, voices, the task of preparing the big meal, and welcoming them all at the same time.

"—and make us truly thankful—"

The familiar words caught abruptly on something in my mind, like a jet hurtling along the surface of an aircraft carrier, hooking on a cable, jolting to a stop.

An image popped into my head from the movie *Top Gun*—Tom Cruise, Meg Ryan, what was the other actress's name? The one who came out as a lesbian not too long ago? I could picture her. God, my mind was like a sieve.

Diana was trying to have a baby. The thought was punctuated consecutively with exclamation point, question mark, exclamation point. !?!

Kelly McGillis. As soon as I thought it, I saw that sizzling-hot, open-mouthed Tom and Kelly love scene. No doubt it was sacrilegious to be thinking about Tom Cruise and sex and feeling horny while Joe was praying. I was very pleasantly buzzed. Very pleasantly.

I felt reckless.

Uncharacteristically *wild.*

In fact, if I wasn't holding Annie's hand in my left and David's hand in my right, I would pick up my wine glass and take another slug. "*Amen*," Joe said finally.

"Praise the bread, praise the meat, good God, let's eat," one of the Ohio cousins said, and all three kids giggled.

"I'll vote for that. Pass the turkey," Jamie said.

"Don't be shy," Joe said to Molly, seated on his right at the other end of the table, "or you'll go hungry."

Hands reached for bowls and serving platters. "While we're all in one room, let's make our plans for Christmas," Lillian said.

The very pleasant fuzziness that had filled my head and loosened my joints suddenly turned to something else, something that cleared my vision and filled me with adrenaline. I looked at my mother-in-law and noticed that she had gotten her hair "done" for this weekend, and was wearing a sweater I didn't recognize. Saw the way her lips pressed together when she was intent on what she wanted. She had glasses but resisted wearing them and so she squinted just a tiny bit as she glanced around the table. I realized suddenly that I resented the way Lillian was always so put together, never, ever had a hair out of place or a gravy stain on her shirt or garden soil under her nails. I resented it so much in that moment, it nearly choked me.

"It's on a Monday this year," my mother-in-law went on. "It'll be so nice to go to Christmas Eve mass together, then maybe we could let the kids open one present. On Christmas, we can have a big brunch and open the rest. We'll have a ham like always. I can buy it and bake it at my house." She looked at me. "I could make that fruit salad that everyone likes. How's that sound?"

Oddly, I was keenly aware of Pat looking at me, though I kept my eyes on Joe. He was reaching for the gravy boat and saying something to Molly. Molly laughed.

"I don't know what my schedule is yet, Nana, but I'm pretty sure I have to be back at work the day after Christmas." That was Jamie.

"Our office is open the day after the holiday," Hope said. The dentist office where she worked as a hygienist.

"I don't like that," Clara said. I could imagine squash. Or maybe green beans. Oysters. Last year, I'd had to go out to the kitchen and make my niece a peanut butter and jelly sandwich, no crusts, because Clara didn't want turkey or mashed potatoes or any of The Big Meal and she didn't like *crust*. I had waited for some other adult to say no, to tell Clara to sit down and politely taste everything. But that had not happened. In fact, Hope had asked if I had strawberry jam because Clara didn't like *grape*.

I looked at my mother-in-law and smiled, though I knew it was a mouth-only smile. "Let's get through one holiday before we start planning the next one."

"Well, I know how busy everyone is. If we don't make plans now, they just won't get made."

Suddenly I didn't care if I rocked the boat. *Rock the boat*. Ha. The fuzziness was back, a little, though I'd lost the pleasant buoyancy, that *glow*. Screw my mother-in-law, and the whole Daley family. "I was thinking we'd spend Christmas with my folks and my brother this year. In Arizona."

I felt Joe's head snap up, his eyes lock on. Like the radar lock in Tom Cruise's cockpit. "What?"

"Really?" Jamie said. "That'd be different."

"What?" Annie repeated. "We won't be *here* for Christmas?"

I glanced at Jamie, then at Annie. I ignored Joe. "We haven't seen them since they were here last spring."

"I don't know if I can get away for more than a day or so and maybe not on Christmas at all. Everyone wants to take off over the holidays. Going to Arizona would be—" Annie shook her head. Something in Annie's voice made my mother's radar sit up and take notice. Not a big something, but something.

"Christmas with no snow?" Hope said. "Can't even imagine it. It wouldn't be Christmas."

I glanced at my sister-in-law. *Shut up*, I thought. *No one asked you.*

"Well that would be nice, but I don't know..." Joe said. "That's a really busy time—"

"*Don't even go there,* I dared him with my eyes. *If you think you can get away for seven nights to cruise the fucking Caribbean with your mother and your siblings... Do. Not. Even. Go. There.*

Lillian, looking stricken, said, "Oh."

"Well, it's not definite," Joe said, glancing at me again. "Your folks don't have a lot of extra room—"

My parents lived in a retirement community, in a one story "cottage" with one bathroom and one spare bedroom slash den. The thought of all of us squeezed in there on top of my mom and dad for anything more than twenty-four hours actually made me feel nauseous. But maybe that was the wine.

"We can do Daley Christmas any day, it doesn't matter when," Laura said and I glanced at Joe's sister. Ordinarily, I would have felt grateful to Laura for the support, but this time, I couldn't help but think Laura was feeling guilty herself and was likely picturing *The Calypso* and those fucking palm trees.

"I have the whole week off between Christmas and New Year's. Maybe we could do Daley Christmas at our place in Pittsburgh this year." Everyone looked at Di. Pat's eyes, I noticed, went wide. Diana was not adept in the kitchen. She might understand the compounds in pharmaceuticals, but the ingredients in scalloped potatoes would be as foreign to her as those pharmaceuticals were to me. *But way to go, Di,* I thought. *Thanks for stepping up.*

"We'll talk about it," Joe said. "Going to Arizona, I mean."

Then someone asked for the green beans and the conversation moved on though I knew it would come up again.

When Annie and I were in the kitchen getting dessert organized, the chatter of voices in the dining room dropped noticeably. It wasn't quite a total mute, I could catch the odd word, identify the owner of voices, but it was as if everyone in the room was whispering now. The Ohio cousins had already left the table and were in the family room where I could hear Clara squeal and the yip of the puppy and the television as someone changed channels. When Annie picked up the tray just as Laura said, "Can you imagine water that blue?" I knew, instantly, that they were talking about Lillian's cruise and I also knew that it was no accident I was out of the room. *Clearly they didn't want to talk about it in front of me.*

"As blue as that dish," Laura said in the dining room and I knew she was referring to the beautiful handmade pottery bowl that had come from the local Arts Festival years ago and that sat on the old sideboard, now filled with trailing pine. "Mom, you're gonna love it."

"They have stuff to do besides sunbathe?" David asked. They had forgotten to speak in hushed tones. Annie was no longer in the kitchen.

"You sound like Joe," Laura said. "He asked the same thing."

He did? When?

"There are all sorts of day trips we can take, ports of call to explore."

Joe hates touristy stuff. Hates spending money on touristy stuff. Isn't wild about spending money, period.

"They have snorkeling equipment on board, fishing rods."

And I suppose Lillian wants to snorkel and fish.

"There's lots of stuff to do. Relax. Recharge your batteries. It'll be wonderful."

"Well, I for one think it's really nice." Hope. David's wife. My sister-in-law.

Are you serious? I had never been close to Hope. I had tried, once upon a time, to be friendly, to open myself to a friendship that was more than just relatives by marriage. But it never happened. Hope just had a way of saying things that, best case, astounded me, worst case, made me want to smack her.

I shook my head. By all rights, Hope, also a Daley by marriage, should feel the same way I did about Lillian's cruise. But I should have known Hope would be infuriating about this, as well as everything else.

"I mean, you don't know how long your mother is going to be

around," Hope went on and I almost snorted out loud. I couldn't see any of the faces gathered around my dining room table from where I stood in the kitchen, but I could just imagine the expressions. The sudden silence was telling.

Hope went on. "I think you should all make some special memories. You just never know—"

"Wait a minute," Annie spoke, in the dining room now. "We're going on a cruise? When?"

"Well, not you, not this time," Joe said.

"What?" Annie asked before someone else said something and Clara and Annie-the-puppy came running into the kitchen.

"Aunt Cath Aunt *Cath!* Annie *pooped!* We need a paper towel! Morgan stepped in it!"

And then I couldn't eavesdrop any longer, but grabbed the roll of paper towels and headed into the family room. When I came back out, after cleaning up the mess and urging the Ohio cousins to take Annie-the-puppy outside for a bit, I saw someone had taken the pies and the plate of raisin-filled cookies into the dining room. The coffee carafe, too. The tea kettle was just starting to whistle on the stove. I washed my hands at the sink and then turned off the burner.

"What'd I miss?" I said as I returned to the dining room. Cleaning up puppy poop, while the puppy's owners sat at my dining table leisurely eating dessert, had left me feeling combative.

"You didn't miss a thing," Pat said, winking at me. "Just plans for Lillian's big birthday cruise."

"Oh," I said, feeling the eyes of everyone in the dining room suddenly on me. "I've heard about that." I didn't know where to look. At Lillian? At Laura? Did they all look sheepish? Guilty? As if they waited for me to react, to disapprove.

It wasn't my place to approve or not. It wasn't any of my business what Mark and Laura, Diana and David wanted to do for Lillian's birthday. But what Joe thought about it, how he handled the whole situation, felt tangled up with our relationship, *our marriage.* Some part of me realized I was drawing a line in the sand, that I was forcing Joe to choose. *What should not have ever even been a choice.*

The members of Joe's family all seemed to be watching me expectantly. Waiting. Did they really think I would offer objections? No fucking way. I refused to say anything. Tried to keep any of my thoughts or emotions from my face.

"They booked the boat. It's official. The third week of April," Pat said.

I finally looked at Joe. Watched him cut a piece of pumpkin pie in half and slide it onto his dessert plate. "Great pie," he said, eventually looking at me.

Was he avoiding my eyes? He damn well should be!

David said something about airfare, Diana said something about US Air, Laura said something about Dulles and early morning traffic. I felt, surprisingly, nothing. As if I'd been suspended in time, as if there was pain out there somewhere, hurt, but it hadn't reached the part of me that registered those kind of feelings. Yet.

I could still feel Pat's eyes on me, and I avoided looking at him.

The third week of April.

"That's over our anniversary. Our thirtieth." Everyone looked at me.

"It is? Oh, it is," my mother-in-law said. "Well maybe we can move the trip a week?"

"The boat we want isn't available the next week," Laura said.

That's our spring break at school," David said. "The third week. It's the best time for me to get away for a whole week. Sorry."

"I'm flexible, but I thought Mark had some conflict the next week?" Diana put in.

I was staring at Joe. Could hear the voices, the comments, but didn't really give a damn what everyone else was saying. I wanted to know what Joe would say. Now everyone else was looking at him, too. I could practically see him wishing himself anywhere but here.

"Well, technically, an anniversary commemorates the day you

vowed to spend your lives together. So you could celebrate it any one of those days. Hopefully every one," Hope said.

I glanced at her. She was smiling like she'd brokered a Middle-East peace deal. WTF? *Blow it out your ass, Hope, you moron*, I wanted to shout. I wanted to pick up the pumpkin pie and smash it on Joe's head.

"I suppose that's true." Joe. "We can do something special when I get back." I could feel everyone looking at me again. Waiting.

Something *special?* Not one person in this room, besides me, thought this cruise idea was fucked up? It must be me. It really must be my problem, that I don't get it. I don't get it at all. My glance slid to Patrick who was leaning back in his chair, coffee cup in his hands.

"Happy Anniversary," he mouthed.

———

ANNIE SAT on one of the stools at the counter in the kitchen. She'd taken a shower after everyone had gone, and her hair was still damp, slicked back from her face. Her T-shirt, old and faded, read "Tina Fey for President."

Lillian, Laura, Di, the Ohio Daleys and their puppy, thank God, had gone back to Lillian's condo. Patrick had gone on home to Pittsburgh, claiming he had work for a client to do tomorrow. Everyone, except Patrick, would be here again tomorrow. Jaime and Molly had disappeared in the car, Jamie claiming he wanted to show Molly "around."

"How's the new cookbook coming?" Annie asked, fiddling with a paper napkin on the counter.

"So far so good. When my editor suggested a cookbook featuring holiday recipes, I thought I'd never have enough. But I do. Easily."

"Like your Chesapeake scalloped oysters. And spicy pumpkin dip. I think it's cool you're writing cookbooks."

"Kinda dumb luck."

"Give yourself more credit. You've been cooking amazing food for forever. You're a master at taking care of us all and the house and the gardens. And Father J, too. It's a full-time job."

Annie had always been a kind person, the one who noticed when someone was left out, or off a team, who remembered others' birthdays, who offered to cut the neighbor's grass. It was just how she was wired. It was part of what made her a good nurse. So her pep talk wasn't really a surprise. But there was something about it that made me glance at her. She was now shredding the paper napkin into strips. After a moment, during which I stacked clean saucers and coffee cups in the cupboard, she asked, "Are Dad and Nana Lil and everyone really going on a cruise?"

I sighed. I didn't want to talk about this. Not now. Not with Annie. "I guess so." The numbness was still there, but so was the knowledge that the cruise was scheduled over our thirtieth wedding anniversary. "It appears they're making the plans."

"That sucks."

"Don't disagree."

"You should say something."

"Nope. I should not."

"Why not?"

"I've told your dad exactly what I think of the whole idea. But it's not my place to tell Aunt Laura or Uncle Mark, any of them, what they can do for their mother."

"I can't believe that Nana Lil would want to have a birthday without all of us.

Well, believe it.

It just sucks," Annie said again. "And over your anniversary, too."

I paused, the dishwasher open before me, a glass in each hand. "Tell me about it," I said.

I looked at Annie again. I thought she looked thin, washed out, but maybe it was just the fact that her hair was wet, her face bare of makeup, not that Annie ever wore much.

She swept all the little pieces of paper napkin into a pile and with her fingers, carefully worked to arrange them into a stack. Abruptly, she changed the subject. She had something on her mind. "What are you going to buy with the money you make from the new cookbook?"

Huh? "Oh, I don't know. We need to put a new roof on the house. Maybe do some outside painting."

"What about that convertible? The one you've been talking about for forever."

"That's just kidding around. Can you see me in a convertible?" I asked. "There's not that much money in writing cookbooks. And a convertible is not really practical."

"Screw practical. You should do something crazy, something fun, like buy a cool car. Especially if Dad is really going to go off on some cruise without you. On your anniversary."

"Maybe he won't go," I said. "Maybe he'll tell Aunt Laura and Uncle Mark that he doesn't want to go." Of course, I'd been hoping that Joe would do just that. That ultimately, he would not go on the *bleeping* cruise.

Annie kept playing with the pieces of napkin. "Not what I heard."

"What did you hear?"

"Dad said that he agreed with Aunt Hope and that an anniversary was about celebrating years, not one specific day. So technically you have three hundred and fifty-eight other days to celebrate."

"When did he say that?" My heart seemed to constrict inside me.

"When everyone was leaving and Dad was out in the driveway saying goodbye..."

"You know your dad. He doesn't like confrontation." Or commitment. If I hadn't gotten pregnant thirty years ago, we still might not be married.

"You should tell them it sucks. The whole idea is dumb."

I sighed. "I've already said it all to your dad." I shrugged. "Besides, if I have to ask him not to go, I don't know if I want him to stay."

Annie looked at me and I could almost see the moment when she grasped what I meant. I felt a surge of emotion, gratitude for a compassionate and giving daughter. Again, I thought there was something in Annie's eyes, those blue-gray eyes that were just like my own. What was it?

"That just sucks," Annie said.

"I know," I said.

Chapter Five

Joe was asleep in his recliner when I walked through the family room. The room looked like a tornado had blown through or else as if it had been the site of a WWE championship bout. Furniture had been pushed or pulled out of place. Magazines and books from the coffee table had been piled on the floor but someone had knocked them over, so magazines had slid partly under the sofa, the rest lay in a messy heap. There was a suspicious wet spot on the old rug, about the size of puppy pee. One section of the newspaper lay on the old bureau, another section was on the floor beside Joe's chair, beneath Trouble who didn't even lift her head when I came into the room.

After the cousins and extended family had all left, Joe had disappeared here into the family room. Had he not noticed the wet spot? The bleeping magazines? How was that possible? Annoyance shot through me. I shook Joe's shoulder, rougher than I would have probably had to.

"Hey." Joe sat up suddenly. "Hey. What time is it?"

Trouble lifted her head. "Almost 11:00." I answered him.

"C'mon girl. Let's go out before bed." The dog rose stiffly to her feet. She was getting to be an old girl. Aging just like the rest of us, I thought, patting the big head, the solid shoulders.

Trouble followed me to the kitchen where I opened the door to let her out to do her business one last time before she found her way to the dog bed in the pantry. Annie was in the dining room now, on her laptop. I could hear the tapping of keys.

"'Night, honey," I said as I passed. "See you in the morning."

"Okay, Mom. We're going to the cemetery, right?"

I was touched that Annie seemed to cherish what had become tradition between us. It was something private, if not exactly secret, that the two of us shared every holiday. "Yep. First thing. I assume everyone will likely come over from Nana Lil's for lunch."

"Okay. If I'm not up, wake me."

When I got to the bedroom, Joe was propped up, reading a trade magazine in bed. Clearly he'd rallied after his little nap in the recliner. He glanced at me and smiled. After thirty-plus years, I knew that smile was an "I'm horny" smile. Clearly, he was remembering our activity in the kitchen this morning. I moved into the bathroom and closed the door.

I stared at myself in the mirror over the sink. My face looked pale, a faint web of lines fanned out from my eyes. My lips were dry. All that wine today. I licked them, leaned closer to the mirror, tilted my head to one side, then the other. I straightened and extended my chin. I pressed one hand against the base of my throat. God, the skin there looked like something from the turkey I'd stuffed this morning. Was it saggier than last week? Last month? Did I look as old as I felt? What did others see when they looked at me? What did Pat see?

No. No. No. Do not think about Pat.

My eyes, the pupils, were pinpricks in the bright light. I stared into the iris, gray steely blue. What was in there?

What. Was. In. There.

I could almost feel Joe in the bedroom, waiting for me to come out. I was not aroused, that was for sure. The resentment I felt about Lillian's Cruise had simply wiped out any passion or desire before it could even take root.

How could Joe not get that?

I slipped on my nightgown.

He was still awake and the look in his eyes definitely said horny. *This is why women fake it,* I thought, pulling down the covers and sliding into bed, my back to my husband.

"Ahh. There it is again," he said rolling toward me.

"What?" I asked over my shoulder.

"That smell. Your lotion or cream or whatever. It makes me crazy." His hand felt around for the bottom of my nightgown.

I reached to switch off the light as Joe's hand slid up my waist, along my ribs, warm against my bare skin. His thumb flicked over my nipple. He made a sound low in his throat. "It's been three weeks." His hand lifted my breast, as much as he could through the night-gown, his thumb still playing with my nipple.

What?

He counted the days? Why does that sound like an accusation? Why does that make me feel guilty? Because it was on me that we hadn't had sex in three weeks.

In another part of my brain the thought formed, *Joe thinks this is foreplay? Reminding me of how long it's been since we've had sex?*

I fought the urge to scream, to push him away while he continued to fondle my breast. Emotions flared: Anger, and hurt, and desire became rage, pure and simple. How close they were: love and hate. I thought I might explode. I shut my eyes, not that Joe could see my face.

He counted the fucking days?

The days since our last fucking?

I sought a picture of something, anything, that would arouse me. I'd read the *Fifty Shades* books. I tried to picture Christian Grey. Those kinky sex toys. The bedroom. That *bed.* Suddenly I thought of Patrick and felt a corresponding surge deep inside.

No. No nononono. Pat was married. I was married. He was my brother-in-law. But who would know? Who would ever know what was in my head? It was committing adultery in my head. If I knew Joe did that, it would break my heart. *More than it was already broken?*

Joe pulled up the hem of my nightgown. Thinking about fictional characters wasn't wrong, was it? If it helped a person maintain intimacy in their marriage on the nights when that person was not. In. The. Mood.

I shut my eyes again. Put Pat out of my head. I conjured up a scene from a western romance I'd read. I'd just watched *The English Patient* not long ago. Ralph Fiennes. Oh, Ralph, I thought, as Joe's mouth found my breast.

A fantasy filled my head. My body responded, but to what? What Joe was doing? Or to something—someone—in my imagination?

Fifty shades of adultery.

Later, after Joe had rolled over and the sound of his steady breathing, not quite snoring, filled the room, I lay and stared up at the ceiling. Three weeks. Three weeks. Three weeks.

———

In the morning, as he showered and dressed, Joe hummed. Some country song. I didn't know it, but I heard him actually sing part of the chorus. Something about a horse trailer on a Cadillac. Joe loved country music. I could practically *feel* his good mood. His high spirits. It made me want to scream. To hit something. *Were all men so pathetically predictable?* Give them sex, no matter how uninspired, and they were pleasant and agreeable? Happy.

It was like feeding a parking meter.

Bitterness at being so used filled me until I thought I'd choke. How often did I let my dissatisfaction and my hostility slide, in the interest of marital accord?

After the sound of his footsteps moved down the hallway, I practiced deep breathing. Concentrated on feeling oxygen fill my lungs and the warmth and softness of the down pillow under my head, the flannel sheets against my legs. In a while, the anger was gone, sifting down like the raisins in a box of bran flakes. An image of a cereal box full of nothing but raisins popped into my head. I opened my eyes and glanced at the clock: 6:23.

When Annie hadn't appeared by 8:30, I went upstairs to wake her. She opened her eyes almost as soon as I opened the door.

"Hey. I'm awake," she said, her voice sleep-roughened.

"Okay. Just checking," I whispered. "We should probably get going so we can be back in time to fix some lunch."

"'K." Annie took a deep breath, rolled over and stretched. "I'll be down in ten minutes."

The door to Jamie and Doug's room was open a crack and I could not resist the urge to peek in at my oldest son. I couldn't help but remember the countless mornings when I'd come up here, opened the doors, called to the boys to get them up for school. I'd often had to shake Doug and pull his covers off to wake him. He slept like Joe, like the dead. This morning the windows gleamed, the waves and bubbles in the old glass glittering and making odd patches of light on the walls. I stared at Jamie's bed. It took me a moment to grasp what I was seeing. There was long hair on Jamie's pillow. Not Jamie's. Two hands were visible above the covers and another gripped the side of the bed. There was a leg and a foot, also not Jamie's, and a big lump under the covers at the middle of the bed. I heard heavy breathing, a soft wheeze, a muffled cry.

I pulled away from the crack of the open door. Pressed myself against the wall. Felt my heart pounding in my chest, the scalding heat of embarrassment on my face. My son and Molly were having oral sex. The picture of what they were doing froze behind my eyelids like a Polaroid. Sex. That shouldn't be a shocker. He was a healthy, normal adult male. But knowing something in your head, and seeing it with your own eyes was entirely different.

Something soft and warm suddenly bumped my hand and I almost shrieked aloud, until I realized it was Trouble. No doubt she'd slept on the rug at the foot of Annie's bed. I hadn't heard her. Keeping my hand on the dog's head, I moved to the stairs and down them as quietly as I could.

———

"WHAT'S IN THE BAG?" I asked Annie, glancing at my daughter as I backed out of the driveway. Annie wore a white down jacket and a pink and orange scarf wrapped in a big knot around her neck. Dark sunglasses. In one hand she carried a flat paper shopping bag, the kind you got when you buy a greeting card; in the other, she carefully held a bright red mug of pale herbal tea wafting steam. It was a beautiful day, sunny, but cold. The heater was on and blowing full blast but warm air was just now starting to pour from the vents.

"Did you get breakfast? I didn't mean to rush you. I just thought I'd start the car and get it warmed up. We could have waited until you finished your tea."

"That's okay, I'm not really hungry. This is fine."

"Smells good. Ginger?"

"Yeah. Supposed to be good for an upset stomach."

"Uh oh," I said. "Hope you're not getting the flu."

"I'm fine."

I shifted the van into drive, and glanced at Annie. She took another sip of tea. I could really smell the ginger now, the aroma filling the inside of my minivan. Again, for a reason I couldn't pinpoint, my mother's radar spiked, my heart clenched in my chest in a familiar way. Worry. Love.

Annie was, like the boys, generally very private about her life. She'd never had a serious boyfriend, always keeping a whole group of friends, guys and girls, around her. She'd been an athlete, a tomboy. Never a "girlie girl." Oh, she'd had plenty of dates with guys, but they always seemed to be guys who were friends, who remained friends long after the dates were over, or dates that included several other people and things like all-night bowling or ice skating or hikes and bonfires with hot dogs and s'mores.

I heard her sniff and when I glanced over, I saw that there was a tear shimmering on her cheek. My breath caught. I swallowed and looked ahead again, feeling the ache in my heart as if it were being squeezed by a giant fist. *Should I ask? Or should I wait for her cue?* "Everything okay?" I finally said. I strived for a blend of casual and caring. Loving but not interfering.

Annie took a deep breath and I heard the catch in it before she seemed to gather herself.

"I've been seeing this guy. His name is Corey. We met at a picnic this summer. One of the nurses at the hospital had a barbeque for the fourth of July."

I nodded. "Hmm." Wow. This summer. Four months ago. Just the way Annie had said *at a picnic*, I could tell there was more to the story.

"He's older," Annie said.

"Older?" I asked.

"Forty."

Whaaaat? I thought, feeling the muscles of my jaw tense as I fought to keep my mouth closed. I knew without a doubt that allowing any disapproval, any judgment at all to show would mean the kiss of death for this conversation. But inside my head, I was shouting *What? You're only twenty-three. Who is this guy?*

"I really like him. I know I shouldn't, but I can't help it." This was a glimpse into the mind and heart of my daughter the likes of which I had never heard.

Because of his age? I took a breath. Cleared my throat. *Careful, careful.* Reminded myself that Annie was an adult, that she did not have to be sharing these thoughts, and depending on how I reacted, she might not do so again. Suddenly, I was reminded of how I'd felt, what I'd thought—what I'd been *doing*—when I was Annie's age. The revelation was like seeing Jamie and Molly in bed this morning all over again. *Tread carefully.*

"What's he like?" I asked. "Is he local? From Pittsburgh?" Not commenting on *older.* For now.

"He's a lineman for a gas company. Buys leases and negotiates deals with people who have gas under their property. He has an office in the city, but he travels a lot. He's from Alabama. He played football at Auburn. Linebacker. He looks like a linebacker. He's blond. Blue eyes. Southern accent. Got that southern charm thing...."

"Hmm," I murmured, smiling, enough to keep Annie talking, not enough to offer even unspoken approval or criticism. *Forty years old.*

"He likes to fish. Likes everything outside. Hunting and fishing. Typical southern boy," Annie spoke with a kind of pride in her voice that I recognized as that rush that accompanies a new relationship. Infatuation. And then I thought, *They're sleeping together. Of course they are.*

Sex for a forty-year-old man was different than sex for a twenty-three-year-old girl. Than for a twenty-three-year-old guy, for that matter. A forty-year-old man was worldly, experienced. He'd likely already been there and done that in the relationship department. A forty-year-old man had already experienced all the firsts with someone else.

I had never met him, but I didn't like him already. In my mind, he was jaded and exploitive, a predator, little more than a pedophile. Not very Christian, I would admit it. The guy should be hung up by his horny little dick. Horny big dick. God. Mental headshake, mental headshake, mental headshake.

I glanced at Annie and saw the resolute line of her mouth. Corey had done something to hurt Annie. That would explain Annie's mood, the absence of the bright-eyed smiles that were characteristically Annie. I had sensed that there was something wrong. "What happened?" I asked.

Annie took a deep breath. "I'm just disappointed we can't be together over the holiday. I understand it's hard for him, but I thought maybe Sunday, Sunday night even. Now that isn't going to happen."

"Is he traveling somewhere? Visiting family or friends? Does he have to work?"

I felt Annie look at me, though I kept my gaze on the road. I'd learned from experience—all those road trips to baseball, soccer, golf tournaments—the kids felt freer to speak if a parent's eyes weren't on them.

"He's with family. His family." There was a challenge in Annie's voice, defiance.

"You mean he went back to Alabama?"

"I mean with his family. Two kids. In Pittsburgh. And his wife."

What? "He's married? Oh, Annie." And now I did look at my daughter, pulled the car over to the side of the road. We were only about a half mile from the entrance to the cemetery, but I turned in my seat so I could see Annie better, with no distractions. The hell with not looking directly at her.

For some reason, I thought Annie would cry, would want a hug, her mother's arms around her, but Annie appeared to be finished crying. She still wore the dark sunglasses so her eyes, and what was in them, remained a mystery. Her mouth was pressed into an unyielding line.

"He's married?" I asked again, so there could be no mistake.

"Yes, Mom. He's married. I didn't plan it, okay? It just happened. For him and for me."

How many times had I heard the "other woman" use that lame excuse on talk shows and in movies? *Oh, my God. My daughter, Annie, is an "other woman."*

"Don't say anything. I mean it. Don't preach. You don't have to. I know what you're going to say. Once a cheater, always a cheater. It's against the laws of man, and God. It's the lowest kind of woman who steals another woman's husband. Thou shall not commit adultery."

"That just about sums it up."

"Don't, okay? I get it."

"Apparently not. He's married, Annie. Seriously?"

"Serious as a heart attack. She was his high school girlfriend, she got pregnant, they got married too young. He doesn't love her."

I opened my mouth to speak, to tell my daughter just what I thought of that line of reasoning, of those *excuses*, but something stopped me, something as effective as super glue between my lips. I sat there, staring at Annie who stared defiantly back—defiant—Annie!—my mind a blur, racing with all the things I was thinking and feeling. Annie looked not at all sorry or remorseful or guilty.

At a complete loss as to what to say, what to *feel*, I pulled back out on the road, my mind and heart reeling. I drove the half mile to the entrance of the cemetery and parked. I got out and Annie got out, the slamming of our doors loud in the empty silence.

We walked through the stones of the graveyard, the ones here closest to the road very old, lichen-covered, their engraved names and dates worn so that they could barely be read. I didn't speak, though I was thinking, thinking, thinking, about what to say. Annie, too, was silent. The sound of our footsteps through the longish grass, of Annie's coat rustling as she moved, was all I could hear, that and the voice in my head.

We are not finished talking about this. We have to talk about it. Could I let Annie leave, go back to Pittsburgh, to her job and her life there without telling her... What? What could I tell her that I hadn't already? More importantly, what would Annie *hear*?

But I couldn't, wouldn't have that conversation now.

Here.

I took a deep breath and held it in my lungs for a long moment. Put Annie and her revelation out of my mind. I closed my eyes, found the place I needed to be in my head, in my heart, when I was here, at my daughter's grave, the daughter whose death certificate said Crib Death. Now such a document would read SIDS, Sudden Infant Death Syndrome. A tidy, descriptive four letter acronym for a loss that was shattering and indescribable.

This cemetery was beautiful, as cemeteries go. It was old, some of the surrounding trees so big I would not be able to wrap my arms around them. When Nora had died, there had been a rusty and crooked iron fence around the whole cemetery, listing under the weight of tangles of wild honeysuckle the gates bent and unable to close, if anyone had wanted to close them. A few years ago, that original fence had been replaced with a new one that was straight and sturdy, the steel pickets pointy like arrows, the whole thing powder-coated a dark green. I liked the old fence better, though I understood the necessity of replacing it.

At this little cemetery, several miles from town and removed from houses or any buildings at all, the grass was mowed once or twice a summer by the local 4-H club. I liked thinking about 4-H kids here, poking among the stones, working the way young kids work, distractedly, talking and giggling, with ponytails or barrettes in their hair, braces on their teeth, jeans and ratty tennis shoes with holes in the toes. Some veterans came before Memorial Day, to put little flags on the graves of fallen comrades. I knew other people must come, occasionally, because every once in a while, there would be a bouquet of flowers, sometimes handpicked wildflowers, sometimes a formal arrangement from a florist. There were no other Daleys buried in this cemetery, but I had no memory of Joe protesting my choice of a plot here for Nora.

After I had come back to myself, after some time had passed, I had supposed that was because at the time, he was numb, too. I sighed. In some ways, it seemed almost impossible to conceive that twenty-nine years had passed. The memory of the pain of that time was imprinted in me somewhere, my head or my heart, I didn't know which. The anguish was dulled but not entirely gone or forgotten. The power of it could still catch me unawares, though that happened less frequently after all these years.

Today, as I'd expected, there was no one else here. In the far corner, along the fence, not far from an ancient lilac bush, my infant daughter was buried. Annie and I walked unerringly up to the stone. Straggly grass had grown up along the edge, dried leaves tangled in it.

The Cruise

"What was she like?" Annie asked. *Her sister.*

My youngest child asked the same question about my oldest almost every time we came here. The asking, and answering, was part of the rite, the homage we paid Nora. Maybe the holiest part. Nora had died before she was three months of age, too soon for there to be stories of milestones, or achievements, birthdays, or holidays. Annie knew that, and she knew what I would say, the things I would remember but she asked just the same.

And just the same, I took a deep breath, mentally girding myself for the ache of remembering. It was softer now, the sorrow, but it would still come. I didn't mind Annie asking the question. I didn't mind the sorrow, either. But I still knew I needed to prepare the place in my heart where it would burrow in.

"She was like every child, such a miracle. It's overwhelming how much you love them. No one can ever begin to describe it adequately or to understand it, really. You have to experience it. What you feel for your children is so powerful it changes who you are inside. Forever." I glanced at Annie. "She had more hair than you or your brothers when you were born. Thick, dark, silky baby hair. I had no idea where such hair came from. No one on the Daley side had hair like that. No one on my side, either. She was an easy baby, never fussy. I was so happy."

"What about Dad?"

I glanced at Annie. This question, too, was not unexpected, but I sensed more to it this time.

"He was, too. Happy. He never seemed to be nervous, like some new dads. He held her and changed her diapers. He would dress her and talk to her. He didn't seem nervous, but I wasn't sure I trusted him to care for her."

"I can't really see Dad with a baby. He's kind of awkward."

"In my defense, I think my feeling so protective was probably normal. I loved her—all of you—so fiercely." I glanced at Annie, smiled ruefully. "A woman I used to babysit for who lived next door to Grammy and Poppy once told me that she could throw her husband in front of a train before she could let anything happen to her kids. I was shocked when she told me that. I didn't believe her. Until I had Nora. Then I understood. One day, God willing, you will, too. Understand that kind of mother's love. "

Annie smiled as if she did understand but didn't comment.

I had never talked about this before, but the time was right. Of course Annie could do the math, she would have known for years, since she was old enough to subtract five from nine and arrive at "oops," that I was almost four months pregnant at my marriage. Joe and I were married in April, Nora was born at the beginning of September, and she was a full-term baby. How does a mother tell her children, her daughter, she broke the rules of the Church, of God, without endorsing that choice, that behavior? "It took a long time for me to believe that your dad did not regret marrying me."

"What?" Now Annie looked shocked. "Why?"

"The typical reason. I didn't know if he really wanted to get married. To anyone. Or if he was only marrying me because I was pregnant."

Annie stared at me. I shrugged. "Things were different then. I expect it was normal for a girl to think that."

"I knew you were pregnant. But I thought you and Dad were in love? I thought you were crazy in love."

"I was. I was totally infatuated. It was love at first sight for me. I think he was so inexperienced with girls he enjoyed the novelty, the —" I grimaced wryly "—the perks. He got more confident though. Just about the time I got pregnant, I was starting to sense that he was feeling—" I pursed my lips, trying to think of the right word, "—restless."

The confession was intimate and, even after all these years, it made me feel vulnerable. Embarrassed even. But Annie needed to know. The choices Annie was making, had made, earned her this truth.

"Dad?" Annie sounded dubious.

"Don't get me wrong. He told me he loved me. He said he did. Yes. But we were young, so young. I was barely twenty-one. Your dad was only a little over a year older." I shook my head. "Your dad had never had a girlfriend before me. A serious one. It was only natural for him to feel that way. Restless." I sniffed. "It's a lot easier for me to say that, to think that, now, as a mother with children of my own. I didn't feel so understanding then. Especially after I got pregnant. But now I can only imagine how—" again, I struggled to find the right word, "—trapped he must have felt. Of course, Nana Lil was really upset when she found out."

"She was mad?"

"Oh, I don't know if mad is the right word. Disappointed, certainly. Unhappy. It wasn't what she wanted for your dad. When we told her we were getting married, she was shocked. The look on her face was not a good one." There had been no hug, no congratulations. "I would probably have some of the same feelings if one of your brothers found himself in the same situation. But I don't think I'd blame the girl. I hope I wouldn't." But wasn't I blaming Corey, the smooth-talking, gas company lease negotiator?

No. I'm blaming him for adultery.

"But it all worked out. You and Dad have been married for almost thirty years. You had all of us."

"Yes, and gave up sleeping soundly forever more." I smiled. "The bane of motherhood. You never sleep again. Even when your kids are grown up, you never stop worrying."

"They never found out what happened?" Annie asked this question, too. Every visit here.

"Crib death. SIDS, officially."

"It's not genetic." This was a statement, not a question.

"No doubt you know more about that than I do now. You and your brothers were at risk. And I didn't stop being terrified until you all turned a year old. But I don't think your future children are more at risk for SIDS because you had a sister who died."

Annie looked at me for a moment, then back down to Nora's gravestone. "He's going to divorce his wife."

We were back to Corey. I didn't speak for a moment, running through what I could say, what I sensed Annie *wanted* me to say. I settled for asking a question, putting the ball back in Annie's court. "Is that a good thing? If he divorces his wife, the mother of his children?"

"I don't know," Annie said, surprising me. And I recognized an honesty that was almost painful to behold. "I thought it was. I really like him."

"You thought?" I pressed. "Past tense? What changed?"

Annie looked at me, then glanced down at Nora's stone before shaking her head and giving a little snort. "The fact that you asked me and didn't totally freak."

I couldn't help it, I laughed. Pulling my daughter into a hug, finally, feeling her pressed up against my chest, smelling her hair and her skin, I felt a lifting of the heaviness that had been in my heart, though it wasn't entirely gone. "That doesn't mean I approve."

"I get that."

"There are kids, Annie. Children. You need to consider them, first." He *should be considering them, first.*

"I know. I said, I get it. But things are different than when you were my age. People aren't so old-fashioned now."

You think fidelity is old-fashioned? "Don't do anything rash. Think about it. That's all I'm saying." *I don't want you to be hurt. He'll hurt you just like he's hurting his current wife. His children. If Corey is the right one, he'll still be the right one in a month or two or six. In a year.*

Is there a "right one?" I used to think there was, that we all had our perfect match somewhere on the planet. That being with the "right" one was good and easy and right. *Or is marriage just when two people both decide to stick it out, to overlook all the "wrongs" and to go to bed in the same bed and wake up every morning and simply keep putting one foot in front of the other?*

Is marriage merely commitment?

Brushing the silky wisps of Annie's hair back from her temples, I kissed my daughter's forehead. "I love you. I love you more than anything in the world."

"I love you, too. Don't tell Dad. About Corey. Not yet."

I looked at my daughter. "Oh, honey. He's your dad."

"I know. I'll tell him. But just not yet."

I studied her face. Features that were so precious to me it made my heart expand to fill my chest. "Okay. For now. What's in the bag?" I asked nodding at the flat paper bag Annie had carried from home.

She smiled and carefully opened it up, reached inside. Pulling out three perfectly golden ginkgo leaves, she laid them on the little lip of the marble tombstone. In the bright, cold light of November the leaves looked like jewelry. I'd envisioned ginkgo leaves on a breakfast-in-bed tray just a few weeks ago. Bone of my bone, I thought, looking into my daughter's eyes.

"Pretty, huh?" Annie asked.

"Beautiful." I smiled, feeling tears pushing against the back of my eyes.

"Did you bring it?" Annie looked at me.

"Of course," I said, blinking, reaching into my coat pocket. Scraped and washed clean, the wishbone from yesterday's turkey was an odd memento. I had no doubt that others would think it irreverent or even disrespectful, but we didn't. And we were the only ones who mattered.

The tears were coming harder now, hot and stinging; my nose started to run. I gripped one side of the wishbone with the little finger of my right hand and held it out to Annie, who gripped the other side with her pinky. Then looking at my daughter, my only living daughter, I pulled, feeling Annie pulling, too.

Oh, Nora, I thought. *Oh, baby, I will never stop thinking about you, loving you, missing you.* I felt the tears sliding down my cold cheeks, sniffed at the pressure building inside my head. The ache in my chest was whole and pure and familiar. I couldn't speak now if I wanted to.

With a bright snap, the wishbone broke and Annie was left holding the bigger piece. Through tears, I smiled, seeing that Annie's eyes were full, too, that her cheeks showed the glimmer of tear tracks.

I wiped my eyes, my face. Sniffed again and took a deep breath, hearing it catch on the pain in my heart. "Thanks for coming with me," I said, eventually, to Annie. It was what I said every time.

"You're welcome." What Annie said every time. Like a priest and his congregants. A prompt and a response. Practiced and familiar.

Annie laid her piece of the wishbone beside the leaves, and I put mine there, too. Both pieces would be gone the next time I came here, I knew from experience. The ginkgo leaves, too. Whether the bones would blow away in the wind or be carried off by a raccoon or something else, I never knew. It didn't matter.

"Let's go home," I said then. "We have a hungry crowd to feed."

———

THE REST of the weekend was the mass of confusion I had known it would be: people, food, mountains of dirty dishes, and one small puppy with bladder and bowel control issues. The house looked like a tornado had passed through and in a way, it had—a whirlwind of Daleys.

Jamie and Molly's flight was at noon Sunday, so the two of them had left just after 8:00 a.m., with Annie, who would deliver them to the airport on the way back to her apartment. The letdown on departure day left me feeling hollow inside. Melancholy. I knew the visit to the cemetery was partly responsible for the emotions that lay heavy inside my chest, but not solely to blame.

After the kids left, Joe went to the office and I lost myself in the mundane and mindless tasks of righting the house after a holiday weekend.

I was standing in the kitchen debating if I had enough time for a cup of tea before changing clothes for 5:00 Mass when my my cell phone rang. I glanced at the little screen as I picked it up. Helene.

"Hey," I answered.

"You survived the weekend."

"Is that a question?"

"Not really. You answered. So you obviously did."

"You sound a little cranky."

"Yeah, well. Happiness is overrated."

"What happened?" I asked.

"Erick got married."

"What? I thought you said his wife threw him out. I thought he *was* married. He divorced her and married someone else already?"

"He is. Married. And she did. Throw him out. But he took her to Antigua over the holiday and they 'renewed their vows.'"

I couldn't help it, I laughed. "Which vows are those? 'I promise to cheat at every opportunity, to make a pass at every woman who is warm and breathing and who stands still long enough?' What a schmuck."

Helene didn't respond, and the silence was full of something that gave me pause. "What?" I finally said.

"He took her to fucking Antigua. We went to Antigua on our honeymoon," Helene said and her voice was tinged with a kind of agony that I could feel in my chest. Erick truly was an asshole.

"Oh, Hel," at a loss for what else to say. "Let it go. Living well is the best revenge. You know that. He isn't worth one thought, one tear, one regret."

"I know that. I know it in my head. But I can't believe he can still get to me. I am so pissed off. I want to rip his shaved head off and put his lying, cheating tongue through the shredder. I'd like to run his dick through there, too." Helene gave a shaky laugh that had a bit of a sob mixed in. "The bastard. The shithead. The fucking asshole."

"C'mon. Don't hold back. Tell me what you really think."

At that, Helene did laugh, though I could still hear tears in her voice.

Just then, footsteps pounded on the porch and the kitchen door opened and Joe came in. Cold air came, too, in a rush. Seeing me on the phone, he looked at me, his eyebrows raised in question.

Helene, I mouthed. Joe nodded and moved on into the laundry room to take off his coat and boots.

"I hate the son-of-a-bitch. I mean it. I hate what he did to me, to Jules." She paused. "But it's Erick. And besides everything else, he is good. I mean he is *very good* in bed. He knows how to push my buttons." A picture popped suddenly into my head: myself in bed, naked, my back arched, my nipples taut and hard while a head, a mouth descended. I could almost feel warm breath on my skin, smell the scent of male body, the image was so vivid. It actually made me horny. I didn't know who the man was. It was not Joe. Definitely not Erick.

"I've never told you this, but twice after we were divorced, we slept together. I know I shouldn't have. Not after what he did. But I couldn't stop myself. It was Erick." Helene had known and loved Erick since high school. It had taken them years to get together, years during which Helene had met and dated other men, had even been engaged to one. But she could never get past Erick. I suspected she never would.

Joe came back into the kitchen and eased up behind me, nuzzling his cold face into my neck. Mr. Doofus. I cocked my head, rolled my shoulder, gave him a push away and he headed off to the family room. Was he really that oblivious to what was between us, or more accurately, what was *not* between us? His cluelessness was actually staggering. It tightened the knot of all the emotions I was feeling. Made them hard, hot, bitter. Trouble was beside me suddenly and I reached down and gave the big broad head a pat.

"Do you think it was wrong? To sleep with him?" Helene asked. "I mean, how fucked up is that?"

I thought of the warm breath, the taut nipples, the man in my imagination who was *not* Joe. Experienced, suddenly, an almost overwhelming craving for toe-curling sex, for *passion*, for lip-tingling, lust-fueled oblivion, and wondered, in the far back of my mind, what I would do to have it. Sex with Joe lately had been more anger and guilt than anything else, sex that was so much a lie, I should have to confess it to Father J.

God, life is complicated.

"No. If it was good for you, I do not think it was wrong."

———

THE VAN WAS cold and tiny snowflakes began to hit the windshield with discernible clicks. *Sleet.* The air smelled sharp and arctic. It seemed to have turned from autumn to winter in one afternoon. I hunched my shoulders, glad I'd worn my heavy coat. Father J would have the thermostat in the sanctuary turned up, once we got to church.

"I'm glad the kids left this morning, if the weather's going to get bad."

"It's just a little squall. Nothing that's gonna stick," he said about the sleet. He kept a close eye on the weather. Everyone in the trucking business did. Especially anyone in the trucking business in the northeast in the winter.

"Still," I said, feeling slowly warming air begin to blow around my feet.

"They'll be fine," he said, referring to the kids. He never worried. Never fretted.

It felt like he was belittling my concern about the weather. I resented the way he was so cavalier about our children's safety and well-being. At the moment, I resented just about everything about Joe.

"I can't believe we're going to be late," I said. "Again," I added. I couldn't help myself.

"Relax. We'll slip in the back. Father J will never know." He said that, *relaaaax*, as if there was something wrong with *me*. As if not wanting to be late was a character flaw of *mine*.

"I don't care about Father J knowing. It just annoys me that we're going to be late. There was no reason for us to be late tonight." Joe put on the blinker to turn left onto Piper Road and I said, "Stop. Stop the car."

Joe glanced at me, but did not stop.

"Where are we going?" I said, though I knew. Just about every week, regardless of weather or circumstance or anything else, we drove two miles down Piper Road to the little condo complex where Lillian lived now "on our way to church." But it wasn't on our way, it was two miles the wrong direction, then the same two miles back into town. And Lillian had a car of her own. And Lillian was perfectly capable of driving herself to church. It was ridiculous that Lillian had to attend church with us.

Grrrraaahhh. The scream was only in my head, but I thought I might explode from keeping it there. I felt my anger flare hot and fierce.

"Stop the car, I said. I mean it."

Joe glanced at me and at first I thought he was going to ignore me, but then he glanced in the rear-view mirror and pulled over onto the berm. "What? I told Mom that we'd swing by and pick her up for Mass this evening. We pick her up for Mass all the time. What's the big fucking deal?"

Joe rarely swore. When he used the "f" word, I knew he was mad. I actually felt a surge of satisfaction. His true emotions were finally showing. He might be as angry as I was.

I swallowed down on all the words that were in my head, pushing on my tongue, begging to be let out: *Because we always swing by and pick up your mother. Because I don't want to take your mother to Mass tonight. Because I don't want to take her to Mass ever again. Because I think I hate your mother. I think I hate you.* I shut my eyes for a moment, noticing absently the air coming from the vent was finally warm.

"I'm not going," I said, opening the door and getting out, feeling the sting of icy snowflakes against my face. The gravel seemed especially rough through the soles of my wedges which were suited for church, not hiking along the road. Cold wind blew my hair around my head and whipped at my pant legs. "I don't feel well; I need some air." Walking home from here was irrational beyond words.

"Don't do that," he said.

"Do what?" The sleet blew into the door, making the passenger seat wet. A sudden gust of wind tried to pull the door out of my hand.

"Get back in the van," Joe said. "It's not a big deal. We aren't going to be that late."

"Do what?" He clamped his jaw but finally answered me. "Act crazy."

Act *crazy*? And the implication that it wasn't the first time, that it was a chronic character flaw, made the fury inside me practically lava-like.

"I can't. I can't go." I could not sit in the van and ride to my mother-in-law's home, listen to her chat on the way to church, sit through the service beside her, thinking what I was thinking, feeling what I was feeling. It was the height of hypocrisy; I could hardly imagine thoughts or emotions less Christian. If I stayed in the van one more second, I would explode. Suddenly, a wash of heat burst upward from my collarbone to my scalp, despite the frigid air, the freezing sleet. Perspiration popped out on my forehead and beneath my nose where it ran together with the sleet.

Great fucking timing.

"I'll walk home," I said, my hand still on the open door. "You go on. Pick up your mother. You're going to be late enough as it is."

Joe was looking at me and I could see the anger in his eyes. Because I was being irrational and getting out of the van and walking home, or because his wife was drawing a line in the proverbial sand about his mother? I didn't wait for him to say anything, just slammed the van door and started walking, stumbling a little on the uneven gravel, wondering if he would actually do what I said.

Go on. Pick up your mother. It was only a mile or so home from here. I could walk a mile, even in heels. Even in this weather. The wintry air, the freezing rain, actually felt good on my skin. I took a deep breath as the van eased off the gravel berm and onto the road. I didn't look back, but I heard Joe accelerate and drive away.

Chapter Six

The landline phone was ringing as I opened the kitchen door. Ignoring it, I draped my soaking coat over one of the stools and stuck a cup of water in the microwave. I didn't feel like talking to anyone, and I wanted a cup of hot tea.

I felt Trouble suddenly beside my leg. "Hey, girl," I said. Ignoring the still ringing phone, I went down the hall to our bedroom, took off my totally wet and likely ruined shoes and my damp clothes and pulled on a pair of sweatpants and an old sweatshirt. I found some wool socks and slippers. I used a towel to dry my head and face.

Back in the kitchen, the phone was quiet. I made my tea before settling in the family room with an afghan. I found a rerun of "Law and Order". The original one, with Lennie Briscoe, Detective. Like tomato soup and grilled cheese for the brain. My hands were freezing and I wrapped them around the mug.

The landline phone rang again. Again, I ignored it.

The phone rang again. Good grief. Nothing on my cell phone, though, so not one of my kids. Resentfully, I got to my feet and went out to look at the caller ID. Lillian Daley. *Well, shit.* I glanced at my watch; Mass was over already? The phone rang again while I stood there.

I picked it up. "Hello?"

"Cathleen. Oh, thank God. Where have you been? I've been trying to call."

"Why? What's wrong?" My heart immediately stopped beating and lodged itself in my throat.

"We're at the hospital. Joe fainted. Thank God he wasn't driving."

"What? He *fainted*? Where? When? Is he okay?"

"In the parking lot, before Mass. I've been trying to call you."

"Is he okay?" I asked a second time, "Is Joe okay?"

"Yes, yes, they think he's okay," Lillian said. "But they're going to run some tests. He needs stitches. He's got an awful gash on his head."

Oh, God. "I'll be right there." *Am I responsible for this?* I could hardly fathom it. He was in good shape. Well, for a fifty-two-almost fifty-three year old man, he was healthy. *My God. What if he'd been driving?*

"He might have a concussion. He really hit the ground hard. Oh, and Cath? You need to bring your insurance card. Joe didn't have his with him. He doesn't have his wallet."

I closed my eyes and pinched the bridge of my nose. Joe never carried his wallet if he could help it. He didn't like the bulk of it in his pocket. In some far, dark, part of my brain, mean, snarky Cath smirked. *That's* why you called me. You need an insurance card. "Okay. I'm on my way. I'll get dressed and then I'll be there."

———

THE LANGSTON COMMUNITY HOSPITAL sat at the western edge of Langston, not too far off the interstate. It was a four-story brick building, built originally during the period when charmless, four-story, dark brick buildings were the sign of prosperity and progress, especially in a town that had once boasted a brick and tile factory. Inside, the waiting area was empty except for a TV turned to CNN with no sound. The woman sitting behind the check-in desk looked up as I entered. When I asked for Joe, she directed me with a nail painted a pale green.

The curtains around the cubicle were partly closed, but I heard voices and looked in. I saw my mother-in-law first, sitting on a chair against the wall holding clothing. A nurse was doing something to the head of the person lying on the bed, some poor soul with a big white neck brace in a hospital gown, who was attached by a half dozen white cords to a monitor and who had an IV running to his hand. And then, shocked, I realized the poor soul was Joe.

Oh my God. Lillian had said *stitches.* I had had three active children; I knew stitches. They didn't require neck braces and IVs and monitor cords attached to the chest.

"Here's Cath," Lillian said and Joe, unable to turn his head, rolled his eyes in my direction. The nurse kept wiping off the blood that had run into Joe's hair and around his ear. There was more blood on the underside of his jaw, too.

"My God." I said, shocked. "What happened?"

"Ahh, jeez," Joe said, and I could hear annoyance in his voice. "Mom panicked. I just got a little light-headed. Had a...you know...a head rush. Fell and hit the damn door frame of the van." Already, his eye was puffy.

"Hit it hard, apparently," I said, wondering fleetingly, guiltily, if there was some real medical problem, something seriously wrong. "You look awful."

"It's not as bad as it looks. I don't need this—" and he reached up as if to remove the neck brace.

"Dr. Randolph wants you to keep that on until they do the X-rays and CAT scan," the nurse said, pushing his hand down. "Better safe than sorry."

"Do they know what happened?" I asked Joe. "I mean why you passed out?"

Lillian spoke. "They're running some tests. They took blood. They want to rule out a heart attack," she went on, clearly embracing her role in this emergency.

I focused my attention on Joe. "What?" *A heart attack?*

The nurse had finished cleaning up the blood that had dried on his face and was gathering up the used gauze and paper packets. "Could have just held the tubes there under my head," he said. "Damn cut was gushing like a fountain."

"His blood pressure was low," Lillian said. "That's why they're giving him an IV."

"As soon as they're ready in radiology, we'll get you down there," the nurse said, checking the clear bag of fluid hanging on a rack attached to the bed. "How are you feeling now, Mr. Daley? Still lightheaded?"

"No, but it's kinda hard to tell laying here with this thing on my neck. I've got a killer headache though. A Chrysler minivan packs a punch."

"You're doing X-rays and a CAT scan?" I asked the nurse. *To rule out a heart attack?*

"Doctor's concerned that he may have snapped his neck or his spine when he hit the car," she said. "The X-ray is just to be sure he didn't fracture his skull." She pulled off the blue gloves and tossed them in a garbage bin.

The nurse went out, leaving me and Lillian with Joe, one of us on either side of the bed. There wasn't another chair in the space, so I stood. It occurred to me to step closer, to take Joe's hand or to give him a quick kiss. Once I would have done so, but tonight, for some reason, I could not bring myself to move.

"It's all liability crap," he said once the nurse was gone. "They gotta do all these damn tests just to cover their asses. Gonna cost a fortune."

"What happened?" I asked again.

Lillian started, "We'd just parked and were getting out of the van when Joe fell. Passed out. He just crumpled. It made an awful noise when his head hit. The parking lot was empty, everyone had already gone in."

No kidding. That's usually the case when you're fifteen minutes late.

"I just stood up too quick. Got a head rush." Joe sounded more pissed off than scared. "There wasn't any reason to call the ambulance."

"You called the ambulance?" I asked, glancing at Lillian.

"I didn't. Mackey Strohmer called 9-1-1," Lillian said. "I didn't know what to do. Your head was bleeding so much. When Joe fell, I couldn't get him up. I ran inside to get help and Mackey was sitting in the back row. By the time we got back out to the van, Joe was conscious and trying to sit up, but Mackey made him lie still on the ground until Kevin Vanderlin got there. Then he took charge until the ambulance came. It was pouring rain. Poor Joe was soaked."

"Kevin Vanderlin?" I asked. "The police came?"

"He heard the 9-1-1 call," Lillian said.

"It's a head wound. They always bleed a lot. Probably costs a few hundred bucks just to pull that ambulance out of the garage," Joe grumbled.

"Stop it," I told him. "That's why we have insurance."

"There wasn't any need to call 9-1-1," he insisted. "I didn't need an ambulance. And two police cars."

"Well, you're here now," I said, not sure what I should think, or feel. The image of Joe prostrate on the ground, Mackey Strohmer and Kevin Vanderlin in the middle of the church parking lot, police lights flashing, siren wailing, the people who lived across from the church huddled around on their porches, Mass goers exiting the service, checking out the excitement, all in the pouring rain slash sleet was vivid and even comic.

Worry, fear, niggled. *Why would Joe pass out?*

Then there was the anger I'd been nursing before Lillian's call. Anger that would now take a back seat to Joe's drama. That anger didn't dissipate, didn't diminish, it just kind of got pushed aside by some other emotion. "They need to find out why you passed out."

"I told you. I told the doctor when they brought me in here. I told the nurse. I just stood up too quick."

Just then, the nurse appeared. "They're ready in radiology now. We'll get you down there for films. Then the doctor can suture that wound."

Lillian said, "We didn't have your insurance information when they brought Joe in. I told them you could bring it. I can take it out to the desk so you can wait here. In case they bring Joe back. " I experienced the aggravating but oh, so familiar frustration of having to deal with a mother-in-law who incessantly Tried Too Hard at a time when I did not want to deal with her.

"I imagine it'll take a little while to get a CAT scan and X-rays. I couldn't believe it when Joe collapsed. When his head hit the car it made an awful sound—"

"He didn't say anything? He just fell?"

"No, he didn't say a word. Not about feeling lightheaded or dizzy. He didn't seem himself, though. Do you think we should call the kids?"

The kids? Belatedly, I heard the "we." Do you think *we* should call *the* kids.

Lillian went on. "I didn't know if you might want to tell them what happened—"

"Oh, God, no. No, *we* should not call them. There's not really anything to tell. Yet. We don't know anything, except that he needs stitches."

Lillian nodded reluctantly but clearly she disagreed. "That's true." She readjusted her coat and Joe's shirt in her arms. "Do you want something to drink? I could run down to the snack bar while you wait here." She made a move to rise. "Do you want to sit down? Joe said you weren't feeling well—"

I clamped my teeth together and looked at my mother-in-law. Joe's mother. Felt the pressure of unspoken words and undeclared emotions expanding as surely as if they were being pumped up with a compressor.

The space enclosed by pale blue curtains suddenly felt too small.

"I was upset." I couldn't keep it inside. "We were running late. Again. I really hate being late. I always have."

Joe needs to choose. His mother or his wife. And not just when it comes to church transportation. Is there something wrong with me that I need Joe to do that? At that moment, I had the sense that something shifted, something elemental, something significant, like a mammoth gear, settling into place. Unbidden, almost shocking me with its truth, came the thought, *It's too late for choosing.*

I stared at Lillian now and saw, all of a sudden, not the woman I'd always known as Joe's mother, through the lens of daughter-in-law, but a stranger, as if I'd never seen Lillian Daley before. At the same time, I realized it was not Joe and not Lillian who had changed. It was me. And now that I'd experienced that clarity of vision, I felt almost weightless. Floaty.

I wish to be anywhere but here. I knew with certainty that was nearly premonition, this is how Bonnie felt right before she went through the doors of that first bank with Clyde. How Thelma and Louise felt when they backed up before throwing it in drive and hitting the gas that last time. The sensation was oddly exhilarating.

"You definitely should have driven yourself to church tonight," I said finally. *Tonight, last week, last month. Maybe for the past thirty years.*

"Oh. I could have. Joe should have called—"

"Joe would never make that call. You know that as well as I do." I realized I had my hands in my coat pockets and that in my right one, there was an old balled-up tissue. I squeezed it. "Go home," I said. "Take my van and go on home. My van *is* here?"

"Oh, yes. I drove it over from the church, after they took Joe in the ambulance."

"We'll get it from your place tomorrow sometime. There's no need for you to wait."

"But—"

"I want you to go home now, Lillian." It suddenly occurred to me that I rarely called Lillian by her given name. I called her Nana Lil, the same as the kids.

"If you're sure—"

"I am. I'm certain."

"Do you want me to take the insurance information out to the desk before I go?"

For God's sake. "No. I want you to go home. Now."

———

THREE HOURS and seventeen minutes after I arrived at the ER, a nurse wheeled Joe out to the exit in a wheelchair, and though I could tell he wasn't happy about it, he didn't say anything. "Mom took the van?" he asked now as we crossed the parking lot.

"Yes. I told her we'd get it at her place tomorrow."

The parking lot lights—nearly as bright as daytime—shone on the planes of Joe's face. I'd thought they would put a bandage on the cut on his head, but apparently that was old school. I could see the short dark line of the stitches, just under the curve of Joe's right eyebrow. His eye was puffy and already starting to show bruising.

The rain and sleet from earlier had changed to fat, wet snowflakes that melted as soon as they hit the ground.

"I don't know why you're pissed at her," Joe said.

"It's late. Let's just go home, okay?"

Joe climbed into the passenger seat before I opened the driver's side door and climbed behind the steering wheel, started the truck, and pulled out onto the road. "Be careful, that snow is gonna turn to ice. The roads are probably slick."

"I think I can manage. Not my first time behind the wheel. In November. In Pennsylvania."

Joe ignored that.

"I can make you something to eat when we get home," I said.

"You haven't eaten since lunch. Maybe that's why you got lightheaded."

"I'm not hungry."

Bite your tongue. Do. Not. Respond.

"You have a headache?" I asked. "They said you could take some Tylenol—"

"For Christ's sake, I'm fine. It's a few stitches. I cut myself worse shaving. Give it a rest."

I bit my cheek and kept my gaze on the view in front of the headlights. We rode the rest of the way home in silence. Once home, I busied myself in the kitchen. Joe went straight to our bedroom. It wasn't long before I heard the pipes rattle and knock and the distant sound of water running. Joe was taking a shower.

Just then, my cell phone buzzed. The caller ID said Father J. Of course Father would call. I supposed I should be grateful he hadn't come to the hospital.

"Hi, Father."

"I understand you had a little excitement this evening."

"Ehh, a little."

"Well, I wanted to check on Joe."

"He's fine. He cut his eyebrow, got a few stitches. He'll probably get a black eye. But no concussion. Nothing broken. We got home a little while ago."

"Did he slip on some ice? The weather this evening has been awful—"

"No. Apparently he was dehydrated. It made him lightheaded."

"Goodness. It gave everyone quite a fright; we said a prayer for him at Mass."

"He'll appreciate that, I'm sure." Joe would be mortified to know the spectacle in the parking lot had led to congregational prayer on his behalf. "He's in the shower at the moment, but I can have him call you back?"

"That's okay. I was just checking in to see if I should add him to my hospital visitation list for tomorrow."

"He'll be grateful to know you were thinking of him, Father."

"And how are you?" Was he asking because I missed Mass and not because of the "little excitement in the parking lot?"

"I'm fine."

"Well, good night, Cathleen. I'm glad to know Joe is okay. And you, too. God bless."

"Same to you, Father."

———

My van was sitting in the driveway when I got down to the kitchen in the morning. Joe had recruited someone from the warehouse into shuttle duty. I was grateful. I had a lot to do today. And I didn't mind at all that I wasn't going to have to see, or talk to, Lillian. I had to assume Joe was feeling okay. I didn't know for sure as he had not left me a note, and I hadn't seen him this morning before he headed to the warehouse. No doubt he'd have a respectable shiner, if the puffiness and bruising of last night were any indication. I tidied the kitchen, made sure Trouble had fresh water, gathered my own shopping list and the one I kept for Father J.

The Foodrite was surprisingly busy after the holiday weekend. Christmas music played overhead; the store was artificially bright and chilly. It smelled of the cinnamon-scented pinecones at the door and of apples and produce. There were two registers open, and I pushed my half-full cart into the closest one.

"Well, hey," Jules Fialka said, from the other register where she was checking out. Before she'd retired, Jules had been the administrative assistant for the president of the little liberal arts college in the next town. She was about the same age as Lillian, and likewise a widow. The two were friends.

"How's Joe this morning? I heard about his accident. Holy moly. How scary. It knocked Lillian's socks off, him passing out like that, and getting taken away in the ambulance. There's a picture on Facebook. Joe looks terrible. No wonder Lillian freaked." Jules made a face.

"There's a picture on Facebook?" *Oh, my God.* I was pretty sure Joe had never considered there would be pictures. On the internet.

"Mackey Strohmer. You know. The kid with the hair," Jules went on, motioning to her neck and what I assumed was the mullet Mackey Strohmer sported. "He musta taken it when they were putting Joe in the ambulance."

"Thankfully, Joe's not a Facebook kind of guy," I said.

"Lillian said his blood pressure was low."

No doubt Joe was the subject of lots of conversations this morning: an ambulance, two police cars, middle of the church parking lot during Mass. The price of living in a small town.

"He was dehydrated. They gave him IV fluids. Took some X-rays to be sure he didn't break anything."

"Well, tell him I hope he's feeling better. He shouldn't scare his mother like that." Jules laughed.

"I'll tell him."

Just then, I heard my phone ding with a text.

> Jamie: Bummer about Dad. He's okay?

How did Jamie hear? Lillian? Facebook? I'd meant to text the kids, but I hadn't done that yet. Clearly, the news was out and had reached Minneapolis. I could assume it had reached Kansas City and Pittsburgh, too.

I texted back, the groceries on the conveyer belt moving slowly.

> Me: He's fine. No fractures. Slight concussion. Was dehydrated.

I wanted to emphasize that.

> Jamie: What a klutz. I'll call him later.

"Paper or plastic?" asked a smiling Robert, the six foot four special needs adult who had to be the happiest grocery store clerk on the planet.

Me: Love you.

I texted before setting the gallon of cider on the belt.

———

THE KITCHEN at the rectory was empty when I got there, a cereal bowl and a coffee cup rinsed and left upside down on the drain board of the sink. Father J was a neat man, leaving minor disturbance in his wake. I marveled at how for a big man, he took up little space. I set to work making soup to freeze—ham and bean, turkey noodle with corn and kale, the corn coming from the stash I'd frozen in the summer, and minestrone. I made some beef stew for Father's dinner and put it in the crock pot, enough so there would be leftovers for either lunch or dinner tomorrow. I made an applesauce cake, using applesauce I'd made and frozen earlier this fall. After eight years cooking for Father J, I knew a lot about the priest, things that felt almost intimate. His all-time weakness was a root beer float. He liked cauliflower raw but not cooked. He loved store-bought gingersnaps, the hard ones, dipped in his coffee. After almost sixteen years of cooking for two different priests, it didn't feel like a job anymore. It had become more, not just because of the cookbooks, but because I could really apply myself to cooking and gardening, to something creative and satisfying, for an audience of more than myself and Joe and our kids. Cooking for Father J wasn't the same as mothering, but it filled the hole my children left...at least a little.

Cooking was, if not mindless, then automatic; my brain able to think about other things while I chopped, measured, tasted. Joe and I had had plenty of arguments in our thirty-plus years together. What married couple didn't? I'd never found those arguments troubling, or threatening. This, now, what I was feeling, was different. It was bigger, stronger, darker.

The garage at the rectory was mostly empty and cleaner than most garages. No coolers, no lawn mower, no tools, no junk. Along the house wall, there was the chest freezer and a spare refrigerator, avocado green, a hand-me-down from a parishioner who had traded up. Father J's car, an older model white Lincoln, practically as long as a school bus, was parked in the middle. I carefully balanced the three containers of soup in one hand while I opened the chest freezer with the other. The lid stuck a little, so I tugged harder, until it opened suddenly and caught the edge of the stack of the containers in my left hand. The top two flipped and dropped while I scrambled to catch them without success. Both containers hit the concrete of the garage floor and lids popped off, soup splattering all over my shoes, my pantlegs, the side of the freezer, the floor.

"Shitfuckdamn," I cried, the expletive erupting spontaneously, as I looked at the chunks of ham, the pieces of carrot, the noodles and corn, the broth running toward the edge of the brown carpet remnant beside Father's car. "Ah, shit," I said again, feeling the sudden, hot press of tears. The garage suddenly smelled of soup.

"Cath?" Father J said from the doorway.

Scalded with embarrassment, worse than any hot flash, I squeezed my eyes shut and took a deep breath. Opened them. "Oh, Father, I'm so sorry. I didn't know you were there."

"Looks like there was a small mishap—"

"You could say that. But don't worry, I'll clean it up."

"I'm not worried at all. Let me help." He was wearing black trousers and his black shirt and clerical collar and an old blue cardigan sweater.

"That's okay. Really. I can get it. I'm sorry you heard me—" *swearing.*

He was looking at me, his eyes and his face so full of compassion, of concern, I could feel the tears burning again at the back of my own. "Are you sure you're okay?"

The anger, the angst, the worry, the niggle of fear, my *discontent*, all clambered to be let out. *Donotcry. Donotcry.*

I cleared my throat, beat down the anger and the angst. The tears. The impulse to bare my soul. I was not ready to do that. To say the words out loud. I hadn't gotten used to even thinking them: *I don't love my husband anymore. I think I might hate him.*

I could feel soup soaking through my right pant leg. "Yes, yes, I'm fine. I'll get this mess cleaned up—"

"You know, Cathleen, being a priest doesn't preclude me being a friend." Father J always saw too much. "I'm a good listener."

"I know that. I'm not ready to talk about it, though."

"*It* being whatever is making you unhappy?"

I stared at him. "*It* definitely being what is making me unhappy."

"Something we can talk about over a cup of tea?" I had once confided in Father J that, not being raised in the Catholic church, I had never grown accustomed to, or comfortable with, the idea of confession. We had taken to sitting at the kitchen table having tea once in a while. It wasn't confession, but Father J let it slide. Father J was a big-picture guy that way.

"Maybe. Sometime. Not today."

"Okay. Raincheck?"

"Raincheck." I gave him a smile that I knew didn't reach my eyes.

It was a sucky day. I wished I could go back to bed and start over. A mulligan. A do-over. Or else just stay there with the covers pulled to my chin.

———

I MADE a version of shepherd's pie for dinner, maybe the ultimate comfort food. I wasn't sure who needed the comfort, but it sounded good to me. White cannellini beans, corn and some chopped, canned green chilis mixed with leftover turkey and enough leftover gravy to hold everything together, a little cheddar and cream cheese in the mashed potatoes. Not a terribly inspired variation on the original, but I'd had lots of notes and emails from people who bought and enjoyed my cookbook, who said they really liked how I gave them ideas on how to amp-up tried and true dishes. I also got notes and emails from people who said my recipes and stories reminded them of their grandmothers—ouch—and even two from women who wanted Father J's contact information.

I didn't profess to be a gourmet, no Julia Childs or Emeril, I was more like a combination of Betty Crocker and Erma Bombeck, crossed with a little Martha Stewart. More than just collections of recipes, my cookbooks—the first and the one I was trying to finish now—included little *vignettes*, my editor called them. I wrote about family and food-related memories, about my garden and life, both here in Langston and on the rural, eastern shore of Maryland where I'd grown up, and sometimes, about faith and life in the church, as a cook for a small-town priest. My publisher promoted me as the James Herriot of the kitchen.

I knew Joe was home when Trouble got up from her rug and moved to the door, her tail wagging. When Joe came in, he looked tired, and in no better mood than he'd been after returning from the hospital emergency room.

I was right: the shiner that had been just a promise last night was in full bloom this evening. Below the dark line of stitches along the edge of his eyebrow, Joe's right eye was one big bruise. I tamped down the pang of guilt and inexplicable annoyance and put a smile on my face.

"Hey—" Joe said, barely glancing at me. Absently, he reached down and fondled Trouble's ears. Her thick tail banged against the dresser and her face looked like it was smiling.

"How's your head?"

"It's fine." The way he said that, I knew he was tired of people asking. He was in a bad mood. He moved through the kitchen toward the mud room to take off his coat.

I opened the oven to take out the casserole. "Dinner's ready. Whenever you are."

"I'm not that hungry. Didn't eat lunch 'til late."

"What'd you have for lunch?" I called.

"Just a burger." There was a pause, or maybe there wasn't. Maybe the pause was in my head, but I heard it nonetheless.

"Bob's Chill 'n' Grill?"

"Yeah, Mom ran over." Of course she had. I knew what Joe was going to say next, *knew it: She was checking in.*

She was just checking in."

"I'm sure."

"What's that supposed to mean?"

"I'm sure she was checking in. God forbid she mind her own business."

"I kinda *am* her business. She's my mother."

"You're almost fifty-three years old. Not six or sixteen. If there was anything important for her to know, I'm sure you'd share it with her." *Would you share it with me? Why does it feel like you're hiding something from me?*

He looked at me with the patronizing expression that made me want to pull out my hair, or his, and began to flip through the mail on the counter.

"Don't look at me like that," I said, feeling a sudden flare of anger.

"Don't look at you like what?"

"You've got that smirk, that condescending smirk I can't stand, on your face. Like what I'm saying is amusing in some way."

"I don't think what you're saying is amusing. Why are you so pissed at my mother?"

I stared at Joe, smelling toasted cheese and the cumin and the chilis, the warmth of the dish seeping through the padding of the oven mitts. A flurry of words and emotion, black and hot and jagged, filled me, my chest, my throat. I had a barely resistible urge to throw it, the whole damn casserole, to smash it against him. "I'm wondering why family counts for something now, when it suits her?" I said.

"Are you talking about the fucking cruise again?"

"Do you not see how hypocritical it is, for your mother to have to be an integral part of our lives on a daily basis, but when it comes to vacation, then not so much?"

"Jesus," Joe rolled his eyes. "Are we back to that again?"

We're not back *to that. We never left it.*

"I'm sure she won't want to go if she knows how upset you are. She didn't plan it."

"No. Maybe not. But she didn't squash the idea like a bug, either. And neither did you."

Some part of me understood that I was probably being irrational and that my anger, my angst, about Lillian's cruise was unreasonable, no matter who was responsible for planning it. But the anger was so big, the angst so combustible that it consumed me. Whatever was inside me that was sane and reasonable had evaporated. Tears burned the back of my eyes and pushed up from my chest. I didn't know if I'd ever felt as overcome with frustration and fury. The lump in my throat tasted sour, of bile.

Do not cry. Do not cry. Do not cry.

Who are you, Joe Daley? I do not know you.

You don't know me.

You are fucking clueless.

I was, all of a sudden, exhausted. I stared at Joe, seeing the way his nostrils flared, the purple bruise around his eye, the line of stitches black and jagged, his face hard and closed.

The two of us stood staring at each other, the animosity palpable. *I don't like you. I don't like you at all.*

————

I FOLLOWED Joe into the family room and I could tell by the set of his shoulders he was bracing for a fight. "What did the tests show?" I asked, changing the subject. "Last night. At the hospital. I assume you got the results from someone today?"

He scowled, and one hand came up and scrubbed his head hard, so that I could actually hear the bristles of his hair. It was something he did when he was irritated. I saw him wince. No doubt a result of the wallop his skull had taken ala my minivan. "Nothing. It's not a big deal."

I stared at him. "You passed out a second after climbing out from behind the wheel of a car. Which you were driving. On the road. You were taken by ambulance to the hospital. It is a big deal."

"It won't happen again."

"You can't know that."

"I can. I do. I had a reaction to some pills George gave me and I stopped takin' 'em."

"Pills? What pills?" George was our family doctor. He'd graduated from high school with Laura and played baseball with Joe and his brother, Mark.

"Pills. You know, Vitamin V. The little blue pills."

"You mean Viagra?"

He looked annoyed. Pissed. Defensive. "Yes. Viagra."

"You're kidding." My mind was trying to wrap itself around the idea. Joe? Taking Viagra? Part of me wanted to laugh. Viagra was a punchline on late night TV. Men who took it were the butt of jokes. "You don't— You haven't—" I struggled to find the words that were appropriately sensitive.

Joe looked, if possible, even angrier, his expression dark. I knew he was embarrassed. I could understand, obviously, it was a very personal, private sort of topic.

"Why?"

Joe just stared at me.

Cheerleader Cath: Now who's clueless?

"Okay, dumb question. But why didn't you tell me?" I said. I thought back to the last time we had sex. Had he been uncharacteristically virile? Or had it been just the opposite? Had he been unable to perform at any time? I couldn't recall that.

He shook his head like it didn't matter. "It's like that song, 'I'm not as good as I was once, but I'm as good once...' You know." He flapped a hand. He never could remember the right words to songs. He was famous for making up his own.

"I can't believe it."

"For God's sake, Cath. I'm getting old. I can't—" He stalled, his mouth clamping down on the word. Finally, "I don't...last as long. I don't know if it's me or just age. Sex—" He fumbled with the explanation. But I understood. There had been times, more than a few, when Joe came so quickly, I had just given up on reaching my own climax. But that hadn't been a sudden thing. It had been a gradual one. Something that had evolved over time. Over years maybe? I just assumed it was a function of routine. Of monotony.

"You should have told me."

Joe taking Viagra. Joe having a reaction to Viagra. I should have felt sympathetic. Compassionate. But instead, it just felt like one more thing that Joe couldn't get right.

When I imagined the spectacle outside the church last night, I almost wanted to laugh. People were apparently talking about it on Facebook, for Pete's sake. They'd added him to the prayer list at church. If they only knew. They were praying for Joe's hard-on. And in some far, distant corner of my—yes, I'll admit it, petty—brain, I thought: Wasn't it just typical that Joe wanted to make sex better, but he didn't see anything wrong with the fucking cruise? Suddenly the weight in my chest felt more like despair.

He shrugged. "It doesn't matter now. I'm not taking them anymore."

Chapter Seven

The next morning, I was in the den preparing to work on some of the essays for the new cookbook, but first checking my email. This morning, there were three emails forwarded from my publisher. Fan mail. Before I wrote *Cooking for Father*, I had no idea cookbook authors got fan mail.

I had gotten notes from people who wanted to comment on one or another of the essays, the anecdotes:

—About the stifling August day I decided I'd make and can a batch of tomato sauce using tomatoes from my garden and just the old wood-fired cook-stove in the summer kitchen as a way to pay homage to the women who had used that stove, and the summer kitchen, a century before me. I'd never sweated so much.

—About saving the seeds from the last apple from the last heirloom tree in the old orchard that used to be our backyard, and finding an Amishman who grafted the seedling into a new tree. Which I planted in the backyard near where its ancestors had grown.

—About my first experience planting strawberries and being unable to keep deer out of the patch, despite my best efforts.

I got lots of questions—I didn't know there would be readers who would not understand the terms "macerate" or "fold over. In the interest of keeping me humble, I'd received plenty of emails and notes from readers who wanted to tell me how they made this or that recipe better by tweaking ingredients or changing them altogether.

While working my way down the list of incoming mail, I saw I'd received yet more responses to my "poll" about the "family-only" cruise. Lately, these were mostly from women I didn't know, had never met, but who had been forwarded the poll from friends I had sent it to. It really was turning into quite the survey. I should mention it to my editor. Maybe there was a book in it. Ha. I snorted.

As I opened an email, there was the sound of a vehicle pulling into the driveway. I got up and went to the kitchen door, looked out, saw Joe's sister, Diana, climbing out of her car.

Diana? Dropping in on a weekday morning? Di and Pat lived and worked in Pittsburgh. Besides, Diana was just here for Thanksgiving. Surely she hadn't driven up from Pittsburgh just to check on Joe?

Opening the door, I called, "Hey. This is a surprise." The understatement of the century.

"Hi. Yeah. Mom is already worried about getting all her Christmas shopping done. And decorating." Di stopped on the porch and rolled her eyes. "I took the day off so I could help her. And I can bring up the boxes of Christmas stuff from her basement. Save you the job." Something Joe or I normally did for his mother each year after Thanksgiving. If we didn't just go do it, Lillian would call and remind us.

"How is Joe?"

I held the door. "Come on in. He's okay. Sore head and a few stitches."

"Mom said he's lucky he didn't break something. Gave her a scare." Di shed her coat and draped it on the back of one of the island stools before taking a seat. I still could hardly wrap my head around Diana stopping in on a weekday morning.

"I'm sure."

"She told me all about calling the ambulance, seeing Joe taken away on a stretcher. Sounds like it was quite the event."

"She probably didn't have to call the ambulance," I said. "Joe was pretty embarrassed about that. But you know your mom, she's gonna knock herself out to help." I didn't generally criticize Lillian, not to her children. But the rules didn't apply anymore.

"Well... You know Mom."

I did. "You want some coffee? Tea? I just made myself some."

"Tea sounds good. Thanks."

"So what's up?" I asked, busying myself filling a mug with water and sticking it in the microwave, getting the box of tea bags from the pantry. We'd just spent time together over the holiday weekend. And Di wasn't a small talk kind of girl at any time.

"I was hoping I could ask a favor. Was hoping you'd talk to Pat."

"Talk to him? About what?" I set the box of teabags on the counter and slid the sugar bowl and a spoon close.

"About having a baby. Starting a family."

I remembered then what Patrick had said about invitro and Di wanting a baby, suddenly, surprisingly after twenty years of marriage. I tried to calculate, again, just how old Di was? Forty one? Forty two?

"Yeah. Not what you were expecting, huh?" Di sort of laughed.

"Well," I hedged. "I guess I thought you'd long ago made the decision not to have a family. You've always been so committed to your job."

"I know. I am, have always been. I'm not sure what's changed exactly." Di laughed, awkwardly; so Di. "I suppose it just hit me that my window of opportunity is closing."

I didn't know what to say to that. "You know I'm an advocate for motherhood—parenthood. Obviously..." But having a baby because the alarm on your biological clock is getting ready to go off isn't necessarily the best reason. "What's Pat think?" I asked instead. As if I didn't know.

"That's why I was hoping you'd talk to him."

"He's not so sure."

126

Diana took a deep breath and I thought she might cry. Diana was *not* a crier. She was more likely to laugh in the wrong empty spaces in a conversation.

"I know it doesn't make sense. I can't explain it. Why I want a baby now.

I've researched it. I know all the statistics. I understand the science.

Of course you do.

My OB has me on folic acid and prenatal vitamins, and I've had acupuncture. I know," she said, "some people think it's a joke, but there is data— It was worth a try. Nothing to lose— And now I know those needles really don't hurt. Ha."

"Wow," I said. The microwave dinged and I took out the steaming mug and slid it over to Di.

She picked up the string of a tea bag and dropped it in the hot water. "I think if Pat hears from another mother, you know, it might help him understand. I've given him the data. He's seen it all. But he's . . . not convinced."

"There are a lot of things to think about—" I said. "I don't know the *data*.... But I do know that things get...riskier...for older women. There are increased chances of birth defects—"

"I've done all the pre-pregnancy screening. And the pre-natal genetic testing options are pretty amazing. Chorionic villus sampling is less than one percent risk for miscarriage and 99 percent accuracy detecting chromosomal abnormalities."

Just because you can identify those issues, *abnormalities*, I wanted to say, doesn't make dealing with the reality of them any easier. I also didn't say that it wasn't my place to try to talk Pat into fatherhood.

"I knew you would understand."

Did I understand? Joe's little sister was so smart in so many ways it was almost scary. When other young women her age had been dreaming of white princess gown weddings, Di had been splitting atoms or something, wearing white lab coats and safety goggles. The maternal instinct had not been on her radar screen. "Understand wanting to be a mother?" I said.

Trouble pushed up against me and nudged my knee. I hadn't heard her get up from her rug by the dresser. I reached down and smoothed her broad head, her silky ears. "Of course I understand that."

"Will you talk to Pat?"

My children were my *life*. Being a mother was the most important thing I would ever do, without any doubt it defined me, and created the world I lived in here on Earth, and that my soul inhabited on some other level. But that was me. What Pat said on Thanksgiving day sitting on the back porch slugging back Pinot Grigio straight from the bottle suggested he felt differently.

"It's a very personal decision. Maybe the most personal one. I'm not sure it's my place to try to persuade someone else about becoming a parent."

Di's face almost looked like she was going to smile. Again, awkward and just socially inept. She had Joe's eyes and now suddenly there was something in the gray depths that made my heart ache. It made me feel insensitive and guilty.

"Okay, sure. I can talk to Pat."

―――――

THREE DAYS LATER, I had a Historic Langston committee meeting at the Presbyterian Church. I was parking the van when my phone rang. L. Daley, my cell phone said. I had not talked to my mother-in-law since telling her to go home from the emergency room after what I had come to think of as The Van Incident. In the past, I would have felt compelled to call Joe's mother, if not the night we got home from the ER, then the next day to patch things up, to smooth over any hurt feelings or offense Lillian might have taken. But I hadn't done that.

"Hey, Lillian," I answered.

"Hi there. I hope I'm not calling at a bad time—"

"I'm just getting ready to go into a committee meeting. What's up?" I knew I sounded short, but I really didn't care.

"I was calling to see if you and Joe wanted to come for dinner tomorrow?"

"No" would be the honest answer and the one that sprang almost immediately to my lips. But the politically correct one would be, "Sure, thanks for the invite." I said nothing.

"I talked to Joe this morning and he said I should check with you. He said he feels fine. And he assured me he's drinking more water. I had no idea dehydration could do that."

"Hmm." I rolled my eyes. Clearly, Joe was not going to share with his mother that it was *Viagra* that made him pass out. I really did not feel up to dinner with Lillian, and more discussion on dehydration and its side effects.

"Thanks for the invitation, and Joe could certainly come, but I'm going to Pittsburgh for the day tomorrow. I thought I'd do some Christmas shopping and have dinner with Annie."

I hadn't thought about it before, about going to Pittsburgh, but decided just that moment. Annie's revelation still weighed on me. It was a lose/lose, a painful situation that would not end happily—for some, if not all.

"Oh, that sounds nice..." Lillian said.

There had been a time when I might have invited my mother-in-law to go with me. But not this time. Besides, there was Diana's request. Much as I was not looking forward to it, and hadn't quite decided how to advocate for Di, for parenthood, I would text Pat and see if he could meet me for lunch.

"Would you like me to run over and let Trouble out during the day?" Lillian asked.

Gahh. I reached out and swiped some dust off the dashboard of the van. Lillian's desperation to be integral in whatever was happening in our lives made me want to scream.

"No, that won't be necessary. I'm going to take her with me. She loves to ride in the car and the weather is supposed to be good."

After I disconnected from Lillian, I pulled up Pat's contact and sent him a text.

> Me: Hi. I'm going to be in the city
> tomorrow. Are you free for lunch?

Then I went inside to the committee meeting. I didn't get a response for almost a half hour when my phone dinged.

> Patrick: Chill. On Banker Place, off Fort
> Duquesne Blvd. 1:30 pm ok?

I'd heard of Chill. It was new—very contemporary, very hip, and the food was supposed to be amazing. Pat knew I was a foodie, an amateur one, no doubt, but still... Again, there were the unspoken words, the silent, implied intimacy, just by his choice of restaurant. Pat was telling me that he knew *me*. Despite my best efforts, it sent a surge of warmth through me, a kind of warmth that was almost forgotten, it had been so long since I'd felt it.

I texted back.

> Me: I was thinking Subway or Panera.
> Something handy to your office. Want to
> talk to you.

The response was immediate.

> Patrick: Chill. 1:30.

And God forgive me, the hot rush, the guilty pleasure was like having the taste of water on my tongue after a pilgrimage through the desert.

The drive into Pittsburgh would take me less than two hours and I knew Trouble would sleep the sleep of happy yellow dogs on the back seat the entire way. Pat's invitation to a fancy restaurant made me rethink taking the dog, but in the end, it was the invitation to a fancy restaurant for lunch that decided me. Somehow, having the family dog in the car was like insurance against staying too long, or forgetting the things that were, that should be, important: Family. Husband. Dog.

And today, the weather really was perfect. Sunny but not too cold, in the fifties, not bad for the beginning of December in Pennsylvania, and I knew if I parked in the shade, and left the windows cracked, the van would be comfortable for Trouble for the two hours—tops—that I was allowing myself for lunch. With Pat. At Chill.

The parking lot beside the restaurant was crowded, even a little after 1:00 on a weekday, but I found a spot in the row facing the building. I took a deep breath, pulled out my phone to check for a message from Annie. I'd texted her when I decided to come down to the city, but had not heard back from her yet.

I hooked up Trouble's leash and took her for a quick walk around the block. Setting the water dish I'd brought between the two seats in the middle of the van, I filled it from a gallon jug. Trouble watched from the middle seat, but didn't move, except for her tail, which wagged a little. She was happy to stay, to wait.

Slamming the door and pushing the button on the key fob to lock it, I took a deep breath, feeling a tangle of emotions. Now that I was here, I was having second thoughts.

Diana had confided in me, had asked me to talk to Pat. He was my brother-in-law; he had been my friend for a long time. There was nothing to feel guilty about. But there was that...*undercurrent*...of something else that was almost imperceptible. Almost.

Then with perfect timing, the sensation struck me, a faint, electric prickling against the inside of my skin, becoming almost immediately a bloom of scalding heat, as if a star had exploded somewhere in my core. Sweat popped out on my nose, on my forehead, along my hairline, between my breasts and at the curve of the small of my back. I ran my fingers through my hair and fluffed it, trying to get cooling air to my scalp. Yanking the purse off my shoulder I shrugged off the jacket I wore.

I would have unbuttoned the top four buttons of my sweater if it had four buttons. Lacking that, I flapped the hem to create a draft of cool air on my skin.

Hot flash. Like calling the Titanic a fender bender.

Just then, a black car pulled into the spot beside my van, and I saw it was Pat. Under the pretense of waiting, I leaned back against my van, feeling the cold steel through the layers of my clothes, against my back and my butt. I'd be happy to stand here for another half hour while the sweat dried, but Pat got out and walked around the front of his car, his eyes on me with the expression he always seemed to have when he looked at me.

He wore a gray suit and a white shirt with a navy blue and gold striped rep tie, polished and big city, masculinely stylish. Like something from a glossy cosmopolitan men's magazine. He looked totally at ease and comfortable. The mustache and little goatee—whatever it was called, it suited him and I was not generally a facial hair fan— that, and the sharp planes of his face gave him a bad boy vibe. Even the strands of gray in his longish dark hair just added to the aura that read as worldly, knowing, experienced. There was always that sense I had with Pat of waiting, and watching, as if he could read my mind.

"Hey," he said, walking up and stopping just shy of touching me, his dark brown eyes holding mine, finally leaning in to kiss my cheek. I caught a whiff of cologne, something musky and expensive and suit-and-tie smelling.

And damn my soul to hell. It made my heart leap to see the look in his eyes, the approval, the *attraction,* that he was shameless about allowing me to see.

"Have you been waiting long?"

"No, not at all. Fifteen minutes. Had time to take Trouble for a quick walk."

"This is a nice surprise." He just looked at me, finally taking me by the hand and leading me toward the entrance. "They're holding a table for us."

"I really hope I'm not messing up your day."

He glanced at me and smiled, as if I'd just made a joke. "You're not."

"I've heard about this restaurant. It's gotten some amazing reviews. I'm excited to try it."

He just smiled at me again as he pulled open the door and held it for me, leaned down and whispered in my ear, "I'm glad you're excited." I felt the thrum of that whisper all the way down to my girl parts.

Pat ordered wine and waited impatiently while a tall, thin Black man spread white linen napkins on our laps, deftly opened the wine bottle, and went through the whole wine-tasting routine.

"I'm glad you texted," he said, once the sommelier had gone, picking up his wine glass and holding it, waiting for me to do the same in a little toast. "To nice surprises."

We clinked glasses and I took a sip. It was light and crisp, faintly apple-ish, like autumn in a bottle. I shrugged. "I had an unexpected day off, and I thought I'd come down and do a little Christmas shopping, then stop and see Annie after she gets home from work."

"She's a busy girl. I know Di talks to her sometimes, or texts. We don't hear much from her. Which is a good sign." Pat smiled at her. "She doesn't need to hang with her boring aunt and uncle."

Thankfully then, a young woman wearing a pair of red plaid leggings under a black skirt with a white blouse approached our table with menus. She had blond hair pulled up in a bun held in place with yellow pencils and a tiny diamond stud in one side of her nose. I looked up at her, and she smiled. "Hi. Welcome to Chill. I'm Adele." She laid a page in front of each of us. "Our menu changes every day, depending on what's in season and what's available from the fish market and the butcher. Check your menus and please let me know if you have any questions. But take your time, enjoy your wine." She smiled again and moved away.

I studied the menu. The choices were interesting, and nothing you'd find on offer in any of the four or five restaurants in Langston. Things like like caviar-topped deviled eggs and bean and lamb cassoulet. I glanced at Pat, assuming he would be studying the selections as well, but he was looking at me and hadn't touched his menu. I smiled. "I really would have been happy with Subway."

He smiled back. "You're happier here."

I nodded and grinned, unable to help myself. "You're right."

"I know," he said and how he said it made me feel light as air. It was a long forgotten but wholly addictive sensation. *It's the wine*, I told myself. *Stop drinking* now.

I looked down at the menu again, unable to hold his gaze. I attempted sunshiny chatter. "This will inspire me. I'll want to go home and cook."

Pat watched my face, evidently sensing the way I felt awkward, suddenly, waiting patiently in that way he had for me to relax. The look on his face said he would be happy to wait all day and like it. It sent another spike of pleasure through me, God help me. It was Just Wrong to make the comparison, but I could not recall the last time Joe paid me this kind of attention. I lived with Joe, we were married, for God's sake; we'd been together for thirty-plus years. He didn't need to be focused on me like I was oxygen and he was drowning. Joe knew me and I knew Joe.

You didn't know about the Viagra, said a little voice in my head. Cheerleader Cath.

"Uh huh. So what's wrong?" he said.

I laughed. "Why do you think something's wrong?"

Pat just looked at me with a not-quite smile on his face. "Annie?" He guessed.

I knew that anything I told Pat would not leave this table and I really needed to talk about Annie and Corey. "She's been seeing a guy... A man..." I hesitated.

He half-smiled indulgently. "And that's a problem because?"

"Because he's married. With two children." Pat's expression didn't change, didn't reflect the shock that I felt, still, even now when it was not new news to me. "You don't look shocked."

He shrugged. "It's not shocking. It happens, Cath. It's not remarkable, not really."

"Maybe not for you. I find it pretty damn remarkable. It's not how she was raised."

Pat looked at me, his gaze holding mine and after a moment, he nodded, his eyes full of something I didn't want to understand but was afraid in a way that I did. Absently, I thought again that this Pat, the beard, and the suit and tie, and gold cuff links Pat, was like a different species of Pat from the one I'd met all those years ago in Pollock Commons at Penn State.

Forgetting my earlier pledge, I picked up my wine glass and took another drink, a healthy slug this time. Pat's gaze was relentless, patient, and finally I had to meet it. "It's not okay, it's not acceptable," I said. "That Annie would break up a marriage, that she would hurt another woman, and children, in that way."

"Did you tell her that?"

"Of course I did."

Pat nodded. "Of course you did. What did Annie say?"

"Oh, she was defensive and full of rationalization. She sounded like a pathetic cliché. He doesn't love his wife, his wife doesn't love him, blah blah."

Pat watched me. He was a very good listener. He always had been. "Don't you think that people can make mistakes?"

Part of me wondered what mistakes he meant: Marrying the wrong person, or cheating on a spouse? I was unable to look away from his eyes. "Don't," I said finally. "Don't do that. Don't make me feel guilty," I said. "About being here."

Pat studied me, as if he were thinking about how to respond. "What's Joe think?" he finally asked.

"About Annie? He doesn't know... It's Annie's news to share and she hasn't shared it. Yet."

Pat cocked his head, his brows raised.

"Did Di tell you about him passing out? Joe. His ambulance ride to the ER?"

"She told me. I texted him. He said he's fine. Got dehydrated."

Yeah," I said. And though I was fairly certain Pat heard the "there's more to the story" note in my voice, he let it ride.

"You know that Diana came to see me a few days ago?"

Pat didn't flinch at the change of subject. "And she's recruited you to talk to me."

"She thought I would understand. Why she wants suddenly to have a baby."

"Is that why you're here?" he asked.

"I wish you wouldn't look at me like that," I said, avoiding the question.

"Why?" he finally asked.

"Because I just told you what I think about marriage vows. And people who break them. I need you to be my friend."

Beneath the table, shielded by the white tablecloth, I crossed my legs. I could see how it happened...cheating. Sin.

He smiled, then. And the tension was almost gone. "If that's what you want—" he said.

"That's what I *need*."

He was a lawyer. I had no doubt he knew prevarication when he heard it.

———

JUST THEN, our waitress appeared beside our table. Her appearance was perfectly timed. "Can I bring you an appetizer or maybe soup? Chef Franco has made a pumpkin bisque and a red snapper and mussel bouillabaisse today. Both are wonderful."

I glanced back down at the menu, my mind slow to change gears. "I'll have the pumpkin bisque and the grilled shrimp with corn salsa, please," I said finally.

"The pork tenderloin. A small salad," Pat said and handed the page to the woman. After she'd walked away, he looked at me, gently though, there was nothing intense about it...or *not much* intense about it. "You're beautiful," he finally said, smiling.

"Hardly," I scoffed. "I'm old and tired. Cranky sometimes." I had a flabby stomach. Stretch marks. Fat thighs. I was embarrassed to even let Joe see me naked anymore. Though Joe didn't seem to mind how my body looked. On the other hand, Joe needed Viagra.

"You *are* beautiful. To me. You always have been. Not pursuing you was the biggest mistake I ever made," Pat said.

"Why are you telling me that now? Why didn't you ever tell me before? Before I was married?"

He shrugged and it was self-deprecating. "You snooze, you lose? Joe got there before me."

"You snoozed for a long time. Joe wasn't moving at warp speed. We'd known each other for almost five years before we married. If I hadn't gotten pregnant with Nora, I don't know if he would have ever gotten around to popping the question."

"I was young, inexperienced, but even I could see that you were...infatuated...with Joe." He hesitated over the word. "Everyone could see it. I guess I thought I needed to wait until you got over it. Until you were ready to move on."

"And then I got pregnant."

He shrugged. "You're right, though. That's hindsight. Whatever kept me from speaking up then—youth, inexperience—it was a mistake. I just wanted you to know that."

"I have a happy marriage."

"Do you?" he asked.

"It's not perfect, but what marriage is? We're like everyone else. We have some ups and downs."

"Bullshit."

"You have a wife. A wife who wants to have a family."

"There is not going to be a baby. Di and I... Our marriage..." He held up both hands, didn't finish the thought. "What you are to me is separate and apart from that. Always has been."

"Friends," I said.

He looked at me, that little smile on his mouth. "Sure." He was silent for a few moments, I thought he was listening to the music. Jazz, a piano somewhere. "But it could be more."

"Are you talking about an affair? A fling? Do you really think I'm a fling kind of woman?"

"Do I think you could give yourself up to something that would make you very happy? You *should*. And no. An affair won't be enough. For you, either."

I was surprised at the intensity in his voice. And I knew suddenly, with a certainty that was as bold and black as if it were written on the white damask tablecloth between us that Pat would demand to see my whole, naked body. My whole flabby, stretch-marked, naked body. That he would require sex with the lights on. And all clothes off.

It hurt to swallow, my mouth was so dry. *Something* hurt. Had Joe ever professed his love for me like this? Suddenly I didn't care if it wasn't fair to make comparisons. The pleasure was so fierce I ached with it. I could hardly bear it. It was a physical thing, as quantifiable as pulse or blood pressure or temperature. If only there was an instrument to measure it. Is this what I wanted? Is this what was wrong with me? A need for this feeling, this sensation?

Cheerleader Cath was doing some kind of writhing dance, a combination of a belly dance and a strip tease.

My phone buzzed in my purse then, and after a moment when we just looked at each other, Pat laughed humorlessly.

I grimaced apologetically. "Do you mind, just let me check, in case it's Annie? I texted her that I was coming down to the city, but haven't heard back from her yet." I dug in my purse and pulled out my phone, glanced at the caller ID.

I shook my head. "It's Joe. I'll call him later."

"Have you ever had an affair?"

"Of course not." I couldn't keep the reproach out of my voice.

"Being a good Catholic girl—"

"I was raised Methodist."

"Were you never once tempted? Not even in your head? You never imagined what it would be like with someone else?"

I took a deep breath, closing my mouth, giving me time to think what to say. I could smell the faint scent of the perfume I dabbed on the inside of my wrists. I'd worn the same scent for years. This morning, I'd applied it to my wrists, and between my breasts and at the top of my thighs.

Heat pushed up from below my collar toward my face at the memory, and at the thought of what had been going through my mind at the time. *What had I been thinking? Why did I do that?*

Pat waited patiently for me to answer. His dark eyes held mine, his expression almost amused. As if he knew about that dab of Chanel CoCo. The look in his eyes—the sense that he knew my secret, secrets, that he desired me because of them, not in spite of them.

"No. I was never tempted. My children and my family were my priority," I finally said. "The kids came first, before a career or a job. Before Joe even. Being a mother was everything. And I loved it. It made me very happy. It felt important, more important than anything else. Especially after Nora died."

Now I couldn't tell what Pat was thinking, his eyes were darker than ever.

Adele brought our food then. Pat sat back in his chair while my soup and his salad were placed before us. We looked at each other and I smiled, appreciating the excuse to change the subject. "It smells delicious."

We talked food and we ate. Maybe it was just that I was really hungry, or maybe it was the wine I'd drunk, but it was perfect, the soup, the shrimp, the salsa. "I'm not sure who I am anymore. What I am," I said into the quiet after a while.

Pat paused, cocked his head at me.

"I'm not a mother, not like I was, not in a way that consumes my life, day in and day out. For so long, that's who I was. Now I don't know."

"Does that mean now you could be tempted?"

"Not hardly."

"Is that a challenge?"

I snorted. Didn't even credit that with a response.

"You are a talented, beautiful, passionate woman."

"You are very good for my ego."

"I could be very good for you in a lot of ways. Just give me a chance." He smiled. Serious or more kidding around? I couldn't tell. "Are you happy?" He asked and watched, waited patiently, for me to respond.

Tears suddenly burned in the back of my eyes. I had to clear my throat before I could speak. I chose not to answer the question. "I've forgotten how to be a woman who is not a mother," I said instead. *Why am I telling Pat something so private, so intimate? Why haven't I had this conversation with Joe?*

"I don't know how to be me anymore," I said. "I'm not sure who me is."

There was a certain relief in saying the words and a sense of...revelation. I studied Patrick. He was simply listening. No judgment on his face or in those dark eyes but a great deal of understanding and compassion. And desire.

The leap of desire in my own body was unexpected. It was like bubbles in my chest. I had to swallow down on the nearly unfamiliar jolt of pure lust that hit me and made me feel as if I wouldn't be able to stand if I tried. *I don't do lust, not like this. Not wild and reckless. Not for a long time anyway.*

It has to be the wine.

I stared at Pat and shifted uncomfortably in my seat.

"I know," he said. That was all.

Oh, my God. Could I do that? Have an affair with Pat? "Who would it hurt?" I said.

"What?" he said.

I said that out loud?

"My kids. Joe. Diana. Lillian," I said.

He didn't speak. What could he say? I had said it all. He reached for the wine bottle.

"No. Seriously. I don't want any more," I said, covering the top of the glass.

"Why not? What else do you have to do today? What could be more important than talking about this?"

"Go look at a car. Buy a car," I said without thinking.

"What?" The look on his face made me want to laugh. Pat stared back at me, his eyes warm, the corners of his mouth curved in a smile.

"Come with me? Please. It'll be fun." The words were out of my mouth before I could weigh them. I felt suddenly buoyant—a great, helium-filled kind of joy that was so full of promise it pushed against my chest and made me smile.

"A car? What kind of car?"

I reached for my purse and my phone. "It's been kind of a family joke. For a while now. I've been saying I was going to buy a convertible. But always sometime down the road—after the kids were gone, after Joe retired, always after *something*. Annie thinks the time is now. She brought it up again when she was home for Thanksgiving. Sent me a picture of one at a dealer near her apartment a couple of days ago." I found the phone and pulled it out, scrolled through the messages to find the picture Annie had sent. "I don't know about buying. But I'd like to see it. Let's go look at it? Let's drive it? If it's still for sale? Here." I opened the message with the picture and held it out to Pat.

He took the phone and held it up so he could see the picture. "Whoa." He looked appraisingly at me, brows raised. "A Z4 Roadster. Nice." He nodded, amused and, maybe, surprised? He handed the phone back to me, grinning now.

"You think it's funny that I'd want a car like this?"

He shook his head, still smiling. "Not at all."

I glanced at the picture again. The sleek red car said, vra-vra-vroom, and wild thing. My minivan said make way for groceries, and soccer mom. Had I felt like this when I was younger? Or was it some-

141

thing new? Oh, God. Was this...desire...inside me simply a mid-life crisis? Was I a cliché? I swiped the pic away, then dropped the phone back in my purse.

"What's Joe think?"

"About buying a convertible? No idea. I didn't ask him. It doesn't have anything to do with him. It's a car for me."

He grinned. "So a fuck-you gesture."

"Maybe. Kind of." I hedged. "It's a whim. A fancy. But I have been talking about it for a long time."

"I went to Europe after college on a whim. Changed my life. I'm a big fan of whims." He stood up, took my hand and pulled me up. "Let's go indulge yours."

Chapter Eight

"I need to walk off the wine I drank. Besides, Trouble could use a walk. Do you think we can leave our cars parked here?"

I reached to open the sliding side door of my van. When Pat didn't respond, I turned and immediately he was against me, so that my back was pressed to the cold steel. His hands came up to hold my face, his thumbs stroking the curves of my cheeks to the corners of my mouth. His hands shook, and that made me remember again the soft, tender young man Pat once was. Then he was kissing me and his lips were warm and gentle, but urgent; I could sense that he was holding himself in check, trying not to frighten me. The mustache was tickly, and my first thought was how he was different from Joe. I couldn't stop the comparisons. Couldn't remove Joe from my head.

The differences made my heart stop, made guilt push hotly up into my throat. "Stop," I said. *What am I doing? I'm married* .

Pat pulled back, though his hands were still gently holding my face. The shaking had stopped. He smiled as his thumb brushed lightly over my lips. I couldn't read what was in his eyes. "I'm not sorry. I've wanted to do that for...forever, I think."

Oh, my God. This, this...sensation, this effervescent high... It was like all the clichés: balm to my bruised soul, moisture to my parched spirit, a drug. A barbiturate. Opium. Addicting. It felt so good, so delicious. It was wrong. It was *so* wrong. It was Satan with the apple; it was more tempting than original sin. It *was* original sin.

The warmth between my legs had begun to melt my resistance, my good sense, my better judgment. Sin. Sin. Sin.

Pat stood back then and dug into a pocket for his keys. I watched him open his car door and reach for an overcoat on the front seat. It was still warm in the sun but I could feel the cold and the damp beginning to creep up from the river on the other side of the building.

"Get your dog and let's take a walk." He looked at me as I just stood there, unmoving. "That kiss was on me, all on me. Put your guilt away already. You didn't do anything, you didn't kiss back."

"I didn't stop you."

He shook his head. He did read my mind. "There's nothing for you to feel guilty about. I kissed you, you didn't kiss me. I'd swear it on a stack of Bibles." He reached out one hand, one forefinger, traced the edge of my mouth. "I wanted to give you something to think about. Remember what I said. You are so beautiful."

I just stared at him. My mind was fuzzy.

He gave my hip a little slap. "Dog. Coat. Walk," he prodded, smiling at me now, his gaze suddenly unreadable. "Let's go."

"A souvenir or a sales pitch?" I asked, not moving. *That kiss.*

His mouth quirked. "Both," he said as he took my hand.

An hour later, my cheeks and nose cold, my brain feeling much more sensible, I followed Pat as he drove to the suburb where Annie lived. There'd been a little awkwardness, after we'd returned to the restaurant parking lot, as we'd worked out logistics. Pat suggested I follow him to Annie's neighborhood, where we could park one car and then ride together to go check out the convertible. *The convertible. I was going to actually test drive a convertible.*

He pulled into the parking lot of a mini mall. I pulled into the spot beside him in the little lot and rolled down the window. We were only a few blocks from Annie's apartment. The drive from the restaurant alone in my car had given me time to have second thoughts. *What was I doing?*

As if he knew what I was thinking, he said, "Just park your van and get in the car, Cath. I'll drive from here. Trouble can ride in the back seat."

"She'll be fine here in the van. It's not hot and I'll leave the windows cracked. After that walk, she'll sleep on the seat happily."

I poured some more water from the gallon jug into her dish. "You comfy, girl?" Trouble wagged her tail, smiling. "I won't be long. You hold down the fort, okay?"

I opened the door and slid into the front seat of Pat's black Audi. It must be new; it still smelled new. The interior was a pearly gray leather, the seats low slung. It was the kind of car a very successful city lawyer who wore crisply starched white shirts with cufflinks would drive. "This isn't your first time doing this, is it?" I said.

"Car shopping?"

"No. Managing the logistics of being with some other woman when you shouldn't be."

"You're not *some other woman.*"

"You're not answering the question."

"I'm supposed to be with you. We had lunch. You haven't done anything wrong. Yet. But if you want to, just say the word." His eyes were bright; he was teasing. But he wasn't.

My skin flooded with heat and it was a moment before I could rule out a hot flash. It was desire...and a sense of loss so—shockingly—crushing I wasn't sure I could swallow, all rolled into one great wad of emotion. *Oh, Mary, Mother of God.* I shut my eyes.

"Just put your seat belt on, okay?" he said, and when I opened my eyes, he was smiling gently and something had changed in his expression.

That feeling of being *worshiped*.

"Just tell me where we're going. I'm very curious to see you in a hot red sports car."

"A mid-life crisis car, you mean?"

"I didn't say that."

I grinned at him. "You didn't have to." I reached back for the seat belt and buckled in. "But if that's what it is, I don't care."

He shrugged. "Why shouldn't a woman who is smart and funny and creative, who has made a life of putting everyone else first and is at all times practical and eminently sensible, have a totally impractical car?"

Joe would have one hundred and ten reasons, at least, why it was dumb to spend money on an impractical sports car, and would just in general be negative about the whole adventure.

"A woman who is beautiful in a way that makes it hard for me to breathe, who is crazy sexy." Pat paused, did that almost smile thing with his mouth that had nothing to do with the look in his eyes. "And so passionate she doesn't know what to do with it."

I stared at him. "You think I'm crazy sexy? And passionate?" He knew what to say; he surely knew what I needed to hear.

"You are kidding, right?" Pat said, as if it was nuts that I was asking.

His reaction, this conversation, this whole afternoon, made me feel almost giddy with an excess of emotion. I wanted to close my eyes and savor the feeling even though it was *wrong*. It was filling some part of me that I hadn't realized was empty and that felt sooo right.

I snorted. "Now you're just blowing sunshine, as Joe would say." I reached in my purse for my phone. Still no texts. No call from Annie about meeting for dinner. "The dealer is called Bach Motors. Do you know where it is?"

He grinned. "That's where I bought this car."

The salesman either remembered Pat or he recognized the car Pat was driving. He proceeded to address most of his comments to Pat, which was annoying on the one hand, and kind of a relief on the other. I could look, walk around the car and run my hand over the shiny red surface without having to deal with any high-pressure sales pitch.

The reality of being here, looking at this car—red, shiny, cold in the December air—felt so removed from the joking I'd been doing for years about having a convertible it was almost surreal. Not to mention I was here with Patrick. The whole afternoon was surreal. That kiss I didn't want to think about because guilt would surely swamp me when I did. Guilt because I didn't feel guilty? How crazy was that?

The salesman asked Pat, "Your wife a lawyer, too?"

"No. She's a chemist. But my friend here is a chef."

That definitely got the salesman's attention. He didn't know what to say. He still directed most of the rest of his spiel to Pat.

I opened the driver's side door and slipped into the seat, glove-soft leather an elegant, creamy tan color, while he droned on. Gripping the steering wheel, I looked out over the hood. It felt so different from my van or Joe's pickup truck. It made me smile.

It's just a car, for pity's sake. But I couldn't stop smiling. "Can we take it for a drive?" I interrupted the salesman.

"Of course." He looked surprised that I'd asked, not Pat, but in a calculating, bright-eyed way. "Just let me get a plate."

Still gripping the steering wheel, I glanced at Pat standing beside the car on the passenger side. He'd put on sunglasses at some point and I couldn't see his eyes. The little smile on his face was amused. "How's it feel?"

"Fantastic," I said, grinning, surprised at myself. I loved it. *Loved. It.*

I'd never driven a convertible, never even ridden in one, that I could remember. I had no idea where this desire to have a convertible came from. It *was* a joke: "When I get my convertible..." akin to "when hell freezes over." It occurred to me that the joke was so long-standing that a convertible had become something more than just a fun car. It stood for something, it meant something; it was a metaphor. A symbol. Now that I was sitting in one, I decided that it changed me. Holy moly.

The salesman returned and popped a license plate onto the back, then practically jumped to show me the power controls for the seat and how they worked. I wanted him to shut up and go away. I wanted to drive the car. I wanted to own this car.

"You want to put the top up?" the salesman asked.

"No. I want to drive it with the top down," I said.

"You'll probably want to turn on the heated seats, then."

We were only a few blocks from Annie's apartment complex, but I turned in the other direction. I could feel the heat from the seats beginning to seep through my coat and pants. It was a delicious sort of sensation while cold air blew past my face and caught in my hair. People on the sidewalks stared at us. Some laughed and waved. We were on mostly residential streets so I wasn't going fast enough for the wind to really blow us. I felt a need to be on a highway where I could go fast. Where the wind would whip at us; I didn't care how cold it would be.

I glanced at Pat. He was sitting turned a bit in his seat so he could watch me. He still had that half smile on his face. I couldn't read his expression, his eyes hidden behind sunglasses. He reached over at one point and slipped my hair behind my ear. "You look good in that seat."

"I need a hat. Or a scarf."

"Oh, I don't know. I kinda like the tousled, wild woman look."

I didn't even spare him a glance at that. I took the road that led in a winding way farther from the dealership, from development and traffic. Soon enough, we were on a country road with the occasional house and subdivision, no traffic lights and few stop signs. I picked up speed, so that my hair was blowing not behind me, but into my face. I didn't know that would happen. Note to self: Pull hair back when riding in a convertible.

Pat hadn't moved or turned in his seat or said a word after the wild woman comment, which I appreciated. I didn't want to talk. He just watched me. I could feel the smile on my face, which was cold; no doubt my nose was red. I could smell everything, whatever was in the air. It was so *immediate*. It was wonderful. This was wonderful.

After about a half hour, I turned around at an old service station that was closed and boarded up. Taking a left, then a right, I found myself on the road that passed Annie's apartment complex. As I drove by, I slowed and scanned the parking lot.

The blue RAV4 that Annie had bought after college was parked in her spot. "Her car is here," I said. "That's weird. I didn't think she'd be home from work just yet. She hasn't texted."

"You want to stop?" Pat asked. "Go see her now? Show her the car?"

There was no traffic in either direction so I stopped in the middle of the street, debating. Annie had sent me the picture of this car. Annie was the one who had been encouraging me to actually *buy* a convertible, instead of just talking about it all the time. I wasn't sure I was really considering buying a convertible, but I kind of wanted Annie to see me in it. It had something to do with how I saw myself, becoming reacquainted with the Cath that had been lost, but I couldn't put that into words.

On the other hand, there was Pat. The reason I was sitting behind the wheel of this car, driving a convertible—top down—in early December when the temperature hadn't hit forty degrees. That opened the door to a whole raft of questions I'd just as soon avoid.

"Maybe she rode with a friend today—" I said.

Then I saw Annie. There were two people with her, and I realized, belatedly, there were two little kids running around, chasing each other. At the same moment, I recognized one of the people with her: Joe. What was he doing here? I couldn't see his face, but I could see Annie's. She looked...defensive. Clamped jaw, determined, resolute. I knew that expression well.

The other man...was that the married older man boyfriend? Corey? It had to be him. Of course it was, the two little kids belonged to him. He was a stocky guy, which surprised me for some reason. I hadn't pictured him like that. Even from this distance he looked older. Mature. Something in the way he carried himself. And was he *bald?*

"My God. Joe has more hair than he does."

"Shaved head," Pat said. "The boyfriend, we assume?"

I glanced at him. "Can a married man be a boyfriend?"

"Apparently so."

"He's short. And heavy. Shorter and heavier than I imagined."

"Big boy."

"Annie said he played college football."

Corey, if that's who it was, called the kids to him, pointed at a car in the parking lot. The two little boys scampered over to the car and climbed into the back seat. Corey pulled the duffle bag from Annie's shoulder—I hadn't registered the duffle bag—Vera Bradley pink and lime green paisley, the same bag she'd used when she'd come home for Thanksgiving. Annie and Joe stood just looking at each other for a long moment before Joe reached over and gave her a big hug. Watching that made my heart clench in my chest. Then Annie and Corey got into the car. Before I knew it, they were pulling out of the parking lot, never even noticing me and Pat and the red convertible, still idling in the street.

Pat didn't say anything and neither did I. I was still wrapping my mind around Corey the married-man-with-two-kids as stocky. And bald. Not what I'd pictured. I'd assumed that though he was nearly two decades older than Annie, he would be at least young-looking. More a boyish, baby-faced Kurt Russell than a middle-aged James Gandolfini. He looked nothing like the nice boys Annie had dated.

A car horn honked, so loudly and unexpectedly I jumped in my seat. Glancing in the rearview mirror, I saw there was a car behind me, unable to pass on the street since I was effectively in the middle of it. I put my blinker on and pulled to the curb. The horn caught Joe's attention. He was looking, and I was hard to miss: sleek red convertible, top down. Patrick.

"Nice ride," Joe said, standing beside the car at the curb. He leaned down and put both hands on the hood and pushed, hard, so that the car bounced on its springs. Pissed. Confused. *What the hell?* in his eyes, and the emotion from his conversation with Annie in there, too.

Without speaking, Pat and I had both climbed out of the car when Joe had looked our direction. But I didn't want to talk about the convertible. Or Patrick, either. Yet. I wanted to know what happened with Annie. And Tony Soprano. And what was Joe doing here?

"What was that about?" I asked. "With Annie. I assume that was Corey?"

"You know about him? Her *friend?*" Joe said, and I knew by the way he said it that that was how Annie had introduced Corey. I guess that answered my question. A married man is a *friend*. Not a boyfriend.

"She told me about him at Thanksgiving."

"Well thanks for the heads up. She's dating a guy old enough to be her father and you forget to tell me. An old guy with kids."

"She asked me not to say anything. She wanted to tell you herself."

Joe scowled and made some noise in his throat.

"Why don't I take the car back to the dealer?" Pat said as he handed me my purse and held out his hand for the key at the same time.

All of which prompted Joe to look at the car again. "Am I missing something? My wife driving around in a convertible with you in December?"

"Nah," Pat said, adjusting the driver's seat and the rearview mirror. "Not a thing. Just a test drive. My dealer had it on the lot."

"If you say so. Four wheel drive would be a hell of a lot more practical," Joe said in typical wet blanket Joe fashion.

"But not nearly as much fun," Pat said, winking at me.

"Thanks for lunch," I said.

"Anytime."

After Pat disappeared down the street, I asked Joe, "What else did Annie say?"

"I assume there's more to that story. A sixty-thousand-dollar car? Lunch?"

Eye on the ball, Joe, I wanted to snap. The car is not important. Lunch is not important. "Annie?" I said.

"She said, 'Dad, I'd like you to meet Corey,' and the guy said, 'Nice to meet you.'"

I wanted to slap Joe for the sarcasm. I could feel my jaw tightening. "What did you say?"

"I said, 'Nice to meet you. What the fuck are you doing with my daughter?'"

"Seriously."

"What do you think I said? What could I say? I was caught a little with my pants down, no thanks to my wife." I ignored that jab.

"I wanted to take the guy out behind the building and kick his ass. He's got to be twenty years older than her."

"Seventeen," I said, thinking that Joe wouldn't know the first thing about taking someone out behind the building and kicking anyone's ass. His bluster, so predictable, annoyed me. Though if I had to say how I wish he would have reacted, I wasn't sure.

"Well, that's fine, then," he said. "Just seventeen. That makes a big difference."

"What else did you say?" I asked again. I was more worried about Annie.

"I said 'I'm Joe, Annie's dad.' But Annie could tell I was not very happy."

"I'm sure she could."

"How long she's been seeing this guy?"

I shrugged. "Since the summer I think."

"Jesus. And I'm just finding out now? What's she thinking?"

That she loves him and that he's going to leave his wife. "Where are they going? I texted her several times today and she never responded."

"They're going to Michael's cabin for the weekend. What the hell is Laura thinking? I suppose Laura knows about this guy, too? She know how old he is? That he's got kids?"

"Laura's Michael?" The mystery man who had a fishing cabin somewhere in West Virginia?

"Apparently one of his kids tried to flush her phone, Joe said. "Yesterday. What the hell? She hasn't had a chance to replace it. A new phone is gonna cost her a thousand bucks. Maybe more."

Typical Joe. Focused on the wrong thing. "I'm sure Corey will help her pay for a new phone."

"Whatever. They're actually on their way to the phone store now. Before they head off to BF wherever. She looked pretty shocked when she saw me."

"I can imagine." And I could. No doubt she'd felt blindsided. Did she think I'd betrayed her trust and told Joe about Corey? Surely not. Not after her dad's reaction.

"What *are* you doing here?" I said. Then because that sounded accusatory, "I didn't know you had a trip down to the city today."

"I didn't know either 'til lunch time. We ordered some new tires for the Hyster and the dealer called to say they were in. If I'd known sooner, you could have brought the truck and picked them up. But after they called, I thought I'd come down, surprise you and Annie. Take my girls to dinner. Guess I'm the one surprised. *Big* fucking surprised." He scowled at me. "Did you see that guy? He's old enough to be her father. Christ, I have more hair than he does." Joe's rant made me want to slap him. "I can't believe she's seeing an old, divorced guy—with kids—seriously enough to go away for the weekend together and it's a big fucking secret." Doing what he always did in an argument: make it all about him.

"He's not divorced," I said, almost curious to see his response to that.

———

ON THE WAY HOME, in the welcoming, warm solitude of my van, serenaded by a station playing nonstop old-school Christmas music and soothed by the soft glow of dashboard lights, I had sorted thoughts of the day into two major groups: Everything Annie. And Everything Patrick.

Now, I was standing at the kitchen counter, stirring the contents of a container of yogurt, more vigorously than necessary, waiting for Joe to come inside when my phone rang inside my purse. Jamie.

"Hey, Mom."

"Hey yourself. What's up?"

"Everything's good. You're not mad or anything are you? Upset?"

"Mad? Why would I be mad? At you?"

"Well, I thought once Dad told you the news, you'd call."

What news? I felt stupid asking. "Oh?"

"Yeah, when I talked to him yesterday. I told him I'd send you a picture of the ring. You're seeing it first. I just picked it up. Check your email."

Ring? What ring? "Oh," I said again. "Okay. Checking now..."

"This is on the down low, okay, Mom? Keep it to yourself. I want to surprise her."

"Molly?"

"Who else?" Jamie laughed. "Yeah. Over Christmas. I can fill you in later."

What? Jaime bought a ring? For Molly. Jamie is going to propose? And Joe knew yesterday?

Just then, the door opened and Trouble led Joe into the kitchen. The dog danced right over to her food dish, stood looking up at me, tail wagging, doggy grin still evident, clearly happy about a day spent riding in the van, having walks in strange places, and the status of the shrubbery at the front of the house.

Joe gave me the raised eyebrow, "who's on the phone" look. I ignored him.

"Oh, wow, honey. That's big news. Exciting." I turned my back on Joe so that the edge of the countertop pressed into my hips and I was staring at the knife rail on the backsplash.

Joe knew this yesterday and he didn't tell me?

Cheerleader Cath: And *you thought you were the one with secrets....*

"I'm heading to the gym. You can try calling later, but Molly and I might be going to a movie or something. Love you."

"Love you more," I said and, oddly, could hardly get the words past the swelling in my throat. The marble, hard and cold against my hips, was a counterpoint to what was in my chest.

"Who was that?" Joe asked.

I turned around slowly, now feeling the countertop against my spine, a distraction. I barely noticed Trouble still standing at her dish, smiling, tail still wagging.

"Jamie." I waited to see a reaction on Joe's face. "He just wanted to be sure I wasn't mad. Or upset. About his big news. Since he hadn't heard from me."

There was definitely a flicker of something in Joe's eyes. Surely he hadn't just forgotten to tell me? Though honestly, nothing would surprise me these days.

"I can't believe you didn't tell me. About him buying Molly a ring."

"That's the pot calling the kettle black. I can't believe you didn't tell me about Annie's boyfriend," he said. "Who's fucking married." *Or the lunch with Pat, or what the hell you were doing in a convertible together....* Joe didn't say that, but I felt like it was there, in the air, between us. But maybe that was just my conscience.

I stared at him seeing every feature, every quality of his face that was oddly at once familiar and as strange as if I'd never seen him before.

He spoke before I could decide what I wanted to say, and his tone was so conciliatory, I could tell he was taking a page from the How To Deal With Angry Customers book. "I'm sorry. I didn't mean to keep Jamie's news from you. You were just so pissed again about Mom...I thought I'd wait and tell you later.... And then..." He waved a hand.

"And then?" I repeated.

"And then you were gone to Pittsburgh for the day. And now we're here and Jamie called before I had a chance to tell you...."

"I wasn't pissed," I said. "I was annoyed. At your mother."

"Because she invited us to dinner? It was just dinner."

"Not because she invited us to dinner. And it wasn't *just dinner*. Because when I told her I was going to Pittsburgh, she practically fell over herself offering to come take care of Trouble during the afternoon. She tries too hard. She's too invested in our lives. And you know what? Until a few weeks ago, I didn't mind, I mean, I minded, but I didn't *mind*. I just let it ride; it was just your mother being your mother."

"What's different now? Why are you so pissed at her all the time?"

I scowled at him, but let the *pissed* ride, too. "Actually, I don't think I'm mad at her as much as I'm mad at you."

"That's pretty obvious. I can't do anything right these days."

Gahhhh. What was it about that comment that made my blood pressure ratchet up?

"What's going on have anything to do with you riding around Pittsburgh in a convertible with my sister's husband?"

I didn't quite understand why I was so angry at Joe. Why he annoyed me. All. The. Time. And it wasn't Lillian's Cruise. Correction: It wasn't *just* Lillian's Cruise. No doubt that had lit the fuse, but it wasn't the fuel. "I was riding around Pittsburgh with Patrick because I wanted to test drive that car. I've been talking about having a convertible for a long time."

Cheerleader Cath was standing in front of a furnace, one that looked suspiciously like the brick patio pizza oven I'd seen in a magazine recently, heaving chunks of wood into the opening until flames were leaking through the joints in the masonry.

"You've been joking about that for years. Whatever's bothering you is not about a convertible and you know it."

This was one of those times Joe was more astute than I gave him credit for. He was right. It wasn't about the convertible. Or the cruise. Or maybe it was about both of those things, and so much more.

"I'm sorry I didn't tell you about Jamie," he said. "I thought I'd have a chance to tell you today. But the day just got away from me."

"Yeah. I get that," I said. Which was neither condemnation nor forgiveness.

"And that guy Annie's seeing? Corey? He's still married? With kids? Really?"

"Really."

"He getting divorced?"

"I don't know. Annie says he is. At some point."

"Well, fuck. What's she thinking?"

"She's thinking that she loves him. And Jamie's going to propose?" Speaking of love.

"Yep. At Christmas. That's why he called me," Joe said. "Molly's family is going skiing somewhere. Colorado I think. He already talked to her dad. He wants to propose there. On the top of a mountain."

On Christmas? So Jamie wouldn't be here? It would be the first time ever all of my kids wouldn't be home for the holiday, we wouldn't all be together. Which, in the big scheme of things, was no biggie at all. Not really. Not compared to death or cancer, or Alzheimer's or homelessness or oh, so many things. And he'd be missing being here for a good—happy—reason. I should be happy about the news. And I was, for Jamie. Absolutely. But there was something else, too. Something achy. Something...*lonely*? I tried to name it but couldn't find the words for it. It had nothing to do with liking or not liking Molly. It was about me. About feeling old, suddenly.

Joe didn't say anything for a moment, neither of us did. I was thinking about a Christmas without Jamie and about the new stage of my life I was apparently entering and why that was so hard, so depressing. Joe stood at the opposite end of the island, his coat open, his hands shoved in the pockets. "You and Pat looked pretty damn cozy together in that car. What was that about?"

"Diana asked me to talk to him. We went to lunch. The test drive was just one of those silly, spontaneous things.... Not a big deal." The brilliant, faceted joy I had felt flying down that back road, the air icy sharp in my face and smelling of winter, had slipped away like dirty water down a drain.

"What did *Di* need *you* to talk to Pat about?"

"About having a baby."

"What? Who's having a baby?"

"Diana wants to. Thinks she wants to."

"Seriously? Now? Hasn't that ship sailed? She's—" I could see Joe doing the same mental math I'd had to do. "Forty-three. Why now? And why did you need to talk to Patrick about it? Shouldn't she be having that conversation with him?"

"You'd have to ask her that. All I know is that she drove up here the other day to talk to me about it. But you're a parent. You should understand why someone would want to have children."

"I do understand why people want kids. But she kinda made her bed a while ago. It's just like Di to come late to the party. I'm still not sure what Diana wanting a baby has to do with you in a convertible in Pittsburgh. In December."

We were back to the damn convertible. I wanted to pull out my hair. I took a deep breath. "It was nothing. I mentioned to Pat that Annie had sent me a picture of that car for sale. That I kinda always wanted a convertible. This is no secret, Joe. I've been talking about it for years."

"You were kidding. Joking. "

"No, I wasn't.."

Something shifted in his expression, his mouth opened the slightest bit, then closed, like he was going to say something and then immediately decided not to. He was surprised. Did he ever *listen* to me? "I didn't think you were serious. Jesus. A convertible." He shook his head, though I didn't think he realized he was doing it. "What would you do when it snows a foot? A car like that makes about as much sense as tits on a nun."

"You don't have to be crude. And I'm not thinking it would be my only car. *Our* only car."

"What do we need another vehicle for? An *impractical* vehicle."

I stared at him. *Practicality has nothing to do with it*, I wanted to shout. I hated how everything about Joe made me angry these days. Hated how...*ugly*...that made me feel.

He stared back at me and I could see he was clamping his jaw, watched his eyes. I could practically read his mind. He was going to change the subject. "I called Laura on the way home," he said.

"About Annie and Corey using Michael's cabin? What did she say?"

"She didn't answer. Mom said she's at a meeting or conference or something in San Francisco."

Lillian again. Had Joe told her about Annie and the married man with kids? Even after almost thirty years, I could still remember Lillian's distress/shock/horror at me being pregnant before marriage, at the *scandal* of that.

"But I'll read her the riot act when I talk to her. What the hell is she thinking? Encouraging...*facilitating*...Annie's relationship with a married man."

"It doesn't really surprise me that Laura would facilitate a weekend for our daughter and her married lover. That's as messed-up as the 'family only' cruise and apparently that was her idea, too—"

"Oh, good Christ." Joe dragged a hand over his head, then scrubbed at it the way he did when he was frustrated. "You really need to get over that."

The condescension in how he said that made my blood pressure spike; I could literally feel the force of it. It made my vision almost blurry. "Get over it?"

"If that's the reason for the convertible, the hot-trotting all over Pittsburgh, lunch with Patrick, all of that...? You definitely need to get over it."

I stared at him. *Get over it* like it was my problem? "There's so much wrong with that statement, with you saying it and thinking it, I don't even know where to start."

"C'mon, Cath. That cruise for Mom is just not that big a deal."

I wondered, in some far distant place in my mind, when Joe and I had stopped speaking the same language. It was a big deal. It was so big a deal I couldn't get past it, past Joe's lackadaisical concern over how it made me feel. Even if my outrage over the damn cruise was crazy, irrational, shouldn't Joe care how it hurt me?

I closed my eyes for a moment, trying to order my thoughts and calm the rage that was making me feel dizzy. "You know how sometimes you hear about a person who has a car accident and when they run tests to be sure she doesn't have a concussion, they find a brain tumor? A tumor they wouldn't have found if she hadn't had the car accident?"

Joe was looking at me as if I had a brain tumor.

"That's how big a deal that stupid cruise is. It's the car accident."

"What the hell are you talking about?"

"I'm talking about what's wrong. Don't you understand?"

"Honestly?" He was still looking at me like I had grown a second head. "No."

I took a deep breath. Blew it out. Felt, suddenly, the burn of tears behind my eyes. "How did we get here?" I asked on a barely there whisper. It was all I could seem to manage.

But Joe heard it. His eyes changed suddenly; there was a flicker of something unsure, tentative, in them that hadn't been there before. "Help me out. What's *here*?" He still sounded frustrated, annoyed.

Were all men so *clueless*?

You don't get around to sharing family news with me. Big family news.

Our daughter is seeing a married man.

You're taking Viagra.

I contemplated sin.

You're going on an almost unimaginably luxurious cruise. Without me.

Our children are grown and gone. Their lives are effectively separate from ours, from mine, now. I am no longer a mother first, everything else second. That's a huge change. Monumental.

Chapter Nine

"Hi, Mom."

"Cathleen. Well, this is a nice surprise. You don't usually call on a weekday morning. Is everything okay? What are you up to? What's happening there?"

Last night, I wanted to hit Joe with the bedside lamp when he fell asleep with the lights on and was snoring so obnoxiously I could feel it through the floor when I came out of the bathroom.

"I was just thinking about you. It's snowing here and I'm making Aunt Mary's bread recipe. This kind of day makes me melancholy. It's so quiet. I miss the kids, I miss being a mom. I'm feeling...out of sorts, I guess—" I left that statement hanging. My mother was not generally the kind of mother you bared your soul to; she was not warm and not fuzzy. "Did you feel like that when Sammy and I were gone?"

"Of course. Have a little nip of chardonnay. That's what I always did. Do."

"No you didn't. You don't even like wine."

"Not really, but I read somewhere that wine doesn't make your breath smell like alcohol."

"I don't even remember there ever being wine in the refrigerator."

"Of course not. When we lived in Delaware, I kept it in the cupboard above the oven. Here, I keep it in the little pantry."

"After it was opened?"

"Well, sure. It's alcohol. It's not going to spoil."

I shook my head. "What are you doing today?"

"Oh, I'm crocheting a baby blanket for Esther Rose, next door. Her granddaughter is having a baby. Your dad's golfing."

"I still can't believe that dad has taken up golf."

"Oh, he loves it. He goes out and plays at least nine holes every morning. It's good for him. And it keeps him out from underfoot. He'd make me silly if he was home all the time."

Maybe it's that Chardonnay that makes you silly. Is that how you dealt with Debra Patterson, by nipping on Chardonnay? Joe hasn't cheated on me, not with another woman. Would I feel any angrier if he had? After Debra Patterson, the woman my dad cheated on my mother with, no one in the family, least of all my mother, ever mentioned her name. She was the woman who was not spoken of.

"Doesn't Dad miss the water? Fishing? When I talk to him on the phone, he never says..."

I could almost hear my mother shrug. I had never really understood how she had convinced my dad to leave Delaware. But he had been different after Debra Patterson. Had he loved her? Had she made him feel the way lunch with Pat had made me feel? Had the revelation about Dad and Mrs. Patterson made Mom as angry as I was now? Angrier? After all, Joe hadn't cheated. If there had been any cheating, or thoughts of cheating, I was guilty of that.

Had my mother discovered a dark reservoir full of mean and ugly deep inside her? Had she been unable to even look at Dad without feeling hateful and bitter? Had she subsequently wanted something she couldn't name?

"He doesn't have time to miss the water or anything else," Mom went on. "He keeps busy."

We chatted some more, and when we hung up, I realized I was

still full of a rage that was foreign yet perversely also as familiar as the freckles on the back of my hand.

This morning, Joe had left his wet towel in a pile on the vanity in the bathroom. He'd left the milk and the box of Raisin Bran out on the counter, though he'd put his empty bowl in the dishwasher. The coffee maker had been left turned on, the coffee mug he'd used on the counter next to the milk. I'd wanted to throw the mug through the fucking window.

But was Joe right? He wasn't the angry one. I was. The wet towel, the milk, the cereal, the spoon, the coffee mug...all that was same old, same old.

Did I really think I was going to be able to talk to my mother about what I was feeling?

You had that time with Dad and Mrs. Patterson. That was hurtful. And surely that made you mad, too?

I am so angry *these days.*

―――

I DIDN'T SEE Father J until Friday. He stopped into the rectory kitchen midafternoon on his way to visit a parishioner who'd been hospitalized. I had made a fresh pan of apple crisp and had just taken it out of the oven and the whole house smelled of baking apples and cinnamon.

"Cathleen. What ambrosia are you making me now?"

"Apple crisp. Dessert for dinner. Would you like a sample now?"

"There's an apron in God's Heavenly kitchen with your name on it. Bless you."

I laughed as I got out a bowl—Father J liked milk on his apple crisp—and a spoon. Father J dug in, rolling his eyes in pleasure. "At the risk of sounding sacrilegious, if we served your apple crisp instead of the sacrament, I do believe world peace would be a very real possibility."

I laughed. "Can I use that quote in my next cookbook?"

"Of course. How's Joe this week? Any lingering side effects after that fall?"

"He's fine. No side effects." *That I know of.*

I wiped the counter, around the coffee maker, the condensation that was forming on the plastic milk jug, then around the cutting board where I'd been chopping vegetables. When I glanced at him, he was finished with the apple crisp and was watching me, his face, his eyes full of gentle patience. "Would you like more, Father?"

"Yes, of course I would, but I'll pass. I'll have some after dinner."

"Chicken cacciatore. With brown rice. And I'll leave ingredients for a tossed salad. I made that apple and wheatberry salad you like and poached a piece of salmon for the weekend."

"Ahh. Sounds delicious. But everything you make is wonderful."

"Thank you, Father. You're a pleasure to cook for." Father J appeared to be in no hurry. "Stop looking at me like that, Father."

"Like what?"

"You know exactly like what. Like you have all day to wait for me to tell you what's on my mind."

"There's something on your mind?" he asked with mock innocence.

I laughed. "I'm really not ready to talk about it yet."

He nodded. "Okay." But still he didn't move from the table except to pull the Sudoku book from under the newspaper and unclip the ballpoint pen. He glanced at his watch. "I think I'll wait to make my hospital visits until after my four o'clock meeting with Mrs. Lamb at the elementary school. I hate to visit with someone who might need to talk, only to have to hurry away for an appointment."

"You're pretty smooth, Father."

"You think? Felt a little obvious to me."

I smiled, my eyes burning suddenly as if I was going to cry.

"Do parents ever stop worrying about their children?" I asked eventually, picking up my knife and sliding a red bell pepper onto the cutting board. It was easier to talk when my hands were busy, when my eyes could be on something else. Without looking, I could tell that

Father was paying me the same courtesy, his eyes on the puzzle book, pen in his hand.

"My mom used to say 'a mother is only as happy as her unhappiest child.' Obviously, I can't speak from first-hand experience, but based on my experience as a professional listener, the answer is no. You never stop worrying about your children."

I rubbed my nose with my forearm, then scooped up the chopped pepper using the edge of the knife and my hand and dropped it into the sauté pan. I'd already browned the chicken thighs and they sat on a blue plate, awaiting the sauce.

After a bit he asked, "Which one?"

"Annie," I said and kept chopping, trying to find the right words. "She's seeing a man, an older man, who has two children. And he's married. My daughter is committing adultery." I felt the shame of it all over again, saying the words out loud.

I glanced up at him finally and saw that he didn't look shocked. There was no outrage there, no judgment, just compassion. And not only for Annie. For me, too. I didn't want to cry, but sensed that the tears would come if I let them. I took another deep breath, and suddenly they were gone, the tears. It was as if the anger that had been my constant companion of late pushed aside the urge to weep like I pushed the papery brown skin of the onion I chopped into the trash. I could not seem to shed the anger. I kept vigorously chopping and adding the vegetables to the pan. Turning up the heat a little, I stirred.

"This is what you've been worried about."

I wasn't sure if that was a question or a statement, but I didn't answer or clarify, merely shrugged my head noncommittally. "Adultery is a mortal sin." According to the Church, my sweet precious daughter was headed for the pits of Hell. But in my heart, I just couldn't, didn't, believe that.

"Yes. It is. But I don't think that God sees the world in black and white. I truly believe Our Father appreciates shades of gray. And I'm not talking about the books."

"You know about those, Father?"

"Of course. I'm a priest." A smiled played about his mouth. He raised his eyebrows. "Who better to know about those books?"

I snorted and grinned.

"And I also know that you've been at the center of your family, taking care of everyone for almost all of your adult life. You're a nurturer. It's your gift."

"It's not easy to change that, Father, if you're suggesting I just stop worrying. Let go and let God." *Blah blah.*

"If it was easy, everyone would do it."

"Is that the wisdom of Our Lord or Tom Hanks?" I almost felt...annoyed. Father J and I joked about and replayed quotes from movies and popular culture all the time. What was wrong with me?

He smiled unapologetically as if he knew what I was thinking and it didn't bother him. "Worry is a no-confidence vote in God?"

"I thought it was depression is a no-confidence vote in God?" I stirred the vegetables a bit while I could feel Father J sitting quietly, waiting, something which was always notable to me; he was such a big man, so full of life. I had the sense that he would sit all afternoon, if necessary, his meeting at 4:00 p.m. be damned.

"That too," he said.

I stopped stirring and looked up at him. "I think that Doug might have a drinking problem."

He nodded, still not looking shocked or distressed. "It's not uncommon."

"Doug has always been the child who causes me sleepless nights. And my worry for him has always been different for some reason. Like I've known in my gut that the bottom was going to fall out, it was just a matter of time." I was revealing something I'd never even said to Joe, because saying it out loud made me feel disloyal.

"Your children are all adults now. You can't make, or unmake, their choices for them. Our journey to God is meant to be personal. And to have speed bumps. And potholes."

"Their speed bumps are breaking my heart."

"I imagine Our Father feels the same way." He smiled at me, his trademark kind, caring, nonjudgmental smile.

I sniffed. "I suppose so," as I dropped the cutting board and the knife into the sink. Picking up the wooden spoon, I stirred the contents of the skillet almost vigorously, pushing the onion and pepper around in the sizzling oil. It wasn't just Annie. Or Doug. It wasn't just being an empty nester. I didn't realize how vigorously I was stirring until I pushed a heap of half-sautéed vegetables over the rim of the pan onto the stovetop. The gas flame sizzled and flared up.

Father had leaned into to the table and sat with his chin in one hand watching me, his expression still ever benevolent and patient. "I go shoot some hoops in the park at the end of the street when I need to blow off some steam."

"Maybe I'll borrow your ball."

"You're welcome to it. Anytime," he offered. "Do you want me to talk to Annie?" His gentle eyes held mine.

"No. But thank you for offering. She won't be happy to know I've told you about her...relationship. And I guess I'm hoping she'll break it off, that it's not serious. Though I think that actually makes what she's done worse."

"I can understand how worry about a child can weigh on a parent. On you, Cathleen. But we are all tempted. You know this. It is part of what makes us human. None of us are without sin. None of us."

"Oh, Father," I said, stirring, unable to look at him. "I seem to be questioning everything these days. My life. My values. I'm so mad lately. At Joe mostly. I don't know if it's because of my age, menopause, you know. It's a bitch." I glanced at him.

He nodded, his lips still flirting with that little smile, but his eyes were warm, full of understanding.

"I mean so mad it's changed who I am. How I see others...how I see Joe. How I see myself."

"A crisis of faith?"

"I don't think faith has anything to do with it."

"Faith has everything to do with everything."

I raised my eyebrows and no doubt the scorn I felt was apparent. "For you, maybe."

Typically, Father J didn't see the scorn, didn't judge me by it. "For all of us. Prayer—faith—can solve lots of problems. I've seen it happen."

I was disappointed. "That's your advice? Pray? Have faith?"

"It is." His eyes held mine. "And don't do anything rash."

Like divorce? Could Father J read my mind? "I told you about the cruise—the unbelievably luxurious and expensive cruise—my in-laws are planning for 'family only.' No spouses invited. I can't believe how angry, hurt, resentful I feel. I can't seem to get past it. To find, or be, the person I was before I heard about it."

"I understand why you'd be hurt."

"You might have some idea. But you can't know, or appreciate, the history. The *context*," I stressed, trying to explain that it wasn't just The Cruise.

"No, I can't."

"I wasn't unhappy before. I wasn't angry. At least I didn't know it if I was. I was actually content. Life was—is—good. I have a wonderful life. Which is why it makes no sense that I'm so pissed now. Furious. What is wrong with me?"

Father J watched, listening, still with no judgment. No condemnation. In fact, he looked as patient as ever, which was unreasonably annoying. Infuriating.

"Tell me to stop being selfish. Spoiled. Entitled. God. I hate entitled people. Tell me to suck it up and be happy for Joe and my mother-in-law and all of her kids. Be the bigger person. Well, I just can't," I answered myself. "I'm just too mad.

"It's like there was a tiny hairline crack in the sidewalk of my life that has now broken completely open. And a bitter, resentful, ugly genie popped out. I can't put her back. I can't seal up the crack or pretend it isn't there." And I didn't know where to put that genie. The bitch.

"It's okay you feel that way. Give yourself some grace. Maybe it seems like a giant crack now, but down the road, when you look back, you'll see it wasn't so big. Or maybe it is big, but it's the crack on the top of a soufflé and it's a good thing. Or at least not a bad thing. Not a terminal thing. Maybe something good will come of it. Don't give up on yourself. On your life."

"You're reaching now, Father. A soufflé?"

"It's the first food analogy I could think of."

I gave a laugh and smiled at him, just to let him off the hook. I didn't want a pep talk. Not even a Father J one. I did what my mother always does when there is dissent or upset that she can't or doesn't want to deal with. I patronized and changed the subject. It makes me crazy when she does it. And it made me annoyed at myself that I was doing it now. Jesus. Was I becoming my mother on top of everything else?

I felt oddly raw, and tender. Father J seemed to sense it. "It sucks getting old," I said then.

"Yeah, but it beats the alternative," he said, smiling now. He let that rest for a moment, let me take a deep breath and lay the wooden spoon down on the counter.

"Talk to your kids, to Annie and Doug," he said. "Give them your counsel, and then allow them to find their own way."

"I know. I mean I will, Father. I'll try," I corrected.

"You and Joe have made a life together, a family. You need to remember its worth when you are weighing your anger, your resentment, and your hurt. And not to belittle those emotions, but don't nurture them, either. Sometimes we have to go out of our way to find goodness. In others and in ourselves."

I just stared at him. His advice felt ambiguous. I wasn't sure what he was suggesting.

"Remember your gifts. Those evolve as life changes. Don't do anything rash," he said again. "Trust. Have faith. Pray. Think about what you want now, what's important to you at this stage of your life.

Allow time to give you some perspective. We all need that sometimes. A change in perspective. It's healthy."

Time. I glanced at my watch. "Oh." I said. "Your meeting, Father."

"It's quite all right. I like to give Mrs. Lamb the occasional opportunity to admonish me. Things run smoother all around when I give her reason to rap the proverbial knuckles." He wagged said knuckles at me, his fingers like the rest of him, large, the backs dusted with sandy-red colored hair. Father J still looked like the shot-putter he'd once been.

"Father."

He grinned and pushed the puzzle book and newspaper back toward the center of the table and stood up. "Shameless, I know. But I go with what works."

I laughed and the tension, the anger, I'd felt somehow seemed to ease out of me.

———

THE SKY WAS flat and colorless. The little skiff of snow that had fallen a few days ago had melted except for shaded places where it still hugged the ground, providing the only relief in the otherwise bleak landscape along the interstate. It was an ugly kind of day that suited my mood.

The Daley-Hallowell company holiday party was at the end of the week and I had a boatload of stuff to get done. We always hosted, which meant the house had to be cleaned and decorated. I cooked and baked an assortment of food that included traditional favorites as well as one or two new offerings I thought would appeal to the group.

Normally, I loved the party, even though it was a lot of work. The decorating, the food prep, buying or making little gifts and favors; it all gave me great pleasure. For someone with my skill set—another phrase Joe learned at some conference or other and used with regularity—the company Christmas party was an event that was right up my alley. But, for the first time ever, I was wishing we held the party at the Holiday Inn, like some other local businesses. I wished I could just postpone Christmas for another month or two. Or skip it this year all together.

I pulled into the Walmart parking lot—crowded already. I was digging my shopping list out of my purse when my phone dinged with a text. Annie. I hadn't really spoken to her since the afternoon in Pittsburgh, other than to hear from her that she got a new phone. As far as I knew, Joe hadn't talked to her either.

> Annie: I have to work on Christmas Day
> and the day after. I have Christmas Eve off.
> But I have plans, so I won't be able to get
> home. Just FYI.

What? I read the words again while my mind resisted, wouldn't let them settle so their meaning could be absorbed. *No.* There was a wealth of information in those few words, more that wasn't said than was. Christmas without two of my children? It was unimaginable. So different from past Christmas tradition that I literally could not imagine it. The very idea made my heart hurt.

I tried to accept that this went along with what Father J had counseled: That my children were adults, living their own adult lives. But it didn't make me feel any better. I was circling a huge pile of Feeling Sorry for Myself, I knew that, but this news felt like one more Jenga block being pulled from the stack of my life. How long until the stack collapsed?

FYI, Annie had texted. I *hated* FYIs almost as much as LOLs.

> Me: Oh, no. That's a bummer. Jamie won't
> be home either. He's going skiing with
> Molly's family. Poor Doug. He'll have to be
> the token Daley child this year. Can you get
> home sometime? To see Doug and to open
> presents and stuff? Maybe we could come
> to you?

In a funk, I sat in the parking lot outside Walmart, not realizing at first that I had crumpled my shopping list in my hand. I'd decided on miniature topiaries for favors for the company party this year, using terracotta flowerpots, large cinnamon sticks, and gobs of clay to hold them in the pots, oranges and whole cloves. Red ribbon. Party favors and gifts that were food—or at least kitchen-related—were my "schtick." People expected it now. My editor wanted me to include some of those crafty "recipes" in the holiday cookbook as well.

Could I leave Joe?

Whoa. Where did that come from?

The image of a gerbil spinning away on a wheel to nowhere filled my head. Like today, like this. Spend untold hours sticking whole cloves into oranges. Who cared about that kind of thing except me? I'd had to special order bulk whole cloves on the internet. I paid shipping, for God's sake.

The frickin' time and thought and care I put into the things that consumed my existence. My children, cooking, food, the garden, our home. It had been my *life*. Never before had I felt so inconsequential, so trivial. "Remember your gifts," Father J had said. "They evolve." Blah blah.

Or you just chase your tail forever, run on the damn wheel. Like the gerbil.

When I'd gotten pregnant in college, I'd never given any thought to doing anything other than what Joe and I had done. Get married. Part of it was the times, they were different then, but even so, had I had other options, like having the baby myself, not getting married, I would not have taken them. I'd loved Joe, I'd wanted a family, the traditional version, two parents, other siblings. Would Joe and I have ended up together if I hadn't gotten pregnant? I used to wonder that, but not for a long, long time. Had it been a mistake?

No. I could never think that because without Joe and our marriage there wouldn't be Jamie and Doug and Annie. Or Nora. The most important things in my life. But did having children mean I had to stay married? Had my marriage been a mistake?

I knew middle-aged women who were divorced, and they all, every last one of them, wore an aura of desperation, as palpable as scent. Lonely and Pitiable No. 5. Did I really want to leave Joe? Was the peace worth the price? Would peace even follow? The idea of change that dramatic, that severe, that *terminal*, was terrifying. But did I really want to stay married because I couldn't bear the cinematography of divorce?

No response from Annie. Dropping the now crumpled shopping list back into my purse, I opened the message app on my phone and typed Helene's name at the prompt. *Did it scare the shit out of you when you got divorced?*

Then was struck by how stupid the question was. I'd been Helene's 911 countless times during the weeks and months her divorce had dragged on. I had had a front row seat to Helene's pain. And fear. Even now, more than a decade later, the scar was still apparent, still raw. Divorce had changed Helene.

I backspaced. Typed. *Do you ever regret getting divorced?*

Just as dumb. Deletedeletedelete. *How did you know? That divorce was the answer? That you could survive it? That life would be better? Is your life better? How did you know?*

That was a stupid question. Helene had caught the asshole in his exam room with a dental hygienist. Erick had been, likely still was, a serial cheater. Because once a cheater, always a cheater.

Joe had never cheated on me. Not that I knew of. I had not suffered that indignity. *But you might have cheated on him.* Cheerleader Cath did one of those jumps with one leg straight and the other bent. *You did cheat on him, in your head. That* made me think of Annie—my daughter the adulterer. I laid my forehead on the steering wheel and closed my eyes. My hands shook.

Do I really want a divorce? Do I want to leave Joe?

A couple of deep breaths later, I contained the vast, dark, hollow unknown that was somehow connected to the shaking in my hands, at least enough to push the send button on my phone.

174

Me: Can I have the number for your divorce
attorney?

Almost immediately, my phone buzzed with an incoming call.

"What's going on?" Helene asked.

"I don't know."

"Why are you asking me about my divorce attorney? Did Joe do *something*?" Something being code for *cheat*.

"No, no. Not what you're thinking. It's just that he's making me nuts."

When Helene didn't respond, I realized how that must sound. Complaining about how Joe chewed his food and how he didn't *listen*, how he was so inherently *clueless*, how I was so *angry*. When Erick had cheated. "I'm in a funk I can't seem to pull myself out of. I can't decide if it's something more. Something bigger. Something fatal."

"Menopause. Hormones. You'll feel better tomorrow. You'll feel better in ten minutes."

I don't think so. "Maybe."

"Everyone gets a little overwhelmed this time of year. Even you."

"Even me? What's that mean?"

"No doubt you're baking 250 dozen Christmas cookies, you're going out in the woods somewhere to get pine boughs to make your own decorations. No, you probably planted a pine tree in your yard fifteen years ago so that you wouldn't have to go out in the woods. You're knitting sweaters for half the town. You're making your own wrapping paper and weaving the ribbon for bows."

I couldn't help myself, I laughed. "Only twenty dozen cookies." I didn't tell Helene that I hadn't planted pine in my yard, but a number of years ago, I did plant two holly bushes, a male and a female, so that I'd have my own source of red-berried holly every Christmas. I wasn't making wrapping paper—this year. Because a couple of years ago, I bought a commercial-sized roll of brown kraft paper and used pine cones dipped in red and green and silver paint to roll on a design.

"And no sweaters this year. Scarves. And only ten. For the rectory committee."

"Good grief. No wonder you're in a funk. Go to the store like normal people and buy gifts and decorations and cookies."

"I wouldn't actually care if we didn't celebrate Christmas at all this year."

"You love Christmas."

"Not this year. Jamie and Annie won't be home, the first time ever we won't all be together on the holiday. The thought makes me so sad I can hardly bear it."

"Boohoo. They're grown up. They have lives. It's not the end of the world," Helene said, and beneath the words, I heard the admonition that was reminder and rebuke together: Helene had had years of holidays without her daughter because Julia spent every other Christmas with her father. I felt a flush of shame, and apology. It was all part of what I was asking Helene, though. About life after divorce. Did I want to divorce Joe? Was what was wrong *that* wrong? I laid my head on the steering wheel again, feeling it press against my skull in a pleasantly distracting sort of way. I closed my eyes.

"We're not talking about Christmas," Helene said. "What's wrong?"

"I feel old." I took a deep breath, the little ridges of the steering wheel pressing into my head. "I am old."

"You're not old. You're just older. What does that have to do with divorce?"

"I have thirty mini topiaries to make."

"What?" Helene burst out laughing.

I supposed it *was* funny, though I couldn't even manage a smile. "Favors for the company Christmas party. Thirty frickin' clove-studded orange and cinnamon stick topiaries to make. In four days, I've got fifty to sixty people coming to my house for a holiday party for which I will make all the food. Baked ham and cheddar thyme biscuits, homemade chicken tenders on skewers, pots de chocolate, sugar cookies cut out in the shape of big trucks and decorated with Daley-Hollowell green and white and yellow icing."

"You like doing that stuff. You always have. It's why you write cookbooks and make crafty things like orange-studded topiaries and truck-shaped sugar cookies instead of writing software or cleaning teeth."

My forehead was starting to throb where the steering wheel was gouging it. I pressed harder, perversely enjoying the pain.

"Joe will buy gifts for me and wrap them. That will be the extent of Joe's Christmas preparations. I'll shop and buy the gifts for all of our children, my parents, Joe's mother, and I'll find some kind of 'thoughtful but inexpensive' holiday tchotchkes for his siblings and their families and for my brother and his family. All of the Daleys will gather—at least the ones within driving distance—at my house to celebrate with a dinner that for the most part I will cook. I'll shop for and prepare the food. I'll send the cards, I'll orchestrate Christmas from the first day to the fucking twelfth day. And all the days in between."

There was a pause while I could tell Helene was gearing up to respond. But what she said wasn't the sympathy I expected. "Oh, my God. Listen to you. You want some cheese with that whine? You made your bed, girlfriend. But if you don't like it, unmake it."

"Easier said than done."

"You need a vacation. One with sex. Hot, steamy, bone-melting sex."

"Ha. Not gonna happen."

There was a telling silence, at least it felt telling to me. "Why not?"

"Why not? Because we've been married for almost thirty years. Our bone-melting sex days are behind us. I don't think sex is the answer. Not sex with Joe."

"You're married to Joe. Joe is the only option in that department."

For obvious reasons, spelled P-A-T-R-I-C-K, I ignored that observation. "I went to lunch last week with Patrick." I told her about that lunch, what Pat said, what I said, how he kissed me.

There was a long silence. "Patrick your brother-in-law, married to Joe's sister?"

I couldn't decide what it was I heard in my friend's voice. Shock? Disappointment?

"I don't love Pat. I like him. As a friend. He's always been a friend, someone to talk to, who understands me differently than Joe."

"Oh, God. That's what Erick said. What they all say. 'She understands me better—'"

I flinched at the vehemence of Helene's comment.

"I didn't mean..." I started to say.

But Helene continued, "That's the oldest one in the book. You're a cliché. There's nothing novel about adultery though everyone committing it seems to think they're the first. They're special." I could hear simple anger, and maybe pain, in Helene's voice.

I had so badly wanted to talk to someone who would understand how angry I was, someone who would empathize with the rage and resentment I felt toward Joe, I had lost sight of the fact that Helene would never understand adultery, or even the temptation of adultery. Not after what Erick put her through. Thank God I hadn't told her about Annie, the adulterer. "Oh, Hellie. I'm sorry. Forget I said anything. Forget I texted."

"You're not serious about divorce? You're just blowing off steam, right?"

"I don't know. I'm so... Mad. Pissed off." I realized I'd sat up in my seat, was watching activity in the Walmart parking lot without really seeing it. I put my head back down on the steering wheel, finding the narrow view of the floor and my feet somehow soothing. "What am I going to do?"

"You can't divorce Joe. You've been married for almost thirty years. This is temporary. This...what you're feeling. You love Joe."

"I do love him. But right now, I hate him. Everything is wrong, somehow, and I don't know why. Or when it got this way. What I feel for Joe is not what I used to feel."

"Of course it's not. You're not the same person you were twenty or thirty years ago, either. But you have a life that most of the rest of us would give up a kidney for."

I closed my eyes.

"I wish I was still married," Helene said. "I dream about it, you know. And in my dreams, I'm Mrs. Erick Altonmeyer. I'm still with Erick and he's not a shitbag. He doesn't cheat on me and we're happy. Jules has a family."

The revelation surprised me. Helene's divorce had been bitter and painful and so destructive as to leave scorched Earth in its wake.

"They're so real I wake up feeling light, like I'm filled with helium. Those dreams kill me." I heard her take a deep breath and for a moment, there was just that, the two of us breathing, no words. "I'd be happy with a good one," Helene said then. "No once in a lifetime grand passion required. Not movie-star handsome. Just a *good man*."

It sounded so easy, so simple, so reasonable. *A good man*. I made my hands into fists and squeezed.

"Listen," Helene finally said. "It doesn't really matter what's holding your marriage together. If it's not enough for you, then make something more. You're the queen of making stuff, Ms. Topiary. You didn't ask for my opinion, but that's what I think."

And just then there was movement to my right, and a tapping on the passenger side window which startled me so that a rush of adrenaline flooded my system and ignited a hot flash. I hadn't had one of those for a couple of weeks. Lillian tapped again to get my attention then opened the door. "Cathleen. I didn't know you had an errand to Walmart today. We could have come together."

———

I was literally up to my elbows in sugar cookie dough when

Trouble barked once, suddenly, and stood with her tail wagging, watching the kitchen door.

"What do you hear, girl? Who's coming? UPS? FedEx? Santa making deliveries?" I laid the cookie cutter and the spatula down beside the rolling pin, wiped my hands on the dishtowel and moved to the door.

Both Sandy the UPS driver and Albert the FedEx guy brought dog treats when they delivered packages. Trouble loved them both. Though Trouble loved pretty much anyone and everyone who breathed. The cookies weren't iced yet, but I could give whoever it was a couple warm from the oven.

Before I could reach the door, I heard stomping and then it opened and it was Joe. Cold air poured into the room. It wasn't quite 2:00.

"Hey. What are you doing here? Something happen?" Joe never came home in the middle of the day.

"I told you I'd be home."

"You did? When?" And there it was, that flash of annoyance that was becoming all too familiar.

"This morning. Before I left."

I walked back to the batch of cookies I was in the midst of cutting out. Picking up the spatula, I worked it under one of the truck shapes on the counter, transferred it gently to the parchment paper on the cookie sheet.

"Those are cool," Joe said.

"I found the cookie cutter online. I thought I'd make cookies for the party, but I ordered one—a cookie cutter—for every family, too."

"Did we get them anything else?"

"You mean besides their Christmas bonus? I was going to make mini topiaries. But I didn't feel like it."

"Mini-what?"

"Topiaries. We talked about it."

He shook his head, got the apologetic look on his face that I knew. Too well.

"Clove-studded oranges. Cinnamon sticks."

"Oh, yeah. Sorry. Forgot."

"Well, it doesn't matter because I didn't make them." *Didn't have time. Didn't feel like it. Didn't want to.*

"Don't worry about it. No one will miss them."

I shook my head. Of course they wouldn't. Joe always gave Christmas bonuses, but what I gave at the annual holiday party had always been something handmade. All this... I glanced at the cookie dough...

What was I doing it for? *Who* was I doing it for?

When Annie, and even the boys, had been younger, I liked thinking up this kind of project because they could help. It was the kind of memory I had wanted them all to have of the holiday. It was part of the season for me: cookie baking, cut-out cookies, fancy sugar, giving of my time and effort and caring—myself.

"You're right." I looked up at Joe. "No one will miss the mini topiaries. What are you doing here?"

"I came home so we could go get the tree."

"Tree?"

"You know. The big green thing with lights and tinsel? Smells like pine, feels like pine. Star? Ornaments?"

"I know the Christmas tree."

He *was* a good man.

When had that become not enough?

"C'mon. Let's go get a tree."

"I've got all these cookies to make—"

"They're not going anywhere. Throw a paper towel over them and finish them later."

I felt a spike of annoyance. I had two pounds of butter in this dough. I couldn't just "throw a paper towel over them and finish them later." But I could put the dough in the fridge. Make the cookies later tonight or even tomorrow. Regardless that I had plenty of other stuff to do tomorrow.

"Why didn't you let me know you wanted to go get a tree this afternoon?"

"I wasn't sure I was gonna be able to get away. But I'm here now. Let's go. C'mon."

Typical Joe. Because it was convenient for him, I should adjust my schedule to accommodate his. I could feel myself clenching my jaw and I made a conscious effort to stop, took a deep breath.

Make something else, Helene had said. "I was just going to run down to the courthouse. The Boy Scouts are selling trees there— Besides, if Jamie and Annie won't be here..." I started.

"Well, we'll be here. And Doug. And we have the party. We're not having some kind of lame-ass Charlie Brown tree. We're going out to Lanyards, like we do every year."

Our marriage was falling apart, and Joe wanted to go on as usual.

Make something more Helene had said.

I owed him that. Didn't I? Joe and me.

And Jamie, Doug and Annie.

Almost thirty years of marriage. Full circle. I'd come full circle.

Chapter Ten

ven though it was a weekday, the tree farm was doing a fair amount of business. Only two weeks 'til Christmas. Thirteen days, actually, but who was counting? The afternoon was perfect, though already the shadows were getting long.

A teenage boy wearing a bright red jacket with a Lanyards Tree farm logo asked us what kind of tree we wanted. "Fir," Joe said, and the kid pointed us in the right direction. Joe pulled the tree cart thingee and I held the leash with Trouble.

There had been a time when we had to allow a couple of hours for tree selection. For each kid to pick a preferred model, to debate its qualities, and compare it to the others. Sometimes those debates had turned contentious, when the kids were younger. Once, Jamie had snatched Doug's cap as they'd stood arguing, and had raced off down the rows of pine trees with Doug in pursuit. At some point, Jamie had tossed the hat into the tree tops as he ran, and the whole family had spent another hour looking for it. Joe had been pissed, and I had been frustrated. All three kids recalled that episode with hilarity when it came up now.

"Hey." Joe was ahead of me in the row between trees. "You

remember the time we spent half the damn day here, looking for Doug's hat?"

I smiled. "I was just thinking about that. He was so mad." The reminiscence was nice, warm. Our shared joy in our children, the pleasure of remembering, was sweet. Even recalling a time when the boys had been fighting. That was the luxury of memory: time and distance.

"How 'bout that one?" Joe had stopped and was pointing with the tree saw.

"Too fat," I said, almost on principle. We couldn't take the first one we saw.

"How 'bout that one, over there. On the other side of the short, squatty one?"

I looked at the tree he was pointing at. "Maybe," I said, cocking my head, studying the tree in question, finally leading Trouble around to inspect the other side. "Nah. There's a big bare spot over here." We walked on, the tree cart squeaking.

"I worried about them so much," I said after a bit, thinking in particular of times when that worry was justified. I didn't even let my mind get near enough to touch the memory of the morning I'd found Nora. Even after all these years, I didn't let myself think of that day, though surely all the rest of motherhood, for me at least, was limned by the appearance of the police, the coroner, the funeral director, the black, aching, irretrievable loss that followed. "I still do."

Joe was silent for a while as we walked to where the trees petered out at the end of the field. "You worried too much."

"What?" I stared at him.

Joe had stopped walking, the handle of the cart in his right hand, the saw hanging from his left, swinging a little bit. "I've heard other guys say the same thing. It's normal, I guess." He didn't sound convinced. "They took up all of you."

"I suppose they did."

"It's different now. Will be different."

Hadn't I been thinking the same thing, not all that long ago? Of renewed intimacy that was manifested in my head by images of me and Joe in a convertible, a road trip, lots of road trips, the sun on our shoulders. Like a couple in the Viagra commercials on TV. Ironically.

"You—we—" he amended and I knew he was patronizing me, "need to learn how to be without them."

Thanks, Dr. Phil. "They're all I ever wanted: Kids. A family."

Joe smiled at me. "You still have me."

Had he felt like he competed with them, the kids? Hadn't we been mutually consumed by the job of raising our children? I felt like I had to defend myself. "After Nora, I couldn't stop thinking or worrying for one second. For fear of what would happen if I did."

"That's crazy. You weren't responsible for Nora's death. It was one of those things. Beyond your control or mine."

"I won't ever feel that way. Will never be able to stop feeling guilty. Hypervigilant."

"We're not just talking about Nora here, are we? They're adults now, and Nora is gone. When do you start living your life again? When do we get our life? Your hormones will get back to normal; you'll like having an empty nest. That's what people say."

Hormones? You clueless idiot. He thought it was that easy? It was all I could do not to turn and scream at him, while his words filled my head: *That's what people say. What people?* Joe had been talking to *people* about me? *I could just imagine that conversation. Men talking about women's hormones.*

Cheerleader Cath scoffed, dropping her pompoms on the bleachers.

If it didn't piss me off so much, it would make me laugh.

And then, I had the revelation I knew with sick certainty was truth: *Lillian.*

"Your mom said it. You had a discussion with your mother about me. About menopause." It wasn't a question.

"It mighta come up."

"Oh, Joe. Seriously. Is there nothing about our marriage that's sacred? About me? I'd almost rather you talked about it with Chip at work or with Jack Hastings. But your mother?"

"Hey. It's a big deal for you—for women," he amended. "She's been through it." He waved a hand. "I wasn't telling her anything she didn't already know."

"What does that mean? Because it's obvious to the whole world that I'm going through menopause?" I didn't know if I wanted to kill him or cry.

Joe looked at me and the expression on his face was genuinely perplexed. "What?"

"Do you realize that after almost thirty years of marriage, I've learned to keep things to myself because I never know what might end up for Lillian's consumption? There's this huge part of me that you don't share, or know, because somewhere along the line, you stopped deserving to share it. Do you understand that? I can't trust you to keep my secrets."

"What are you talking about? I don't tell her private stuff. What secrets?"

The urge to kill him had passed. The urge to cry, too. I was suddenly too weary for either. "Forget it." I pushed past him in the row between trees, walked to the end and turned into another, the cart squeaking somewhere behind me so that I knew Joe was following. "This one's good." I pointed, changing the subject.

"Too small," Joe came up beside me.

"No, it's not. It's just the right size," I said.

"What about that one?" Joe pointed the saw toward a candidate. The tree had a nice shape but was easily ten feet tall and more than half that around.

"Too big."

"No, it's not. Just because all the kids won't be home doesn't mean we're going to forego the holiday. Or a nice tree."

"I didn't suggest that we would *forego* Christmas." Although hadn't I just expressed such a wish to Helene? "Or not get a 'nice' tree. I just don't want one that'll take me hours to decorate." *And undecorate after the holiday is over.* "This year, a smaller tree is appropriate."

"*Appropriate?* What the hell does that mean?"

Because, I wanted to say. Because I say so.

"I think we should put a big tree in the front hall, by the stairs. We could put another smaller one in the living room. Really do it up this year."

I stared at him. "Are you out of your mind?"

"What's wrong with that? You used to talk about putting a big tree in the front hall."

"Years ago. When there were kids around to help decorate." *To make the effort for.*

"Doug will be here."

"Yeah, but only for a few days, and he doesn't get home 'til the night before Christmas Eve. There's no point in having two trees, one huge one. It's too much work."

"Nah, it's not," he said, and something about how he said it, or the way he was looking at me felt like a line drawn in the sand. "This is the perfect year for a big tree. For two trees."

"Joe. No. We're not going to put that tree up in the house. It's too big. We won't be able to even walk past it in the hallway, it's so fat."

"Yeah, we are."

"I'm not decorating it. I'm not un-decorating it."

"I can manage to put some lights on a damn Christmas tree. I think I can do that."

"Sure you can." I gave Trouble a tug and walked back toward the truck. For some inexplicable reason, I wanted to laugh, the kind of laugh that was fueled not with good humor, but with something else, something murky and fragile.

———

JOE CUT THE HUGE TREE, as well as a smaller one, one that I'd approved with a curt nod, barely even looking. The two trees were duly drilled and shaken and snugly twine-wrapped at the red barn. Joe chatted with Mack Lanyard, owner of the tree farm; I smiled and nodded and said little and wished I was anywhere else in the world.

At home, I went straight into the kitchen and set to work finishing the sugar cookies, letting Joe unload the two trees, my normal-sized one for the family room, and the humongous one that Joe had insisted on that was never going to fit in the house. I needed some space and the kitchen was my refuge. I'd tackle the tree—my tree—later.

When the kids had been young, we'd put the tree up as soon as we returned from Lanyard's. I would make hot chocolate, and play Christmas music, and tell stories about all the ornaments as I unpacked them, about where they'd come from, or what had inspired their selection, as the kids hung them on the tree. I'd made the task a ceremony; it had become tradition.

I gave the kids a special ornament each year. The collection of ornaments was stored in big Rubbermaid containers in the attic, one for each of my children, for when they had their own homes and Christmas trees.

Did this tradition matter to the kids, or Joe? To anyone but me? If I went to Walmart and bought all new, generic Christmas balls, would anyone care?I stood at the counter, cutting out sugar cookies and watching Joe with the stupid tree he'd picked. He hadn't even gotten it entirely into the hallway before it had become apparent that it was oversized for the space. He'd glanced into the kitchen at me, but I'd pretended to be focused on the cookies. This time, I didn't even have to say I told you so. Though I wanted to shout it, believe me. I took the high road. Father J would be proud.

I poured myself a little glass of wine and that made me think of my mother. Hiding wine in the pantry. I could hardly wrap my mind around the idea except for what I heard in her voice when she told me. I knew it was the bare naked truth. Joe took the tree to the front yard, where it lay on its side in the approaching dusk. I watched him from the kitchen window as I worked. Honestly, he'd never taken this kind of effort with any Christmas tree before, not with any Christmas decorations, period. I watched him get the big stepladder from the garage. He fiddled around with the tree and an old five-gallon bucket, then I saw him bring a spool of wire from the garage.

What does he think he's proving?

At the sound of a car starting, I looked out to see Joe in his truck pull out of the driveway and head toward town. *Now what?* I shook my head. The huge tree was up. It looked odd, I thought, a big fir tree right in the middle of the front yard, where no tree had ever stood before. A good strong wind, of which there were plenty in central Pennsylvania in December, would blow it over. *Good grief.*

It was almost dark before Joe returned, but in the light from the front door and from inside the garage, I could see there was an assortment of white plastic shopping bags on the ground next to Joe's tree. *What a doofus.*

———

MY TREE, the normal-sized one, was up, stuck in the Christmas tree stand we used every year for two dozen plus years. Still bound up with twine like a green fir mummy, but it was upright. I did a quick rearrange of the family room furniture to make space, went out to the kitchen to get my scissors. Through the window, I noticed Joe was apparently staking the big tree using wire and something metal that clanged when he pounded it with a sledgehammer.

The ground was likely frozen and I could hear the sharp *clink clink* of the hammer hitting steel. *This whole exploit could have been an episode from* Home Improvement. I hoped the stupid tree blew over five minutes after he got it staked up. What a ridiculous idea. A cut tree displayed in the middle of the front yard.

I went back into the living room and began to string up lights and unpack ornaments. I hung the green tissue paper and bent clothes hanger wreaths, three of them, one from each child—second grade. I refilled my wine glass and turned on some Christmas music. There was the sound of a car. I refused to get up to look. Joe going somewhere for more supplies. A passerby, stopping to see if Joe had lost his mind.

I was just hanging a miniature replica of a Converse high-top sneaker, one of Doug's ornaments when the front door opened and Joe and Lillian came inside. *Oh, just fucking great.*

"Wow. Smells good in here," Lillian said.

"Sugar cookies. And Christmas tree," I said.

"Joe told me you were swamped, trying to get everything done before the party. Baking cookies and decorating."

"I ran into Mom downtown," Joe said. "When I was at the Dollar Store."

"It sounded like you could use some help. You always take on so much, with the company party, and with everything else you do—"

Oh, save me, Holy Mother Mary and all the bleeping Saints. "That's really nice, but we're in good shape. I have the cookies baked. We got the tree..."

"You've never had a tree outside before, have you? It'll be beautiful, once you get it decorated."

"No, *we* never did." I glanced at my husband. He was leaning up against the back of the sofa, his arms crossed. "It was Joe's idea."

"Well, put me to work," Lillian said. "I can do something—" She began to pull off her gloves and unbutton her wool coat.

"We're good, Mom. Really." Joe said. "In fact, I think we're done for now. Cath wants me to take her to dinner. She said something about the Lodge."

I did? Joe's expression was open and honest. He never looked at me. "As soon as I get the lights on the tree in the yard," he added.

"Oh, nice." Lillian smiled. "I haven't been there in years. Your dad loved to go there."

"We haven't been there in a long time, either. But I promised Cath."

What are you talking about? I stared at Joe. He was moving toward the front door, deftly steering Lillian in that direction. We were hosting a party for fifty people in two days. I had stuff to do. There was no time for a leisurely dinner at the Lodge tonight.

"Well... Have a nice time."

"Thanks for the offer though," I said.

Lillian stopped and looked back. "I can come over early before the party. I'm sure you can use some help—"

"You don't need to come early," I said. "I have everything ready." Well, not everything, but I did not want or need Lillian's help.

"See you then," Joe said, finally ushering his mother out the door, Lillian talking about something or another. Before he closed it, he turned and gave me another wink.

That fueled my annoyance, like pouring gas on a fire. Could he really not tell how I was feeling? Was he really that clueless? *Wink this.* I thought, flipping him the bird.

There was the sound of Lillian's car starting, but Joe didn't return to the house. After a little bit, I picked up my wine glass and moved to the window to look out to the front yard where it was full dark now, Joe and "his tree" lit only by the spotlight at the corner of the garage.

He had traded the small stepladder for the big one and was perched on the top of it, draping a strand of twinkle lights around the tree, an extension cord snaking across the driveway and into the garage. I watched for a while, then I went out to the kitchen, took my coat off the hook and went out the kitchen door and around the side of the house to the front.

Joe glanced down from the top of the ladder.

"Why did you tell your mother we were going to the Lodge for dinner?"

He shrugged. "It seemed like an easy way to get rid of her."

"Get rid of her? Since when do you want to 'get rid of' your mother?"

He got to the end of the strand and climbed down the ladder. "Because we didn't need her help. Not tonight."

Any other night it would have made me unreasonably happy that

Joe felt that way. "This tree looks ridiculous. Our address is Sweet-mill Road, not Rockefeller Center."

"I think it looks nice. Christmasy. Or it will. Soon as I get the tinsel on it."

"Tinsel? You can't put tinsel on a tree outside. It'll just blow away."

He climbed down the ladder. "I'll wire it on. I got a whole pack of small zip ties. And I got her anchored real good." He patted one of the guide wires he'd rigged and staked into the ground. "This baby's not goin' anywhere. Not 'til I take her down."

"Or I do. You're conveniently never around when it's time to take down the Christmas decorations."

I could see him smile at me in the strobing of the twinkle lights, intentionally ignoring my mood, which just annoyed me more. No doubt I was picking a fight.

"Rockefeller Center, where all the people ice skate?" At that, Joe grabbed my hands and pulled me into an exaggerated dance, trying to move his feet in the dried, brown December sod like he was gliding backward on skates. I tugged to free my hands, but he wouldn't let go. "We can't skate, but we can dance."

"You can't dance *or* skate. You can't dance on a dance floor where it's smooth and there's music."

"Who says I can't dance?" He yanked me closer. His hands held mine tightly.

"Stop it. Let me go. This is ridiculous. We're in the front yard."

"So what. Joe Daley is dancing with his wife. Under his kick-ass Christmas tree. I'll dance with you out here, then I'll make love to you under my tree. I don't care who drives by and sees."

"No, you won't. Stop it." I yanked on my arms, but Joe only held tighter. He was trying to be funny, but there was something under the joking that was sober.

He bent his head down and tried to kiss my mouth. I turned my head so he hit the corner, part of my cheek. "You used to like to make love outside. You were wild and crazy. C'mon. Let's get wild tonight. How long has it been since you felt the grass on your hiney?"

"Never when there was frost on it. The grass. I mean it. Let go."

"No." He stopped dancing and looked down at me, my hands still firmly held in his. "I want to make love to my wife. You are my wife." And he kissed me again, this time hitting my lips. His mouth was warm and he tasted like Joe, a taste so familiar that it barely registered with my senses, so it was a shock when I felt a corresponding tug deep inside. As if my synapses had fired without my acknowledgement. Like Pavlov's dogs.

There was a sense of inevitability. As if every action, every word, all day had been leading to this moment. It had been a long time since I had felt aroused, stirred the way those nerve cells down deep were being stirred. *Patrick did it. He fired you up.* Cheerleader Cath.

My lips pushed against Joe's, hard. I wanted the almost-pain that was lip against teeth. I wanted to bite Joe, in a sudden and furious need that had its root in anger.

Joe's hands were inside my coat, the coat I hadn't bothered to zip. They were cold, even through my sweater. A cold that felt delicious against my steaming flesh. *Damn the hot flashes.*

He ran his hands around my ribs, the calluses on his palms almost, but not quite, tickling me, until they met in the back. I felt the palm of one of his hands pressing against the small of my back, rubbing there, feeling the moisture that leeched from my skin unbidden.

"You're sweating," Joe said against my mouth. There was wonder in his voice.

I tried to pull away but again, he tightened his clasp.

"Where you goin'? We're not done dancing."

"Joe. This is nuts—" I started to say, but he kissed me again, pressing hard, and I sensed he felt the same need, the same near-anger that I did. That the need was too big, too rough, too ravenous.

I was aware, suddenly, of something cold and rigid behind my thighs and realized that Joe had steered me to his truck, to where the tailgate was down. He pushed me against it, his hands moving to my legs, the back of my thighs, to lift me so I was sitting on the tailgate. His mouth never left mine.

"Joe—" I tried. "Stop—"

"You stop," he said, and he tasted of sugar cookie. "Stop fighting."

"We can't do this—"

"Sure we can. I know it's been too fucking long, but I still remember how."

"Ha ha," I said, feeling a surge of something—guilt?—at the implied criticism, before his mouth pressed against mine again, stealing my protest.

It was different, this need, this hunger I was feeling now, different than what I used to know, once upon a time, in the years when I had been "wild," when I'd been young. When I'd given up myself to Joe, to the love I felt for him, when I'd let myself be lost in the sensations.

Now—this—was more calculated, more specific, more self-centered. There was more thinking. There was thinking, period. I knew what I wanted. I knew what I liked. What turned me on.

"Here," I said, pushing his hand where I wanted it. "Softer." Had I ever demanded my own pleasure like this?

"Oh, babe," Joe said. "Oooh, babe."

"Stop. Wait." I took a deep breath, thought my lips felt tingly. "Now. More. Harder." This was all for me. And I felt no apology for that. I didn't care what Joe wanted.

I shifted around, felt Joe pop the snap on my jeans and push the zipper down. Leaning back on the truck bed on my elbows, I lifted my hips so he could tug my pants and my panties down, over my hips, where they caught at my ankles. The steel of the truck was frigid on my backside, my ass, my thighs, but it still felt good.

I pushed his shoulder hard until he dropped his head between my legs and I had to close my eyes with the overwhelming desire to melt into a puddle. I'd never really been comfortable with oral sex, though Joe had wanted to, or at least he used to want to.

I want this. Now. And fuck it. I don't care who drives by and sees. "Ohhhh," I whispered.

His fingers gripped my hips, the cheeks of my bottom, his fingers grazing the cleft between. At one point, I reached down and directed him to the right spot, needing him to be *there. Now.* "Harder," I said. "Oh, harder," feeling no shame at all, none, for my need.

I had never known so clearly what I wanted.

I did not come though I came close and finally, impatient, his own hunger too big, Joe yanked my shoes off, pulled down my jeans and my panties and tossed them on the driveway. He tugged at his belt buckle, unsnapped his own jeans, pushed them over his hips and leaned suddenly over me, driving into me.

"Stop," I ordered, and my voice was steely, as cold and hard as the truck bed. "Put my legs up. Push them up. That's right. Like that," I said.

"There," I said, directing him to a nipple. Use your tongue. Oh, yes. Don't. Stop." I waited until I was close, very close again. The word barely more than a breath at the tail end of a gasp. "Now." When I came, the strength of my orgasm did make my lips tingle and bright spots flash behind my closed eyes.

There was something revelatory about this expression of want. This *knowing*. I recognized the feeling—it was elemental, primitive— but it had been gone from me for so long, buried under the demands, the wants and needs of others. It was empowering; I felt empowered by acknowledging what I wanted.

Is that all it takes? Is that the answer to happiness? Knowing what you want? It was as if something that had been lost, was found.

"Wow," he said, nipping the tip of my nose. "You wild thing."

"Oh, stop! That was crazy. Nuts. What if your mother had come back?" A thought occurred to me. "Oh, my God! What if Father J had shown up?"

"I'm pretty sure Father J knows about sex. Second hand, though. Hopefully. My mother, too." Joe still sounded amused.

"Not on your life. Your mother never did *that*."

"Well," he said, and I could hear laughter in his voice. "I can't imagine it. But you never know." He leaned in and kissed me again, fast and hard.

"Stop. I need to go inside. Clean up."

I tried to push past him, so I could jump down from the tailgate. I could feel the trickle of warm semen on the inside of my thigh. The air was cold now, my legs felt chilled, and my butt, but surprisingly, not uncomfortably so. I was still wearing my socks.

Ignoring my efforts to get up, Joe leaned down and pressed his forehead against mine, his arms braced on either side of my legs. "I've missed you."

I was not in the mood for postcoital snuggling in the driveway. "No need for Viagra today, huh?"

The expression on his face changed suddenly and I knew my comment had been snarkier than I'd intended. Did I want to embarrass Joe, to shame him? Did I turn the attention on him, before he could turn it on the wanton who had just demanded oral sex on the tailgate of a truck outside in the driveway?

What had come over me? *What a bitch.* Cheerleader Cath.

———

I CLEANED UP THE KITCHEN, put the cooled sugar cookies into plastic containers, and did a couple of things to prep for the party that would be here in about forty-eight hours. Joe had already gone back to our room. He was lying in bed with his reading glasses on and a magazine folded across his chest, asleep. I went into the bathroom and turned on the shower. My legs had warmed up but my feet felt cold, the kind of cold that only a hot shower would fix.

When I came back into the bedroom, warm now and wearing an old plaid flannel nightshirt, Joe was watching me, the magazine still on his chest. "Feel better?"

"Yes. Much." Suddenly, I felt awkward at the intimacy between us. A little embarrassed. I pulled back the covers on my side and realized Joe had turned on the electric blanket. "Oh, that feels really good," I said sliding my legs in. *For now. Until the next hot flash.*

"Roll over; I'll rub your back."

A little sex, and bang, just like that, things were good for Joe. As if whatever had been wrong between us was swept away, gone like the smear of ketchup on his plate at dinner, washed down the drain. "I'm sorry I said that. About the Viagra."

Joe tossed the magazine onto the floor and rolled over so he was facing me. I watched him open his mouth, then close it, start to speak then stop. Finally he said, "I thought it was me."

I knew, somehow, what Joe meant and I felt sorry for that, too. Sorry and embarrassed and inadequate because I knew it wasn't him.

"I miss you." He leaned in and kissed my shoulder through the flannel of the nightshirt. "I thought I wasn't satisfying you. I guess it's age. I mean, it *is* age. I thought maybe sex wasn't good for you anymore. Because of me."

The idea that Joe might have doubts, that his normally robust self-esteem might not always be as robust as I thought made him seem vulnerable somehow. It touched me...and more guilt followed. "It's not you," I finally said. "You're fine." The look on his face told me "fine" might not be enough. "I mean, you're *good*."

Just then, his cell phone rang. We both laughed. "Just let me be sure it's not an emergency—" and he rolled over and looked at the caller ID. "Just Mom."

The phone rang two more times before it stopped.

A lock of my hair had slipped down over my forehead and Joe reached up and brushed it back. One of his legs snaked over and hooked mine, pulled my legs closer. He wasn't wearing underwear and I could feel he was aroused. Partly aroused. *Seriously? An encore? Or a victory lap?*

His cell phone erupted, the vibration buzzing against the wood of the bedside table.

"God damn it," he said again, rolling back and grabbing the thing. "Mom again. Jesus."

"You'd better answer. It might be important."

"You're important. This is important," he said, but he answered. I knew he would. "Hey." I could hear the tinny sound of Lillian's voice. "Oh, we didn't get there." He wagged his eyebrows at me, the half-smile turning into a full-fledged grin. "Nah. Something came up." Joe thrust his hips into mine. Still grinning. "We'll go another night. What's up?"

Joe must have pressed the phone tighter to his head because now I couldn't hear Lillian. "I could. But it's not really my business." he said. "No. I guess. Yeah. Whatever. Okay. When I get a chance."

I could tell by the resignation in his voice that he'd given in. He'd do whatever it was his mother had asked. Or at least he'd say he would. Then, often, he'd get busy and never do whatever it was Lillian had wanted. I could never decide if he really "forgot" or if he simply hoped the problem or whatever would just go away. Which-ever. It was so Joe. "What's she want you to do now?"

"She wants me to call Patrick. It seems he's moved out. Moved into a hotel. You forget to tell me something? He didn't mention leaving my sister when you had lunch last week?"

"He left Di?"

"Apparently," Joe said. "Did you know? That he was going to move out?"

"No. I mean, I could tell that maybe things weren't—aren't—rosy. He just vented a little. Which was—is—especially worrisome given that Di wants to have a baby. I told you about that. But whatever Pat did, it's between him and Di. Not me. Or you. Or your mother."

"I'm not understanding why he needed to vent to you."

"What's to understand? We're friends and we're married into the same family. Who better to talk to? We're both 'out-laws'."

"Is this about the cruise again? You and Pat *vent* about that?"

"It's not the cruise. The cruise is just—" I thought about telling him of my analogy again, the cancer, the car accident, but I knew he wouldn't get it.

"It's a stupid idea. Hurtful and so outrageous that I can hardly believe it—" I was saying the words but they were so tired. In my defense, I hadn't raised the subject this time. Joe had.

"It *is* a stupid idea. But I didn't dream it up—"

"No. But you're not going to tell anyone how you feel. You wouldn't want to rock the proverbial boat—or sailing yacht. That's the problem. If you think it's a stupid idea, why don't you say so? This thing with Patrick and Di is more of the same. Why can't you tell your mother you're not going to call Pat? That it's none of your business? It's none of her business, for that matter. Why didn't you tell her that?"

"I didn't have to tell her that. If I don't call Pat, she'll figure it out. I just don't see any point in turning everything into an argument."

"And I do? Is that what you're implying? That I turn everything into an argument?" I felt my mouth open with incredulity. Like a cartoon character.

"Everything lately. If it's the cruise for Mom, you can get over that already. I'll tell Mark and Laura I can't go."

"Can't go? *Can't* go?" I thought steam really must be coming out of my ears. "Sure you'll tell them that. Because that takes all the responsibility for the decision off of you and lays it on me. Why don't you tell them you think it's a stupid, hurtful idea that should have never made it out of committee? Why don't you tell them you don't *want* to go, not on a trip like that without your wife, or your children? Over the week of our thirtieth anniversary, though since we can *technically* celebrate that anytime during the year, I suppose that's irrelevant. That *family* clearly means something else to you than it does to them, or your mother."

"Jesus, Joseph and Mary! What's the difference?"

"The difference is you, having a fucking opinion for once. Taking ownership of it. Stand up to your mother and your siblings! Surely, even you can see there's a difference between I *can't* go and I *don't* want to go—"

If you don't feel that on your own, if I have to tell you to feel it, it hurts even more. It raises the hurt to a whole different level. You really are clueless.

"They never said you couldn't go!"

I took a deep breath and tried to lower my voice. This argument had become a broken record. The realization made me weary. Beyond weary. "If they wanted to plan a vacation that included everyone in the family, they wouldn't have gone about it like they did. It's wrong and exclusionary and disrespectful of all of us. It's a slam to you, too, you're just too oblivious to see it. It disrespects the idea of family. It's changed how I see you and everyone in your family. It's changed how I see me."

I looked at Joe. "I... You..." I tried to find the words. "I'm annoyed with you more than I'm happy. I feel so...angry...so much of the time. It seems like everything you do, everything you *don't do*, makes me crazy. Mad. Pissed off. I can't get past it. It would be easy to blame how I feel on other people, you, your mother, but that wouldn't be fair. What's wrong is not you. Or her."

"What are you saying?"

I looked at Joe, sitting at the end of the bed now. I knew that face, knew the hair and the ears, his eyebrows, those freckles, the beginning of the paunch, the smell of him. I knew this man so well. We had an almost thirty-five-year shared history.

You're a great guy. You're a hard worker, you're honest, you're a good person. You can check all the boxes on the husband list: provider, good father, good son. You're faithful.

I'd be happy with a good one. A good *man, Helene had said.*

Joe was a good man. Is it human nature, to never be satisfied? I have a good man but I am so angry I can't see those things.

Joe watched my face as if he was trying to read my mind.

"I can't stop being angry at you. I feel so much rage. And I hate myself for it. I hate you for it. It's...toxic." I took a deep breath, looked down at my hands. I was hurting Joe, I knew, and though I was sorry about that, I felt resolute, too.

And so powerful, so momentous, the weight of the words caught, like a fist, low in my throat.

For a moment, there was silence, only the sounds of our breathing in the room. "Don't you ever feel unhappy? Unsatisfied? Disappointed? Angry? Hurt? Do I never fall short of your expectations?" I said, finally.

Joe looked at me like I'd grown another head. "I don't think about it. You're just you. We're just us."

"That's...." What was that? Nuts. Sad. Pathetic? I wanted to shake him. "Do you think we'd have gotten married if I hadn't gotten pregnant with Nora?"

"What?"

"Are you asking me if I love you? If I loved you then?"

"I don't know. I guess I'm wondering if we would have made the same choices thirty years ago if we hadn't been forced into them."

"We weren't forced into anything."

"Kinda we were. I got pregnant. We weren't married. Back then, that was a big deal."

"We loved each other. We woulda gotten married regardless."

I had loved Joe to distraction. I'd lost myself in my love for him for a while. Joe hadn't been consumed with me the same way. And after thirty years, I understood that Joe never would be consumed like that. He just wasn't wired that way. But he did love me. I knew that.

"Yes. I think we would have gotten married. I loved you. Then. I love you now." We stared at each other. "You ask me if I'm ever unhappy....unsatisfied. Which even I am smart enough to know means you are. Unhappy and unsatisfied. I mean. I'm not totally clueless."

I didn't respond to that. There wasn't anything to say because he was right, but somehow I knew with a certainty that was hard and dark, we'd crossed a line.

IN THE MORNING, I felt physically battered. I hadn't slept, could not stop my brain from thinking, from replaying the argument. I had not abandoned our bed, but I had spent the night rigidly avoiding even approaching the Mason Dixon line of our queen-sized mattress. I had looked into the darkness and listened to Joe's breathing and could tell that he never really slept, either.

This morning, I took my cup of tea into the den and sat down at my computer. Joe had gotten up early and gone to the office without saying a word. Now, I should be getting ready for the Daley-Hallowell Christmas party. In just over twenty-four hours, people were going to be coming to my house, expecting food, drink, a party. I had the truck-shaped sugar cookies to frost. A double batch of sweet cream biscuits to make. I needed to run the vacuum, clean the powder room. But fuck the sugar cookies. Fuck the whole damn party.

My email homepage opened and there where I could not miss it, flashing bright and colorfully, on the right-hand side of the page was an ad for swimming suits—the very same retailer from whom I'd purchased two tummy-toning, ass and boob lifting one-pieces. Swimming suits for a cruise I was never invited to be a part of, a tangible spandex and Lycra reminder of the distance between my perception of my life and the reality of it.

I had so much to do. The company Christmas party. Cooking for Father J. Christmas here, without two of my kids. Joe. The idea of shucking it all, even Christmas, the holiday that I lived for, that no doubt unresaonably summed up what family meant to me, made me feel almost dizzy, like I'd stood up too quickly after kneeling.

Where would I go? Somewhere warm and sunny. Somewhere I can wear those new bathing suits. It suddenly wasn't a matter of *if*, but *where. How far? When?*

The idea was so powerful, so compelling—the notion of warm sun and an ocean breeze, and most of all an absence of the angst that felt like it had been chewing me up for weeks—that I had to close my eyes for a moment. There was a warmth in my chest, like that same sunshine was glowing and warming me from the inside out. *I am going.*

Oh, God! Could I really do it? Yes.

And that decision, made that spontaneously, felt like the most right decision I'd ever made. Where was I going? As spontaneously as I had made the decision to go, I knew. *Charleston.*

I'd always wanted to go there—despite Joe's contention that it would be crowded, and touristy, it would be hot and humid and buggy. It was beautiful and historic and the food was supposed to be amazing. It was the home of *Charleston Receipts*, one of the most iconic cookbooks of all time and one of my favorites. For some reason, just the names of the women who had donated recipes for that cookbook inspired a yearning that I knew made no sense: Mrs. Thomas A. Huguenin (Mary Vereen), Mrs. R. Barnwell Rhett (Virginia Prettyman), Mrs. William Granby Dodds (Louise Hutson)....The recipes themselves: Charleston Light Dragoon Punch (serves 300-350!), Crème Vichyssoise with Curry (Delicious for a "Three O'Clock Dinner"), Cinnamon Flip, James Island Shrimp Pie. I could drive there. There was something about the notion of the southern low country that evoked memories of my growing-up years in Delaware, along the rivers of the eastern shore, something that was wired into my DNA, that smelled of sunbaked mud and water and an ocean not too far away. Something that was missing here in west central Pennsylvania. Fresh fish. I missed fresh fish.

Charleston. It made no sense. But at the same time, I could not resist the pull. The thought of the absence of angst almost made tears come to my eyes. A niggle of guilt tried to make itself felt, but I stifled it, like I would a flare-up on the stove, as effectively as dropping a lid over it.

Change your perspective. Isn't that what Father J had recommended? Renewal. I needed some renewal. I'd wanted to hit Joe with a lamp. The urge had been more than just a funny story I'd share at the Christmas party with other wives about a snoring husband. The Christmas party. I didn't care about the stupid party.

And everything was mostly ready, and I was sure Lillian could take over. Would take over and be happy to do it. The thought of my mother-in-law loose in my kitchen was almost enough to make me change my mind.

When would I go? Tomorrow. Before the party. If I'm going to miss the party, then might as well go in an hour. As soon as I can pack my suitcase. For how long? Forever. The thought was fleeting and dazzling as a comet.

What about Christmas?

It was going to be different this year anyway. Jamie would not be here, Annie would not be here. The thought of that made Charleston, a beach, fish, sunshine, an ocean breeze, even more achingly appealing. It was a physical sensation so fierce it made my throat hurt.

Was going to Charleston leaving Joe? What else would you call it? I thought suddenly of Father J. He would be disappointed. Would he? *Change your perspective.*

I opened a new tab on my computer and typed in "Charleston SC Craigslist." Under the heading *housing,* there was a listing for *sublets/temporary.*

Just then I heard the faint sound of a car door at the same time Trouble lifted her head and thumped her tail. Now what? Who would be stopping at 8:37 in the morning?

Before I got to the door, Joe came in, carrying a large wooden three-tiered tray in one hand and a fancy silver serving platter under his arm. He was wearing a green Daley-Hallowell insulated jacket and there were snowflakes on his shoulders. Cold air followed him in. "Hey," he said. Everything that had been said and unsaid last night was in that one word.

"What are you doing home?"

"Mom dropped these off at the warehouse. She thought you might want to use them for the party."

"The party." I was still thinking about sublets/temporary, furnished, pets welcome. Walk to the beach.

"Hey, you don't have to use them. She was just trying to be helpful," he said, misreading the look on my face. "It's not a big deal."

"You came home just to bring those?" I tried to switch gears but it was difficult. I wanted to think about the smell of the ocean, walking to the beach.

He shrugged and I could see the uncertainty on his face. "I didn't feel right just leaving this morning without talking to you, but I didn't want to wake you up. If I know you, you didn't sleep much."

Now the words we both said the night before sat in the middle of the kitchen, like a second, big island, like an elephant. "I'm glad you're here, actually. I need to tell you something." A city full of history. Fresh fish. Sunshine. Sand.

"That sounds ominous."

I didn't respond to that; my brain was scrambling, trying to think how to tell Joe what I had decided. It was probably good he'd shown up so unexpectedly. I could have spent all day thinking about how to say it when realistically, there was no good way. I did not want to be here for the party tomorrow. The idea of going through all those motions was absurd, when I'd made a decision about leaving, when the pull of a different place, an angst-free place, caused an almost physical reaction inside me. I couldn't do it. *Just tell him.*

I bit my lip, swallowed. "You know I've been upset lately. You told me last night you've noticed. No secret there."

"You're stressed, babe. You've got the new cookbook. And there's the party and the holiday. Plus all the stuff you normally do. Cooking for Father J. I get it. I haven't been as much help around here as I could be."

"It's not that. It's not you. It's me."

To his credit, he didn't disagree. He stood in the kitchen doorway, his green jacket still on but unzipped. He'd put the three-tiered tray and the silver platter on the counter and had his hands on his hips. "I know you've probably got a hundred things on my honey-do list. All shit for the party. I can come home early tonight to help."

"I'm not going to be here for the party."

"What? Why? Where will you be?" He had a little bit of a smile on his face like what I was saying was a joke and he was just waiting for the punch line.

"If I don't get out of here, I think I'll implode. Explode. It's destroying me. This anger that I feel all the time. It's like I have a wound and the scab keeps being pulled off. I need to go somewhere and let it...heal."

Joe shook his head but didn't say anything. I could see the cloud of emotion moving beneath his face as clearly as if he were a mood lamp. "Go where?" Defensive.

I pulled my top lip between my teeth. "I don't know. I'm not sure it matters."

"Like to visit Annie? Or Helene? For a couple of days."

"No. Not like that. By myself."

"For how long?"

I shrugged. "I don't know." As long as it takes.

"You're leaving me."

I opened my mouth to say "no" but couldn't make myself. "I don't know," I finally said.

"What does that mean? Either you are or you aren't."

"I guess I'm thinking of it more like a sabbatical."

He just stared at me like he was waiting for me to begin speaking English. "I don't know what that means. A sabbatical."

I took a deep breath and felt, somehow, despite the look on Joe's face, relief at having said it. It was out. "I don't either, exactly."

"Jesus. You can dress it up however you want. It's leaving." There was confusion and hurt and anger in his voice and I waited for guilt to hit, for remorse to swell inside me, but I felt, oddly, removed. Untouched.

"Yes. I guess it is."

"You want a divorce?"

That question made me feel something. Sad. "I didn't say that. That's not what I'm thinking about now." And that was true.

He just stared at me like he didn't know me. "Jesus. Where? Where are you going?"

"I'm not sure. South. Where it's warm. Sunny. Charleston, maybe."

The muscles of Joe's jaw had tightened, his eyes had changed. I could tell him this was a chance for our marriage to heal, for me to heal, so that we could still have a marriage. But I couldn't bring myself to say that. I didn't know if it was true.

"When?" he asked.

"As soon as I get packed."

"Oh." He was shocked, I could tell, though there were so many other emotions at play that shock at my ETD was lost among them. "Okay. I guess you won't be here for the party, then."

"No. Everything is ready, though. I've already made all the food. I just didn't ice those sugar cookies."

"Well don't worry about that." Now he sounded snarky. Bitter. I understood. I was leaving. Oh, my God. Was I really leaving? Fear suddenly filled me, like a flare, like a hot flash. I thought my fingers might be tingling. Was I really leaving? Cathleen Daley leaving her husband?

"What will you do?" he asked and I knew he really did not understand. "Where will you stay?"

"I don't know. I'll work on the cookbook. I'll sit on the beach. There are a couple of places on Craigslist. Or Airbnb.... I need to do this, Joe."

"How long are you going to be gone?" It's almost Christmas. He didn't say it, but I knew he was thinking it.

"I don't know." I took a deep breath and felt it catch. "As long as it takes? If I have any chance of getting past all this *anger*, I have to do this."

"Well, by all means, do it then."

"Don't be that way. Please."

"What way is that? This is new territory for me. My wife has never left me before. Because whatever you call it, it's leaving."

I took another breath and let it out slowly. "I'll have my phone, and my laptop. I need to finish the copy edits on my cookbook. You can call. Or text. Or email."

He stared at me. "Well, thanks. What about the kids? What're we gonna tell them?"

"I haven't really thought about what to tell the kids. There's no good, or easy, way to explain. I haven't really thought that far ahead."

"But far enough ahead that you found a place to stay in Charleston. South Carolina. A week before Christmas." Joe's expression was closed.

The conversation seemed to stall there, the two of us just looking at each other. I thought Joe's face looked white, paler than usual, but maybe that was my imagination.

"Say that I'm going on vacation. I'm going to work on my cookbook."

"They're not stupid, Cath. Vacation? By yourself? Right before Christmas?" I noticed he didn't say we're not the kind of married people who vacation apart. "What about the party?" he said. "When you're not here, it's gonna be pretty obvious something's wrong."

"I'm sorry about that. But I can't stay and pretend everything is normal. I just can't stand around in a red sweater, passing out ham and cranberry chutney biscuits and refilling the punch bowl. I can't do it. I'll let you know when I get there," I said at the same time I was struck by the outrageousness of the statement. The momentousness. "I'll talk to the kids, if that's what you want."

"Huh," he snorted. "What I want doesn't really matter, does it?" Before I could respond to that, he said, "Sure. Whatever."

Whatever? I was going to Charleston.

Chapter Eleven

My first view of the brick carriage house apartment was across a broken macadam driveway, and the "carriage house" looked more like a garage, what I could see of it hidden under some kind of very vigorous vine. Yes, it was Charleston, it was a nearly balmy, almost unseasonably seventy-one degrees. It smelled distinctly different from home, dusty and almost spicy, but there was no ocean, no sound, no river, not even a glimpse of a marsh. The building was old, but not antebellum old. If I had to guess, I'd say the building had been built in the late 1800s. Victorian era. Still, I was here. It wasn't what I had imagined—*what had I imagined?*—but it felt somehow okay. The bubble of emotion that had swelled as I got closer and closer seemed to be filled with something light, something warm.

I hadn't wanted new and shiny, and I didn't want to be in a "complex", I wanted to be in "real" Charleston in a place with imperfections and history and provenance. All things that spoke to me. But whatever the vintage, it was clearly going to cost me the proverbial arm and leg to reside here, even short-term. When, if, Joe ever found out what the rents were in downtown Charleston, he would have a stroke.

An old, faded yellow VW Bug was parked in the driveway, in front of the single garage door. I carefully pulled in behind it. "You stay, girl." I told Trouble as I got out. "We'll take a long walk. Soon. I don't know about you, but I need to stretch my legs."

Even in December, it had the feel of vacation. The earth was greener, trees, shrubs, there were still some flowers. Trouble sat, trusting as ever, on the middle seat of the minivan, her eyes following me as I shut the driver's side door.

I'd hoped to have time to drive around the city of Charleston proper, to get the lay of the land, before heading here, but I'd worried about being late for my appointment with the owner. The traffic, both on the highway and on the main streets before I'd found this neighborhood had been terrible. This street was, thankfully relatively quiet. The ad for this apartment had said *walk to shopping, restaurants, rivers.* I wanted to be able to walk to water.

I heard music that seemed to be coming from inside the garage just as an older woman opened a pass door on the side. She was maybe late sixties, wearing a pair of baggy white pants, clogs, and a faded blue button-down shirt marked with splatters of something. She had what Annie would call Earth Mother hair, gray and coarse-looking, pulled back into a braid that hung over one shoulder and fantastic, large, dangly silver earrings.

"Hi," the woman said, smiling. She had piercing blue eyes and a no-nonsense handshake. "Yo'ah heah to see the apahtment? Cathleen?"

"Yes. You're Krystal? I'm at the right place?"

"Y'ahr." *You are.* "I'm Lucinda, Krystal's mother. She's the one who owns the buildin' but I was goin' to be heah workin', so she asked me to show you the apahtment. It's upstairs. C'mon. The steps are 'round back." Lucinda's speech was slower than what I was used to, as if the words were thicker, coated with molasses, the vowels and consonants stretched until they were like a different language altogether. I loved it. It made me smile.

I followed her, passing by the door to the ground floor of the garage where the music was coming from. I caught a whiff of something musky. Sandalwood. A set of black metal stairs climbed the back wall to a small, square landing, where an awning shaded a periwinkle blue-painted door with a window in the top half. The yard behind the garage was jungle with a thick green wall of boxwood edging the back of the property.

"Do you live here, I mean in the house?" I asked, nodding to the glimpse of red brick beyond the hedge.

"No. My dawtah bought the carriage house about five years ago. She had the apahtment finished upstairs; I have my studio downstairs. I live over on Johns Island." Lucinda opened the door at the top of the stairs and I followed her inside.

Two skylights had been added to the roof and sunshine filled the space. That was my first impression, that and color—blues, greens, gold, bright splashes of orange and pink. It was one big room, with a short run of dark green cabinets, with a stainless fridge and a stove on one side and a big, antique poster bed taking up almost all of the space on the far wall. The comforter on the bed was a shimmery golden yellow, the exact color of an egg yolk; there was a daybed upholstered in a red and cream cut velvet, an old highboy, an armchair covered in a graphic orange and pink print fabric, and a lime green ceramic garden stool. The daybed and the chair made up the "sitting room" part of the space. The only door in the room was painted a robin's egg blue.

"This is the bathroom," my tour guide said, opening the door. Inside, there was a clawfoot tub and a pedestal sink the size of an aircraft carrier with two curvy legs. The floor in here was tiny, octagonal black and white marble tiles. There was another door beside the sink, this one painted sky blue, that Lucinda opened to a large closet slash laundry room. When we stepped back into the main room, I saw there was also a tiny bistro table and two cane chairs against the wall beside the refrigerator. The floors in the main living area were wood, old and golden colored. A couple of paintings hung on the walls, one a massive, frameless abstract of blues and grays, the other was a landscape, a street scene, in a thick ornamental gold frame, the lacquer on the canvas aged and dark.

It was like a jewel box full of rich, saturated colors. Fabrics that made me want to touch and run my hand over them: velvet, satin, a glazed chintz. The Craigslist ad had included photos, but the reality was so much *more*. It was charming in a hippie artist meets grandma's attic sort of way. I loved it. And better yet, I could see myself here, sitting at the little bistro table, my laptop open before me, or on the daybed slash sofa with a book, and Trouble at my feet. "You can walk everywh'are. They'ah bunch of shops and restaurants in this neighborhood. You could walk to the historic district, down to the Battery. The City Maw'ket. Of course there's a bus. I can give you the names of a couple of good places to eat not too fawh. I think there's a list in one of the drawers." Lucinda nodded toward the little kitchen. "My partner and I ah just gettin' ready to go to Texas to visit his son for a couple of months. You'll have the place to yourself."

"How about the beach? Can I walk there? It's important that I can get to the beach. I have a new swimming suit." *Two.*

"You want to swim? There ah a couple of parks you can walk to that ah on the rivah. Of course, the best beaches are on the islands. Folly Beach, Sullivan's Island, Isle a Palms. But not until May, at least, for swimmin'."

Would I be here in May? Will I have effectively left my husband if I stay here until May? How long can I afford to stay? I stared at Lucinda who smiled back, unaware of what I was thinking. "Owah beaches ah beautiful."

"I have my dog with me. She's older, very well-mannered. The listing said pets are allowed?"

"Thass fine. We're big dawg people."

There were four other apartments or condos on my list, and surely dozens more if I spent time searching the internet. If Joe were here, we'd look at all of those and even then, he'd be reluctant to commit. If this was the cheapest place, and a beach was right outside the door, he'd dither. My breath caught suddenly, as if panic and buoyancy both pushed up my throat at the same time. I'd never chosen a place to live by myself. For myself. "It looks perfect. I'll take it. How soon can I move in?"

———

To Joe,

> Me: I'm here. Arrived this afternoon around 3:00. Just wanted to let you know. I'm sorry for the text. I tried to call but got your voicemail. I'm sure you're busy getting ready for the party.

> Me: I talked to all the kids yesterday. I told them I was on sabbatical for a little bit, working on my cookbook, but I think they all read between the lines and suspect it's more than that. I know you don't understand why I'm doing this, but I have to be somewhere else, somewhere you're not, until I stop feeling so angry. I am sorry for leaving you in the lurch, but if I didn't leave, I was going to become my anger and there would have been nothing else left.

> Me: The snail mail address here is 119 ½ Gloria Alley. Charleston.

To Helene,

> Me: Hey. I'm in Charleston. I needed a break. Not sure I need your divorce attorney's number yet, but I'm thinking about it. Seriously. I told myself this trip would be about working on my cookbook, for which I have a deadline in a month, but so far the only thing I've done is read three tabloids. What is wrong with me?

Helene: There's nothing wrong with you. Nothing that a couple of days of R&R won't cure. You don't want to divorce Joe. You just need a little time to find your way back to happy and content Cathleen. The Cath who loves her life and her family, including her husband.

Me: You really think I just need some R&R? I'm not so sure.

Father Julius: I'm sorry I missed your call yesterday. I did get your message. I appreciate your thoughtfulness; I'm sure I won't starve! You have the freezer and the pantry well stocked.

Father Julius: Is there a good time that I can call you later? I think we should talk. It's not unusual for people to need space and time to reflect on personal challenges and trials. If a short sabbatical—a retreat— can provide the opportunity for that reflection and for healing, I'm all for it. But I do think we should talk. God's blessing on you always.

Helene: I know you're upset and your feelings are legitimate, but I think there's a chance that your perspective has just gotten skewed.

Me: I'm not upset, I'm so ANGRY that it has damaged me somehow. And I know that's CRAZY. There are women the world over whose lives are really, truly bad, or hard. And I, a woman with a charmed life by any standard, am so ANGRY that I took my toys and my dog to Charleston. I am an unreasonable, spoiled, selfish, unsympathetic bitch. WHAT IS WRONG WITH ME?

My mother sent me a text. A text. Who taught her to text?

Delores Keen: This is your mother. Are you on vacation? In December, right before Christmas? Is Joe there?

Delores Keen: What's wrong? You know I can always tell when something's upset you. How long do you plan to be away? P.S. Your dad says thanks for the flannel shirt and the fleece. Your brother and Alice and the kids came over and had birthday cake and ice cream with us to celebrate. Little Sammie couldn't understand why we didn't have 78 candles on the cake. Love, Mom

Helene: Whatever you do, keep talking. I know you think you need some alone time, but emailing or texting doesn't infringe on that. Even talking on the phone. You know you can call me anytime. I'm worried about you. I'm sure Joe is worried. Make sure you talk to him, even if it's email. Don't burn any bridges. Yet.

Me: I sent him a text when I got here. Haven't heard back from him at all. Not that I expect to. I didn't burn it, but I left the bridge behind. I'm in uncharted territory now. Not a bridge in sight.

Jamie: I changed my holiday plans so I can
spend Christmas in Charleston. I'm trying
to see if I can get a flight in tomorrow.
Looks like my only option gets me there
around 5:15pm. Can you pick me up at the
airport? If not, I'll uber. Is there space for
me to crash at your place there? We can
talk.

Me: Don't even think about it! I appreciate
the idea, but I don't want you coming to
South Carolina for Christmas. You have
plans to spend the holiday with Molly, big,
important plans, and I WANT you to go
skiing and have fun and do your thing. I'm
taking a little sabbatical, long overdue,
that's all. I'm fine; Dad's fine. I can't wait to
hear about your big moment, and I expect
pictures! I'll miss you, of course, but I'll be
happy thinking about how happy you will
be! I love you. Maybe I can schedule a trip
to Minneapolis this spring. I imagine you'll
be busy planning a wedding.

Doug: It'll just be weird to have Christmas
without you, and without Jamie and Annie.

Annie: I know you were upset, are upset,
about Corey and his family situation. Does
that have anything to do with the reason
you went to South Carolina? I feel awful
that you're not going to be home for
Christmas!

> Me: Oh, sweetie! Corey has nothing to do
> with the reason I came to Charleston.
> Please don't take that on yourself! The
> reason I'm taking a sabbatical has to do
> with me, not anyone else. I will miss seeing
> you all, but I just need to be away for a
> while. You know I love you more than life
> itself, I always have, always will.

———

DAY THREE IN CHARLESTON. When I woke, Trouble stood beside the big poster bed smiling, her tail wagging and her soulful brown eyes luminous and patient and about six inches away. I couldn't believe I'd slept so soundly. And so long. Then the thought struck me again. *I'm in Charleston. I left Joe.* The novelty of that concept was not yet wearing off.

"Oh, my gosh! Poor girl!" I said to the dog. "I'm coming." I threw off the satin comforter and scrambled to find some pants. "Just give me a sec."

When we came back upstairs after a walk, I made a cup of tea, and parked myself on the top step of the little balcony. I left the door open; it had warmed up—three days before Christmas and it was sixty-three. And gloriously sunny. Over the smell of the tea, there was the spicy fragrance of Charleston, sounds that were different from home. Nothing remarkable, really, just different. Even on this quiet street, there was a sort of *hum* of life going on. And even in just a few days, I'd found the hum lifted something inside me, lightened it. Sitting here on the second-floor stoop just letting it wrap itself around me felt therapeutic.

What would I do today—what was left of today—after my tea and the newest *National Enquirer?* What would I do with my life?

I was considering how I would fix shrimp for dinner when there was the sound of a car door, faint voices. Trouble gave a rough bark, rising with difficulty from the sunlit spot on the floor at the end of the bed. A dark blond head—ponytail—appeared around the corner of the building at the bottom of the staircase and the dog barked again which made the head look up.

Annie!

"Mom!" she called when she saw me sitting at the top of the stairs.

"What are you doing here!" I started laughing. Wanted to cry, suddenly, my heart full, seeing my daughter standing there, purple roller bag at her feet. She looked so beautiful. Her light blue down jacket hung unzipped from her shoulders, a bulky navy and orange and magenta scarf looped around her neck and filled the opening of her coat. She trotted up the steps, leaving the suitcase at the bottom. I pulled her into a hug.

"Oh, honey! How did you get here? You didn't drive?"

She hugged me back then dropped to her knees to rub Trouble's ears, to bury her face in the furry neck. "No, I flew. I wanted to surprise you. I uber-ed from the airport."

"Oh, honey, I'm so happy to see you. I thought you had to work? Is everything okay?"

"Job is fine. I swapped shifts with a couple of other nurses."

"That's a big-time barter. Just before Christmas."

Annie shook her head. "Not a big deal. You're not mad?"

"Of course I'm not mad. Why would I be mad?"

"You said you needed to get away from everyone...."

"No! I wanted a little time away, that's all.... But not from you."

"From Dad." It wasn't a question.

I studied my daughter, unable to resist bringing my hands to her face, holding her cheeks, feeling the delicate bones of her jaw and the curves of her ears and studying the features, the flawless velvety smooth skin, marred only by a few faint freckles. "Yes, from your dad."

"Are you guys splitting up?"

Oh, honey," I said, breathing out a laugh and releasing my daughter's face. "Get your bag and come in! Are you hungry? What can I get you to eat? Isn't this a cool little apartment?"

"I'm fine, Mom. It is a cool place. How long are you going to be here?"

"I don't know. But come in, take off your coat, we'll talk. I was about to prep some shrimp. Fresh shrimp that were probably swimming in the ocean this morning."

"We need to talk. I wanted to come and see you and find out what's going on. And I have some news for you, too."

And I knew, knew in that instant, without Annie saying another word, knew before she pulled off the oversized scarf and shed the down jacket, knew so certainly that it wasn't even a surprise when I saw the baggy sweater and—maybe?— the hint of a bulge. Annie stood next to the daybed, one hand on Trouble's neck, the other resting on her abdomen.

"I'm pregnant, Mom. Please don't be upset. I'm going to have a baby."

I was full of such a mix of emotions I wasn't sure which to lean into first. What I would not do, very intentionally not be, was ashamed. Not for Annie, not for my grandchild, not for myself. I would not be my mother. "I see that," I said and laid both hands gently over the bulge of my daughter's belly, remembering, suddenly, her nausea the morning we went to the cemetery not quite a month ago, the oversized sweaters and yoga pants she'd worn most of that visit, a fashion trend so common I hadn't given it a thought. "Four months?"

"A little more. Eighteen weeks. I think. My periods are still unpredictable. I'm not exactly sure when I conceived. Are you angry?"

"Angry? Not *angry*." I looked into Annie's eyes, and knew she would know immediately if I lied, if I was anything but completely truthful. "Worried. Concerned," I said and smiled into my daughter's beautiful face, the love I felt for her so big, and so powerful. Yes, I was disappointed, but that was a selfish emotion that was about me, and not one I was going to lay on Annie. "Blessed," I finally whispered and pulled her to me and hugged her. Held her and knew that I would forever after remember everything about this moment. Everything.

Annie stepped back and took a deep breath, her eyes glistening and full, and I knew then exactly how she'd felt, worrying about sharing this news. "I planned to tell you and Dad together, when I came home the day after Christmas. I wanted to tell you at Thanksgiving, but I couldn't. There wasn't the right time; the whole family was there. I chickened out. I know you don't like Corey..."

"We don't *not* like Corey. We don't know him." And we have serious concerns about his character, his morality.

"It wasn't planned, but we're happy. I am so happy." And her face looked it; she was luminous, radiant. "I know we have stuff to figure out. It's complicated. But it will be okay."

"I know," I said. "Things have a way of working out." I pulled my top lip between my teeth and thought of all that Annie was going to lose, all she was going to miss out on, the responsibility that was going to change her life, the fact that there would now be a bond, an everlasting, lifelong one, for all of us, with Corey the married man. It was clear that Annie, eyes glowing unrepentantly, was totally ignorant of the weight of those truths.

I could not help but remember how I had felt, telling my mom and dad, and Lillian, this very same news. How scared I'd been, nearly sick with the dread of telling them. How embarrassed, how upset they had been. The shame. The look on Lillian's face that had contradicted whatever she'd said, words I no longer recalled. And Joe had been single, and we were married before the baby was born.

Do people even use the word illegitimate anymore?

"Oh, sweetie. I love you so much," I said, pulling her into another hug, feeling tears burning the backs of my eyes, "You will be an amazing mother." The words I would have given anything to hear my own mother say, words that had never been voiced.

I stuck the shrimp in the fridge, and found Trouble's leash. We set off walking toward downtown. The three of us got as far as the College of Charleston and found a bench, watching people out and about, listening to gulls and pigeons, savoring the warmth, the angle of the sun, the differentness of our relationship. I think Annie felt it, too.

"It's beautiful here. Is that why you came? I mean why here and not...the beach?"

I smiled a little and shook my head. "There are beaches not too far from here. But it's the city, this city, I have always been curious about, infatuated with. There's so much history here. I've read about the city and the low country for years and years. I wanted—needed—to be in a new, unfamiliar place."

Annie was watching me, the expression on her face, in her gray eyes, intent. She was listening, trying to understand. I couldn't tell if she did.

"It's crazy, I know. It doesn't make sense. I just knew in my gut it was where I wanted—needed—to come. As soon as I thought of it."

She nodded again but I could tell she was just humoring me. I wasn't sure anyone would understand why I did what I did, leave home and hearth (and husband and Christmas party) and come here at this time of year, the season that was about family, home, and hearth. I did not really understand it myself. "My favorite cookbook of all time is from here," I said. "*Charleston Receipts*. Very old school."

Just then a blue jay swooped in and landed first on the branch of a tree then hopped to the rail of the fence. A wrought iron fence, the top of each picket a delicate swirl, edged the tiny lot that sheltered the bench where we sat. I had learned that these little spaces, alcoves almost, dotted the city and were called pocket parks. How was that not totally enchanting?

"This fence makes me think of Dad's fence at the cemetery," Annie said.

"What do you mean "Dad's fence?""

"The new fence that Dad put up. At Nora's cemetery."

"Dad didn't put up that fence."

"Yes, he did. Well, I don't think he did the work himself. But he ordered it and paid for it. You didn't know that?"

"He didn't tell me."

"A couple of years ago. He said the old fence was a mess. It was falling down, it was missing parts. He tried to get one that matched, but he couldn't find a design that was the same. So the new one is different, but similar."

"How do you know this?"

"He showed me the two choices and asked me to pick one."

"Why didn't he ask me?" *Why didn't he tell me?*

"I don't know, Mom. Maybe he wanted to surprise you."

"That fence has been there for a couple of years. Three or four even. I'm surprised." Why would Joe buy a new fence for the cemetery where our daughter was buried but not tell me? How did he even know the fence there needed repair? To my knowledge, he never visited Nora's grave.

I felt, suddenly, as if I didn't know my husband at all. And until this moment, I would have sworn I knew Joe Daley better than I knew any other human being on the planet.

"It's beautiful here, Mom," Annie said, stretching and rolling her shoulders. "But how long are you going to stay? Is this permanent?"

"I don't know. I wasn't thinking about that when I came. I just wanted to get away."

"I didn't know you were so unhappy," Annie said. "Though you didn't seem like yourself at Thanksgiving."

"I'm not unhappy. I am—was—mad. So mad I didn't know how to deal with it."

"Mad at Dad?"

"Yes." Furious. And at Nana Lil. And at the whole fucking Daley family, actually.

"So you just left? That's not like you. It goes against everything you ever taught us. You wouldn't even let me quit piano lessons."

"I was angry. I mean *really* angry. So angry that when I heard him breathing, I wanted to scream, or hit him with a lamp."

"Mom!"

"I know."

"Is this because of the cruise for Nana Lil?"

"It wasn't the reason I left. I'm not even sure it was the reason I was so mad. But I guess it was like the match that lit the fuse. The anger I was feeling was changing me from the inside out."

"I can't believe I'm an adult, that I'm going to be a mother, and the idea of my parents getting a divorce makes me so sad. You have to figure it out. Get back together." There were tears in Annie's voice; she blinked hard to keep them from falling.

"Oh, honey," I said pulling her into a hug. "It'll be okay. Whatever happens, it's going to be okay."

————

ANNIE and I were browsing a specialty kitchen store—The Purple Onion—that was jammed with last-minute Christmas shoppers. We'd walked through Waterfront Park and along Rainbow Row and now were poking along, enjoying the low country Christmas decorations and stopping when we felt like it to window shop.

"What is Corey going to do?" I asked. "He can't continue to straddle two relationships."

Can he?

"Now that you're pregnant..." I consciously kept my voice low, glancing at Annie. "I mean, he'll have two families."

The look on Annie's face was one that I knew well. Stubborn. "Lots of people have two families, Mom. It's not unusual. Of course we've talked about it. It's all we've talked about since I found out I was pregnant."

I had followed Annie's lead when it came to talking, wanting to be supportive, be the ear, the loving mother, the rock I sensed she needed. There were so many things I wanted to know, but I was treading carefully, trying not to ask questions that sounded like judgment. Talking while shopping seemed to offer the same kind of comfort talking while driving used to offer when the kids were young. Annie would leave first thing in the morning. I kept my eyes on the road, or in this case the stockpots, and spoke. "Is Corey happy about another baby? In his situation, it would only be natural to feel..." I paused, searching for the right word, "...stressed."

Annie didn't take offense. "He's happy. I mean, I really think he is. He loves babies. He loves me. He says he does."

I looked sharply at Annie. *Was there uncertainty there? He says he does?* "What is he going to do? He's still married to someone else. He has children."

"I know. Believe me, I know. But that doesn't change the fact that I'm going to have a baby in five months, give or take. No matter what, that fact is undeniable." She laid her hands on her belly.

I studied Annie, and to her credit, she didn't look away. Her beautiful gray eyes looked green today; the T-shirt she'd worn under the cable knit sweater was the bright color of grass in April. "You've thought about what you're going to do if things don't...work out...with Corey?"

Annie took a deep breath. "If things don't *work out*, I'll manage somehow."

I studied Annie's face, her expression, saw the determination that had allowed her to chug a gallon of milk, and swallow an earthworm, and refuse to cry over skinned knees or broken dolls. I forced a smile. "I know you will. *We* will," I amended, suddenly struck again by the realization that in a few short months, there would be a baby. The notion was still so novel, so bright and nearly piercing, it made my breath catch and my chest swell. I felt, despite all the concerns, the apprehension and the worry, a kind of warmth and joy.

"What?" Annie asked, watching my face. "What are you thinking?"

"I'm thinking I'm going to be a grandmother." And I felt my face break into a smile that I couldn't have stopped if I'd tried. "I always assumed I would be. I just hadn't thought about it, how I would feel, or when it would happen."

"Well, it's going to happen sometime around the end of May."

"I'll come. Be there when you're laboring. If you want me. For the delivery. You know that, right?"

"I know, Mom. You didn't have to say it."

"Yeah. Yeah, I did."

We wandered, and I stopped to study the offering of cookbooks in the store, looking to see if *Cooking for Father* was represented because I couldn't help myself. I was just going to admit to the sin of pride, when I heard my daughter's voice and found Annie talking to a woman in front of a display of KitchenAid mixers.

"Oh, hey, Mom. I was just telling this lady about the ciabatta bread you make using your KitchenAid."

"I do use my KitchenAid. A lot," I said. "I keep it on my counter. Luckily I have the space and I feel like having it there is a little like having a Mercedes parked in the driveway."

"I know what you mean." the woman said. *Ah knowh what you mean.* "I've never had one of these mixers; I guess I learned to cook without it, so never felt the loss, but I've heard such good things about them. I'm shopping for a gift for my daughter-in-law, which is why I asked your daughter if she had one, if she used it and liked it."

"I don't have one—yet," Annie said. "I live in a tiny apartment with a kitchen the size of a shoe box. Once I have a real kitchen, it will be the first thing I buy. Mom's ciabatta bread is to die for. And you need a dough hook to make it. She makes pierogi dough with the mixer, too, all kinds of stuff. She's an amazing cook. Baker."

I was touched to hear Annie enthuse about my cooking skills. "The ciabatta bread is very easy. I could get you the recipe."

"Or you could buy her cookbook. *Cooking for Father.* It's got the best recipes from all her years cooking for our priests back home. It's in there."

The woman looked at me. "Why, that's wonderful. My brother is a priest. I should get your cookbook to give Barbara with the mixer. Do they have it here? Would you sign it if they have one?"

"It would be my pleasure. They do have a couple of copies here. I just saw them in the cookbook section."

"Splendid. I'll get the mixer and the cookbook. What a perfect gift. I can tell Barbara I met the author, too."

"I was going to see if I could offah any assistance, but you've given a better endorsement than I evah could have." The man from the counter at the front of the store smiled warmly at us all. I hadn't heard him approach. "Evan Pugh," he said and held out a hand that was long-fingered and as elegant as he was. "P'haps I could tawk you into hosting one of ow-wah cookin' demos? A guest chef. We have a kitchen in the back of the sto-ah. They're verah popula. Of course, we would have copies of your cookbooks he-ah as well."

"Hi," I said, shaking his hand which was warm and gripped mine very lightly. "Cathleen Daley. It's so generous of you to offer." I smiled. I'd never done a cooking demo, unless you counted the time I'd made oversized gingerbread men—and ladies—with Annie's first-grade class and the kids decorated the cookies for Christmas ornaments. "But I'm just visiting the city."

"We'll start the demos again after the holidays, and we have a chef already scheduled for the January demo. But February is open. Or March. We usually get twenty-five to thirty people. The demos are verah well received."

I grinned. I'd noticed the kitchen set-up at the back of the store. Black granite, stainless steel, and every high end kind of pot and pan, a fancy commercial cook top, a big oven. A mirror on the ceiling, tilted so that people could watch the action on the countertop. "It sounds very cool."

"Mom," Annie said, and I glanced at her. "February or March? How long are you going to be here?"

I stared at her and honestly my first thought was *your baby is not due 'til May, so until then?*

―――――

WE WERE LYING side by side in the bed, the room dark except for some ambient light, from the streetlights out front. We'd gone out to dinner, Annie's second, and last, night in Charleston, and tried one of the restaurants that headed several of the Best in Charleston lists.

"Thanks, Mom." Annie sighed.

"You're welcome. My pleasure. I'm glad we could go. And that you could enjoy it."

"It was awesome. I just get really tired these days. At the end of a shift, I'm wiped."

"I'm sure. A twelve-hour shift is long when you're not pregnant. And no doubt you're on your feet the whole time." I wanted to ask about work after the baby came, daycare. I wanted to know if Annie would be able to breastfeed the baby. Would she miss out on the pure joy that I had always felt nursing the babies, nestling them in my arms, watching their faces as they suckled? Would some stranger in a daycare be feeding my grandchild a bottle of formula poured from a can or mixed from powder?

Health insurance, sleep deprivation...would Annie and Corey even be living in the same house when the baby came? Would Annie have any help during the nights before she had to work? About a million worrisome fears and questions filled my mind but there would be time for those later.

"Mom," Annie said softly into the darkness. "I'm glad I came. And that you're not mad."

"Oh, honey, I'm not mad. I couldn't be mad at you. I love you so much."

Annie reached for my hand and squeezed. "I love you, too. I don't know if things are going to work out with Corey. I mean I hope they do, but I don't know."

"I know. I understand. But you have us." Together or apart. "Whatever happens." I couldn't tell, but I thought maybe she was crying. "You're going to have to tell Dad about the baby. He should hear it from you."

"I know. I will. After Christmas. If I couldn't tell you together, I wanted to tell you first."

Despite everything, I smiled in the dark and squeezed Annie's hand in return. "Thank you."

Annie took a deep breath and I could hear tears, relief, overwhelming emotion in that inhalation. "Do you think you and Dad are going to get divorced?"

"I don't know."

"I hope not. I mean, I will try to understand, but I want my baby to have grandparents who live in the same house." Now I was certain Annie was crying. "Does that make me a hypocrite? Corey has kids, and if things work out for me, their parents won't be living in the same house."

I didn't know how to answer that. Before I could decide what to say, Annie pulled my hand and laid it against her belly and I felt it, felt the gentle shift, a tiny push, the baby moving.

"Oh!" I said. "Oh! Is this the first you've felt it?"

"No, I've been feeling her move for a little while. But her kicks are getting stronger. Maybe she's going to be a soccer player."

"Her? She?" I repeated.

"Well, we don't know for sure. I didn't want to know before the birth. But I just have this feeling—"

"A baby girl." Thinking of the quickening under my palm as a girl somehow made the baby even more real. A granddaughter. An image of Joe with a pink blanket snuggled in his arms, holding his granddaughter, popped into my head. Joe. He would feel the same way I did. Worried sick, but blessed. Accepting. Joe loved kids. Even babies.

"Mom. If the baby is a girl, I want to name her Nora."

Chapter Twelve

I was working on the copy edits for *Holidays With Father*. Each section of the cookbook, in this case each holiday, opened with what Kandace, my editor, called "a little first-person narrative," what I thought of as an essay. Anecdotes about family, about my gardens or the butcher, about Father Cecil or Father J. Sometimes they documented the provenance of one of the recipes in the book and that meant stories from growing up on the eastern shore as a Methodist—all those pot lucks! I didn't ever talk about faith or religion explicitly. But in any case, I'd become good at tying all the bits of my life together and connecting them to cooking.

I stared at the computer screen for a while, then I looked out the window, not really seeing, my mind thinking a thousand and one things. The essay introducing the section on Christmas felt...wrong.

I had bailed on Christmas and the trappings this year. Or most of them anyway. It was Christmas Eve and there was no tree. No wreath. No cookies. Not one ornament, not one string of lights, not a pine-scented candle. Not one gift to put under the nonexistent tree. It made me feel—

My phone buzzed. I glanced at the screen. Patrick. I debated not answering. Why didn't I want to talk to Pat? I knew he would support me coming to Charleston. But I didn't want his endorsement. Why not? Trying to sort it out confused me and was too much effort for this moment. I pushed the button to answer. "Hey."

"Hey," he repeated. "I hear you're on sabbatical. Charleston. Good for you."

"Well, I don't know if it's *good* for me, but I think it's been good *for* me. If you know what I mean."

"I think I do. It's supposed to be a beautiful city. I've never been—"

"It is. Beautiful. Warm. At least by Langston standards for this time of year. And sunny. For that alone, I'm loving it."

"How long do you plan to stay?"

"I don't know. I was asked to do a cooking demo and book signing here. In March."

"March."

"Yeah. I haven't told Joe that. Keep it to yourself, please."

"Of course."

"I heard you took a little trip of your own. To a hotel."

"Diana's pregnant," he said.

"What? You're kidding."

Pat didn't answer and I listened to the silence pressed into my ear. Pat was going to be a father. Her life, their lives, Di's and Pat's, were never going to be the same. Wow. A thought suddenly occurred to me. Diana and Annie were going to be pregnant at the same time. The realization startled. What would those babies be to each other? First cousins once removed? Second cousins?

"It's a high-risk pregnancy. Because she's over forty. Old eggs, old sperm." He made a sound which I took for laughter without humor. "She's had all kinds of testing. Everything looks good. She's healthy. Was healthy before she got pregnant."

"I don't know what to say. Congratulations?"

"I don't know what to say, either. I'm too old for a baby. Too old for a new life."

"What are you going to do?"

"What can I do?"

"I don't know. I'm the last person to be giving marital advice."

"I didn't call for advice."

I was still having a hard time envisioning it. Pat was going to be a father. He was my age. A baby was a big deal for anyone, anytime. But for someone my age? "When is she due?"

"Late summer. She was pregnant at Thanksgiving though she didn't know it. I didn't know it."

Diana would have been pregnant already when she made the trip to Langston to talk pregnancy and babies with me.

"Well, congratulations," I said again.

"Yeah," he said. "Thanks?"

———

I DIDN'T HESITATE to answer my cell when I saw Father J calling. There was really no point in evading him. The Christmas essay could wait. I wasn't making much progress on it anyway. "Father. How are you?"

"I'm well. You've been on my mind. How are you?"

"I'm okay." Good. I think.

"I had lunch with Joe yesterday. Of course I saw him at Mass on Sunday with Lillian. No doubt I'll see them both this evening, as well."

No doubt.

"You were hoping for some time to find a little peace," Father J said. "Solace. Have you found that? This time of year can be especially lonely for people who are not with family."

"I don't know, Father, I haven't been here that long. And Annie was here. She came and spent a couple of days with me. She left early this morning."

"Ah. She was worried." The way he said that, I understood that he was telling me Annie wasn't the only one.

"She was. And she wanted to talk to me about some things." I didn't feel like I could share the news about Annie's pregnancy yet. Not until Annie had had a chance to tell Joe.

"Talking is good. Have you talked to Joe?" I could tell that he knew the answer to that question before he asked. That was often Father J's way. He didn't *preach*. He gently prodded.

"Not for a couple of days." Or three. Or was it four? When I thought of Joe, we'd been married for almost thirty years, how could I not think about him, but when I did, I still felt the same burn of anger, like bile in my stomach.

"You know I'm not as traditional as some priests, and I try to be open-minded about how relationships work."

"I'm not avoiding having a conversation with Joe, Father, if that's what you're getting at. But we haven't gotten to a place where a relationship discussion would be productive. Yet."

"I really wish you and I could talk in person instead of over the telephone. Maybe we could FaceTime."

I laughed. "FaceTime? Really? You *are* unconventional, Father."

He scoffed. "I just recognize that sometimes I need to trust the instincts of my congregants and that sometimes the desired conventional outcome requires unconventional strategies. But I must say I'm worried about you, Cathleen."

"Don't worry, Father. I'm okay. I really think being here, being away, is a good thing. For me. For now."

Father J didn't respond to that. "Rose Stauffer has been coming in to prepare meals. I think there's still plenty of Cathleen Daley cuisine in the freezer, but apparently the rectory committee is worried I'll starve."

The thought made me feel an odd tick of jealousy. "Rose is a good cook."

"Ahh. She is. But she's not you. You're missed here, Cathleen. Don't become too comfortable being away. You know there's a fine line between being away so that you might find peace and healing, and running away from your problems."

"I know. But thanks for the reminder. Is that coming from you, or Joe?" I couldn't help asking.

"That's coming from both of us. Joe is your husband. He loves you. Talk to him. Keep the lines of communication open. I know you want to work this out, whatever it is that you're dealing with. I know you, Cathleen. Your heart is big, and good, and pure."

I was touched by the praise, though I wasn't as sure of the assessment. What would Father J think if he knew about my impulse to beat Joe with a table lamp?

———

LATER, after lunch, I was still working my way through the copy edits when there was the sound of footsteps on the metal staircase. Who would be coming to my door now? On Christmas Eve?

The FedEx man. With a FedEx box about the size of a shoe box. "Cathleen Daley?" He held out the electronic doohickey so I could sign. "Happy holidays," he said as he handed me the box and trotted down back down the stairs.

The label was handwritten in my mother-in-law's loopy script.

Hmmm. I snorted. What would Lillian be sending me? I hadn't given her this address so she would have gotten it from Joe. I shook the box. It was light; it didn't rattle. I carried it to the counter and found a knife to slit open the packaging. Inside was another, smaller, bubble-wrapped and packing-taped package. I slit the tape holding the bubble wrap to free the small white box. It was in perfect condition but it was clearly an old cardboard box. Very old. Inside that was a hinged blue ring box, also old, the blue silk covering faded.

I noticed the envelope then, separate from the bubble wrap, inside the FedEx box. It was a Christmas card and inside that was a note, on old-school stationery. Before I read the letter, I opened the ring box. Inside, secured in the padded slot was a sapphire ring, the round stone so deeply blue it was almost black. It was a ring I had never seen before, the gold setting intricately detailed, filigreed, almost medieval looking.

I picked up the note.

> *Dear Cathleen,*
>
> *I understand you won't be with us this year for Christmas. I hope you know how much we will all miss you. You put so much of yourself into the holiday celebration; it won't be the same without you.*
>
> *I had decided to pass along the enclosed to you this year for Christmas; it's been long overdue. The passing along, that is. I said something to Joe several months ago, but he suggested I save it for Christmas. Even though you won't be here, I wanted you to have the ring.*
>
> *It came to me from my grandmother, on the Rutledge side, my father's mother, though it belonged to her mother before her. I'd like it to be yours, and after you, Annie's.*
>
> *As you likely know, I gave other rings to Mark and to David to give to their intendeds; when you and Joe married, it caught me off guard. I had not thought about the jewelry I'd inherited, or considered how I wanted to pass it on to my family, my heirs.*

I glanced at the heirloom in my hand. I was very aware that my mother-in-law had gifted her other sons, Mark and David, with rings that they had then given their brides. Joe and I had been the recipient of no such gift.

> *I regret that I will not be able to pass along this ring to you in person. But I want you to have it. In many ways,*

234

you remind me of my great-grandmother Mimi Rutledge. She was betrothed to my great-grandfather before he went off to start a branch of the Merchant's Bank in Vancouver, Canada. She waited for a year and then she decided she was done with waiting and she set off to join her George alone, by herself, across the whole of Canada by train. In those days, it would have been a tremendously forward thing to do, for a young woman to travel that distance alone. I don't ever remember hearing what her parents thought about their liberated daughter making such a trip; the stories were always about Mimi and how bold and fearless she was.

This ring was a gift to Mimi from great-grandfather George when she had my grandmother. Mimi and George had three children; my grandmother was the oldest.

My sincere apologies for waiting so long to give this ring to you. Mimi's strength, and her passion for the man she loved, are what makes me think you will honor this ring, as Mimi did.

Wishing you a holiday filled with peace and the comfort you are seeking. I hope you return home to us soon. Joe misses you! We all do.

With love, Lillian

I turned the front of the Christmas card over, creamy white card stock with an elegant gold nativity. Then I reread the note a second time. Looked at the ring in its silk box.

Mimi's ...passion for the man she loved, that inspired her to leave her home and travel across the continent to be with him, are what makes me think you will honor this ring, as Mimi did....

Was that a jab because I'd left the man I love to come to

Charleston while Mimi traveled across a continent to be with hers? I snorted again. Shook my head.

Was this an apology? Was my mother-in-law extending an olive branch? A bribe?

What am I supposed to do with this?

There was a time when the gift of this ring would have meant a great deal to me, to know that Lillian had accepted me and would cherish me, if for no other reason than my love for Joe. That was years and years ago, though. A lifetime ago. *I don't know what to think about this.*

Was it a tacit reminder that I'm committed to Joe—a guilt trip? It feels intrusive, somehow, and poorly timed. It would be so like Lillian to think she could intercede in some way between Joe and me. Whatever it was, whatever the ring stood for, I didn't want it. More importantly, I didn't need it.

Later in the afternoon, Joe called. "Hey," I said.

"Hey. Is this a bad time?" Joe asked.

"No, this is fine. I was going to call you later. I thought you might be having dinner now."

"Nah. Not yet. We're supposed to go over to Mom's for something in a little bit."

"Doug's there? His flight got in okay?"

There was a pause that only just barely registered on the fringe of my awareness. "Yep. He's taking a shower. It's weird, just him and me here." I didn't respond to that, thinking instead of the way Doug was usually so *loud*; he filled a room, was always so *ebullient*. At every gathering, he talked to everyone, asked a million questions, kept drinks topped off, told funny jokes, laughed fully at others' jokes. Thinking about how hard he worked just being Doug made me miss him, my tender, vulnerable second son.

"Jamie texted. Said the condo Molly's family rented is right at the bottom of the ski slope. They can ski home, right off the lift."

"Yeah, he told me that, too. Annie's coming the day after tomorrow?" I asked.

"Yep. Said she'd be home sometime after lunch on the 26th. I didn't know she was going to see you."

"Yeah. I didn't either. Total surprise. But it was nice. We had a chance to talk."

"Is everything okay there?" he asked.

"Yeah. It's good. I'm getting some work done on the edits for the new cookbook." Just some. If I could stop my compulsive consumption of every tabloid in print form I'd be more productive. I walked a hundred miles a day. I spent hours just staring into space, zoning out. "How are things there?"

"Lonely. Quiet. Too quiet. I still can't believe you're going to miss Christmas here. I can't believe that there's something so wrong with our marriage that you had to leave me."

"I didn't leave you."

"Sure feels like leaving to me." He paused. I'm sorry. I didn't call to argue. It's just not the same without you here. I love you. I miss you."

"I love you, too."

"Then come home. Get in the van and head north. You could be here by breakfast." His voice sounded thick.

"No. No, I'm not going to do that. I'm not ready to come home yet."

Joe didn't respond, didn't say anything, just let a silence settle between us, and I was relieved that more words didn't have to be spoken today. Trouble got up from where she had been sleeping on the rug beside the bed and came over, tail wagging, yellow eyes steady, smile on her face.

"Would it be okay if I come there? Don't answer that. Just think about it."

I didn't answer right away, though I felt a sense of almost panic. I didn't want Joe to come. Did I? "I'll think about it."

"We'll talk to you tomorrow, okay?" Joe said.

"Of course," I said.

"I love you," Joe said.

———

CHRISTMAS EVE IN A CHURCH...NOT the one I had attended as a child, not the one I had attended for most of my adult life. Not a Methodist church, not a Catholic church.

One where I didn't know any person, where I was a total stranger. There were more black people here, in this building, than in all of Langston. I'd never before really thought about that, how white Langston was.

Some of the words were different, the liturgy, the ritual. And the sanctuary was very different. There was the familiar churchy rustling and jostling, the muted sounds of children speaking and being hushed, the sense of excitement, of anticipation. Lots of poinsettias.

The church and service and the people were foreign, but it smelled the same, like every church I'd ever been in—a potpourri of perfume and aftershave, hair spray and old wool, dusty hymnals, fresh flowers, candles, furniture polish. The scents triggered an emotional response, one I had not been expecting. Homesickness. Memories of decades of other Christmas Eves, with Joe beside me, with the kids dressed in "church clothes," the joy that filled me at those moments, all came back in a rush. Tears suddenly burned behind my eyes and I blinked and sniffed, but did not try to hold them back.

This church was beautiful, magical, as all churches must be on Christmas Eve, candles flickering and the air nearly humid with the feeling of goodwill. The minister, standing behind a pulpit in white vestments, raised both arms and said, "Welcome, all ye faithful on this most blessed and holy night," and the service began.

Everything was different. Life was different.

———

I CALLED home on Christmas day, after lunch.

The Ohio Daleys usually came to Langston the day after and

spent several days, Laura and Diana and Patrick, too, so that the week post-Christmas at our house was filled with many, but not all, of Joe's siblings and family. What I had for a lot of years thought of as *my family*, too. I had no idea if those were the plans again this year. I waited for emotion to kick in, but there was nothing. After the tears last night in church, I felt empty of feeling, even homesickness.

My little apartment was warm and smelled of crab and hollandaise sauce and the English muffin I'd toasted under the broiler. I'd only been here a little over a week, but already it felt like there was a wall, an impenetrable divide that separated my here and now from my life in Langston, and it was more than the fact that there was no sign of Christmas in the little apartment.

"Hey," I said when Joe answered. "Merry Christmas."

"Same to you."

"What's happening there?"

There was a pause, and I thought I knew what Joe was thinking: *If you were at home, like you're supposed to be, with me, with your family, you'd know.* "It's quiet. Mom and Di and Laura are coming over later. It's weird."

"It's different," I agreed.

"We had a little problem last night," Joe said and the radar that was born with my children quivered to life.

"What happened?"

"Doug went out to meet some friends. He got busted driving home. Drunk. A DUI."

"Oh, no."

"I'm pretty sure he was under the influence most of yesterday, though I didn't see him drinking anything. You know how he is. Too happy. Talking too much, too loud."

"Oh, Dougie," I said, bringing a fist to my mouth, my heart hurting in my chest. I felt a twinge of loss, of need, a maternal instinct, to be with my son. "I'll come home."

There was silence on the line; I thought at first we'd been disconnected. "I don't think you should."

"What? Why not?"

"I want you to come home for the right reasons. Because you want to be here, with me. Doug is an adult. He did a stupid thing. Well, he was a shithead. But you aren't going to fix it. He's gonna have to do that himself."

"I wouldn't come to make it right. To fix it. But me being away...maybe that made it worse. His drinking."

"Maybe." I could picture Joe shrugging. "But not likely. He didn't turn into an alcoholic in the twenty-four hours that he's been here. It's a problem that's been brewing for a while and you know it. We've talked about it. He drinks more every time he's home."

"Alcoholic? You think he's an alcoholic?" Hearing Joe say the word out loud shocked. At the same time, it wasn't really shocking at all.

Joe's silence answered the question.

"I think I should be there," I said. "So we can show him how much we support him. He needs our support. What's he doing now?"

"He's in the kitchen, washing dishes. I came out to get an armful of firewood. I'm freezing my ass off in the backyard. I told him he needed to call and tell you himself. So when he does, you may want to pretend you don't already know. But I thought a heads up was in order. It sucks to be blindsided by news like that."

Wait 'til he found out about Annie. I almost groaned out loud. "Why does he drink so much? What triggered this...problem? Did we do something? Not do something? Did we fail him somehow?" I said.

"Why do you assume it has anything to do with us? He's a big boy. No one held a gun to his head and made him drink last night. No one told him to get in the car and drive. He made those choices all by his lonesome. But it's a problem that needs fixed. Now."

"He needs professional help."

"Well, he'll need to figure that out, too."

"I still think I should come home. I paid my rent here through the end of the month, but that's only a week away."

"Nope. I don't think so, Cath. Not now. Not because of this. He leaves in two days. You stay there." 'Til you get your head on straight. He didn't say that, but I imagined the words coming from his mouth.

Merry Christmas, Cath. Ho ho ho.

———

My phone buzzed and I checked the screen. A text from Jamie. To everyone: Me, Joe, Doug, Annie.

> Jamie: Merry Christmas! Missing you all!

I glanced at my watch and was surprised to see it had been almost two hours since I'd talked to Joe. I was still sitting at the little table in the apartment, almost mindlessly reading the copy of *Charleston Receipts* I'd brought with me from home.

Another buzz, another text. This time a photo. I tapped the picture until it popped open full-size. A brilliant blue cloudless sky filled the screen, snow-covered mountains rolling into the distance. From the glimpse of cable and green bars at the corner of the photo, it was taken from some kind of lift.

> Me: Spectacular!!

> Jamie: Big news from Colorado. She
> said yes!

Another picture. This one of Molly's left hand held up against the achingly blue sky, a magnificent silver or platinum solitaire diamond ring on her third finger. I felt an unexpected pang deep inside. My son was going to be married. My oldest living child: my first boy, first toddler, first tooth, first haircut, first two-wheeled bike...Jamie owned all the firsts. *All the firsts after three and a half months, because before Jamie, for twelve weeks, there had been Nora.*

My driven, ambitious, perfectionist son. My baby.

Jamie was going to be married. Was it a betrayal of Doug to feel happy for his brother?

Me: Congratulations! So happy for you.

Joe: AWESOME.

Doug: Way to go, dude.

Jamie: We want to get married in the yard.
Small wedding. Mark your calendars for
May. Probably the weekend of the 20th.

In the yard? At the house in Langston? I was swept by a flood of conflicting emotions. Touched that Jamie wanted to be married there, that his childhood home was that important to him. Excited at the idea of planning and hosting such a special event. It felt like the ultimate tribute to me as a mother, as a homemaker, a hostess, a cook. But. But. It also meant the spotlight would be on me as wife. On me and Joe. I would have to return to Langston...and to Joe. But I'd been planning to go home at some point. Hadn't I?

And May? *That's quick. May. Annie's baby is due around then.*

Annie: May is going to be a great month.

———

After the texts from Jamie, I'd decided that today, Christmas, was a beach day. The weather was nice, mild. It was just about as different from the pictures Jamie had sent as it could be. The air smelled of ocean, fish, sand. The sun was bright and felt amazing, the breeze surprisingly, even unseasonably for Charleston, balmy. I found a place to park, helped Trouble off the backseat and out of the van. I clipped the leash to Troub's collar, and we made our way along a path through some dunes to the beach.

We walked along the edge of the water, where the sand was damp and hard. Occasionally, there were other people walking on the beach, a few with dogs Trouble had to greet, nose to nose, her thick tail waving, her mouth smiling. We walked until Trouble slowed, then I found a place far enough back from the water to sit. Trouble plunked herself down, tongue hanging from her mouth. The sand was warm on the top layers, cold below. I had taken off my sneakers and now held them in one hand. I set them aside, petting Trouble's spade-shaped head. The dog was breathing hard, harder than a gentle beach walk merited. She was an old girl, and despite her forever-young spirit, her body was showing her age. "Sucks getting old, huh, girl?" I said, rubbing the ears that I'd rubbed countless thousands, millions, of times over the past thirteen years.

I was going to be a grandmother. I was going to be a mother-in-law. I was the mother of a child, an adult child but a child forever and always, who likely had a drinking problem. Was I going to be a divorcee? What was I going to do? Was I going to stay here? What was my life going to look like next month? Next summer? Next year?

My phone buzzed again. A call.

From Doug.

Doug, my earnest, tender-hearted, always trying-to-please son. Third born, second son, destined to follow an over-achieving older brother. When I looked at Doug, or thought about him, even now that he was an adult and six feet two inches tall, I saw four-year-old Doug, with the round glasses that he had had to wear for a few years, that made him look like a solemn little owl. The Doug who just wanted to be wherever his big brother Jamie was, doing whatever Jamie was doing. Who wanted so much to please. Who wore his heart on his sleeve. Sometime along the way, because Jamie, driven to succeed, to always be first, hadn't wanted to be bothered with a tagalong little brother, Doug's earnestness had hardened, had turned to a sharp-edged humor, a cynicism, a cutting wit that was at once funny and smart and, to me at least, sad. Because Doug *was* smart, he was too smart for his own good sometimes. And he had become a drinker. An alcoholic?

I started to cry.

The phone buzzed again. Doug, calling to wish me a Merry

Christmas, to tell me he'd been busted for driving under the influence. Oh, baby boy, I thought, my heart squeezing hard in my chest. I pushed the button on the screen and put the phone to my ear and tried to swallow the tears, to make my voice clear and bright.

"Hey, honey."

———

THE DAY after Christmas had passed in not exactly a blur, but in a fog. I'd read through more of the copy edits on my cookbook, I'd slept, I'd taken Trouble for a short walk. I'd spent a lot of time thinking about Doug. Now, just before bedtime, Joe was calling.

"Hey," I said.

"Hey." He sighed. After thirty-plus years, I could hear a novel —*War and Peace*—in those three letters and the breath of air that followed them. "So we're gonna be grandparents."

"We are."

"Jesus. I could hear rustling and imagined Joe rubbing his forehead, the way he did when he was frustrated or bothered.

She said she told you last week. Thanks for the heads up," he said, but there was no reproach in it.

"It wasn't my news to share."

"Yeah. I get that," he said, and there was a weight of disillusionment in his voice. He sounded resigned. "I didn't know what to say to her."

"What did you say?"

"What could I say? I couldn't see any point in telling her how disappointed I was, how sad. Sorry that she was having some married guy's kid. Jesus," he said again. I blew out my pursed lips, tipped my head back to stare sightlessly at the ceiling of the little apartment.

"What a Christmas. You're gone, Doug gets busted, now Annie." He sighed again.

"We'll get through it," I said.

"Yeah. We've done it before. She'd be thirty years old."

I felt that comment, the reference, like a jolt to my heart, like one of those heart-shocking machines on medical dramas. Joe never talked about Nora. "Thirty years." I swallowed.

"A lot of water under our bridge."

"I read that book on birth order, remember? I always think about how different the kids would be, how their personalities might be different if she hadn't died. Jamie wouldn't be a first-born. Doug would have had two older siblings. Annie wouldn't have been the only girl. If Nora had lived, we might already be grandparents. We were parents by the time we were thirty. Four times over."

Joe didn't answer. But he didn't pooh pooh what I said, either, or change the subject as he usually did when I talked about Nora. He was such a pragmatist. A realist. The wallowing he was doing on this phone call was in some ways out of character, though it was odd, how I could so clearly picture him. He'd be sitting in the chair in the den, the old wing chair there. I thought of the fence at the cemetery, Nora's cemetery, the new fence that Joe had apparently purchased and never told me about. I wanted to ask him about that but not now.

"Things would have been different, no doubt," he said. "I think about what she would have looked like. She looked the most like me when she was born, remember? She might have been six feet tall with size eleven feet."

I suspected that Joe was humoring me, patronizing me, even, by having a conversation like this about Nora. We'd never done it before, talked about the might-have-beens, the what-ifs. I didn't care if this was Joe humoring me. It felt wonderful. Sad, and wonderful at the same time. Tears suddenly burned against the backs of my eyes. I couldn't speak.

"Jamie's news is exciting," Joe finally said into the silence. "Molly seems like a nice girl."

The mass that clogged my throat made it hard to say anything. I sniffed, short, hard. I didn't want Joe to know I was crying. I cleared my throat. "Yeah," I said. "She does."

"A small wedding here in the yard. I guess that means you'll be coming home?"

At some point. Eventually. I guess.

I didn't speak and Joe said, "I hope you had a nice day." Christmas day he meant.

"Thanks. It was different."

"Well, I guess I'll be talking to you. I love you, Cath. You know that, right?"

"I know that."

But was it enough?

———

AND THEN IT was January and the holidays were over.

The weather here was gorgeous, sunny every day, a blue sky that hurt the eyes, it was so pure. It was chilly, but not unpleasantly so. It made my soul feel light. I thought maybe more than anything else, the sunshine was therapeutic. In Pennsylvania now, the odds were good it would be dreary, I would be wearing snow boots, wool, polar fleece, corduroy and some days, many days, two pairs of socks. It was depressing to contemplate.

Here, in the mornings, I pulled on a turtleneck, draped a scarf, Annie's scarf that she'd left behind, around my neck, and more often than not, felt the blood warm in my veins as I walked with Trouble around the neighborhood, or farther, if Trouble seemed willing.

It was so joyous. In the afternoons, I had taken to sitting on my little west-facing balcony with my face to the sun. With my eyes closed, I could hear the rattle of palmetto fronds in the trees at the back of the yard, and I imagined I could smell things growing: jasmine, wisteria.

There had been no sign of my neighbor from downstairs, the mother of my landlord. The pottery shed was empty and quiet. From the balcony, I could see the yards and the backs of the houses on the next block. Occasionally I saw kids playing, or heard their voices, there was a little traffic on the street out front, but mostly only in the morning and late afternoon. If I chose not to see anyone, Trouble was my only companion. When I drove to the beach though, I often saw the same people walking, the same dogs. It had become routine, almost.

But it was the sunshine that reached into my bones and warmed me, filled me, that healed. I couldn't seem to get enough of the sun.

I had a call from the man at the Purple Onion, the kitchen store, about a book signing and cooking demo. I'd given him my contact info the day Annie and I had met him before Christmas. Maybe making bread or pierogies, he suggested. Could I stop by sometime so we could talk about it?

I was not too sure about doing a cooking demo. It sounded like they generally had a big crowd, and they'd had some famous chefs. Emeril! I was just a housewife. But Evan's manner had been gracious and courteous; he was kindly persuasive. My publisher was thrilled. Any PR was good PR, and publicity like a cooking demo in Charleston wouldn't cost them anything. They would arrange to have extra copies of *Cooking with Father* on hand.

I took Trouble for a walk around the block, which was about all Troub seemed to want these days, then filled her water dish and left her on the rug in the patch of sun under the skylight. I decided to walk downtown to The Purple Onion. I held Annie's scarf to my nose; it still smelled like her which made me smile.

Evan was in the front of the store and as soon as he saw me, his face lit up. "So nice to see you," he said, reaching out to shake my hand, "Cathleen, right?" he said, confirming. "I'm so pleased you'll come to do a demo and signing. Yowah cookbook is just delightful."

I couldn't help smiling, his accent was so charming. Plus, he was wearing a plum velvet smoking jacket and an ascot that looked like a Lilly Pulitzer print.

"I should warn you, I've done some book signings, but never any cooking demonstrations. Official ones, anyway. Pierogis with the

Altar Guild or cookies for my daughter's elementary school class don't count, somehow."

Just then a tall, thin, black woman came from the back of the store. Her features were almost sharp, except for her nose which was broad and flat. There were some graying strands in her hair which was cut in something approximating a buzz cut, but the woman could have been thirty-nine or fifty-nine, she had that kind of agelessness about her. "I have to go now, Evan." She glanced at me, acknowledging me, maybe even subtly tilting her head in my direction, but not smiling, not even a little.

"That's fine. Thanks for your help today," he said. "Marsal, this is Cathleen Daley, a cookbook author who happens to be visiting the city. She's going to do a cooking demo for us. And a book signing. Cathleen, this is my sister, Marsal."

The woman, Marsal, looked at me again, this time inclining her head and holding out a hand, though the reserve was still there.

"Nice to meet you." I smiled uncomfortably. The woman was the definition of aloof. She didn't spare so much as another glance in my direction but moved toward the door.

When I looked at Evan, he shook his head and grimaced. "Sorry for my sister's rudeness. She's part owner, but shop work isn't her thing," he said. "Today I was up against it, though. My assistant manager had a baby last night, six weeks early. One full-timer is on a dove hunting trip in Argentina, and the other left for California yesterday to help her mother who fell and broke a hip. The two part-timers I hired before Christmas went back to school. It's been a perfect storm of lost store help. You don't want a job, do you? Part-time? Just for a couple of weeks?"

I smiled at him, a kind refusal on my lips, but then I thought, sure, why not? I was almost finished with the edits for the cookbook; mostly, I was dragging my feet, poking along, because I had the luxury of doing so. I spent hours walking and sitting at the beach watching the water and the gulls. The idea of a distraction like working in a kitchen store sort of appealed. It was on the tip of my tongue to say I would talk to my husband but I thought, *I don't have to talk to anyone.*

"Sure. I'd be happy to help out. When do you want me to start?"

———

Dear Lillian,
Thank you for the ring.
It's too little too late.
Do you have any idea how ANGRY I am? Do you honestly think that a ring would fix things? Is that why you sent it?

Dear Lillian,
I apologize for taking so long to thank you for the gift of the ring.
WTF?

Dear Lillian,
My apologies for taking so long to let you know that your gift arrived here. I opened the ring and

Dear Lillian,
Really? Seriously? I've been married to your son for almost thirty years, have known him for almost thirty-four, have had four children with him, have buried a child with him, have been present when your other children married, when my husband's brothers gifted their brides-to-be the heirloom rings that you gave them. I ignored what felt like a personal slight, twice. I told myself I was being petty and shallow, that Joe and our children were the most important

things in my life, that happiness, living well, was the best revenge. But the truth is, the fact that you honored those other women in that way but did not recognize the love I had for Joe, or he for me, that you singled us, me, out, in such a way was very hurtful.

Dear Lillian,
Thank you for the ring. I will give it to Annie, and she can save it for her daughter one day.

Dear Lillian,

"CATHLEEN? This is Mina McDonald, Molly's mother. I hope it's okay that I called? Jamie gave me your number."

"Oh, hi! Of course it's okay. Congratulations on your daughter's engagement!"

"Same to you. On your son's."

"Thank you for having Jamie with your family over Christmas. He sent pictures from the ski lift. It looked beautiful. And he and Molly looked very happy."

"I think they are. We couldn't be more thrilled. We love Jamie. What a wonderful young man. And he's very good for Molly."

"Molly is a great girl, too." The image—dark hair, white pillowcase, Jamie's hand, pale white thighs, his head buried beyond—flashed through my mind. I could almost feel the remembered heat scald my face and neck. Was that picture going to be forever imprinted in my head? "It was lovely to have her at Thanksgiving so she could meet the rest of the family. We're looking forward to meeting all of you, too."

"Well, the reason I called was so we could talk, mother-to-mother, about the wedding. The kids are insistent that they only want a small, informal ceremony, at your house. In your yard. Garden. Molly says it's lovely."

"That's so kind of her. It's been a labor of love for a lot of years.

Of course a Pennsylvania garden wedding is fine with us if that's okay with you."

"Well, to be honest, Molly's our only daughter and we'd kind of been thinking of a big traditional wedding, you know, all the bells and whistles, here in Minnesota. But I guess that's not what kids are doing these days, and it's definitely not what Molly and Jamie want. They've been very clear: Simple, no fuss, at home. I guess we should be glad they didn't elope!" She gave a laugh that was almost a bark.

I smiled. Mina McDonald sounded like one of those people who wouldn't know pretense if it jumped up and bit her in the behind. Just based on the sound of her voice, that laugh, I imagined Molly's mom was one of those women who wouldn't flinch when the entire football team showed up for dinner, or when a tree fell through the roof. The kind of woman I'd actually like, not just because we were destined to become in-laws.

"I know what you mean," I said. "I have all sorts of ideas about Annie's wedding. Our daughter. Jamie's little sister. But I just haven't really given any thought to what the boys' weddings would look like."

"Boys are different, that's for certain. Molly has two brothers, so I speak from experience. But just because Jamie and Molly want simple and no fuss, I don't see why a backyard wedding can't be elegant. Can you?"

Uh oh. "Of course not. I mean, it can be very elegant. Classic. Lovely."

"Well, that's why I called. I thought we'd be on the same page about that. I wanted you to know that Danny and I will do whatever you want, or need. Caterers, tent, table, chair rental. All that stuff."

"Thank you. Once we know how many guests they'd like to invite..."

"I do have a favor to ask, though. Would you be able to send me some pictures of your yard? My little girl is getting married, and I'd like to start picturing the place where that's going to happen." Mina gave a gruff laugh, another bark, though her voice sounded suddenly thicker, as if she was having trouble swallowing.

"Of course. I'm out of town now but I think I have some pictures saved on my phone. I'll look and send them ASAP."

———

WHEN I WASN'T HELPING out at the Purple Onion, I spent the daylight hours, and even some of the after-dark ones, walking, sometimes with Trouble, sometimes alone. When the sun was shining, and that seemed like almost every day, I reveled in it. January passed, and then February, then it was March, and fully spring in the low country. Two-plus months, going on three, and I was beginning to realize that the longer I stayed in Charleston, the easier it was to be here. What did that mean?

One day when the daffodils were just starting to bloom, I called Joe at work. "Hey, I've been thinking about Doug. Have you heard from him?"

"Not lately." I heard the rustle of papers. I could picture Joe at his desk in the office at Daley-Hallowell Trucking. There was other background noise, muffled voices. Joe sounded distracted.

"I've texted him several times, trying to sound cheerful and positive, you know. Just 'touching base.' When he responds, it's one or two words. I'm worried about him."

"I can call him later," Joe said.

"I don't want him to think we're checking up on him. That we don't trust him."

"You want me to check up on him, right?"

"Well, he was arrested, for God's sake."

"He has a drinking problem."

"Did he admit to that? I mean, did he really say it like he understood the truth of it, or did he just say it to get you off his back? You know how he is."

"He said he was going to deal with it. That's what he told me. He's an adult, Cath, and it's something he has to do himself."

"I know that. But I can't help worrying.

252

Joe sighed. I could imagine him throwing his head back, the fingers of one hand rubbing the bridge of his nose, his eyes. "I'll try to call him tonight. See how he's doing."

"Let me know what he says, okay?"

"Of course."

After I hung up I googled Alcoholism. Then I googled addiction. Then AA.

I texted Annie.

> Me: Hey. How are you feeling?

> Annie: Great except for morning sickness sometimes. I'm in the third trimester. Not supposed to have morning sickness now. Guess I'm just lucky.

> Me: I had morning sickness all 9 months with each pregnancy. A pnut butter sandwich on plain white bread sometimes helped.

> Annie: Hmm. Will try that. My official due date is May 29. FYI

My first grandchild was coming in about two months. The disappointment I'd felt when I'd learned Annie was pregnant had somehow waned, replaced by this other, foreign, emotion. Anticipation laced with joy. And worry.

> Me: That will be a wonderful time to welcome a new Daley into the family. You'll have the summer to spend with the baby before you go back to work.

> Annie: It'll be a busy month.

> Me: That's okay. Busy and happy. Did you tell Jamie about the baby?

Annie: Yeah. Doug too. They were surprised.

Me: Well, they didn't know you were seeing anyone.

Annie: Do you know when you'll be coming home?

Me: No. No date yet.

Me: I'm scheduled to do the cooking demo at the end of the month. Sometime after that I'll head home.

I remembered the fear, the uncertainty I'd felt driving away from home and Langston when I'd come down here. Now I felt the same way thinking about going back.

Chapter Thirteen

> Helene: Hey. I'm coming to Charleston.
> Driving down. Will be there Thursday late
> afternoon. Get some wine.

The next day, I spoke to Evan at work.

"She's coming because she's worried about me. She didn't say that in so many words, but I'm reading between the lines."

"Because you left your husband in Pennsylvania." I'd been working at the Purple Onion now for three months, the slow season, post-holiday. Evan and I had had plenty of time to talk. Besides having an encyclopedic knowledge of salt cellars and bone china, and what I suspected had to be the largest collection of ascots in the low country, he was a fantastic listener. One of those people who you can tell empathizes wholly. He actually cried when I told him about Doug. And about Annie. Then a few days later he'd given me a pair of hand knit booties in a beautiful lavender color for the baby.

"Yep. She thinks I'm nuts. She doesn't understand why I came here."

"Of course you came to Charleston, it's Charleston."

———

THIS MORNING, her first here in the Holy City, as per Evan's directive, Hellie and I had spent a couple of hours walking, detouring through one of my favorite neighborhoods, then along King Street clear to the waterfront, to the Battery. Now we were sitting on a bench, watching people. The day was sunny, but cold, in the 50s maybe, though the sunshine was heavenly and I still thought I could feel it soaking into my bones. Maybe that was all that was wrong with me? A vitamin deficiency. Maybe after getting enough sun and vitamin D, I would feel like the old Cath, the Cath that baked and cooked and cleaned and painted and gardened and wrote cookbooks, then went to bed content each night. "I have an idea for another cookbook." I told her, my head tipped to the sun, eyes closed.

"That's awesome. What is it?"

"*Celebrations With Father*. Working title. And those would include weddings, receptions, baptisms."

"Perfect timing since you'll be hosting Jamie's wedding. You can take great pictures."

"If it's okay with Jamie and Molly. I don't want them to think I'm commercializing their wedding day. But I do think I can take pictures of the food, the tables and centerpieces, the flowers, that kind of stuff. Not necessarily of them."

"How cool would that be? To know your wedding was immortalized in a book?"

"I'm thinking I could use the same kind of pictures from the baptism of Annie's baby."

There was a pause. "What baptism? Annie's having a baby?"

"Yep. In May." I could feel Helene looking at me so I opened my eyes and told her the rest of the story.

The leaves of the palmetto trees around the park rattled faintly in the breeze. It smelled of water, ocean, fish and the spice of the green things that grew here that had no place in Pennsylvania. From here I could see the sun glinting off the surface of the water in the harbor in arcing shards so bright I had to squint when looking directly at them.

"Hel? What are you thinking?"

"I'm thinking a hundred things. That it's sad. Disappointing. That men suck. That marriage is a joke. Why do I wish I was in one? You're in one and you're still miserable."

"I'm not miserable."

"You're not? Then why are you here?"

I didn't—couldn't—answer that. "Everything is different now. Now that Annie is pregnant. She's going to have a baby."

"Different how?"

"Like all babies. They change life's priorities."

"You're going to be a grandmother."

"I am. I can't quite wrap my mind around it. I mean, I always expected to be one. Just didn't expect it this spring."

"Ohh, Annie," Helene said.

"Ohh, Annie," I echoed.

"What are you going to do?" It was a testament to how well I knew her that I understood the question wasn't about Annie or being a grandmother.

"I don't know. I'm going to have to go home. I have to get my garden ready for a wedding.

"Just for that? Or to stay permanently?"

"I don't know."

"Why not?"

I shrugged. "I feel happy here. But I don't feel it so surely that I'm certain all the anger and annoyance and resentment won't come flooding back as soon as I get home to Langston."

"How could anyone not be happy here? It's lovely. But have you considered that you may just be running away from your problems instead of dealing with them?"

"Of course. I'm sure that's what everyone thinks. But if I hadn't left Langston, I was going to be the pressure cooker that exploded.

The anger was going to eat me alive. The fact that I can feel this mad, just now, sitting here in this glorious place, with you, and can still feel this ugly inside, should tell you something about why I don't know what I'm going to do."

Helene nodded and looked back out toward the water. We sat there for a while not speaking, just watching the other people in the park, watching the sun shine on the water.

"I'll give you my lawyer's contact info, if you still want it."

———

THE DAY AFTER HELLIE LEFT, after walking miles and miles and talking and talking and talking I called Joe at work and Jerilyn answered. "Cath! Hey!" There was an awkward pause. "How're you?"

"I'm fine, thanks." And I did feel fine. "Is Joe there? I've tried his cell and it rings right through to voice mail. I'm assuming he left it at home. Again."

"Ahh. No, he's not here. He's..." there was another pause, "on his way to the airport. He's got an 11:30 flight."

I could imagine Jerilyn, who had worked at Daley Hallowell since she'd graduated from high school and the local vocational school, looking at the big clock that hung in the office.

"Oh," I said, my stomach and its contents feeling like they'd just turned to lead. I'd been distracted by time with Helene. I hadn't really thought about the date. So, Joe had decided to go on the cruise after all.

I could suddenly hear my blood pulsing through my eardrums and the sound of the refrigerator humming into the silence. I cleared my throat, swallowed past the lump of what? Betrayal? Sorrow? Because I should not care. I'd left Langston, and Joe, and come to Charleston. I had no right to be hurt. To feel betrayed.

"Oh, that's right. I wasn't thinking about the date," I said, clearing my throat again. I clicked my tongue, as if I were admonishing myself, knocked on the wood of the little table which made Trouble lift her head, her tail sweep the floor. *Duh. Silly me.* "Sorry to bother you."

"No problem. Do you want me to give him a message? He'll be checking in."

"That's okay. I'll catch him later." Joe was on a plane. On his way to Florida. To spend a week cruising the Caribbean on a chartered sailing yacht.

———

To: Cathleen Daley

From: Kandace Feinstein, Dutton Morrow Publishing

Subject: New book: CELEBRATIONS WITH FATHER

Cath!

LOVE LOVE LOVE this idea! Put together a brief proposal and I'll run it up the flagpole at our next editorial meeting. I can foresee some very poignant essays in this one: your first-born getting married in your garden. Readers LOVE your garden. Then becoming a grandmother for the first time. All good stuff. Weddings, baptisms...What other celebrations were you considering?

Kandace

To: Kandace Feinstein

From: Cathleen Daley

Subject: New book: CELEBRATIONS WITH FATHER

Kandace—

Besides weddings, baptisms/new baby and showers (bridal and baby), I was thinking first communions, graduations, birthdays, engagements, anniversaries. I'm sure I'll think of some others. Do you have suggestions?

Cath

. . .

To: Cathleen Daley
> From: Kandace Feinstein
> Subject: New book: CELEBRATIONS WITH FATHER
> It's too bad you're not Jewish, I have a bar mitzvah to plan and I'd love Cathleen Daley's ideas for that. Though of course if you were Jewish, these books would be COOKING FOR THE RABBI. Ha.
> New job? Retirement?
> Mazal tov,
> Kandace

To Kandace Feinstein
> From: Cathleen Daley
> Subject: New book: CELEBRATIONS WITH FATHER
> New life?

I LOVED THE BEACHES. I'd discovered several places to park and walk, to let the water and the waves, the feel of sand and icy salt water against my feet slowly fill me with a kind of peace. Sometimes the sand, away from the lapping waves, held the sun's warmth and on those days, I'd walk until I found a spot that called to me and then I would sit and just watch, almost mindlessly, the ocean, the clouds, the sea grass moving in the wind, let the briny tang of the ocean fill me up, to push out the ugliness that I hated, that felt like it could kill something inside me. Almost had killed something inside me.

Today, I had brought a huge beach towel and now Trouble lay beside me on it, panting gently, the two of us just watching the water and the other people who were out walking. There were more of those almost by the day, now that the weather was warmer. Somehow, the presence of other people, people I did not know, but who almost always smiled, nodded, and/or spoke a greeting, was comforting.

Joe was sailing around the Caribbean with his siblings and his mother—and a private chef and captain. Was it this same ocean? For maybe the first time since the trip had been proposed, I did not feel the hot flare of outrage. I still felt a small heat, a glow of anger, but it was manageable now. It did not feel consuming. Destructive. There was more ache now, now that I knew he'd gone. Hurt. My chest hurt.

But regardless of what I was feeling, I would have to go home soon. At least for a while. Next month at the latest. My garden would need a great deal of attention if it was going to be ready for a wedding in May. Jamie and Molly had decided on the next to last Saturday of the month. I sniffed, not quite a snort, almost smiling, recognizing that I thought of it that way: *my* garden. Hadn't I abandoned it, as well as Joe, when I came to Charleston? I'd had countless emails from Molly's mother, all of them with the subject line: WEDDING. In all caps. Was it still my garden?

Father J had given up on subtlety and had taken to asking me outright when I was coming home. He'd even told me he had gained weight, which I recognized as a shameless effort to play on my guilt.

Joe was on a private sailing yacht, with a private chef, sailing around the Caribbean. I sniffed again and Trouble looked at me, brown eyes full of love, her tongue lolling.

———

"How DID YOU KNOW? I mean, what made you decide to get help? For your addiction? If that's not too intrusive to ask."

"Sweetie. You can ask about anything. I have no shame left. And if my experience can save someone else, I'm happy to share. Spiritual awakening, carry the message, you know. Yada Yada." Evan waved one graceful hand. "I ended up in the hospital." He was rearranging napkin rings in an antique glass fronted case, the shelves inside lined with royal blue satin. I was polishing the glass, a white cloth in one hand, a spray can of glass cleaner in the other.

"What happened?"

"I'd gotten mugged."

"Here? In Charleston?"

"Yes," He looked at me without apology, though there was so much in his dark eyes that was vulnerable. He was such a gentle man. "I'd been at a bar, one of those establishments that cater to a particular clientele. I'm gay." It was part statement, part question.

"I know," I said. *It doesn't matter.*

"It wasn't just a mugging, strictly speaking. It was a seedy crowd, in a seedy part of the city, and I was an easy target. I was stoned."

Images flashed through my mind of a dark alley, dumpsters overflowing with sour garbage and the ever-present smell of the ocean and too sweet flowers. Evan, in cashmere or the velvet smoking jacket, the green cowboy boots, his beautiful smile, the cologne he wore that I'd come to associate with him, being beaten, crying out. "I'm so sorry."

"It wasn't the first time. My sister sent me to rehab. Wasn't the first time for that, either. But you know what they say," he smiled, and the regret and recrimination—the sorrow—beneath the self-deprecating words pulled at my heart "The fifth time is the charm."

"Oh, Evan."

"Now you understand why my sister doesn't trust me. She's angry."

"She loves you."

"Loves. Accepts. Not the same thing. But it's okay."

"I don't think Doug is doing drugs. I think he's just drinking. *Just* drinking." I winced. "I don't think he's one of those people who drinks every day, all day. I think he doesn't know when to quit. When he drinks, he drinks to excess. Maybe getting busted at Christmastime was a wake-up call? Or is that just the desperate wish of a worried mother?"

"If I tell you I have days when I give thanks for my dad's

Alzheimer's because he can't remember the worry I've caused him....
The curse of loving an addict. Worry. Stress."

"I feel like it's my fault. Like I was a bad parent. In some way, I
fell short."

Oh, sweetie. It's not that simple. Don't give up on him. That's my
most important piece of advice."

———————

"P<small>UDDING OR CUSTARD</small>?"

"Pudding."

"Bourbon butterscotch or chocolate?"

"Chocolate. Dark. Steak grilled or sautéed?"

"Sautéed. Or broiled."

I glanced up the ladder where Evan was perched, replacing a
light bulb in the hanging fixtures that looked like a cross between a
carburetor and a tennis racquet. I was trying to distract him. He
hated heights and the ceilings in the Purple Onion were high, twelve
or fourteen feet.

"Spam with a fried egg or tuna noodle casserole?"

He had me holding the ladder, not that I was going to do much
more than break his fall if he slipped or fell. At my last question,
Evan looked down, his hand with a death grip on the top of the
ladder.

"Don't make me laugh." He truly looked fearful.

"Sorry." I bit down on my grin. Evan was such a food snob. He
was also the biggest clothes horse I'd ever met. Today, he wore a
leather motorcycle jacket, over a white t-shirt with a short red scarf
tied around his neck, and the emerald green cowboy boots. After
more than three months of working at the Purple Onion, I didn't
think I'd seen him wear the same outfit twice, except for the cowboy
boots. Whatever he wore, he wore with pizazz.

I heard the bell that indicated the door opening at the front of the
store, and saw Evan glance in that direction from his perch at the top

of the ladder. From where I stood holding the thing, I couldn't see past a display of All Clad cookware and antique clocks on a gorgeous Art Deco buffet.

"We'll be with you in a moment," Evan called.

A voice answered. "No problem. Take your time." I knew that voice and my breath seemed to catch in my chest. Joe. *Joe is in Charleston? He's supposed to be in the Caribbean.* On The Cruise.

I saw him as he passed the cookware and the clocks, though he hadn't seen me yet. I watched him notice the poster, still up after my cooking demo, with the photo of me that I had decided just might be the best picture I'd ever taken. Joe actually stopped and looked at it. From where he stood, I couldn't see his face, only his back.

He was wearing his green Carhartt jacket, the one with the Daley-Hallowell logo embroidered on the chest. Of course he was. When he did turn, first looking at Evan at the top of the ladder, the thought struck me at once: He was familiar, he was *Joe*, but he looked old. The skin on his face looked loose, his hair grayer, his eyes more deep set. Had he aged in the time I'd been in Charleston, or was this how he'd looked when I'd left and I hadn't noticed?

How did I look to him?

I knew immediately when he noticed me. His face, his eyes, changed somehow, though I couldn't tell what he was thinking.

"Hey," he said.

The ladder wobbled a little bit and I realized I'd stopped holding it. Evan froze immediately.

"What are you doing here? I mean, surprise! I didn't know you were coming."

"Hi," Evan said, now safe and sound on the ground and studying Joe closely. He reached out to shake hands. "I'm Evan."

"Joe Daley," Joe said, shaking. "Cath's husband."

"I gathered. It's a pleasure to meet you. I've heard so much about you and your wonderful family. And seen pictures, too. I would have recognized you anywhere."

"Oh?" Joe said, his brows raised, and I could almost hear him thinking *I don't know who the hell you are.*

"Evan's the owner of the Purple Onion. My boss," I said, answering the question Joe didn't ask.

"Oh, yeah. Cath's told me about you, too."

"Here," I said, reaching to collapse the braces of the ladder and to press the two sides back together. "I can take the ladder back to the storeroom."

"Show me where?" Joe asked, folding the big ladder easily, never touching the shelves of cookware or the table displaying handcrafted table runners made from Alpaca wool from Peru.

"Oh, that would be lovely, thank you. Natalie is due in soon," Evan glanced at the big fat silver watch on his left wrist then at me and winked. Winked! "Take your time."

I wanted to laugh. Joe who stood patiently holding the ladder, studying me, his eyes full of emotion I couldn't quite read as Evan hurried off toward the front of the store.

"Hey," I said again and felt *something* in my chest. I didn't know whether to hug Joe, or scold him for showing up unannounced. Why was he here? I had almost expected it earlier, after I'd been here a week or two, but not now. Why did I feel that way? Because in the beginning I'd still felt tied to Langston, to Joe? And now, after all this time, I'd severed those ties?

"I'm surprised to see you. You didn't tell me you were coming...What are you doing here?" *You're supposed to be cruising the freakin' Caribbean.*

"I came to see you. What do you think I'm doing here?" He said that with a smile, a Joe smile, that—mostly—took the sting out of the words. "You want to show me where this goes?" He hefted the ladder a little.

"Oh, sorry! Sure. This way." It required some care to maneuver the long ladder past displays and tables and shelves, but he moved easily, carrying the ladder as if it weighed next to nothing, as if it wasn't twelve feet long.

The storeroom was through a doorway at the back of the store. I pointed to where the ladder was kept and waited while Joe leaned it up against the wall. There followed one of those awkward moments when two people look at each other and neither knows what to do. Hug? Shake hands? At the same time, I had the thought: he's my husband, it's *Joe*. Joe.

He pulled me close then. Hugged me. I could feel his hand pressing against the back of my head, holding it tight to his shoulder. It felt familiar and foreign at the same time but I couldn't let go and enjoy it. I could feel myself stiffening and knew immediately that Joe noticed. "I've missed you," he said.

Tears suddenly, unexpectedly, burned behind my eyes and I blinked them away, until I could smile at him, until I no longer felt like crying. *Where did that come from?* "I thought you were away…" I cleared my throat, couldn't say it. Even now, I could not mention Lillian's cruise.

"I was. I'm on my way home."

I led the way out of the storeroom and into the tiny office that Evan kept in the back of the space. It was barely big enough for the mahogany table and the leather wing chair, every inch of the walls hung with royal blue colored velvet drapes that Evan had bought at an estate sale and half a dozen old oil paintings of horses or hunt scenes, all in wide, ornate, antique gilt frames. He had a thing for horse paintings. Leaning against one wall was another of the posters Evan had had made from the photo he'd taken of me to promote the cooking demo.

Joe stopped in the doorway and took in the entirety of the office. I grinned. "I know. 'Go big or go home' is his motto. He's partial to velvet."

"Nice picture." Looking at the poster. In it, I was wearing a black turtleneck sweater, my usual winter "uniform" but Evan had accessorized me: a blue scarf the color of my eyes wrapped around my neck; he'd posed me in front of the Baccarat display, which caught the light in brilliant slivers and blurred what was beyond it. I looked sophisticated, and elegant, as much as I ever did and certainly more than I ever felt. My hair shone and my skin looked smooth and creamy against the black of the turtleneck. The blue scarf was the perfect accent. The fact that Evan had brought it from home, that it was one from his own personal collection, said more about his fashion sense than mine. "Thanks. Evan took it to advertise my cooking demo."

"How was that?"

Had I really not spoken to Joe since then? What did that say about our relationship, or my commitment to it?

"It was good. Great, I guess. We sold a bunch of cookbooks and even had people ask about the new one—that's not even out yet. Evan had a big day in the store, sold six KitchenAids in one two-hour window. He's still talking about it. Apparently that's never happened before, even when Emeril was here."

"Wow. That's cool." I knew Joe had no idea who Emeril was. I was pretty sure he didn't know what a KitchenAid was, either.

But he was trying and that touched me. "There were no snafus, which was my big fear. I imagined the worst. I've never cooked in front of such a big audience before. There were thirty-two people watching at one point, and the local television station filming."

"Nice."

"It was a good experience, but I don't think I want to do it full-time. It felt too much like work, cooking in front of an audience. "

"It's good you did it then, and found out you didn't like it. Knowing what you don't like is as important as knowing what you do."

I shot him a look. Was he trying to say something? "Yeah, I suppose. It was good publicity for me, for my next book. Kandace is happy, thrilled, actually."

Did Joe remember who Kandace was?

"I wish I could have been here."

He stood leaning up against the door that closed off the office. It was an antique, too, it had come from a theatre here in the city that had been torn down. The word MEN was painted in gold block letters in the center of the frosted glass panel. It was just the kind of joke Evan liked to poke at himself. He had a very self-deprecating sense of humor that hid, I knew, vulnerability and a lot of pain. It made me feel protective of him. There was a neat stack of papers on the desk which I carefully slid away from the edge so I could prop there. I didn't know what to do with my hands so I wedged them under my thighs.

I studied Joe. The Carhartt jacket and the button-down shirt and jeans were his uniform. The cap he'd had been wearing when he'd first come into the store, a navy Penn State baseball one, he'd taken off, and I assumed it was now tucked in his coat pocket. Joe was a stickler for guys taking off their hats indoors. This afternoon, without his, I could see he needed a haircut. But he looked soo Joe. A little bit redneck, not that he saw himself that way or would chose to change even if he did. There was something about Joe that made him *noticeable*, though. I had never been able to put my finger on what it was that made me think that. It had drawn me to him all those years ago when I'd met him at Penn State. He was comfortable in his own skin, always had been, so much so that he never doubted himself. He saw the rest of the world in terms of how far off his center they were.

"Can you get away for a bit? We could go get some coffee? Or I can come back—?"

"No, no. I can leave. We're not super busy today and someone else is due to replace me shortly. I'm sure Evan won't mind if I leave a little early. There's a coffee shop down the block. Let me just go tell him."

———

"I wish I'd known you were coming." *Aren't you supposed to be on a sailing yacht somewhere in the Caribbean?*

He shrugged. "I wasn't sure you'd want to see me."

"Of course I want to see you. I wish you'd told me... It feels a little awkward. I'm just surprised."

"Because your husband showed up?" He studied my face for a moment, and I noticed again how his skin seemed to have aged. He looked thinner, the bones of his face a bit more pronounced.

"I thought you were on the cruise. With your family." I would never again say that term, *your family,* and not hear irony, mockery, scorn in my head.

A look of surprise passed over his face. "I told you I wasn't going."

"I know. But I thought..." I shrugged, waved a hand. "I called your office a few days ago and Jerilyn said you were on your way to the airport."

"Yeah. To go see Doug. I went to Kansas City, Cath. To see our son."

"You went to visit Doug?" Joe had discouraged me from going and then he went himself?

"You told me you were worried about him. Not that you had to tell me. I was worried, too. "

I didn't know what to say, could hardly process it. Joe, who was generally so oblivious about the world beyond his own, he wouldn't remember from morning 'til night things I told him about myself, about our kids, about his mother. "How was he? What did he say?"

Joe shook his head. "Nervous. Guilty."

"Oh, no."

"Sure. I texted him. Gave him my itinerary. But no question he knew I was there to check up on him. "What did you say?"

"I told him we were worried about him, have been for a while, and that the DUI at Christmas pretty much nailed it down."

"What did he say?"

"He cried."

"Oh, God." I could feel the ache up through my chest into my throat. I pressed my fist against my mouth.

"He promised he had stopped drinking, had joined a gym."

"Do you believe him?"

Joe grimaced. "I wanted to. Until I got to his apartment and found a bottle of vodka in the freezer. He swore he just forgot it was in there, and he dumped it down the sink. But who knows? This is Doug we're talking about."

Doug was a master at saying what he knew you wanted to hear, so you stopped worrying, or being angry, all the while doing whatever it was he wanted to do. I knew he did that, knew in my gut when he was playing me, but I couldn't stop wanting, needing, to believe him. To believe *in* him.

The little coffee shop was getting busier. Glancing outside, I noticed the sidewalks were becoming more crowded with pedestrians, the street with traffic. There was that renewed buzz of activity that came at the end of the workday as people started home. I felt exposed here, having this conversation in a room where people could overhear. I looked at my watch. "I didn't realize it was getting so late. Are you hungry?"

"Sure. I didn't know if you already had plans...?"

"I don't. Other than taking Trouble for a walk. We could take her to the beach then have dinner?"

I had walked to The Purple Onion, so Joe drove us back to my apartment. As I climbed the wrought-iron staircase, digging in my purse for the keys, the thought struck me. Was Joe thinking he would stay here with me? Was he staying overnight? He hadn't told me his plans. But I only had one bed. The thought nearly froze me in my tracks.

He followed me up and into the apartment. Light filtered down from the skylight and at this time of day, this time of year, through the tiny window beside the bed. Trouble was almost always sleeping when I returned; she was sleeping now. The sound of voices and footsteps hadn't woken her.

"Hey, girl," I called, dropping my purse and keys on the table next to my computer and the stack of pages of recipes. "Look who's here."

"Hey, girl." Joe said as Troub struggled to get to her feet, her whole body becoming part of the tail wag. "How ya doin'?" Joe squatted down and rubbed her ears the way she loved. The dog's tail wagged harder, if possible. Joe didn't say anything, didn't comment about the apartment, though I noticed him taking it all in.

My home, albeit a tiny one. "It's small," I said. "But I don't need a lot of space."

"I didn't say anything."

"You didn't have to."

We drove my van to the beach, the park I'd found on the Isle of Palms, my favorite of all the beaches I'd explored. This afternoon, it was sunny, though it was cooler here than it had been in the city and I was glad I'd pulled on a sweater under my jacket. The tide was out, the beach wide and flat, the high tide mark far from where the water lapped gently now, and littered with a tangle of seaweed and shells. I took a deep breath, thinking I'd never tire of the smell of the sea. Gulls screamed overhead, while others stalked or ran along the edge of the tide wrack, searching for food.

"When did we stop trusting him? Doug?" I asked. "God, that makes me feel like a horrible mother, even thinking that. To say it out loud feels reprehensible."

"Because he's played us before. And I told him that that shit won't cut it this time."

"Oh, Joe. We're his parents, we're supposed to believe in him."

"I told him that he's got to get his act together. Going to the gym isn't enough."

"Do you really think that? That's so not like you." I was—literally —astonished. "Sorry. I don't mean that to sound like I'm criticizing."

"What's not like me?"

"You're all about the path of least resistance. Always have been. If Doug promised to get it together, you'd believe him, because that's the easy thing to do."

I didn't mean to be cruel or snarky. It just wasn't the time to beat around the bush. Joe's mouth seemed to tighten a little, though he didn't disagree with me.

Trouble broke into a trot, suddenly, as if she might catch a gull that was scooting along the sand ahead of her. The bird squawked and took to the air.

"I told him he needed to get help. And I was there to make sure he did. It was serious, his drinking, and we were worried, and we weren't going to fuck around."

I almost wanted to laugh at how firm, how stern, Joe sounded. That was so not Joe. It wasn't funny, but for some reason it loosed the tension I didn't know I'd been feeling.

"We don't know that he's an *alcoholic*. Maybe he just hasn't grown up, maybe it's stupid kid stuff. Maybe he just needs to rein himself in. And having me show up and lay it out for him will be enough."

"Maybe... Maybe that's wishful thinking."

Joe shrugged again. There was a piece of driftwood stuck in the sand just in front of where we were walking and he bent down to pull it up. He smacked it against the side of his leg, then tossed it for Trouble, who loped slowly off after it, tail wagging.

"Maybe it is. But I don't think we're ready to admit him to some kind of rehab. I don't think he's that far gone. It's like he just doesn't know how to moderate. Anyway, I don't think I'm ready for that, yet."

"I know what you mean. But I think it was good you went out there. Maybe that kind of reality check is what he needs. Maybe that will do the trick." Though somehow, in my gut, I didn't quite believe it. Doug had gotten behind the wheel of a car and driven drunk. He'd gotten *arrested*. A DUI. My son had a *mug shot*. Those thoughts still made my stomach clench and bile push up into my chest.

Trouble came back holding the driftwood, her tail wagging. Joe took it gently from her mouth and tossed it again. "Jesus. I thought the hard part was over. Once they left home, I thought we were on the downhill slide."

"I don't think there's any downhill. I think it's all uphill from the time they're born."

Trouble watched Joe throw the piece of driftwood again but

didn't chase it. We walked for a while without talking, the dog between us. I crossed the hard-packed sand left by the wash of tide when it turned and found a spot to sit. Joe sat beside me, and Trouble dropped down beside him panting gently.

Later, we went back downtown for dinner, to one of the restaurants I had heard about, and had on my bucket list to try, even though it was touristy and crowded. After we had ordered drinks, we both looked around the room, which was white and simple with colorful art on the walls, and busy with other diners, and then, awkwardly at each other.

I still couldn't quite believe that he was here. I had gotten into a routine of being by myself, of life on my own.

"Trouble is really slowing down," he finally said.

"She is. I took her to the vet last week. She was having a hard time getting up and down the stairs. Diagnosis was old age. Arthritis. She has a couple of lumps—cysts—but they're benign, and normal for thirteen-year-old dogs. She got a prescription for doggie aspirin but nothing else."

"Fourteen," Joe said.

"No. She'll be thirteen this fall."

"Fourteen. We got her the year Jamie broke his collarbone. That was the year he played pee wee ball."

I stared at him. Was he right? Joe remembered something as insignificant as the year we got the dog? Remembered something as trivial as Jamie's broken collarbone? He didn't remember for the eight or nine hours of his workday that we'd been invited to a friend's for dinner. I was astonished that I'd short-changed Trouble a year, seven in doggie calculations, and even more incredulous that it was Joe who had it right. "Oh, my gosh. I've been thinking she was thirteen."

He shrugged. "Time flies."

"It does," I said before the awkwardness descended again.

"Mom dinged up the car the other day. Backed into a light pole at the grocery store. Which was the straw that broke the camel's back. I took her keys. She's now dependent on Jimmy's Taxi Service." Jimmy

O'Keefe ran a sort of taxi and delivery service in Langston and the surrounding area, largely hauling seniors who could no longer drive to doctor's appointments or shopping.

"Or Joe's Taxi Service."

"Yeah. Or that."

"That wasn't an easy conversation to have."

"No. But it was time. She's not happy with me, but she'll get over it."

I studied him. This was not the old Joe. Well...it was, but it wasn't. The old Joe would have waited for someone else to make that decision about Lillian driving, to have that conversation, for the decision to be taken out of his hands entirely. "You're right. It was past time. She shouldn't have been driving for a while now. She could have hurt someone, or herself."

He shrugged again. "She wasn't happy that I didn't go on the cruise, either. Couldn't understand why I didn't since you were off in Charleston, anyway. But I told you I wasn't going to go."

I suddenly felt tears press against the back of my eyes. Unexpected tears; I wasn't even feeling emotional. Where did tears come from?

"When are you coming home, Cath? *Are* you coming home? How long is a *sabbatical*?" He used my word. He smiled, conciliatorily, and reached for my hands across the table, held them on either side of the candle there. "I'm glad you had this break, if it made you happy, if you found whatever it was you were looking for. But hasn't it been long enough? If you really like it here, we can come down again, vacation here. Spend a couple of weeks here together. Hell, we can even look for a place down here, a condo or something. But I want you to come home now. I miss you. We're going to be grandparents. I didn't think I was going to do that alone. I don't want to do that alone." He shook his head and his grip on my hands tightened. "I want us to be grandparents together. Come home, Cath."

I didn't know what to say to that. I couldn't form a response. The plea was still hanging in the air while I led the way to Waterfront

Park after we'd finished dinner, because it was beautiful, even at night. We stopped and watched the pineapple fountain which was lit; we could see lights across the harbor in, and on, the mammoth cruise ship anchored there. The sky was empty of stars or moon, and it was dark and vast and infinite. The air smelled of the sea, as it always did, if you stopped and noticed, and there was that constant sense for me of the ocean waiting, looming, powerful, as if my body reacted to the pull of the tide. I took a deep breath, to draw the smell of the ocean into my lungs and caught a whiff of something earthy. It was not Langston, there was no angst here, no anger, and that made me feel absurdly happy. A kind of happy that didn't have anything to do with anyone else, that was somehow apart from the rest of the world. Part of me resented Joe for showing up and bringing reminders of angst and anger with him.

Home. Was Pennsylvania, Langston, still my home? I felt like I'd made a home of sorts here. And one that gave me a great deal of pleasure. One that was absent the bitter, resentful, corrosive Cath I had become in Pennsylvania. Did I want to go back to Langston permanently? Did I want the life I'd had there? Could it ever be the same again? Would the anger, the bitterness I had been feeling before I left creep back and fill me again?

"What are you thinking?" Joe asked and I realized I had been staring off in the direction of Africa for a while without speaking.

"Thinking about why I came here. About all the thinking I've done since I got here. Ha. Thinking about thinking."

"You mean why you came to Charleston as opposed to say, Paducah or Shreveport? Or why you left in the first place?"

I glanced at him. "Why I left in the first place. Why I was angry."

"Why were you so angry? I still don't understand that." He shook his head.

I didn't answer that. "How is Diana doing? Pregnancy can't be easy at her age. I should have called her, or at least sent her a text or a note."

"She lost the baby. About a month ago."

"Oh, no." I felt the hurt of those words in a place deep inside. I also knew what it felt like to lose a child. Pat had not wanted a baby. What was he feeling? I was surprised he hadn't let me know. "Is she okay?"

"She was pretty devastated, I guess."

"I'm sure she was. She's not young, I mean, it's not like she can just try again. How about Pat? Is he okay?"

Joe shrugged. "Who knows? I texted him. He texted back, but it was pretty short. He's still living in some hotel downtown." Joe shoved his hands in his coat pockets and looked out toward the cruise ship. "I figured you knew."

I looked at him. "No. I didn't know."

"Yeah, well. I think Di has read the writing on the wall. No baby, at least not one of her own. Sounds like her marriage is circling the drain. She went on the cruise. Probably good for her to get away." He shrugged.

"Yeah. Probably." No doubt Diana had needed some recovery time, and surely there would be no better place to spend that than on a sailing yacht in the Caribbean, in the sun, surrounded by family who loved her. I didn't want to talk about Pat and Di. Didn't want to think about them.

There were the sounds of water moving, of the fountain splashing, of the palmettos rustling high over our heads and of the pebbles in the paths under our feet. Joe and I talked about Annie, and about Corey, and our first grandchild, and I thought the sting of disappointment about that, not about the baby specifically, but about the circumstances of his or her birth, was starting to diminish for Joe. I couldn't not think about Nora and feel the ache that accompanied any conscious thoughts of my first daughter. The ache that had become so familiar I couldn't remember not knowing it.

Joe must have read my mind because he said, "I drove out to the cemetery the other day."

"You did? What for?"

He looked at me oddly. "I do go out there, you know. I just don't like talking about it. Don't see the point."

"*The point?* The point could be that I would like knowing you haven't forgotten her." He never mentioned Nora. Certainly he had never told me he visited our daughter's grave. Or told me about that fence.

"She was my daughter, too. I haven't forgotten her. Could never forget her."

"I wish I'd known that."

"Why? Would it have made a difference? About how angry you were. When you left?"

Life felt a little like a game of Jenga, where you had to pull the blocks out one by one without the tower collapsing. It was impossible to know which block would be the one responsible for the fall. "I don't know," I finally answered.

"I'm sorry," he said. "Sorry that we lost her. That I couldn't save her. That I apparently couldn't save our marriage."

I clenched my fists so tightly inside my own coat pockets I knew the skin of my palms would be broken by my nails. Again, I couldn't bring myself to respond, but what I wanted to say was *Me, too! Me. Too.* I'd wondered if the despair I'd felt upon learning I was pregnant had been the reason Nora had died. Karma's a bitch. Who said that? Was that from a movie? This pain, too—the questions, the doubt, the guilt—were all familiar.

"I don't think the reason I was so angry had anything to do with Nora. I was angry at you. With you. So angry I felt sick inside. It was everything you did—do. How you chewed your food, how you fell asleep in the chair every night, how you snore. The way you never fold your towel, the way you leave the coffee pot on—every morning, every single, frickin' morning—even though you know I don't drink coffee. It was making me wild. Bitter. I couldn't stop it. It was like thirty years of anger was eating me alive. I wanted to hurt you. I mean it. I laid in bed some nights listening to you breathe and I wanted to hit you with the lamp. I hated how I was feeling. I hated you."

He flinched. Oh, not truly, physically, but emotionally; I could see him react. I was sorry for that, but he needed to *understand*. I watched him swallow, wordless, and turn his gaze out to the harbor where the cruise ship sat like a small country.

Finally, Joe said, "Wow. Hate. That's pretty strong." There was a hollow sound in his voice that told me he was hurt.

"I hated how I felt more. I had to get away."

He sniffed. "Doesn't bode well for a reconciliation." I sensed him digging his hands deeper into his pockets.

I wanted to say *I know*. But I wasn't sure. Did I want to reconcile? Did I want my old life back? More importantly, could I go back to that life and not end up bitter and angry again?

Joe muttered, "Some of that stuff I can change, I can fold the fucking towels. I can turn off the coffee pot. I probably won't stop snoring. I won't chew any differently. I am who I am, Cath."

"I know," I said. What I meant was *I know you can't change. You shouldn't have to. I don't want you to change.*

"I want you to be happy," he said.

"I want you to be happy, too." *That's why I left. I wasn't going to make you happy if I stayed. I was going to smother you with your own pillow.*

"But can you be happy with me? That's the twenty-four-thousand-dollar question."

After that we didn't speak much. By mutual agreement, we went back to the van, and I drove us home to the carriage house apartment.

Joe dug the keys to his rental car from his pocket, had them in his hand by the time I pulled to the curb. He jiggled the keys, but made no move to get out. This was the moment I had been dreading. "Thanks for dinner," I said.

"You're welcome. It was great."

"Do you want to come up? I have some beer. I don't have anything else. No other liquor, I mean."

"Do you want me to come up?"

"Is that your way of asking if I want you to stay here?" I smiled to show I was joking. Sort of.

He didn't answer, but he didn't look at me either, just followed me up the iron staircase again, waited while I unlocked the door, then followed me into the apartment.

"It's just a little awkward," I said, dropping my purse and keys on one of the bistro chairs at the table. "You're my husband."

"For thirty years. Almost. In five days. But I know what you mean," Joe said. He cleared his throat, pulled out the other bistro chair, and sat down, but he left his jacket on, though it was unzipped. I thought that was a little like splitting the difference; he was here, but he wasn't necessarily committed to staying. Which was good. I didn't know if I wanted him to stay. I wasn't ready to give up my alone-ness.

I hung my coat on the hook beside the fridge, kicked off my shoes, and sat on the edge of the bed. Trouble, lying in her regular spot, on the rug at the foot of the bed, where sun from the skylight cast a warm square when the sun was shining, lifted her head and her tail wagged, but she didn't get up. I looked at Joe. He wanted to talk, that was obvious.

I don't know if I want you to stay here. "The anger that was eating me alive is gone. But the absence of it feels *tenuous*. Fragile. I'm afraid to trust it."

"Why? I mean, why is the anger gone? Because you're away from Langston? From me?" He propped his arms on the tiny table, picking up the pen I'd left there by the stack of manuscript pages, fiddling with it, without really looking at it.

I looked at him, conscious of how my words would injure, but wanting, needing, to be truthful. "Yes."

"But why? Not because I don't turn off the coffee pot or hang up my towel?"

"I honestly don't know. I don't understand it myself. I just felt overwhelmed. I was drowning in anger. I couldn't get ahead of it." I took a deep breath. Realized my hands were clenched and made a conscious effort to relax. Was he listening? Was he *hearing* me?

"I knew in my gut somehow that if I could get away, someplace the anger wasn't fueled all the time, I could get past it, all the resentment, the rage. It wasn't just anger. It was *rage*."

"What were you so mad about? The way I see it, nothing changed, life was the same as it had always been, and then suddenly you decided you were too pissed off to stay and live it anymore." Now he stopped, breathed; I could see him collect himself.

"I know."

"So you're happy here, and you've done a lot of soul-searching, but you don't know why you were so angry, or if you want to come home." It was a statement, not a question.

"The stupid cruise. It was like that destroyed something rational inside me. I don't think I even realized how angry your mom has made me, all these years. She's always been a part of our lives, probably more than she should have. But I wasn't really angry about that, it was just what we did. What she did. How we lived. I took the bad with the good. But when your siblings, or your mom—whoever—dreamed up the idea of a cruise that was for 'family' only that didn't include me, or our kids, or any of the other spouses or grandchildren? All of a sudden, I couldn't *contain* the anger."

"I—" Joe started to speak but I cut him off.

"I know. You didn't have anything to do with that, you didn't plan it, you didn't go on it. But that doesn't matter." I paused, some part of me weighing how talking about it made me feel. Was I still angry? Was the bitterness still there? Maybe, maybe a little bit.

"I'm sorry," Joe said.

"Yeah, me, too."

"In hindsight, I wish I'd have told Laura and Mark to go fuck themselves when they brought up the idea. I was just thinking about Mom, didn't think about how it would make you feel."

Clueless? Did that hurt? Still? Yes. A little. But it felt like hurt, disappointment, not fury. I didn't say anything and I saw the exact moment Joe realized how that sounded: *I was thinking about Mom, not you....*

"Fuck."

I just raised my eyebrows and let a moment of silence say what I didn't have to. "You're lying to yourself about that. You knew it was going to hurt me, you knew it was just wrong. It's why you didn't tell me about it. You waited until Laura and your mom brought it up."

I thought he'd deny it. "You're right."

I tried to decide if that was Joe practicing some form of Socratic selling on me. Patronization as olive branch. "I think I can separate it from you, us, now. The cruise. My feelings about it. The anger. *Mostly.* But it's changed how I think of my life, our life. And more importantly, I think it's changed how I will choose to live my life from now on."

"What does that mean?"

"I'm not sure exactly. I just know that I don't want to ever feel that way again."

"I understand. I mean I'm trying to understand. I am. I don't want you to feel that way again." He rubbed his forehead. "It wasn't easy for me when you left. I was pretty pissed off myself. You just frickin' left. The day of the Christmas party. I was mad and hurt and embarrassed. Humiliated. Which just made me madder. I wanted to understand how you were feeling but I couldn't stop thinking *my wife left me.* Of course it didn't help that everybody knew it. At first, everybody wanted to know where you were, but then everyone stopped asking and that was almost worse, because then I knew they'd all been talking. I could tell they were all looking at me and feeling sorry for me."

Joe took a deep breath, pursed his lips. Finally looked down at the pen in his hands. "I'm sorry. About everything."

"Me, too."

"I'm not staying here tonight," he said suddenly. "I want you to want to be with me." Joe glanced away, uncomfortable, and then back again. "Like that, and in other ways. Just being together. I want that if you want it. I honestly want you to be happy, Cath. I didn't mean to push myself on you by coming here. But I wanted to see you. I wanted to talk."

"Thank you. For that."

We looked at each other for a moment and it was still awkward.

"I'll see you in the morning? My flight is at lunchtime." Joe stood up and pushed the chair back under the table. I stood, too. "But I'll come over before I go to the airport, okay?" And he walked over to the bed where I stood. He leaned down and kissed me on the cheek, brought both hands up to hold my head so he could look into my face, my eyes. "I love you," he said. But he didn't wait to see if I would respond, just squeezed gently, once, so that I could feel the strength in him, and left, his footsteps pounding down the iron staircase.

Chapter Fourteen

O n the morning of our anniversary, I had two text messages
when I woke up.

> Annie: Happy anniversary, Mom! I love you.

> Joe: Happy anniversary. Wish we were
> celebrating together. I love you.

Thirty years. Thirty years was a lifetime. A generation. I couldn't
help but think how much had changed since this day last year. *This
date.*

Last year, we'd celebrated the same way we did most years: Joe
went to work, I went to the rectory, cooked for Father J, grocery
shopped, did laundry, ran errands. It was a day like every other day. I
would have made Joe's favorite dinner: spaghetti with vodka sauce.
He would have given me a card. He usually, but not always, bought
me flowers. Nothing that took much imagination for either of us. We
marked the day, but in a casual, almost indifferent way. Sometimes
we'd talk about our wedding day, each of us recalling different things.

To Joe:

> Me: Happy anniversary to you, too.

To Annie:

> Me: Thanks, baby girl! What are you doing today? How are you feeling?

But there was no immediate response. Annie was likely at work, had probably texted before she started. She was almost eight months along now. I was going to be a grandmother in a matter of weeks.

I had asked Evan for the day off today and on this, my 30th anniversary day, I was going to the beach, I was taking a book. I was going to wear one of my new swimming suits. I was going to savor the sun, the weather, the ocean, the smells, the sounds of waves. Today was the kind of day I'd pictured when I left home in December.

Joe's mother and his siblings were in the middle of their Caribbean cruise. Would I think about them? Not intentionally, though by default because obviously I would think about Joe, and because I was here. Without them and The Cruise, there was little doubt I would be at home in Langston, probably buying onion sets for the garden, maybe raking up winter leaf litter from the yard, and making something special for dinner.

My phone dinged again. Another text.

> Helene: Happy anniversary. Wasn't it just yesterday that we were twenty-somethings wearing chiffon and lace and laughing about life?

> Me: Seems like another lifetime. I guess it was.

> Helene: What are you doing today?

> Me: Just heading to the beach. It's supposed to be 85 degrees!

Helene: Great way to spend an anniversary.
Except that you're spending it alone.

Me: It's okay. I have Trouble. So I'm not
alone.

Helene: Not what I meant. Wish I was
there.

Me: Me too.

Despite what I told Helene, I was not planning to take Trouble to the beach. It was going to be too hot, too sunny, during the middle of the day. The dog would be much happier here, in the cool shade, with the AC. It was hard to believe she was going to be fourteen. In some ways, relative to other milestones, fourteen seemed like a small number. Today, I was married more than twice that many years. But I could hardly remember not having Trouble, could hardly remember when she had not been part of the family. In some ways, Trouble had been the constant. She had certainly been a comfort to me here, in Charleston.

The rest of my life might be changing, but you're here. You're the steady one. You're my grace. My succor. Better than any rosary.

The dog just smiled at me, tail swishing against the rug, as if she knew what I was thinking. "Bye, Girl. Hold the fort. I'll see you in a bit."

When I got back from the beach five hours later, my skin tingling pleasantly from sun and salt water, my mind pleasantly empty, I opened the door of the apartment, feeling the draft of cold air, and saw Trouble right away. The dog was on her side, still in the same spot under the skylight where she'd been when I'd left this morning. I knew immediately by how still she was, that she was dead.

I sat and stared at her body. At the soft pale fur, the floppy ears, one of them scarred from where it had been torn, once, long ago, when she was hardly more than a puppy. The fat tail, almost a weapon, it was so thick and heavy, motionless now. I felt a knot deep in my throat, a lump that seemed to keep me from taking a deep breath.

Ohhh, Trouble.

I didn't know what to do, except to call Joe. But before I could push all the right buttons on my cell phone, I'd thought, *what is Joe going to do?*

You can go home again. I was. Going.

And I simply dragged my suitcases from the closet, lump still hard in my throat. I packed—clothes, computer—and carried everything down to the van. While I was there, I pulled out the old plaid blanket I kept in the back, shook it, spread it open. Then I climbed the iron staircase to the apartment, feeling the ache in my chest like a bruise.

Trouble was heavy—*dead weight,* the phrase flashed through my mind and I had to bite my lip to keep from giving voice to the hurt. I had to get down on my knees and work my hands under her neck and back. It was a struggle to stand, but I did it, my arms around her ribs, under her front legs, one hand clasping the wrist of the other arm. I could smell the familiar doggy smell, and feel the coarseness of her hair coat, the hair that had collected in wisps and clumps under every piece of furniture in the house, and stuck like magnets to dark pants and dark sweaters. It was all I could do to carry the body down the iron staircase and around the side of the building, feeling every uneven brick under my feet, and get her to the back of the van. All I could think about was her smile, her golden-brown eyes so full of love and trust. After laying her on the blanket, I wrapped the fleece around her, covering her. Then I made one last trip upstairs to close the windows and turn off the AC, grab my purse, and lock the door.

I drove all night. Somewhere in northern West Virginia, when the sun was just a hint at the edge of the horizon, I felt the ache in my chest becoming something more, something I couldn't swallow down, or hold in. When they came, I couldn't stop the tears, and I had to pull off the interstate and let them come.

I don't know how long I sat there, the occasional semi truck and car passing me to the left and making the van rock, while I cried a kind of cry that made my eyes burn and my throat hurt. Finding a linty, crumpled tissue in my pocket, I finally blew my nose and dropped my head back on the seat rest and closed my eyes. A sob escaped my mouth, and another, but eventually, I thought the crying jag was over. I wasn't sure I could lift my head or hold my hands on the steering wheel, I felt that wrung out. The GPS on my phone said I'd be home in a little over two hours. It wasn't quite 5:00 a.m.

Things were greening up in Pennsylvania, though the color seemed weak, lackluster, compared to Charleston, even the yellow cloud of forsythia at the corner of the yard, and the crabapple beside the driveway, blooming now. My white house looked just as I remembered it, stately but not grand, friendly somehow, window glass gleaming in the early morning, the deep green shutters looking almost black. Charleston green—I'd picked that color years and years ago without ever having been to Charleston. Looking at those shutters now made me smile and feel oddly sad at the same time. There was no sign of Joe's Christmas tree in the center of the front yard.

His truck was parked in front of the garage and there was a dark gray SUV in the driveway that I didn't recognize at first. Kansas license plates. And then I realized with a jolt: Doug's car. Doug was here? Since when? What had happened?

The kitchen door was unlocked when I turned the knob; Joe looked up from where he sat at the island, an orange coffee mug and a cereal bowl and a magazine in front of him. Some part of me took in the clutter on the counter, the laundry basket on the floor filled with a jumble of clothes, the disorderly stack of newspapers on a chair, the way the sunlight came through the window over the sink, and the familiar smell of the house: coffee, old plaster, maybe bacon.

Emotions passed over Joe's face before he could shield them: Surprise. Shock. Was he happy? I couldn't tell.

"Cath! I didn't know you were coming." He stood, almost

knocking over the stool he'd been sitting on, and came to the door. He moved and I moved at the same time so that we almost bumped into each other. I thought he might hug me, but he stepped back before there was any contact.

"I didn't know until yesterday."

"You should have called or texted. You drove all night?" He glanced over my shoulder, taking in the van.

"Trouble died," I said and felt again the burn of tears behind my eyes. I'd thought there weren't any tears left.

"Oh, geez," he said and then pulled me into a hug. "Where is she?"

"In the van. I brought her home to bury her here," I said, and then realized that it sounded like the only reason I came home was because the dog died. "I needed to come home. There's so much to do...." That still didn't sound right. I opened my mouth to say more, to try to explain, but there was nothing else to say. Not now.

"You should have let me know you were coming." He started to shuffle some of the papers and magazines on the island, pushed them out of the way. I looked around the kitchen some more. It was messy, but not as messy as I'd thought it would be. The little porcelain Santa that I always put on the windowsill over the sink for the holidays was still there.

"I thought you'd be at the office. I was going to wash my face, brush my teeth before I called. Where's Doug? Why is he home? What happened?"

"He lost his job. Was drinking at work. His boss caught him. Fired him on the spot." The muscles in Joe's jaw clenched. "A month ago."

"But you were just there last week!"

"He didn't tell me. Lied, actually. Never said a word about getting canned. He apparently thought about getting another job out there," Kansas City, "doing the same thing at a different company. Though that industry is like every other one. Small. People talk. Maybe he couldn't have. I don't know. But for whatever reason, he decided to 'fess up and come home and get his shit together. Which I'm thinkin' is a good thing. He got home a couple of days ago. The day after I got back from South Carolina actually."

"Why didn't you tell me?"

He looked at me for a moment. "He asked me not to. And you can understand *that*."

I could. Oh, God. Oh, Doug. My too-smart, generous, tender-hearted baby. He was a *good kid*. He was. How did he get to this place? And I wondered again, couldn't help it: Was it something we did, or didn't do? Did we drop the ball somehow as parents?

"I told him I could use some help with a new digital platform we're trying to get up and running. AI. Dash cams, diagnostics for every rig. I mean it," he said when he saw my look. It's new to us and pretty sophisticated. We really can use him."

"But—"

Joe shook his head cutting me off. "He needs to work. He's got legal bills. A DUI's not cheap. And he still has to pay his rent in KC."

"What about his apartment?"

We both paused when we heard movement upstairs, footsteps, a door closing.

"He's trying to sublet it. At some point, he'll have to go pack up his stuff but we'll cross that bridge then. In the meantime, he's got rent to pay. It's okay. It's...good. I think? He's here. Maybe he wants our kind of... I don't know." He shrugged. "Rules. Accountability."

Part of my mind thought *our kind of accountability?*

"More likely he knows word got out about his drinking. " Joe scowled. "But..." and shrugged again.

Footsteps pounded down the stairs.

"Mama!" Doug said as he came into the kitchen, clearly as shocked to see me as Joe had been. My second son was tall, taller than Joe by an inch or two, and lanky, all arms and legs. His dark blond hair was cut short in the same way it had been for years. He was a good-looking kid, what Joe called "clean cut." He wore jeans and a T-shirt and a green zip-up hoodie sweatshirt with the Daley-Hallowell logo on the chest.

He pulled me into a big hug. What was the emotion I glimpsed on his face before I was smooshed against him? Surprise, certainly, and was that embarrassment? Shame? "I didn't know you were coming. Dad didn't tell me." Doug glanced at Joe.

"Yeah, I didn't know you were here, either," I said, not really able to keep the disappointment from my voice.

"I should have told you. I screwed up. I'm not real proud of it. But it's not the end of the world." He leaned down and kissed me on the cheek, smiling at me with typical Doug charm, before heading over to the coffee maker, as if he really wasn't too upset, as if it really wasn't the end of the world.

Why did he do that? Say what he thought we wanted to hear? Act appropriately contrite. I thought suddenly of Evan's sister, Marsal, and her cynicism and bitterness.

Oh, Doug! He was my baby, little Dougie, of the blonde buzz cut and the cowlick and the freckles.

"You look good, Mom. South Carolina agreed with you," he said, pouring coffee into a travel cup. "You got some sun."

And there it was, the flattery that came so easily to him and that seemed so genuine and that made me want to smile, even when I knew he was full of shit. "Oh, Doug. You lost your job? You loved that job. You loved your life in Kansas City."

"It's okay, Mom. I'm good. I've got resumes out and calls in to people. I'm okay." This was the Doug I knew well. Full of optimism, or bluster, or the sunshine Joe would say he was blowing up our behinds. Joe's expression was dark and unmoved.

Doug came over to get milk out of the fridge and I couldn't resist, I reached up and wrapped my arms around his neck and pulled him down for another hug. "I've been so worried about you." Massive understatement. "And I've missed you!" At the same time I had the thought, not so much an actual thought, but an emotion: *I need to fix this; I need to make things right for you*, before it struck me how wrong that was. I could not fix anything. Doug's fix had to come from him.

And as much as I loved my son, and loved the idea of having him here, it wasn't the way life was supposed to be. It wasn't how successful children lived: at home, in their childhood bedrooms. Doug was not okay, or he wouldn't be here. The pretense, the untruths, the lies—the ease with which Doug told them—left a sour taste in my mouth.

But Trouble's body was in the van. My eyes burned with lack of sleep. My back and hips ached from too many hours sitting and driving. I was so exhausted I wasn't sure, suddenly, I could remain on my feet.

Just then, Joe spoke to Doug and the abruptness of his voice jarred me. "Get the shovel from the garage. We need to bury the dog."

"Trouble?"

"Yeah," I said. "She died yesterday afternoon in her sleep. I brought her home to bury her in the backyard."

"Awww," Doug said. "Poor Troub."

"She was a great dog who had a great life," Joe said. "And she's home now where she belongs." He didn't look at me when he said that, but there was no doubt in my mind he wasn't just talking about the dog.

Joe chose a spot under the big maple in the corner of the back-yard, a tree the kids had climbed in, where the boys had once levered a few two by fours and pieces of plywood to build a "tree house," the same tree under which all three kids had posed for prom pictures with their dates. The tree was leafed out, but just, the new leaves tender and bright chartreuse green. Joe and Doug took turns digging.

"She was a great dog. The best," Joe said unwrapping the tartan plaid blanket a bit and rubbing the yellow fur, giving a gentle tug on the yellow ears one more time.

"Bye, girl," Doug said, and I thought his voice was thicker, that there were tears in his eyes. Trouble had been a big part of his childhood.

I couldn't help but think of my journey to Charleston, my "sabbatical," and how comforting it had been to have Trouble with me, how the big, yellow dog had kept me from feeling alone. My nose burned and I blinked to hold back tears. "I'll miss her," I choked out.

"We all will," Joe said.

Joe returned the spade to the garage, stopped in the kitchen to wash his hands, and paused, looking at me. I'd parked my butt against one of the island bar stools, not quite sitting. Not sure, suddenly, what to do with myself. It felt remarkably strange. I was home, it was familiar, mostly, but it was foreign, too. I saw Doug's car back out of the driveway and turn down Sweetmill Road. "Doug left?"

"I sent him on over to the warehouse," Joe said, wiping his hands on a towel. I could tell he felt as uncomfortable as I did. His eyes met mine and held my gaze...like he was telling me something? Like he was looking for a clue to my intentions? There was resolve in his gaze, and wariness. But not happiness. Not out-and-out joy. He was afraid to be happy.

"He's good at computer stuff," I said, clearing my throat. "Maybe he really can help with your new system."

"Oh, no doubt. Most importantly, I'm keeping him too busy to drink."

"You think that'll work?"

He snorted. "Probably not. But I'm not going to make it easy for him.I got rid of all the booze here. Took it to the office and packed it up in a box he'll never find."

I raised my brows and shook my head. "He's old enough to buy alcohol legally."

"I know." He shrugged and studied me a moment. "People have to do what they want to do," he said and I knew he wasn't just talking about Doug again. "He'll work hard, and he can be a big help to us, and beyond that, it's up to him." He took a deep breath and rubbed his nose. "I have a couple of things I have to do today. I can't stay."

"That's okay. I wasn't expecting you to."

"Well, I feel like I should. Stick around—"

"Don't worry about it. I have lots of stuff to do. I'm fine." I smiled awkwardly. He hadn't known I was arriving this morning; I really hadn't expected him to hang out and entertain me, had I? I did have things to do. Had I expected life in Langston to come to a halt because I'd returned home? Had I thought things would be different than the way they'd been for almost thirty years?

No. Not really. I'd known, in the way I knew how to breathe, that it wasn't Joe who needed to change. Like he said, people had to do what they wanted to do. I hadn't gone to Charleston because I wanted, or expected, Joe, or life in Langston to change.

Then why did I go?

To let the anger out.

Is that all?

I'd experienced no epiphanies, had no revelations, had done nothing extraordinary. I'd gotten a job working retail in a kitchen store. Getting paid minimum wage.

Had the anger gone? Was it gone for good?

"I can bring your stuff in from the van before I go to the warehouse," Joe said.

"Don't worry about it. I can get it. There's not that much."

"Okay then. Well, I'll see you later."

Was that a question? "Sure. I'll be here."

He didn't respond, but I could almost see him thinking *Will you? Or will you leave again?* But Joe didn't say that. Which was good because if he did, I'd have to say, *I don't know. I called my landlord to tell her there'd been a death in the family and that I was returning to Pennsylvania. I didn't cancel my lease.*

Joe left for the warehouse, and slowly, I became aware of the sounds that filled the silence of the empty house, sounds that were thirty-years familiar: The low hum of the refrigerator, an absolute chorus of birds, a kind of general white noise that was as unique to this house as its fragrance, and of the angle and the color of the light through old wavy window glass. I found myself sitting at the island in the kitchen, actually thankful to have this moment alone. You *could* come home again. But for me, that wasn't the question. Did I want to stay? Did I want this life? I thought of the tiny apartment and felt a pang of something—loss? Pleasure? Sitting here, surrounded by a room that was as much a part of me as my own skin, Charleston seemed almost like a dream, a fantasy, and as distant as the moon, except for the sense of peace I'd experienced there that was even now almost physical warmth. I never wanted to lose that feeling.

Before I could get up and begin the process of assimilating into life here, in Langston, for however long that might be, there was rustling and a thump as the kitchen door opened and Lillian stood in the threshold, grocery store bags in each hand.

Oh, shitfuckdamn. Not now.

"Oh," my mother-in-law said. "Cath! I thought that was your van. I told Jimmy I thought it was. I didn't know you were here."

"Hi. Yep." I smiled a smile that was just my mouth. I was too tired to deal with Lillian now. "I got in early this morning. Drove all night. Actually, I was just heading up to shower and sleep a little." What was my mother-in-law doing here? With groceries? She called Jimmy O'Keefe's delivery service to bring her over here?

"Does Joe know?"

"Yes. He was still home when I got here. He and Doug."

Lillian would have known about Doug being home. Lillian knew but me, his mother, had not. I waited to see if that notion lit the fuse of the anger. I felt sad, maybe. But that's all.

"How are you?" Lillian was clearly unsettled to find me sitting in the kitchen, as unsettled as I was about her showing up with groceries. It was a reminder that life truly had gone on without me.

"I'm okay. Exhausted just now," I smiled so as not to sound totally ungracious. "How are you?"

Tan. The Cruise. Of course she'd gotten some sun. Seven days sailing around the Caribbean. I wondered when she'd gotten back. Recently from the look of that unseasonable glow.

Beyond the tan, Lillian was wearing a pair of pinstriped pants and a blouse with a bow at the neck and a powder-blue blazer with a silver broach on the lapel, this one in the shape of a hummingbird. It didn't matter if Lillian had nothing more on her schedule than grocery shopping and picking up the dry cleaning, she would wear panty hose. And pumps. She set the grocery bags on the counter and then moved awkwardly to where I had risen from the stool and gave me a hug. "We were out of a few things, so I had Jimmy take me to the Foodrite on the way over."

The *we* didn't escape my notice. Jimmy waited while Lillian shopped? Of course he did. That was Jimmy. Was he waiting in the driveway, now? I glanced out the window but couldn't see the blue van that was Jimmy's taxi. God. How long did she intend to be here?

"That's great. Thank you." Now *I* felt awkward. It was my house and my kitchen, but I had no idea what items we were out of, or what Lillian had bought. I had a sudden thought of the ring that Lillian had sent me before Christmas, that I never had gotten around to acknowledging. Not sending a thank you note for a gift was almost a cardinal sin in my book. And I'd committed it.

"Laundry detergent and coffee and a few other things," Lillian said. "I'm awfully glad you're home, Cath. I've been so worried. About you...and about Joe."

"I'm sure you were. Are. But it was—is—something...between me and Joe." *Don't ask me to say more. Please be waiting in the driveway for her to leave,* I prayed to Jimmy O'Keefe.

"I wanted to call. I even considered coming to see you—"

Thank God that hadn't happened. "There really isn't anything you could have done. Honestly. And you did write to me. And sent the ring. That was...unexpected. I meant to send you a thank you note and I just..." I shrugged.

"I'm sure it was unexpected. I should have given it to you years ago. I don't know why I didn't. I guess I was waiting for the perfect time, which is silly. There is no perfect time. But I wanted you to know...how much you mean to me, to this family. It should be yours, and after you, Annie's."

I waited to feel the tension in my chest that meant words wanted to be spoken that couldn't, shouldn't. But there was nothing, nothing except the great fatigue, the grit in my eyes, the need to brush my teeth, the desire for sleep. "I—" I stood again, and started to speak, to excuse myself to go upstairs and shower.

But Lillian spoke at the same time so I sat back down. "I wanted to send a peace offering, too. I worried that I might have had something to do with your leaving...."

I really don't want to be having this conversation. Not now. In a perfect world, not ever. One of the lovely things about Charleston was that there was no Lillian. Life had been...my own...and Lillian-free.

"You two have been married for so long. You've been through a lot. You have a family together. I hope you can work things out."

"We'll see."

Lillian didn't respond to that but I could see worry in my mother-in-law's eyes, in the line of her mouth. "Did Joe tell you my news?"

"No. What news?" I asked.

"I've rented a condo in Vero Beach. From January through April next year. In the same complex where Jules owns hers. She's promised to teach me to golf." Lillian laughed awkwardly. "She says I'll love it."

I couldn't have been more surprised if Lillian had undressed and run around the yard naked. My mother-in-law? Spending four months in Florida and *playing golf?*

"Really?" For years now, we'd been trying to encourage Lillian to visit Jules in Florida or Mark and Elaine in Atlanta during central Pennsylvania's long, cold winter months, but she was never interested in going for longer than a few days. And most years, she didn't want to go at all.

"Yes. Jules' neighbor has moved to be nearer his children in Texas. But they don't want to sell his condo yet. So Joe talked them into renting to me. For this coming winter."

Joe did that? "Wow. That is big news. You never wanted to spend that much time away before."

"I know. But the winters are getting longer." It sounded like Lillian was repeating something she'd heard someone else say, like a young child. "Well, I'll get out of your hair." Lillian gestured at the grocery bags. "If you don't mind putting the groceries away."

"Of course not." I forced a smile. "Thanks for bringing them."

"I've been coming over every morning to tidy up, and do the laundry and fix something for Joe for dinner, unless he was going to come to my house. Except while I was away of course—"

"Of course. I'm sure he appreciated it. Thank you for doing that." I should have known Joe wouldn't have to fend for himself when I left. Of course he wouldn't. Again, there was no responding curl of anger, though I waited for it. Inside, I felt numbed, somehow, my emotions oddly still. Even mentioning her cruise, indirectly, didn't rouse any reaction.

"Cath—" Lillian started and I felt a sudden nauseating rush of panic. I sensed that whatever Lillian was going to say was going to be painfully awkward. "I'm sure you have a lot you want to do. With Jamie's wedding and everything. That'll be here before we know it."

"Yes. No doubt about that."

"And Annie's baby. A wedding and a new baby, all in the same month." Lillian smiled at me. If she so much as implied some judgment of Annie, I wasn't sure my emotions would remain quiet. "It'll be a busy time. I'm gaining a granddaughter-in-law and a great-grandchild both. You'll let me know if I can help? With wedding preparations? Or with anything for Annie."

Lillian gave me a look that had something of a plea in it. But maybe I was imagining that, though it was clear that Lillian felt as unsettled as I did. "Sure," I told her. "I'll let you know."

"Joe and Doug have been working in the backyard the last couple of evenings."

More of Joe's strategy to keep Doug on the straight and narrow? Doug had never been one to enjoy working in the yard or garden. But

I didn't have a better idea. Even after talking with Evan, especially after talking with Evan, all I knew about addiction or being the parent of an addict—was Doug an addict?—was how much I didn't know. The very notion of having to deal with it all exhausted me.

Let go and let God, popped into my head.

Father J would tell me God speaks to us, we just need to learn to listen.

Father J. I needed to call him. Tell him I was home. I needed to call Evan, too.

"Well they've got a head start, then," I said to my mother-in-law. "I'm excited to get out into the garden and get my hands dirty." And as soon as I said it, I realized it was true. I'd spent hours on the beach, walking, looking at the city of Charleston, at other gardens, but I'd missed working in my own.

The first thing I'm going to do is plant some pansies over Trouble's grave.

"Okay, then," Lillian said, slipping her hands into her jacket pockets, pulling her phone out of one. "I'll call Jimmy and have him come get me. Take me home, I guess. I'm not dressed for gardening."

Thank God. I suddenly had to bite my cheek to keep from laughing out loud, the very idea of Lillian working in the yard, wearing garden gloves with panty hose and Naturalizers was so ludicrous.

"Joe decided I can't drive myself anymore. I don't really under-stand why. I can drive just fine. But he sold my car."

"He told me."

I was so tired I could hardly see straight. Did I need to offer to drive Lillian home? I'd agreed that Joe's decision to take her keys was the right, safe, one, but I hadn't really considered the unintended consequences. It made my mother-in-law that much more dependent on others, and not just Jimmy's taxi service. Joe. Me.

"If you can call Jimmy, that would be great."

There was another of the uncertain smiles, the tentative expres-sion in Lillian's eyes and I could tell my mother-in-law did not know who Cathleen Keen Daley was any longer, and not just because I didn't offer to drive her home. I had become a different person. It struck me, then, suddenly, that leaving Langston and going to Charleston changed the dynamic of my relationship with Lillian, as much as it changed the one between me and Joe.

It had changed *me*.

A re-set. Like when your computer is giving you fits so you unplug it for a few moments and then plug it back in. I almost smiled. I was an analogy Father J might use.

Chapter 15

The first thing I noticed when I opened my eyes was the huge cobweb. I knew immediately where I was, but still felt weird, like an interloper. I'd showered in the master bath, and that had been weird, too, everything was the same but *different*. I had not been able to bring myself to get into the bed that I'd shared with Joe for almost thirty years. Instead, I'd curled up on the couch in the family room.

One of the things I hadn't considered when I left in December was *re-entry*. What it would be like when I came back. *If* I came back. Astronauts and soldiers had special training to manage it because it wasn't easy. No such preparation for me. I was going to have to wing it.

My phone buzzed again where I'd laid it on the coffee table and I realized that's what had awakened me. Annie.

"What's wrong?" I knew immediately, the way mothers know those things, that something was.

"Nothing bad. Not really. My blood pressure is a little high. But I've been put on bed rest. I'm not supposed to be on my feet except to pee."

Now I could hear the fear under the confident, competent, four-years-of-education-and-two-years-in-the-trenches-of-the-NICU nurse's voice.

"Oh, honey. That's really scary, I know. But it'll be okay. Bed rest isn't the end of the world. Where are you?" I pushed the blanket down and stood and went to find my shoes and a sweater without even thinking about it.

"I'm at the doctor's office. I'm supposed to work this afternoon. I'm on at three. But I'll have to take medical leave. I need to call my supervisor. Oh, Mom."

I wished I was there, right there next to Annie, so I could give her a hug or her hand a squeeze. *Thank God I'm here, not in Charleston!*

"Where's Corey," I asked. "He's there?"

"No. His in-laws are here for the weekend. He couldn't get away for this appointment. And it was just a regular check-up. I feel fine. Other than really tired. And fat. And that's all normal. What am I going to do? If I can't work, I can't pay my rent! I can't be on bed rest at home by myself!"

What? He couldn't "get away?"

"It's okay. I'll come get you. We'll figure it out. Don't let yourself stress about it. That can't be good for you or the baby. You can be on bed rest at home. Where your mama can take care of you," I kept my tone light, let none of my own fears through in my voice.

"Home? Where are you, Mom? Aren't you in South Carolina?"

"I'm home. I got home this morning." It was not the time to tell Annie about Trouble.

"You are? Does Dad know?"

"I am. And yes, Dad knows I'm here. I saw him and Doug before they went to the warehouse." I paused. "I can leave in five minutes and be there by..." I glanced at my watch, "four o'clock. We'll pack up some things and head home."

"What about my job, Mom? My apartment? I can't leave Pitts-burgh. Corey can't leave. His boys are here. His job is here."

"Call your supervisor first and let her know what's happening. You're not the first person to have an emergency like this. She'll deal with it. That's her job. The rest we'll figure out. As long as you're okay and the baby is okay."

"But I have OB appointments. Every week now."

"I can drive you down for those."

"And what about when I go into labor?"

"I can drive you down there then, too. It's only an hour and a half, Annie. And there's a hospital here. And obstetricians, if it comes to that. Langston is not the end of the Earth."

"But what about Corey—"

"Corey can come visit you here. It's not ideal, I know. But it's only for a few weeks. You can manage it. We can manage it." *He can fucking manage it.*

"Four weeks of bed rest." I could hear the Annie that never said quit, the Annie that chugged a gallon of milk when she weighed all of seventy-eight pounds soaking wet herself, because her brothers dared her to. The Annie who confidently and competently cared for preemie babies that easily fit in the palm of a hand. "I'm thirty-three weeks. The doctor wants me to get to thirty-seven. That's my goal. I'm not even supposed to drive home from here. They have me on a couch in one of the offices."

"A month. You can do that. One day at a time." *The only way out is through.* It was one of Joe's catchphrases. It popped into my head.

"But call Corey. You need to let him know."

"I can't."

"Why not, Annie?" *Why the hell not?*

"They don't know about us. His in-laws. About the baby. Things are so messed up. His wife has left— That's why her parents are in town."

"Left? Left where?" *Messed up is right. Good God!*

"They're not sure. They're all worried about her. She's bipolar, Mom. It's an actual medical diagnosis, a disease. She didn't just go off on a whim."

Was that a dig at my own sabbatical to Charleston? "Oh, geez. Annie."

"Corey's got a lot on his plate. He's trying to hold everything together for his boys. I thought this was just going to be a regular check-up. Not a big deal."

Holy moley. "But now you need to let him know, Annie. This is important. It's his baby, too." I wanted to wring his neck. He had as much obligation to Annie and her baby as he did to the other children he'd fathered. And to the AWOL wife. I ground my teeth together so hard my jaw ached.

It really hit home, suddenly, how much Corey the married man was going to change the relationship I had with my daughter. "I understand that things are *messed up*." I used Annie's words. "But you need to call him. At least leave him a message. He needs to know what's going on. Can you take a cab? To get home to your apartment?"

"One of my friends is coming. They wouldn't let me take an Uber because my doctor wanted to be sure I'd have help once I got there."

"I'm putting on my shoes now. I'll be there in a little over an hour."

"Does that mean things are okay with you and Dad?"

"Don't worry about me and your dad now. Just relax. Stop stressing. I'll see you soon."

"Thanks, Mom. Mom?" Annie added. "I love you."

"I love you, too."

I thought about calling Joe to let him know about Annie. I even picked up my phone to make the call before deciding it was a conversation better had in person. And the warehouse was on the way to the interstate.

Jerilynn was on the phone when I walked into the reception/office area but her eyes showed her surprise. Was there judgment there, too? Jerilyn thought Joe walked on water. She waved, motioning me into Joe's office. The door was open and I could see him sitting at his desk, typing on the computer. He typed awkwardly, meticulously using the finger placement he'd learned in high school typing class. Of Doug there was no sign.

"Hey," I said, catching his attention.

I watched the mix of emotions cross his face, ending with something very guarded. This was the price I paid for Charleston. There was the sense that we stood at the edge of a great unknown, a future that was completely shapeless. The feeling struck me so suddenly and so forcefully that I almost felt dizzy with the power of it. I had to literally shake my head to ground myself again.

"Hey," he echoed, not really smiling. Uncertain. "What's up?"

"Annie called," I said.

"Yeah?"

"She had an OB appointment today. Her blood pressure is high. She's been put on bed rest."

"She okay?" Joe pushed his chair back from the desk, poised to get to his feet.

"She said she's fine. The baby's fine. But I'm going to go down and get her, bring her home. She can't be on bed rest in Pittsburgh by herself. She's scared. I mean, she didn't say that, but I could tell."

Joe nodded, his jaw tight. "But Corey's been through this before. I mean pregnancy and childbirth. Babies. He knows what they're getting into. At least there's that. Right?"

"Corey's not there. His in-laws are in town. His wife left." I tried to keep my voice neutral. Corey was the father of Annie's baby whether Joe and I liked it or not.

His expression hardened. "What do you mean, his wife left?"

"They're trying to find her. She's bipolar. I get the feeling she's done this before. Left Corey with their kids."

"You're fucking kidding me."

"Nope. Not kidding." I met Joe's look. "Annie didn't tell him about this appointment; she thought it was routine. We can't criticize him because he didn't know."

"He still should be there. I went to every appointment with you."

"You did with Nora. You missed a couple when I was pregnant with the other kids."

Joe didn't argue, but he scowled.

"And Annie says they don't know about her and the baby. The in-laws I mean. So she's by herself at the doctor's office. One of her friends is going to pick her up."

"What a fucking mess."

"Yes, well. I just wanted to let you know that I was heading to Pittsburgh. I had to go right by here anyway—"

Joe shuffled some papers around on the desk to find his cell phone. "I'll come with you."

"Really?"

"Of course. It's Annie."

"I mean, I know you're busy—"

"Not so much that I can't do this. I have a conference call scheduled in a half hour but Doug can take it. Will be good for him to have to step up." I watched him stuff his phone in his shirt pocket and grab his jacket off the hook by the door. "You get a chance to sleep at all?"

"I did. After your mom left."

"Oh, Christ. Sorry about that. I should have called her. I didn't think of it."

"It's okay." I shrugged.

"I'm not sure if her help was more of a blessing or a curse." We'd exited the warehouse and climbed into my van, which had a much more comfortable back seat. "It..." Joe frowned and shook his head like he couldn't find the word, his eyes on the road ahead, "...wrecked me," he finally said. "When you left. Maybe it shouldn't have. Maybe I should have seen it coming," Now he glanced at me again and shrugged. "But it made me crazy having her underfoot and I told her that."

"Seriously?" I could not imagine Joe saying any such thing to his mother. "What did she say?"

"She looked hurt. Made me feel like shit. But she stopped coming over when I was home and started coming after I left for the warehouse. Not every day but every couple of days."

"She comes every day. She told me."

He shrugged again. "But not when I'm home." He didn't look at me when he said it. "She rented a condo in Florida."

"She told me."

"Yep. It's a test run. She's going to spend a few months there next winter. If she likes it okay, she can buy it."

"I never thought she'd leave Langston."

"We had a heart-to-heart. It'll be good for her," Joe said. "Florida." *And us* went unsaid but was as loud in my ears as if he'd spoken the words. "She can make friends. Be busy with whatever. The weather is warm. No snow. No ice."

I nodded, my brain still processing: My mother-in-law was going to spend a few months in Florida next winter. Maybe every winter from now on. "Was that your idea?"

He looked at me. "Yep."

"I got the sense that she's not entirely sure about it."

He shrugged. "Probably not. It's change. None of us likes that. But the place in Vero Beach? It's all golf carts and the condo she's renting comes with its own two-seater. No doubt she'll be happy to be able to drive herself again. She can't kill anyone in a golf cart. They have a little market and a beauty parlor right in the complex. It's not perfect. But it's something."

I nodded and neither of us spoke for a while. Traffic was heavy, lots of big trucks. "I don't want to be the reason you didn't go on your mother's cruise. I don't want to be the reason she moves to Florida."

Joe looked at me. "You weren't."

"If I hadn't made a big deal about it, you would have gone."

He studied me now, glancing at the road. There was a pair of semis ahead of us, but nothing close just now. He didn't deny it. "I don't know."

Chapter 16

Joe dropped me off at Annie's apartment complex, almost exactly in the same spot where I'd stopped the convertible on *that day* and went to fill the van with gas so that we wouldn't have to do that once we had Annie and her stuff loaded up. The tiny lobby was literally as big as a phone booth, with half a wall of metal mailboxes on one side, a glass door and stairs at the back—no elevator. No washers or dryers, either. How would she manage a stroller in here?

I climbed the three flights to the landing on the third floor where Annie's door was to the left and another apartment was to the right. I hesitated just for a second before knocking, tried the knob almost without thinking and found the door unlocked. The living room was dim and warm. She often had a window cracked even in winter. The space was familiar, the rug, the furniture, the pictures on the walls, and it smelled like Annie. The fragrance something I felt in my heart as much as recognized in my head. It was silent in the apartment.

"Annie?" I called softly walking into the bedroom, which wasn't much of a walk. Three or four steps. Almost subconsciously, I imagined a baby here, a toddler, toys, a highchair, bouncy chair, books, Legos.

Would Annie stay here after the baby was born? Would she and Corey raise their child here? Who would take care of the baby when Annie went back to work? Annie had a good job, but could she afford to pay for day care, and an apartment, and a car payment, and living expenses? *Oh, God, what a mess.*

I froze when I got to the bedroom door. The only light was what came though the slats of the window blind: pale, late afternoon sun. Annie was on the bed, on her side facing the door, her head on her arm, asleep. There was a man behind her in the bed, which threw me for a moment. It took a silent beat or two for me to realize it was Corey there, tucked up behind Annie on the bed, one hand propping up his head so that he was looking at me, the other gently, slowly, almost hypnotically rubbing the mound of Annie's belly—a mound so much bigger than when I last saw her that it took me aback, though it shouldn't have.

He looked at me, his mouth curving in an expression that wasn't happiness, exactly, but was something different, something shared, something more to do with Annie. He appeared haggard, every one of his forty-two years. He had a scruffy three-day beard, longish hair, longer than I remembered it from when we'd met him all those months ago. Were his looks what had attracted Annie? That was so not Annie. But then, none of what I knew about this man was Annie.

I was not prepared to see him, had not thought about what to say to him. Oh, God. Joe was going to have a cow. Should I go downstairs and wait for him and give him a heads up? I could hardly pull out my phone and send him a warning text.

Corey's eyes were light in the shadows of the bedroom, light against his dark hair and the beard, dark brows framing those eyes. There was...what...in those eyes? Worry? Exhaustion? In the stillness, my eyes were drawn to his hand, the way it cradled the baby inside Annie, rubbed absently. *Annie's baby might look like that. Those pale eyes. The dark hair.* The thought popped into my head. *His baby. My grandbaby.*

"Hey," he whispered.

"Hey," I whispered back and he slowly eased himself from behind Annie and off the bed and came to me in the doorway. The two of us stepped out into the living room, Corey drawing the bedroom door partway closed behind him.

"How is she?"

He shrugged. "Okay. Worried. More about how she's going to manage everything. Her job. She knows the baby is okay." His voice, his eyes, his expression, the way his jaw was tight, all said something else. Not that Annie's baby wasn't okay, but that he wasn't okay.

"She sounded pretty upset when she called, though she tried not to let on."

His lips quirked, not a smile at all, but something that hinted at mutual understanding. "She always thinks she has to be so tough. She cried a little when I got here, but I think that was hormones. She doesn't want to be a burden."

I met and held his eyes and saw there something raw, vulnerable under the strain that gave me a start. We both loved Annie. "A burden, ha," I said finally. "She has no idea. Though in about four weeks she will. Once she holds her baby in her arms. That kind of love is a gift. Never a burden."

"Yep." He smiled wearily. "But you can't tell someone that. They have to experience it for themselves. Annie will be an amazing mother."

Of course she will! But she shouldn't be one, yet. "I didn't know you were going to be here," I said. "Annie mentioned you have family in town—" I stumbled over that. What were the parents of his wife? They were his family. In-laws. In some bizarre way, they would become my family, too. They would be the grandparents of my grandchild's half siblings. *Oh, Annie.*

"I do." He sighed, but somehow I understood that that sigh wasn't about Annie but was more plain exhaustion. He really looked shot, old beyond his years, even. "Danielle's parents. They've been here for a week. Danielle is...my wife."

My wife. A cow. A whole fucking herd. That's what Joe was

going to have. I didn't say anything, was still wondering how to let Joe know Corey was here before he just walked in the door. Besides, what was there to say? It was weird—wrong—talking about this man's wife, when my daughter was sleeping in the next room, pregnant with his child.

"She's not...well," he said finally.

"Annie mentioned your wife has some...health issues." Mental health issues. I shouldn't feel uncomfortable saying that, but I did. "I'm sorry."

"It's something she's been dealing with for a while. *We've* been dealing with," he corrected. "Medication helps, but she doesn't like taking it. When she stops, this is what happens."

I shook my head. *What* was what happened?

His jaw clenched. "She left six days ago and we didn't know where she was."

"Oh no!" I said. What else was there to say?

"We found her late last night. Well, the Dayton police did. Her dad and I drove out to get her. Just got back a couple hours ago. I came here as soon as we got Danielle home."

Dayton? As in Ohio? "Is she okay? Will she be okay?"

He shrugged. "We'll get her back on her meds. Danielle is bipolar. She's fought depression for a long time. It's not something that can be *cured*."

"You have your hands full—"

He snorted. "My cup runneth over. It's been hardest on our kids. Danni manages things pretty well. But sometimes she just—" He shook his head. "It's not a perfect science. Her parents help, but they live in Quebec. They came down when she went missing."

No wonder Annie didn't want to call Corey with the news from her OB appointment. *But that's just wrong! What's happening in this man's life, with his other family, should not take precedence over Annie, and her health, and the health of their baby.* The thoughts made my throat feel clotted and thick.

I thought I heard the main door to the tiny lobby downstairs open and bang shut and footsteps on the stairs. "Why? Why then?" I asked, unable to help myself. I knew Corey would understand exactly what I meant: *Why did you begin an affair with my daughter?*

"It just happened." He sighed again, and again there was that clenching of his jaw. "It sounds lame. It sounds cliché. But it's the truth. It was just one of those things."

Why couldn't it have been one of those things *with someone else?*

Bottom line was...it didn't matter why it happened, or what Corey had been thinking at the time, or what Annie had been thinking. I had to let it go. And so did Joe.

Corey rubbed a hand roughly around his face; it was something Joe did, in just that way, and it was disconcerting to see Corey do the same thing, the same way. In the quiet in the apartment, I could hear the sound of his beard stubble against his palm. He cricked his neck, the way someone who spent eight-plus hours in a car, who hadn't been sleeping, who was worried and stressed did.

"It's not easy to accept," I said. "Annie is our daughter, our baby. This whole situation is not what we wanted for her. Adultery is not what we saw in her future. Having a baby outside of marriage. With a man who has another family. Who is not even divorced." I had to say it.

"It isn't what Annie wanted. It isn't what I wanted." He looked at me and I could almost hear him say, It's a disaster. But he didn't say that. He said, "But here we are."

"Annie's life will never be the same. I could say it's ruined, but it's not. It just won't be the life she wanted. That we wanted for her."

I was conscious of Annie sleeping just beyond the door to the bedroom, not a dozen feet away from where we stood, and took a deep breath, tried to rein in my emotions, kept my voice low, just more than a whisper. "She doesn't know. She doesn't understand. Who is going to take care of the baby when she goes back to work? Can she afford daycare? Can you? You already have another family to take care of. And it sounds like that family needs you desperately.

Annie's going to be tied to a man who is tied to someone else. Forever."

I had to stop talking and draw a deep breath. "Can you afford two families? Is Annie going to become daycare for your other kids?" I almost winced at that, was nearly appalled at myself for voicing the thought. "I'm sorry. That's none of my business. But here we are." I used his words.

He didn't flinch. "The timing is terrible." *You think?* "But we're not the first people to have a baby that wasn't planned."

Was he referring to me and Joe—and Nora? I didn't know whether to laugh or to slap him, although I'd been thinking pretty much the same thing. We looked at each other without speaking for a moment.

Finally he said, "We'll get through it. We'll figure it out. Give us a chance. That's all I can say."

I smiled at him, humorless, as I heard rustling from the bedroom. "We don't really have any choice."

His jaw clenched at little at that, but in his eyes, those pale blue eyes, I thought I could see resignation. He was not an angry man, or a mean one, but he was obviously a weary one and he couldn't be surprised at how I felt. At how Joe felt. "I know it's not perfect; it's not what you wanted. I'm not what you wanted. But I'm the father of that baby."

"Corey?" Annie called. "Corey?"

"I'm here, babe," he answered, glancing at me at the same time I heard the sound of footsteps coming up the stairs outside Annie's apartment.

"That'll be Joe," I said.

He nodded.

"I need to pee," Annie yelled, and despite myself, I smiled. "I'm getting up to go to the bathroom."

"I love her," he said.

"We all do," is all I could say.

He nodded once, those light eyes still on mine. "I'm coming, hold your horses," he called then as he turned and went into the bedroom.

Joe came in then, with a paper bag from DQ in one hand and a smile on his face, happy, and...proud of himself. That smile did something to me, made me feel protective, somehow, and tender. The thickness in my throat pressed up and back against my heart. Joe loved babies. He loved Annie, in a way that I knew was different from my mother's love.

His baby girl was having a baby, his first grandchild, and I suddenly saw the power of that as if it were an aura around Joe, as if it was something I could actually see, with shape and color. He had gotten Annie a Blizzard on his way back from filling the van with gas. Pecan cluster it would be, I knew without asking, Annie's favorite, and Joe's. It was a little joke between them.

"What?" he said when he saw my face, his own looking suddenly anxious. "Everything okay?"

I nodded my head in the direction of Annie's room, where we could hear voices now, and the bathroom door opening and closing. "Corey's here."

Joe's face changed then. His mouth tightened, and his jaw clenched a little, which reminded me, oddly enough, of Corey. "Well, fuck," he said. A whisper.

"He's going to be in her life no matter how we feel about him. He's going to be in our lives."

Joe took a deep breath and scrubbed his face with one hand and it was like déjà vu. The same way Corey had rubbed his not ten minutes ago. We shared a look and Joe snorted. "I know. Where is she? I want to see her with my own eyes and know she's okay."

"She had to pee. He went in to help."

"She needs help peeing?"

"Probably not."

"Thanks for the heads up."

I shrugged, smiled at him, I couldn't help it. The look on his face was one I knew so well.

"Mom," Annie called. "Is Dad here? What are you doing?"

"He's here. He brought you a treat." I nodded at the DQ bag and urged Joe to move. "Hey, sweetie," I said, stepping into the bedroom. This time Corey was standing at the foot of the bed, his hands in his pockets, looking...wary or...protective? I didn't have time to decide, my attention caught by Annie, reclining in bed, her hands holding the mound of her belly and looking decidedly defensive, though at the sight of me, she started to cry.

"Mom!"

"Ohh, sweetie," I bent down and gave her a hug, squeezing her shoulders tightly, as tightly as I could with the baby bump between us. "Oh, I've missed you."

"I've missed you, too! I'm so glad you're here." The end of that sentence was delivered on a sob.

"Me, too." I smiled, straightening, and studying Annie's face, brushing her hair off her forehead. There were shadows under her eyes, and a kind of fatigue in her features. I remembered those days, when it was hard to sleep and rest well, when I couldn't get comfortable on my back and my hips hurt if I lay on my side, when the baby was big, and active, and my bladder was always full. The memory was so vivid, I couldn't help it, I shook my head.

"Bed rest! I can't believe it. I feel fine."

"It's okay," I said, giving Annie's hand a squeeze. "It's not the end of the world. It's just a little hiccup. And nothing we can't easily manage."

"I know that. But I can't stop crying for some reason." Annie's voice caught on another sob. I could see her biting her lip. Oh, I remembered those days, too. All those hormones running rampant. When I was pregnant, I'd cried at the drop of a hat.

"That's normal. But don't worry. This next few weeks will fly by and then you'll be holding your baby and you'll forget all about this. The most important thing is getting you and this little one to term." I pressed a hand to Annie's belly. It was warm and surprisingly hard.

"Your mama's right about that," Joe chimed in. "We'll get you home and settled in and you'll be fine and your baby will be here before you know it." I saw him glance at Corey, and I knew he was holding it all in for Annie's sake.

"Hey, Joe," Corey said then, holding out his right hand to shake.

Joe stared at the hand, at Corey, but made no immediate move to extend his own. I knew that it was the casual use of his first name that caused the delay in reaching out a hand to shake, not anything more than that.

"Dad," Annie said.

Joe's face shifted, and he extended his hand. There was no question he felt like I did about Corey, because in our world, there wasn't any other way to feel. I also knew that Joe would forgive Corey and forget much quicker than I would.

Joe looked down at Annie again, his mouth breaking into a smile that was pure love. "Princess," Joe said and I moved so Joe could hug Annie, too. He practically lifted her off the bed, rocking her in his arms, the DQ bag dangling from his hand, and Annie giggled.

"Dad, you're going to hurt your back. I'm a whale."

"You're not a whale. You're beautiful. I always thought your mother was beautiful when she was pregnant, too. She always thought she was fat."

"I was fat."

"Yeah, but that just meant you were slower, I could catch you easier." This banter was Mr. Doofus. I wanted to drag Corey by the ear out of Annie's presence and finish our conversation about real life. I wanted to know, to work out the details, to have sorted the day-to-day issues.

"I brought you something," Joe said.

"I see that. Let me guess. A pecan cluster Blizzard." Annie's mouth curved up in a grin.

"What else?"

"I'm gonna look like a soccer ball. I already do."

"Ehh," Joe scoffed. "It's dairy. It's calcium. Practically health food. Good for you."

It made my heart feel light in my chest to see Annie smile. "You're right. Thanks." She took the cup out of the bag.

"You feeling okay?" he asked.

"I feel fine. Except for my blood pressure, everything is good. The baby is okay. We don't know what it is, either, in case you were wondering." Annie glanced at me, spooning a bite of ice cream into her mouth and licking the spoon. "This is awesome, Dad. You're the best."

"I know," Joe grinned. "And you're an astute judge of character." It was what they always said to each other, more of their father-daughter schtick. But this time the words hung in the air. I refused to look at Corey in that moment.

Annie ate another bite of ice cream and changed the subject. Thankfully. "Mom always said she wanted to be surprised at the birth."

"If God wanted you to know, he'd have put a window in your belly," Joe said.

Annie rolled her eyes and licked the spoon again. "Whatever. But the baby is fine. Healthy. Kicks like a mule."

"Gonna be a soccer player, like his mom."

"Or *her* mom," I said.

"How about I gather up some of your stuff?" Corey asked. "The things you want to take with you to Langston. You tell me what, I'll pack it up."

And I was reminded that we weren't just us, just Daleys, just Mom and Dad and daughter—and granddaughter or grandson—there was someone else who would forever after be a fixture in our lives.

It didn't take long to pack a bag for Annie, and we headed home.

When we got Annie settled into the bedroom, Joe told her, "We can make some room in one of the dressers for your stuff. And I'll bring in the TV from the den." We were settling Annie in the downstairs master bedroom so she wouldn't have to navigate stairs.

"You don't have to do any of that. I can go out to the family room to watch TV. There's a couch. I don't want you to give up your room!" Annie looked at my two suitcases still sitting just inside the doorway where I'd carried them in this morning. "You haven't even unpacked yet. This is your room. You should stay in it."

"I wouldn't complain about getting a king-size bed and a good mattress," Doug said. He'd followed us in and was standing in the doorway, eating a bowl of cereal.

"Don't be silly. We can easily sleep upstairs. This way you have a bathroom only a few steps away." I glared at Doug. "There's nothing wrong with your mattress."

"You're right. Especially since I've been sleeping in the guest room. That bed is freakin' awesome. Guess I'll be moving back to the ol' bunk room."

A little voice seemed to speak into my ear: *Reprieve! Question about where to sleep tonight solved!* For now, at least. Thinking about climbing into bed with Joe, like I'd done for almost thirty years, had been one of the things I'd been unable to wrap my mind around. I couldn't just pick up where I'd left off, with nary a hiccup. Now, it seemed that issue had been resolved. At least temporarily. "Just stay put for tonight," I told Doug. "In the guest room. We'll figure everything out tomorrow."

"You won't have to go up or down the stairs at all. I'm sure Nana Lil will come visit. And your old friends."

"My *old* friends are all working. At jobs."

"Yeah, but they'll come over to say hi and hang out. You'll see."

"Dad. None of my old friends are still in Langston. They're all somewhere else. Living their lives."

I spoke. "I know this won't be easy, honey, but you don't have any choice, so we'll make the best of it."

"Only way out is through," Doug said.

"Gee, thanks." Annie.

"Maybe you can start a scrapbook for the baby. You can hook a rug. Something for a baby's room, and someday you can tell your son, or daughter, how you made it…. You know. Lemons. Lemonade."

Annie looked at me but didn't say anything because her lips were pursed as if she'd been sucking a lemon, her jaw clamped. This was mulish Annie.

"I'll get the old chaise lounge out of the summer kitchen so you can sit on the patio. In the sunshine. Get some fresh air. You can supervise while I'm working in the yard." The best way to deal with mulish Annie was to ignore the mulishness.

Annie took a deep breath and moved to dig around in the tote bag until she found a book. "Sure. If it's okay, I might take a shower and read for a little bit," she said.

"Of course, honey." Annie was understandably cranky. But she would come around. She didn't have any choice. Or it was going to be a verrrry long four weeks. For everyone. "I'll go make us something for dinner. You hungry? I haven't had a chance to go grocery shopping; I have no idea what's in the fridge," aside from Lillian's contributions this morning. "But eggs, surely. An omelet?"

"Whatever," Annie looked at me and I could tell she was trying to smile, an apology for her crankiness in her eyes, trying not to cry. "Thanks, Mom."

Later that evening, I gathered up a nightshirt, my toiletries, some clothes for tomorrow, and went upstairs.

"Sorry," Joe said.

"Sorry about what?" I said.

"About us getting the boys' room. There's something wrong with this picture. We should at least get the guest room. You know."

I watched him smooth the comforter on the twin bed, Doug's bed, the bed Doug was apparently not sleeping in now, having taken over the guest room with its queen-sized bed. "It's okay. Not a big deal."

"Yeah. Saves us having to figure out sleeping arrangements."

"What do you mean?"

He shrugged. "I don't know. It's weird. You being here. You've been gone for a long time. It feels like a long time, anyway. It feels like a lifetime. It's weird," he repeated.

"I know what you mean."

He shrugged. "I can't just pick up where we left off." Joe wasn't whispering, but almost. Our master bedroom, where Annie was now ensconced, was just below.

I sat down on Jamie's bed and now the two of us faced each other across the braided rug. "I couldn't do that, either. That would mean having left, being gone, didn't change anything."

Joe shook his head. "I'm still not real clear on what needed to change."

"Me. It was me. I needed to change; I needed to stop feeling so angry."

I felt curiously hollow inside, suddenly.

He made a sound in his throat, like a snort, but not quite.

"What?"

"I won't be able to stop wondering if—when—you're just gonna pick up and leave again."

I opened my mouth to say something, realized I didn't know what to say. I wasn't sure I wouldn't leave again. Had I decided that?

"I'm trying to understand, Cath. I'm trying to give you space, if that's what you think you need. I did give you space. About seven hundred miles."

I didn't want to have this conversation now, not when Annie was resting in our bed in the room right below us. And I wasn't ready to have it.

"What's life look like for me in that case?" he persisted. "If you decide you *need* that again? Just hanging here, holding down the fort?"

———

I INVITED Father J to the house for lunch. I hadn't started cooking for him again, using the wedding and Annie as excuses. It wasn't that I didn't want to cook for him, but just that I didn't want to simply slide back into my old life. Yet? At all?

It was a Friday morning; Joe and Doug were at the warehouse. I had a call scheduled with my editor to go over some of the line edits for the new cookbook. I'd had a load of mulch delivered yesterday, and a yard full of flower beds where I wanted to spread it. During my stay in Charleston, I'd almost forgotten what days like this, a life like this, felt like.

In the ten days I'd been home from Charleston, Father J and I had been trying to connect in person, for a longer talk than the few minutes we chatted after church, and hadn't managed to get together.

Lunch here would give Annie a chance to talk to Father J, too. Of course he knew about the baby, and about her being here on bed rest, but not the particulars about Corey. She needed to own that, for her sake, and for the sake of the child she was going to have.

So I made a pot of cream of asparagus soup with fresh asparagus from my garden and thawed some English muffins for ham and swiss toasted open-face sandwiches. My editor called just before Father was expected, so I was in the den, sitting at my computer, when he arrived. I heard Annie yell from the couch in the family room, "Come on in," and paused a moment, swallowing and clenching my hands once.

"Cath? Are you there?" Kandace asked.

"I'm here," I said, hearing the soft murmur of voices from the family room. Father J was maybe the most empathetic person I knew. Annie was in good hands, but that didn't stop me from feeling a twinge of maternal commiseration for her now.

It took us twenty minutes to go over the edits Kandace had called about, and when I finished and hung up the phone, I could still hear Annie and Father J talking. I couldn't hear what they were saying, but talking was good.

I went into the kitchen and stirred the soup in the crock pot—the best way to keep a delicate cream soup warm—and turned on the broiler to toast the sandwiches. From here, thanks to the quirks and peculiarities of an old house, I could hear bits and pieces of the family room conversation, especially Father J's rumbly bass. I couldn't help myself. I eased over to the little hallway that led into the family room to listen.

"Human beings are extraordinary. And complicated." I could hear that clearly; Father J had a voice meant for gymnasiums and theatres. And pulpits. There was an unmistakable smile in his voice.

Annie's response was muffled.

"I don't know. I think it does. Oh, Annie Bobannie—" It was something Father J called her. Some inside joke between them. "We all doubt."

Annie said something unintelligible; her voice was so soft.

"You're going to have a child to raise up in the glory of God. You know better than me that life is a gift. Always."

I went back to the sink and turned on the water, rinsed out the dishcloth feeling my eyes burning and tears welling. I didn't know how long I stood at the sink, looking out the window, not really seeing anything, with the water running until I heard Annie call out and I realized my cheeks were damp. My heart felt lighter in my chest than it had for a long time.

"Mom! I'm starving. Is lunch ready yet?"

We ate on trays in the family room, Father J telling us funny stories about this year's peewee basketball season, and the team of four- and five-year-olds that he always coached. I had been hearing stories about the little kids on those teams for years; I thought that coaching them was one of Father J's biggest joys. It was practically a rite-of-passage for Langston's Catholic preschoolers to learn to play ball from Father J. He was one of those people who could hardly hold in his laughter when he was telling a funny story, so that Annie and I both were grinning the whole time he told us about the little girl who came to one game wearing a tutu *and* a superman cape. About the little boy who asked him where he worked and if he got "health," which Father J had assumed meant health benefits, something he thought was uproarious. Just looking at him, today wearing a pair of jeans and tennis shoes with a black shirt and the requisite collar, all six foot seven of him, the red hair, the freckles, the big hands and feet, finding so much joy in those little kids was enough to make anyone want to convert to Catholicism. It was certainly enough to make me—and Annie—smile.

After lunch, Father J asked me to show him the yard and the garden, where the wedding would be. "It's a beautiful spot, Cathleen. The work you've done here over the years is clearly a labor of love.

"I'm truly sorry I can't officiate Jamie's wedding. The rule forbidding Catholic marriages outside a church is one I don't understand. But as you know, there are lots of rules I don't understand. I have a long list for when I meet Our Father one day." He smiled ruefully.

"I understand. And Jamie and Molly really want something non-religious. I told you, she's Jewish. Or half Jewish and I don't think conversion is in the cards."

"I'll take my wins when and where I find them. Married in love is the most important thing. What's that?" he pointed.

"Lambs ears."

"I see why."

I laughed. "Yep."

"I'm very glad you decided to come home." He was looking at the plants, not at me.

"Well, I have a grandbaby coming and a wedding to get ready for."

"I hope those aren't the only reasons you returned."

I shrugged. "They're the reasons I returned *now*."

He nodded. "How are things?"

"They're okay. Awkward."

"No doubt. You effectively rebooted your marriage. Just like when you reboot your computer. You know what happens when you do that. Sometimes you have to reorganize your desktop and restart some programs."

I smiled at his analogy. I'd thought much the same thing myself at one point. "Maybe."

"I was worried about you. That you wouldn't find what you needed there, because it was here the whole time."

"I don't know, Father. I think I did find what I needed there."

"Which was?"

I tipped my head one way, then another. "The opposite of anger. Peace?"

"What were you angry about?"

"Ha. Everything. That was the problem. Absolutely everything about Joe made me so mad I couldn't see straight. Everything he said, everything he did, everything. It made me crazy."

Father looked at me intently but didn't say anything.

"I think it was more like a pressure cooker releasing steam than a computer reboot," I said. "I had to wait for the pressure to dissipate, before I could even think about opening the lid. Coming back."

"But you're home now. The anger is gone?"

I sighed. "I don't know. Maybe. I don't feel it, but I don't trust that it's gone. Yet."

"You love Joe."

I looked off toward the woods that bordered the yard. The grass needed to be mowed, on top of everything else. Except the spot where we'd buried Trouble. I wanted to plant some pansies there so we'd always have a way to mark the spot. "I don't know if that matters. Correction. I don't know if that's *enough*."

We moved around to the other side of the back yard, where I had planted delphiniums and foxglove twenty years ago that had spread and multiplied so that this corner was like a lavender cloud much of the summer.

"Did you ever think that maybe the anger, the way you were changing was what God intended?" Father J asked. "That maybe you were supposed to be changed, like metal that gets heated in a forge so it can be made into something else? 'As silver is forged in the fire and gold by the hearth, thus the Lord strengthens our hearts.' My mother used to say that."

"That's lovely. But I didn't like the way I was changing. Not gold, not silver. I was becoming an ugly person. Mean. Petty. Hateful."

"I understand. I can appreciate that you followed your instincts and took yourself away to find peace, to let the anger go before it could destroy you, or your marriage, or your family. I'm not so arrogant that I think only I know God's will. I'm just suggesting that maybe God was steering you to go to South Carolina and you listened."

I didn't respond. I thought of Father J as a friend, not just a priest, but still, he was a priest. He was a man. I didn't know if he could really understand what I had felt, was feeling.

"You've come out the other end, and you're changed."

"I don't feel that corrosive anger now. That is a change."

"Being over, or beyond, the anger is good. Being home is better. But I think you need to figure out what made you so angry to begin with that a trip to South Carolina was necessary. You can't conceivably make a trip like that more than once. At least I hope you don't turn into another Daniel Mazurski."

"Who is Daniel Mazurski? Or shouldn't I ask?"

"My best friend Ollie's dad. When I was growing up. He disappeared once or twice a year, for a day or two, or sometimes for a couple of weeks. No one knew where he went. Well, I didn't know, but I suppose some of the adults in the neighborhood knew. Mr. Mazurski was the nicest guy, quiet. He was always bringing us packs of baseball cards. He took a bunch of us to a White Sox game once. But he just disappeared sometimes."

"What happened? Where did he go?"

"We always speculated about it. That he was a spy, or a hit man. Bobby McCarthy said he maybe had another family somewhere. Ollie gave him a black eye for that."

We'd made a full circle of the back yard and had returned to the patio between the summer kitchen and the house. I sat in one of the old cast-iron garden chairs there. Father J sat down in the other, and stretched out his legs, the Asics running shoes looking huge at that angle, and clasped his hands over his waist. I could see he was wearing argyle socks with his sneakers. Pink and olive green and black. They made me smile. His huge feet made me smile. I glanced at him and saw his eyes were closed, his freckled face tilted up to the sun. His red hair glinted.

"Where did he go? Mr. Mazurski?" I asked, stretching out my own legs, tipping my face up, closing my eyes.

"To some dive bar—bars—down near the docks. Some of them aren't really even bars, not open to the public kind of places. He went down there and drank himself unconscious. Eventually, he'd come home and hold it together for a few months, or maybe a year, then he'd just fall off the wagon. He was one of those guys for whom there's no moderation. It was all or nothing for him." Father J said all this with his eyes still closed and his face tilted to the sun, like a sunflower. I never opened my eyes or looked at Father J but I could tell by the sound of his voice.

"Did Ollie know?"

"Oh, I suppose he did, at some point. When we got older, it wasn't so much of a secret anymore. But he died while I was at seminary."

"Mr. Mazurski?"

"No, Ollie. He got leukemia and died within a few months."

"Oh, that's sad." Now I opened my eyes and looked at Father J. He had his lips pursed and he nodded his head. His eyes were still closed, his faced still tipped to the sun.

"It is. He never married. The first time I got home after his death, there were three shoe boxes on my bed. My bed and my room look the same as they did when I was ten. Mom hasn't noticed that my feet hang over the footboard now. He grinned.

"What was in the shoe boxes?"

"Ollie's mom had brought over his collection of baseball cards. He wanted me to have them. Some seven hundred and fifty-six cards."

"Ohh," I said. "That makes my heart hurt."

"I know what you mean. Oh, do I know what you mean. Our legacies aren't always the things we plan for them to be. I have those shoe boxes in my closet. Every now and then I take them out and look at the cards. Those players were our heroes."A sparrow, or a wren, I could never keep them straight, flew by with a piece of dried grass in its mouth. I watched it land on the top of the light beside the summer kitchen door. Almost every year a bird built a nest on that light. It was amazing to watch how industrious those tiny birds were, and to see the fruits of their labors take shape.

"Joe told you about Doug? About his drinking?" At the moment, I wasn't sure if Father J's story about Ollie and his dad was intended to address my sabbatical to Charleston, or to open the door to a conversation about Doug.

Knowing Father J, maybe, likely, both.

"He might have mentioned it. It's not unusual, you know. There are so many temptations these days."

"It was so much easier when they were little. The kids, I mean. When the biggest worry I had was if they'd get picked for the team, or if they'd pass chemistry. They don't tell you that. When you become a parent. That you never stop worrying."

"You know what I'm supposed to say about that, right?"

"What?"

"Don't worry. Let go and let God."

I snorted. "Some priest with no children might say that."

He smiled. "Agree. I imagine your life is not your own ever again. Not that it ever truly is *your own*, that's our misconception. That we're in control. We never are and He always is. But I get your point. I like thinking that God feels the way you do, the way other parents feel, about their kids. Worried, so much in love that it hurts His heart when we screw up or things go bad. That's the way I like thinking of Our Father."

"Will he be okay?" I glanced at him. "Doug."

"Pray for him. Pray, talk to him, pray some more. Addiction is manageable."

I noticed the choice of words: addiction is *manageable*. Not curable. "I don't even know if he is an addict. He might just be making dumb decisions."

"Maybe," Father J said, and I wasn't sure if he believed that or if he was just holding out hope for me.

"I'll pray. Joe will kick his butt. He already has. Figuratively, I mean. Has him working on some computer tech sort of project at the warehouse."

Father J smiled again. "Tough love. That's Joe's style."

"Yes, it is. Remains to be seen if it's effective."

"Doug has to admit he has a problem. You know that."

"I do."

"Admit it and want to take steps to manage his addiction. Until then, love and prayer."

I bobbed my head: love and prayer, love and prayer.

"I'm here if you need to talk. You know that. I'm here for Doug, too."

I nodded. "Thanks."

"I thought I'd ask him to help me start a summer golf league."

"Golf league?"

"Well, you know we have the adult winter basketball league. Most of those guys would play golf in the summer. You don't think Doug would want to help?"

"I think Doug would help with whatever you asked him, Father." Though I couldn't even begin to imagine Doug hanging out during summer evenings playing golf with the middle-aged men of the parish—for me, and I was sure Doug would feel the same. But it was next to impossible to tell Father J no. Father J smiled to himself and reclined again in the chair, as much as the chair would allow him to recline. He crossed his hands behind his head and tilted his face toward the sun once more.

"Do you think Jamie would allow me to offer a blessing at the wedding? I won't do the service, but I believe I could offer a blessing. I would be honored."

"I think he and Molly would like that." And I thought they would approve. It was the kind of small thing that would make their ceremony personal, without making it "too religious." Jamie's expression.

Father was smiling again. "I'm really missing your cooking, Cathleen. Dorothea has done a great job, filling in, but she just told me the other day that her daughter is counting on her to babysit this summer, when school is out. When the wedding is over and after Annie has her baby, perhaps you'll be ready to resume your duties in my kitchen?"

"I miss cooking for you, Father." It was a hedge and I felt a small twinge of guilt. I just didn't know if I was staying in Langston. But I wasn't ready to talk about that indecision now, today.

I changed the subject. "Did I tell you my parents are coming Monday? So they can 'help get ready for the wedding.' My mother makes me crazy, as I'm sure I've told you before. I don't know when we last spent more than a few days under the same roof. I may be the one with an alcohol problem before it's all said and done. Not to joke about that—"

"I understand," he said with a smile. "I would say 'we all have our cross to bear' but I wouldn't want to joke about *that*."

Now I smiled. How did he do that? Make it feel human and forgivable and almost holy all at the same time to be able to vent? "Definitely not."

"Oh, Cath. I've missed having you to talk to. And of course I've missed your cooking. I'm glad you're home. It's where you need to be."

Chapter 17

L ater, when I returned from running a couple of errands, there was a phone ringing somewhere. In the family room, on the coffee table. Annie's phone. But no Annie. I grabbed it and headed down the hall toward the bedroom. "Annie, honey. Corey is on the phone."

My daughter was curled on one side, covered with an afghan, when I got to the doorway. I watched her shift awkwardly, turning the mound of her belly under the blanket, pushing the pillow under her head so that she was marginally reclined.

"Thank God. I've been trying to call him all day," Annie said, reaching for the phone. "I forgot I left it out there."

"Why? Is something wrong?" I handed it to her.

"No, I just wanted to talk to him. He texted earlier and said he might not be able to come this weekend." The first Corey had been able to plan a trip up since Annie had started her tenure on bed rest here.

The phone rang again. "Mom?" Annie waited, phone held to her chest, looking pointedly at me, clearly expecting me to leave the room before she answered.

"Oh, sorry," I said, waving one hand before turning again and disappearing into the hallway.

"You can bring them here. My mom won't care."

Corey's boys, I concluded. Clearly they had been the topic of conversation even before this call.

"He won't care, either." *Joe.* I didn't know that Joe *wouldn't care.* "I mean, they both need to get to know everyone. They're going to be Daley grandchildren, too."

This was something I hadn't considered. Our future "step-grand-children," little kids who'd had nothing to do with this situation, their dad cheating on their mother, their family falling apart, their lives being totally shaken up. My heart ached for them. It wasn't their fault.

"You can play catch in our backyard as easily as you can in yours." Pause. "I know it's important. They're important. But so am I. So are we! Our baby is important."

Oh, Annie! You and your child are always going to have to share him with another woman, other children.

"I need you. I want you to come up and be here with me. For just a day. Is that too much to ask? I'm stuck lying here, all by myself, growing our child."

All by herself? What were we, me and Joe and Doug? Potted plants?

"The least you can do is be with me for one fucking day!"

Annie was crying now. I could hear it in her voice and much as I wanted to go back into the bedroom and comfort my daughter, I knew that this was Annie's anguish. Annie's life. This was reaping what you sow and there was nothing I could do or say to make Annie feel better.

———

Sunday turned into one of those surreal days that just kept unfolding in bizarre ways from the get-go. Joe and I had gone to early mass. In a surprise move that I was still processing (and trying not to question, Doug had gotten up and gone with us. We'd left Annie sleeping. Lillian preferred mass at eleven, so she was not present, which made for an uncommon, but lovely (in my view) Daley contingent.

When we got home, I made French toast and sausage, at Doug's request. The shower in the master bedroom was running when I went to check on Annie. "I'm making French toast. You want some?" I called through the bathroom door.

There was a long moment of silence, when I wondered if Annie hadn't heard me. I was just getting ready to ask again when she answered. "Yeah, sure," but not sounding particularly enthusiastic. Still sulking then.

I fixed Annie a tray that looked like something staged for a magazine, with a purple flower, bright orange juice and a banana, the French toast with a pat of melting golden butter, browned sausage on a blue willow plate, on a pale yellow linen placemat. I even got out the good silver and a cloth napkin. It wasn't just food and drink, it was a small act of love. It made me smile, though it remained to be seen if it would cheer Annie.

Another cookbook idea? *Small Acts of Love from the Kitchen.* No doubt Kandace would love it.

"Thanks, Mom," Annie said, studying the tray, then looked up after a moment, her gray eyes glassy with tears, when I settled it on her lap. "I'm sorry I'm being such a bitch."

I smoothed her honey-colored hair, which was darker now, still damp from her shower, "You are. But I love you anyway," I said, smiling. I decided to let her wallow in her self-pity for a little while, thinking to chase, or coax, her to the patio for some fresh air later.

Doug and Joe sat at the island in the kitchen, between the two of them demolishing almost two pounds of sausage and half a loaf of French toast. Joe had the local newspaper spread out and Doug was looking at Golf magazine. The two of them sat in companionable silence, the kitchen smelling of coffee and sausage and maple syrup.

Joe offered to do the cleanup which surprised me. It was a small thing, but a momentous thing all the same. I had not left Langston and gone on sabbatical in Charleston because Joe didn't help around the house. But his offer to wash up, the change in roles, felt like an acknowledgment, an affirmation, that things were different. We were different.

"Okay," I said. "Thanks."

The doorbell rang. Nobody rang our doorbell. It was at the front door. And everyone used the kitchen door, everyone who knew us. Even the UPS man and the pizza delivery people knew to use the kitchen door. "Who's ringing the doorbell on a Sunday morning?"

Doug looked up from his magazine.

"I'll get it," Joe said.

"Hey," I heard him say and something about his voice made me get up from the island and move to the doorway to the family room where I could see down the hall to the front door.

It took me a moment to realize it was Corey. And obviously his two boys, one very young, holding his dad's hand and carrying a suitcase, the other, older, looking sullen and uncertain, wearing a baseball glove.

Oh, my! This was a surprise. Did Annie know they were coming? I moved to join Joe at the door. The two boys were both looking up at him. How old were they? Three and ten? A very unhappy ten. The three-year-old looked like a miniature of his dad. The older boy was darker, finer boned. Like his mother? I didn't know what to say, what to do, felt the uncomfortable lull, knew without looking at his face that Joe didn't know what to say or do, either.

"Hi," I said, moving to the door. "Come on in. I'm Cath," I said to the older boy, holding out my hand. He stared at it for a moment before shaking it, tentatively, the way young boys who haven't shaken very many hands shake. The ball glove, which seemed inordinately huge, he held in his other hand. The younger boy held out his hand to shake, too, and I smiled. He was adorable, big blue eyes, chubby cheeks. Those eyes were so solemn, watchful. What I'd thought was a suitcase in his hand was a barn, with a handle. There was one just like it in the attic. "What's your name?"

"He's Alexander," the older boy said.

Alexander just stared up at me, then at Joe, his eyes wide, his expression so serious.

I smiled at the older boy. "You must be Adam." I wasn't sure how I remembered that.

He nodded, still looking sullen. I smiled at Corey, a smile that was polite, a well-mannered hostess smile, at the man who was the father of our future grandchild. Maybe grandchildren. He was wearing a red windbreaker over a light blue polo shirt and jeans. The shirt made his eyes look really blue. I thought it was his eyes that were his most compelling feature; it was those light eyes you noticed. But I couldn't get past his *age! You were in college when Annie was born!* But now he was here, on our porch, and I could feel the two pairs of young eyes standing to either side of him studying me. Awkwardness filled the doorway like another person.

"Come on in," I said after a moment that was filled with words no one spoke. "Annie will be very happy to see you." Joe still hadn't said anything.

"I thought we'd surprise her. She sounded a little discouraged on the phone the other day. I know this has been hard for her. I would have let you know, but I don't have a cell number. For either of you—"

"It's fine. Not a problem." I smiled again, and the term *pasted-on* came to mind. "You want to go get Annie, Joe?"

"Sure."

I led the trio into the family room. Doug stood in the doorway to the kitchen. "Doug," I said. "This is Corey. Annie's...friend."

There was a pause while Doug processed that. "Oh. Hey," he finally said, coming into the room to shake Corey's hand. "Nice to meet you. "He glanced at me when he said that and I could almost see him thinking, *isn't it?*

"You, too," Corey said. "I've heard a lot about you."

"Yeah? Hopefully it's not all true. That would be bad."

Corey gave a little laugh. "Don't know. Remains to be seen."

"Who are these little dudes?"

"Adam. And Alex."

"Hey. Nice glove," Doug said. "You a southpaw? Me, too." I hadn't registered that it was a left-handed glove.

"I am. He's not," Adam said, nodding toward his brother.

"You wanna go outside and play a little catch?"

Adam looked up at his dad, as if to see if that would be okay.

"I guess," Adam said to Doug then.

"You want to come, too?" Doug asked the younger boy.

He nodded, big eyes glued to Doug.

"He can't catch anything," Adam said.

"Yeah, well. Practice makes perfect. Let's go find a glove. Two gloves. I bet we have one that'll fit him. Because, you know, little brothers rock." Then the younger boy let go of Corey's hand and took Doug's in a moment of nearly mind-blowing bizarre-ness.

Just little boys stuck in the middle of this mess. "I hope it's not an inconvenience—" Corey was studying me with those eyes.

"It's fine. Annie will be thrilled."

And isn't that who we all care about? The one thing we have in common?

Until your baby is born, yours and Annie's, then we will have him, or her, in common.

I could hear Doug's voice as he rooted in the mudroom cupboard for baseball gloves, talking to the two boys who would be his nephews. Step-nephews?

Uncle Doug.

———

My mother called then to let us know they were ahead of schedule, and would arrive mid-afternoon. Today. Not tomorrow. My parents would get to meet Annie's married lover the very day they arrived. And his two children. Ugh.

"The wedding isn't for three weeks. She told me they would come early, *to help with stuff.* I tried to tell her it wasn't necessary."

"If I know your mom, the rice will still be on the sidewalk, the cans still rattling from the bumper of the newlyweds' car, and she'll have her bags packed," Joe said.

I looked at him. "You're right. That's her MO. She'll be in the car ready to head home to Tucson by 7:00 a.m. the morning after the wedding."

He swatted me on the rump. "Be glad they're coming. They're not perfect, but they're your parents. I'm sure you can find stuff to keep them busy and out of your hair."

"You're remembering the time they were here and Dad decided he'd go to the warehouse with you."

"He swept the floor, and fixed a hinge on a closet door, and broke down a bunch of boxes for the dumpster, as I recall. He was actually helpful. But I know they get under your skin. Your mom in particular."

"I have lots of stuff to do. I'm not sure how much of that they can actually help with, though."

He shrugged. "They can keep Annie company. Your mom will love stepping and fetching for the princess."

"Maybe." I took a deep breath. I hadn't been able to tell what my parents really thought about Annie's baby. Of course I'd talked to them after Annie shared her news—I think my mother had called me the second she'd hung up—but it was difficult to tell over the phone. Was there disappointment? Judgment? "If they say anything to make Annie feel bad, I swear I'll strangle them both."

"No, you won't. You'll just vent about them at night, in the dark, when we're in our little beds. Like a slumber party."

I looked at him. "They're not little beds. They're actually extra-long twins. And you're right. I will vent. I'm sorry in advance."

"No need to apologize. I'm a good ventee."

I smiled ruefully. Sighed. "Okay, then. I'll get another couple of packs of ground beef out of the freezer. They'll be here in two hours. Ready or not."

"That's the spirit."

Later, as Joe awkwardly shaped some of the thawed burger into patties much too large for today's dinner crowd, and I chopped celery for potato salad, Joe said, "If Doug pulls out the ping pong table, we'd better draw the line. You took Solo cups out with the lemonade. He's equipped."

"Lemonade pong?"

"I wouldn't put it past him. He's introduced just about every other yard game except maybe horseshoes."

"He's being a thoughtful big brother and entertaining the boys so Corey can talk to Annie."

"Yeah. That's what's making me nervous."

I watched his hands clumsily working the ground beef into another patty. "Make some a little smaller?" I said. "We've got some young kids to feed, too."

He nodded, pulled off some ground beef, began to shape a small hamburger patty. I heard Annie laughing, which made my heart warm. Annie needed this day. I just wasn't sure it was the kind of day my daughter was ever going to be able to count on, given Corey's situation.

I opened the fridge to get out the ketchup, mustard, and three different varieties of pickles which I sat on the counter. I pulled out one of the crisper drawers to look for some American cheese. "Do you know how many times you've helped me make burgers? I mean actually make the burgers, not just man the grill as they cook. In thirty years of marriage, I don't think you've ever diced an onion before."

"Sure I have."

I looked at him and could see that his eyes still looked weepy, thanks to the big sweet onion I'd had him chop. But his expression was wide-eyed and innocent. It occurred to me that there were a lot of days in my memory when Joe was present, but I'd not really *seen*

336

him. He'd just been Joe. Ever since I'd gotten home from South Carolina, I felt like I'd been seeing him with different eyes. Now, as he looked at me, his hands messy and full of partly-formed hamburger patty, the look in his eyes mirrored what was in my own. I knew instinctively that he was thinking the same thing, that he was seeing me differently, that I was suddenly, or maybe not so suddenly, but at the moment anyway, someone different. Not just Cath.

What did Joe see? Did he think I was attractive? When was the last time I'd even given that a thought?

As if he knew what I was thinking he smiled at me, one of those little smiles that made a dimple in one cheek but barely moved his lips, and like it had years ago, that smile made a tiny zing shoot through me. It was one of those moments out of time that I wished I could freeze-frame. A blip of a second.

"You can't avoid Corey forever," I said to Joe. "And while I appreciate your help in the kitchen, you—we—need to make an effort. To talk to him. To talk to the boys. To let them—Corey and Annie—know we're supportive."

He took a deep breath and dropped the last roughly round patty onto the piece of waxed paper I'd put on the baking sheet. He grimaced. "That obvious?"

"That you're hiding out in here? Like I said, when was the last time you helped make burgers? Maybe go see if they want more lemonade?"

"Okay," Joe said. He'd missed a tiny spot when he'd shaved this morning and whiskers glinted in the sunlight that came in the window over the sink. Bending down, he pressed a kiss to my forehead, nothing more than a fly-by peck, before washing his hands and disappearing out the mudroom door with the pitcher of lemonade. It was the first kiss of any kind since I'd returned from Charleston.

This one was so quick, so unexpected, afterward, I couldn't recall the expression on his face, or what might have been in his eyes.

———

My parents arrived, and met Corey and his boys. Then, as if she had some sort of intuition, or radar, Lillian showed up. The rest of the day became the kind of chaotic blur that I used to lose myself in: lots of people, lots of food, hostessing. Today, however, I felt removed, as if I was watching from a distance.

As ridiculous as it was, I couldn't stop thinking about Joe kissing me, that peck that lasted less than a second. I caught myself watching him.

I'd moved to Charleston for nearly four and a half months. With no warning or discussion and no real reason that Joe could understand. I wasn't sure I understood it, really. My leaving had to have hurt him terribly, and worried him, and potentially damaged the relationship we had built over more than thirty years together.

Why did I no longer feel the anger and annoyance that had driven me to leave Langston and go south to Charleston?

Nothing particularly note-worthy had happened while I was in South Carolina. In fact, my months in Charleston were especially non-noteworthy: I worked on my cookbook. I worked at the Purple Onion. I walked on the beach a lot. I walked a lot, period. It was especially true in my mind now. The houses, the streets and sidewalks, the shops and flowers and gardens, the smell of the ocean and the rivers and the scents of flowers blooming were all a blur. The most noteworthy thing that had happened in those four and a half months was Annie coming to visit and finding out my daughter was pregnant. What happened to my anger? Until I figured that out, life here felt precarious. Temporary.

The guys were playing catch now; Corey and Joe were playing, too. The younger boy, Alex, had finally given up the ghost and was asleep on the family room sofa. Corey stood next to Joe and threw across ten yards of backyard to Adam, the older son. Joe was throwing to Doug who was standing next to Adam. Fathers on one side, sons on the other. I couldn't remember the last time Doug and Joe had played catch. Joe and Corey were talking about something but I couldn't hear what. I didn't feel any more certain about Corey, didn't feel any happier or less worried about Annie starting a life with this—older—married—man, who looked nearly like a contemporary of Joe's as they stood side by side.

Leaning back in the chair at the round patio table, my legs stretched out before me, I relaxed for a moment. The late afternoon sun came through a gap in the trees beyond the yard and it felt pleasantly warm. I looked around. Annie was on her lounge chair, almost dozing. My mom was in the chair beside her, her feet propped up on the little metal coffee table, a pile of soft mint green work-in-progress baby blanket in her lap, knitting needles clicking softly as she talked to Lillian, who sat primly in a chair on the other side of Annie while sipping at lemonade from one of my great-grandmother's crystal glasses.

Of course. Never mind that I had set out a stack of plastic cups. I waited for the flare of irritation but it didn't come. Had I just needed a vacation?

"Cathleen." My dad stood in the doorway behind the screen, one hand holding a SOLO cup which I knew would be full of iced tea, lots of ice. "The FedEx guy is at the door. He's got a package. A big one. Where do you want him to put it? What'd you order? A telephone pole?"

"I didn't order anything. Why would FedEx be delivering on a Sunday?"

"Amazon Prime," Annie said.

"I didn't order anything from Amazon Prime," I said, getting up and heading into the house. "I didn't order anything at all."

"FedEx doesn't do Amazon deliveries anymore," Doug said, between tosses to Joe.

"That's right, they don't," Joe said, chiming in from the shipping committee.

"The FedEx guy said it's for Cathleen Daley."

"Oh, my God," I said when I saw the package. It did look sort of like a telephone pole. Roughly round, probably more than a foot in diameter, and I guessed maybe eight or nine feet long, wrapped tightly in white plastic and strapping tape.

"There's a box, too," he said, fetching it from the truck. "Minnesota," he said, reading the label as he handed it to me. "You have a nice day."

The return address said Apple Valley, Minnesota. Handwriting that was bold and curvy and unfamiliar. "Molly?" I said. "Molly is from Apple Valley."

"You want me to open it?" my dad asked, digging a folding knife out of his pocket—the knife he never went anywhere without—and looking at me. He'd left the cup of iced tea somewhere.

"Sure."

He slit the plastic and peeled the wrapping back to expose tree limbs. Each one a couple of inches thick. Four of them. The bark was gray and mottled. "What in the heck—?" Taking the box from my arms, dad slit the tape on it, too.

I sat down on the front porch step and opened the flaps. Inside the box, carefully wrapped in tissue, was a white cloth of some kind decorated with blue embroidery. On top of the folded cloth was a pale pink envelope. "What is it?" Joe asked, coming out on the porch. "Firewood?" he said, seeing the poles in the yard still partly wrapped in plastic. "Cost a frickin' kidney to send those by FedEx." Of course Joe would think about logistics and cost.

Ignoring him, I opened the envelope and skimmed the note. "It's from Molly's mom."

"Jamie's in-law's sent us firewood?"

"It's a chuppah. Or chew-pa. I'm not sure how you pronounce it. For the wedding. Maybe."

"Maybe? Maybe what?" Joe said. "What's a chuppah?"

"She says that it's Jewish tradition. This is the same one that Molly's brother used for his wedding. And two cousins. She wanted to send it so it was here. She's hoping Molly and Jamie will use it."

"Jewish? Is Molly Jewish?" My mother.

"Molly's mom is Jewish," I said.

"I thought they wanted to get married in the back yard," Joe said.

I rolled my eyes. "They do. They are. This is like a trellis, I think. But covered with this cloth, instead of flowers."

"Oh, my," my mother said. "Methodists don't have all those sort of...*frills*," was the word she finally settled on. Which was better than *nonsense*, which is what I thought she was going to say, would have bet money she was going to say.

Criticize was what my mother did, subtly or blatantly. For as long as I could remember.

"Catholics have lots of *frills*," Joe said, winking at me.

———

WE'D EATEN the burgers and dogs, the potato salad and the baked beans, I hadn't moved yet to get the ice cream I thought we'd have for dessert, when my mom spoke, in her "let me have your attention please, I'm going to say something important," voice that made me want to squirm. The two little boys were back out in the yard with the croquet set again and I just heard the older boy say "You dumb-ass. You get yellow. I get blue." I glanced at Corey, but he either didn't hear or pretended not to hear, or else he was just afraid to interrupt my mother. "As you all know, Cath and Joe celebrated a very important milestone this year. Thirty years is a special anniversary."

Now I did cringe, though I hid it with a smile that no doubt did not reach my eyes. When I glanced at Joe, he was grinning at me. Did he know about this? Or did he just find my mother funny? He knew she often embarrassed and annoyed me.

"Your dad and I didn't get to help you celebrate on the actual day of your anniversary, but we wanted to give you something really special to commemorate the occasion." *Commemorate. Occasion.* These were words my mom did not use in everyday speech. I could imagine her thinking about this moment, making this *presentation*, and writing it in her head in the car during the drive from Arizona.

I hadn't noticed my dad getting up and bringing a huge gift bag out onto the patio. Joe was sitting across the table from me and he winked again. What was with all the winking?

"Oh," I said. "Wow. I wasn't expecting this."

"Well, you're not too old for a little surprise. Either one of you." Mom glanced at Joe.

I pulled away the several puffs of white tissue paper jammed in the top of the bag to reveal a cheap black wood picture frame. I pulled it out, uncertain. It was a big, economy-style frame, without glass, bordering a piece of dark blue poster board, the front heavy with...silver dollars. A pattern of silver dollars glued to the poster board in the shape of a three and a zero. Thirty. There must have been...thirty. It looked more than a little like a second grade art project. I could see the pencil lines where my dad hadn't erased them.

I looked up at my mom and then to my dad, both with proud smiles on their faces. The expression "pleased as punch," flitted through my head.

I knew some of these silver dollars, if not all of them, had come from the cache of coins that they had accumulated over the years. Some of the really old ones had once belonged to my dad's parents. They—parents and grandparents—believed silver dollars were special. Valuable. Though I knew they had no idea of the actual *value* of the coins. They were not sophisticated numismatists, not by a long shot. I glanced again at the ones on the poster board and could tell some of them were solid silver, truly old coins, but some were newer ones that were some other metal, not silver.

"Thirty years is nothing to sneeze at," my mother said. "And my...have the years flown by."

"Thank you," I said, looking down at the silver dollars glued firmly to the poster board, and running a finger along the pattern, oddly touched. For some reason, when I looked up, it was Corey I was looking at. What was he thinking, sitting here at a picnic table, covered with used paper plates smeared with ketchup and mustard, baked beans and potato salad, the faint smell of grilling meat still in the air, surrounded by Annie's extended family, some of them anyway, people he'd never met before today? He was smiling, a polite, detached sort of smile. I understood the detachment. I did. But...

What's hers is yours, pal, I wanted to say. *We're going to be family to her child. Your child.*

"Yeah thanks! That's pretty awesome," Joe said, about the poster. "That's a lot of silver dollars!"

Was I going to be expected to hang this...*artwork*...on the wall somewhere? I wasn't at all sure what we were supposed to do with it.

"Thirty," my dad said almost curtly, impatiently, a fleeting glimpse of the persona that had been my dad all of my growing up years and that had mostly, but not entirely, seemed to have mellowed into something else since the move to Arizona. Since his affair with Debra Patterson. I could just picture him at the little workbench in the front of their garage, which was all the work bench space my mother allowed in Arizona, meticulously drawing the big numbers on the poster board with pencil, then carefully gluing the coins to the cardboard and then fitting it into the frame, which my mom would have made a huge production about getting. No doubt it involved a special trip to the store, on a day when nothing else could be planned because of the frame shopping trip.

I had to bite my lip suddenly, fighting a grin, which I knew was not the sufficiently awed and impressed reaction my mom and dad expected, but because I also knew that Kandace my editor would love this story. Kandace would love *everything* about this moment, and would encourage me to capture it in an essay: a backyard picnic table, red solo cups, paper plates, an anniversary celebration, that would accompany a recipe for homemade ketchup or kitchen sink cookies. She'd told me many times that it was the small-town, "real people unpretentiousness" of my family, of our life, that was appealing not just to her but to cookbook readers everywhere. I wanted to look at Joe, to catch his eye, but knew what I'd see if I did and then I'd never be able to keep from laughing, so I kept my gaze on the silver dollars.

———

JAMIE CALLED AFTER DINNER. "Her mom just doesn't get it. I mean, she says she understands we're being married in the back yard, for Christ's sake, but then she does stuff like this. It's driving Molly batshit."

I was sitting on the lounge chair on the patio where Annie had perched for most of the afternoon, but it was chilly now, and dark. It smelled of damp earth and new leaves. The faint sound of voices and then a laugh track on the television came to me through the screen door in the laundry room. Corey and his boys had left for Pittsburgh an hour ago.

"I'm sorry, Mom," Jamie said.

About what? Oh, yeah. Molly's mom was driving Molly batshit.

But what was Jamie apologizing for? His language, or for the fact that Molly's mom had sent the chuppah?

"You don't have to apologize. It's not a problem." The language or the chuppah. And I was having no problems with Molly's mom. "I just wondered if you were going to use it. Poppy and Grammie got here this afternoon so they could help with wedding stuff. I'm sure Poppy would be happy to put it up...."

"Not necessary. Tell Dad to throw it in the garage. When I get home, I'll wrap it back up and we can ship it back to Minnesota."

"It wouldn't be too big a deal, to put it up—"

"I know. But it's such a Jewish thing, and we both want the wedding to be secular, not religious. Think a justice of the peace courthouse ceremony, but in the back yard. Our friend Pete, the guy who's gonna do the service, is Baptist. Father J and Molly's uncle, the rabbi, are gonna be there. That's as much religion as we want."

I winced. I'd assured Father J that he could offer a blessing. "I get it," I said, though apparently I was as guilty as Molly's mom at inserting myself.

"That's why we're getting married in our yard. Because if Molly's mom had her way, the whole thing would be over-the-top crazy. We want simple. Just a wedding in a yard with you know, all the wild-flowers."

Wildflowers? I shook my head and rolled my eyes. Typical. Did he think all those plants and flowers grew there naturally?

"If Mrs. McDonald calls, whatever she wants, just tell her we got it covered."

"Got what covered?"

"Everything. Anything. The yard. The flowers. The ceremony. The chairs. The food. The photographer. It'll be perfect. I'll be home in two weeks. And I'll have time to help with stuff. Molly is coming Wednesday before the big day. She'll be able to help then, too. I'm not sure when the McDonalds are coming. Hopefully ten minutes before the ceremony."

"Jamie!"

"Sorry. It's just that Mrs. Mac has been so, you know...Jewish mother about everything."

"Well, it's her only daughter getting married. I'm sure she just wants the day to be special." No pressure, Cath. "I'd feel the same way if it was Annie getting married." *Which she's not. And may never be if Corey won't divorce his wife.*

"How is my pregnant sister? Ready to pop?"

"What do you think about your sister having a baby? About being an uncle?"

"It's Annie's life. She's lived it pretty well up to now. Doubt she'll shit the bed. She texts ten times a day. Twenty. Tells me what you're doing for the wedding. Every detail."

"Seriously?"

"Planted zinnias yesterday. Whatever those are. Bought a bunch of new flower pots. Washed all the windows. Told me about Doug, too. I didn't know he lost his job and was living at home."

"I didn't realize you didn't know. I'm sure he's ashamed to tell you. You're the one person he's looked up to and admired his whole life. I thought about asking you to talk to him, but I didn't know if that would be a good thing or a bad thing," I said. "Your hero rubbing it in your face that you failed."

"I'm not his hero, mom. He didn't fail. He just fucked up."

"Yes, you are. You've never realized that. Did you know about his drinking? I mean, did you have any idea it was a problem?"

"He's too smart for his own good. I always feel like he's bored," Jamie said. "He'll get his shit together eventually. Figure it out."

We got rid of all the booze in the house. I know we shouldn't have to do that, but we did."

"We're having booze for the wedding."

"Of course," I said. "That's one day. Doug will have to *figure it out*."

"It'll be the whole weekend. And yes, he will." There was that challenge, that sibling rivalry thing I could hear in his voice.

Then Jamie spoke again, and now I could hear the laughter in his voice. "Annie's pregnant to a married guy and stuck on your couch. Doug's a drunk who lost his job and is living at home. There's gonna be a wedding in a couple of weeks in the yard and seventy-five guests to feed, and a crazy Jewish mother-in-law driving everyone batshit. Geez, mom. I'm glad you're back."

I could feel the smile spread across my face before the laugh erupted from my mouth, unbidden. Jamie could always do that.

But the day wasn't over yet.

After I finished talking to Jamie and went inside, it was to find my dad and my mother-in-law in the kitchen, sitting at the island, in the middle of a conversation.

Today my mother-in-law was wearing navy pants, what women of her generation called "slacks," a white blouse with a bow at the neck and a soft blue cardigan sweater. Navy blue Naturalizer shoes. Attractive in a prim, proper way, her white hair cut neatly short. She was so much of a certain style, and class, that was light years different from that of my parents; it was disconcerting to me when they were in the same room. They'd always been polite with each other, my parents and Joe's mom, they were just *so different*.

My dad was wearing a cheap golf shirt that had a logo I didn't recognize embroidered on the chest and also a stain where he'd dripped something and the bulge of his belly had caught it. He was oblivious to the stain and the belly. And the logo for that matter. He was wearing white sneakers, the kind with Velcro straps, and a pair of Bermuda shorts that looked like they'd seen better days. It was, I knew, his daily uniform. No doubt his suitcase upstairs featured a selection of similar shorts and shirts. And the odd sweatshirt and a pair of jeans.

He still had a red SOLO cup of iced tea in front of him and today's paper open beside it as if he'd been reading the local news. He'd changed the inner tube on one of the kids' old bikes today so Adam could ride it, and there was still some grease or oil on his hands. Or maybe it was the grease and oil that had been there for all of the years I could remember, even when they were clean, a kind of stigmata. My dad was—had been—a mechanic, a machinist. He was always fixing or repairing something. There was nothing he couldn't mend, patch, or make. He was the definition of blue collar. "How's Jamie? Everything okay?" he asked.

"He's good."

"He hasn't changed his mind? Decided to stay single and go fishing and hunting anytime he wants?" He was making a joke, the kind that made him proud of himself. I also recognized it was a statement about his own life. He didn't get to fish, or hunt, whenever he wanted. He didn't even get to live where he wanted to live. It was my mother who had decided they'd move from Delaware to Arizona.

"No," I smiled. In many ways, it was hard to reconcile this man with the one I remembered from my childhood. "The wedding's still on."

"Well, good. That little filly knows what she's got. She'd better hang on. That Jamie's a pretty special kid."

347

"She's a lovely girl. He's pretty lucky, too," Lillian said. "Have you met her yet?"

"No. Saw some pictures, though. She's pretty cute. Smart, too, sounds like. Gonna be a lawyer. Jamie calls and gives me the update." My dad was proud that the kids called him occasionally. As if he'd been conferred with some special favor. "What about the tent?" he said now to me.

"Tent?" I said.

"Yeah, you know. The thing that came in the mail."

"Oh, the chuppah. No, they don't want to use it. Jamie said he'll pack it up and ship it back to Molly's parents' house when he gets home."

"I can pack it up for him. Might as well make myself useful. Hey, Lillian was telling me she's gonna spend this winter in Florida. Be a snowbird," he said with you-didn't-tell-us-that recrimination in his voice.

"Yeah. Big news, huh?"

"It'll be good for Mom," Joe said, appearing from the family room behind me, his hands on my shoulders, massaging. "She won't have to deal with snow or ice. Just lots of sunshine and ocean breezes."

"You think the weather on that cruise was great, wait 'til you live somewhere it's like that all winter," my dad said.

Despite myself, my gaze jumped to Lillian. My mother-in-law looked at me and I could see the regret that the topic had been raised in my presence. She hadn't mentioned the cruise since I'd been home. I hadn't asked about it, either.

"Sounds like quite a trip," Dad said to Joe, saving her. "Those boats are something. Got big diesel engines on 'em."

Standing right behind me, so close I felt his legs against mine, I could tell Joe shrugged. "I wouldn't know," he said. "Didn't go. Didn't have any interest in a trip like that without Cath."

"That's what Lillian said. I told her I wasn't surprised. The two of you celebrating your thirtieth anniversary. I didn't remember it was thirty but your mom informed me. She keeps track of that stuff. Those silver dollars were a big surprise, huh?"

I wanted to laugh but settled for rolling my head to one side so Joe could reach the tendons that ran along the side of my neck. "They were."

There was more talk about winter in a warm place. Joe kept rubbing my shoulders and I tipped my head, first to one side then the other. Beyond the pleasures of a neck massage, it was Joe, touching me, something that had only happened tentatively, mostly inadvertently, since I'd been back. This felt different somehow.

"Well you can sit here and talk all night, but I'm going to bed," Joe said, tapping my butt. "I have an early call. G'night."

I'd had good intentions of re-grouping on the bedroom situation once my parents arrived, but since they'd arrived unexpectedly a day early, and since that day had been full of Corey and his boys and a picnic, the musical bedroom game hadn't been played. Joe and I were still in the boys' room, Annie was still in our room downstairs, Doug was still in the guest room, and mom and dad were in Annie's room. I sighed. Oh, well. We'd have to readjust at some point before Jamie arrived the week of the wedding because he was going to need a bed to sleep in. But I kicked that can down the road tonight. When I came out of the upstairs bathroom, I heard the sound of voices, muted, from the bottom of the stairs, from the master bedroom. Not the television. The light was still on, Annie was up. Talking to Corey? Maybe Doug.

I'd noticed that Doug had been spending time with Annie, odd moments of the day, sitting in the old easy chair in the corner, his feet propped on the end of the bed, the two of them watching television or reading, or just talking.

There was laughter, suddenly, from the master bedroom and curious, I went down the stairs, my bare feet nearly silent on the treads, and peeked around the door frame. My mom was sitting on the side of the bed, both hands spread over the mound of Annie's abdomen, a smile on her face.

She and Annie both looked up. Annie had an expression on her face that I recognized, the kind of joy that came with being a mother, even a prospective mother. Clearly she was still basking in the fact that Corey had come and spent the day. It was the happiest she'd looked since she'd been here sentenced to bed rest. *I hope you only ever know that happiness, but I fear that you won't. I know that you won't. No one does.*

"My great-grandchild is an active one," my mom said. Even from the doorway, even through the over-sized t-shirt Annie slept in, I could see the baby moving under my mother's hands, where a knee or an elbow traced for a split second the curve of Annie's belly. "She's doing back flips."

"Maybe he's dancing," Annie said, grinning.

"Or juggling." The two of them looked at each other and laughed some more.

Annie put a hand on her belly on the opposite side of my mom's so that there were three hands cradling the mound of the unborn baby. "I'll just be happy when she or he has her, or his, own real estate to do whatever. I wasn't prepared for this bed-rest contingency. I'm using up my maternity leave and she, or he, isn't even here yet." Now I could hear a seed of concern, of fear, in Annie's voice.

"Don't you worry, dearheart. That makes for stress and that's not good for the baby or you. It'll work out. Things always do. The important thing is that you love the child and know that we all love you both."

I stared. *Who are you and what have you done with my mother?* When I'd broken the news to my parents about being pregnant with Nora, my dad had slammed a kitchen cabinet door so hard it had splintered in half and fallen to the floor.

"Times are a lot different now than in my day. Than in your mother's day." She glanced at me. Was that an apology? "Single mothers today have so many more things going for them. You're smart and strong and you have your mother and your dad. You'll manage just fine."

I met my mother's gaze until Annie spoke.

"Thanks, Grammie." Annie glanced up at me. "Mom and Dad aren't so sure."

"I never said things won't work out," I defended myself. "We're both just worried about you, about your job, your life."

I stopped short of saying anything about Corey's situation; I wasn't sure what my mom knew about that, what Annie would have told her, or wanted her to know. My mother patted Annie's hand where it held the mound of her belly. "Your job is to rest and grow that baby healthy and strong. Corey seems like a very nice man. He's a good dad to those two little boys. They're so polite and respectful and they like you, too. You'll make a wonderful family."

Okay. Clearly Annie had not told my mother the particulars.

Regardless, my mother's attitude was just what I'd expect. Unless something impacted her directly, she was just oblivious. She'd always been that way to a degree, but over the years, it had gotten worse. She had gotten worse.

My mom got up then and kissed Annie on the forehead twice before slipping past me in the doorway. She'd lost weight. And she seemed to be slouched most of the time, as if there was an invisible string attached to her sternum, pulling the points of her shoulders together.

It was one of those moments when I could suddenly see myself in twenty-plus years: my physical self. I, too, was going to sag, to shrink, to hunch.

"I suppose your dad's already in bed," my mom said, her mouth pulled into a tight line.

"Yep. I could hear him. Snoring."

"Shheff," my mom shook her head and rolled her eyes, the sound she made not quite *shit*—my mother didn't, rarely, swear. Had contempt always been the constant in their relationship, at least her for him?

———

351

JOE WAS asleep on top of the covers on Jamie's bed when I went back upstairs. He startled awake and looked at me, for a moment as if he was unsure where he was.

"Sorry," he said hoarsely, his voice already gravelly with sleep as he pushed himself up and tried to focus on me. "You in the kitchen all this time?"

"Downstairs. Talking to Annie and mom."

He nodded and lay back on the pillow again, twisting his shoulders as if he'd gotten a crick in his neck. "I'm shot. I'm getting old, babe."

"Looking at my mother, I was just thinking the same thing, about myself."

"You look great. As hot as the day I married you."

I snorted. "You are clearly overdue for an eye exam. Seriously. I was just noticing how thin she's has gotten, and that she's walking around half hunched over most of the time."

"I caught her having a smoke behind the garage after dinner."

"What?"

"Sorry. I thought about not telling you. I know you'll just stress about it."

"God damn it. She said she quit." My mother had been a smoker for as long as I could remember, although over the years she'd become very defensive about it, no doubt because she knew we all disapproved.

"Hard habit to break, I hear."

"God damn it," I said again. Annoyed because it was somehow just like my mother to criticize and find fault with others, my dad in particular, but not hold the bar quite as high for herself.

Pushing the covers down with my feet, I lay looking up at the ceiling. The two bedside lights, one next to Doug's bed, one next to Jamie's, cast round shadows. The windows were cracked open, and the sound of peepers, those tiny frogs whose chirrup and trill marked springtime in the northeast, seemed louder now that the house was quiet. It was a sound associated with this time of year, with the last of the frost coming up out of the ground, the scent of chlorophyll and leaves greening up, of warm days, chilly nights. I didn't think it would ever smell like this in Charleston, in any season.

"I doubt you're gonna change that leopard's spots at this stage of the game."

"She was just downstairs talking about how excited she is for a great-grandbaby, while at the same time, she's apparently out behind the garage killing herself."

"Let it go. It is what it is. Or, rather, she is what she is."

I reached up and turned out the lamp. Joe followed my lead and turned out his, too. Now we lay in the darkness.

"I could go for a glass of wine," I said.

"Or a beer."

Chapter 18

"You awake?" I asked Joe softly. It was still weird, being in the same room, but not the same bed.

"Nah."

"I changed in Charleston. Or maybe the going is what changed me."

"Is that a good thing?" he asked after so much time passed I thought he had fallen asleep.

I closed my eyes and considered. "I think so. Leaving here, leaving you, and knowing I was leaving everything that was familiar, comfortable, *normal*, was so hard; it was *formative*. "It was the hardest decision I've ever made."

"It wasn't easy for me, either."

"Oh, Joe. I know it wasn't. It couldn't have been. I'm so sorry about that. I didn't mean to hurt you."

Yes, you did. Mean to. You were *so* angry. Cheerleader Cath.

He didn't respond to that, either. The two of us lay in silence while the room seemed to grow lighter as my eyes adjusted to the darkness. The framed picture on the night stand, of Doug and two high school friends on the golf course at the country club, caught starlight or moonlight; I could see the sheen of the glass. "It was a selfish thing to do," I said eventually.

"But if it fixed whatever was bothering you..."

Fixed. Bothering. It was so like Joe to over-simplify, to see things in black and white.

It was the hardest *choice* I ever made," I said, not answering the question. "Choosing to go. Just getting in the car and driving away. It changed me," I said again.

He didn't respond to that but I thought I heard him snort, though I wasn't sure. I could see the lump he made in Jamie's bed, but I couldn't see his face or his expression.

"I think I would have left you if I hadn't left you..." I said.

"I guess I'm glad you left, then." Joe's lame attempt at making a joke.

"Are you?"

"I love you, Cath. Even when things aren't perfect."

"I didn't leave because I didn't love you, or because you're not perfect."

Now he did snort. "Didn't you?"

I couldn't answer that, or rather, I had to think about what to say, how to express it, before I answered. A moth hit the screen in the window next to my bed. I could hear it fluttering against the mesh. The smell of the night was like something wired into my DNA. Nearly thirty years in Langston, almost all of them in this house. Thirty years was a long time. More than half my life. I took another deep breath, felt it fill my lungs, felt my chest expand to hold it. Finally I spoke. "I love you. I never stopped loving you. Though it felt like it, when I left."

"I understand how the idea of mom's cruise made you mad, how it *upset* you. It was a line drawn in the sand for you. But it didn't matter. It wasn't the big thing you made it out to be."

"You remember when the Abbott's dog got hit on the road out front? How when Mitch found it and tried to pick it up, it bit him? That's how I was before I went to Charleston. I was so hurt, Joe. You say it didn't matter. It wasn't important. But it hurt me. That anyone in your family—*my family*—aren't we one family now? After almost thirty years of marriage, aren't we in it together? The fact that any one of them would propose something like that, and everyone else would go along with it—"

I could feel just a twinge of the hurt, the way you feel an echo of the pain when you rub a long healed scar. It's there, but it's almost as if your mind knows the sensation because the wound itself doesn't really pain you anymore. I'd always have the scar. And I knew I'd never see my in-laws the same way again.

"I'm sorry," was all he said. There wasn't anything else he could say. When he spoke again, his voice was full of something, some emotion I couldn't quite identify. "We have a life together here. I mean the life we have is here."

"I know."

"Are you home to stay?"

I didn't answer. I didn't know.

———

JUST ABOUT TWO WEEKS LATER, on Friday morning—eight days 'til Wedding Weekend—I was in the kitchen making spanakopita. The food for the reception was being catered, but I had invited Molly's parents over on the Thursday evening before the wedding, and I was making some things for that, figuring a casual gathering on the patio, apps and cocktails before a simple dinner. Spanakopita I could make today and put in the freezer and bake at the last minute. The frozen spinach was thawed and spread on paper towels on a baking sheet, drying, butter was melted in a small saucepan, the phyllo dough was on the counter, though still packaged so it wouldn't dry out, when my phone buzzed.

Doug and Joe were long gone, off to the warehouse. My dad was out in the garage, working on the Adirondack chairs from the back yard, tightening joints and sanding in preparation of giving them a new coat of paint. Lillian had picked up my mother and the two of them were running errands. Annie hadn't made an appearance yet, and I thought to let her sleep. Her opportunities for sleeping late were fast coming to an end. For about the next twenty years.

My phone buzzed again and I glanced at it. Patrick. I hadn't talked to Pat for a couple of months, not since Charleston. I hadn't even called or texted him after I heard about Di losing their baby. I had no excuse for that. I'd sent Di a card and a note, but Pat was a friend, had been a friend for a long time. I still really didn't want to consider why I had been avoiding a conversation with him. "I'm a terrible friend. I should have called after I heard about the baby.... I'm so sorry."

"As you know a baby wasn't my idea, just the opposite. But once I knew there was one, it did something to me. Made me think. I'm not even living at the house, for God's sake. When Di miscarried, I felt more...sad...than I thought I would. Even though in my head I was thinking it was the best outcome."

"Are you back at the house now?"

"No. No plans to move back. It's a legal separation."

"I'm sorry."

"I would make it official, divorce, but Di wants to wait. To take more time. To think about it. Typical Di."

"Maybe that's not a bad thing. She just lost a baby."

"I know. The reason I called. One of the reasons. I think it would be better if I miss the wedding. I don't want to make anyone uncomfortable even though Di says it would be fine."

"I understand how you feel. But it would be fine. You're our kids' uncle. You're a friend. That's never going to change."

"I appreciate that. It's how I feel, too. But no doubt it would be a little awkward for Joe. For everyone else."

"I think it would be okay, but we'll understand whatever you decide."

"Second reason for calling. I have some paperwork for Joe. A deed actually. I have no idea why it came to me at the office, now, other than that I was the attorney of record and the county must have that contact info. Though it's not like Joe hasn't lived in Langston for fifty years."

"What are you talking about?"

"For the transfer we did five or six years ago. Honestly. Someone in the clerk's office in the courthouse there must have been doing some housekeeping or something. I'll have my assistant mail it, but I wanted to give you a heads-up. Didn't realize you'd never gotten it. Not that it matters, the filing at the courthouse is the important part, and that was done, I checked this morning."

"I have no idea what you're talking about."

"The cemetery. The deed."

"The Nixon Road cemetery?" Where Nora was buried.

"Yes."

"Why would you—Joe—have the deed for the Nixon Road cemetery?"

"After he paid the back taxes on it. He—you—own it. You didn't know?"

"I did not."

"Well. I don't know what to say. I have no idea why Joe wouldn't have told you. The church that once owned that cemetery is no more. Hasn't been for a long time. The taxes hadn't been paid for years. Not that they were a lot of money. I think the county approached Joe. They—someone—knew he'd put the fence up. There wasn't anyone else who had any interest in maintaining it."

"The 4-H kids maintain it, as much as it's maintained anyway. You know, mowing, trimming, raking leaves."

"Yeah. Probably. But they wouldn't pay the taxes and apparently the county got tired of carrying it. I mean, not that there's anything they could do, really. But Joe said he'd pay the taxes."

I shook my head. Felt a bubble of something light and effervescent percolating inside my chest.

"Do me a favor and pretend you don't know? I didn't mean to out him. If he hasn't told you, maybe he didn't want to cause you any heartache, knowing the cemetery was more or less abandoned."

"Not abandoned," I said. "Not forgotten."

I couldn't believe it. Joe bought the cemetery where our baby daughter was buried. Why wouldn't he have told me? He hadn't told me he was the one who replaced the fence, either. Tears burned and my eyes filled as I hung up.

Then there were footsteps on the porch and someone knocked on the kitchen door.

When I opened it, I was surprised—shocked—to see Helene standing there.

"Oh, my gosh! What are you doing here?" My heart really did expand in my chest.

Helene grinned and leaned in for a hug. She smelled like expensive perfume, something exotic, her hair long and naturally wavy, the gray in it serving to make her look sophisticated and elegantly blasé. Her coat was a bright coral pink trench, the kind of coat I would see and admire but would never choose, opting instead for classic black or gray, something that would "last forever."

"I was in the area—"

"Oh, nuts." I couldn't stop smiling. "You didn't just happen to be in Langston—"

Helene grinned. "No, I was in State College, so not far. It was a no-brainer to come up to see you. I've been thinking about you. I haven't really talked to you since you got back. I figured you'd be up to your eyeballs in wedding prep and I'll see you next weekend. But you'll be busy with your family then. As you should be. How's it going?"

"Wedding stuff?"

Helene nodded. "That and other things..."

"I'm not doing any of the wedding day food. Molly's mom hired a caterer and a bartender and servers. 'So I can enjoy the day.'" I made air quotes. "The rental company is bringing a tent and putting it up Wednesday. Joe and Doug and my dad will get the tables and wooden folding chairs Thursday. I'm going to cut flowers and make small centerpieces for the tables early the morning of. There's no dancing and no music. The kids want the ceremony, the entire event really, to be simple and almost Quaker-plain. To answer your question: Wedding prep is not too bad, considering."

"You're a frickin' saint. Or a super mom. But I've always known that."

"Eh." I waved a hand, laughing. "It's not a huge crowd; we've had more than one event here over the years with almost as many people. It's manageable. It's all outside. We'll have the tent in case it rains. But so far, the weather forecast looks good."

"How're things otherwise...with Joe..." Helene's eyebrows rose into the broad sweep of her forehead.

"What were you in State College for?" I asked, ignoring the question for the moment. "You look very happy." I hung the pink trench coat on a hook by the door. "Want some coffee? Iced tea? I have cinnamon buns."

"Cinnamon buns sound amazing. But I shouldn't."

There was about Helene a sort of energy, a kind of sparkle, an almost palpable hum. I was so happy to have her here. "A man. To answer your first question. I've been in State College with a man. On a date."

"What man? What kind of date?" I looked at Helene's face and knew. "Never mind. I get what kind of date."

"It didn't start out to be that kind of date. But it ended up that way." She bit her lip and I could tell she was biting on a grin.

"What man?" I asked again.

"Don't laugh. Don't judge."

"Not Erick?"

"God, no. Justin. I met him online. And he's a Penn Stater, too. Isn't that crazy?"

"A dating website?"

"Yep."

"Well... Who is he? What's he do? Details."

"He's a computer guy. You know, IT stuff, like me. He does work for the government, too, defense contractor stuff. Stuff you can't talk about."

"And he was in State College because he lives there?"

"No. He had a meeting there, and I hadn't been back for a long time; a trip to Happy Valley just sounded fun. So we had our date there."

"Divorced? Widowed? Tall? Short?"

"Single, never married. Good-looking sort of like Matt Damon. Average height, maybe just shy of six feet." Helene looked at me and bit her lip again, her eyebrows raised. "Younger."

"Like how younger?"

"Pool boy younger."

"Please tell me he's older than Jamie."

"Barely."

"What? Seriously?"

"No. Yes. I mean he's forty. Almost. Thirty eight."

"You're kidding me?"

"Nope." Helene grinned.

"Well, it appears that the date was a success."

"That's one way to put it."

I just stared at my friend, not sure what to say, what to ask, where to start. *A thirty-eight-year-old?* I couldn't help but think about Annie, and almost twenty-year-older Corey. But if Helene could look like the cat that swallowed the canary, she did just now.

"We matched. We had seventeen hearts. That's how the website marks the things you have in common. Seventeen. That's a lot."

"Well, sure. Justin what?"

"Justin Tennant."

"Mom." Both Helene and I looked up to see Annie standing in the doorway to the family room. She was wearing the huge blue T-shirt that had a picture of a fish and said Just for the Halibut and a pair of pink boxers with yellow dogs all over them that she'd had for years and kept in her dresser here. I knew that the elastic waistband of the boxers was so old it had lost its stretch, but they fit perfectly under the bulge of her belly. "Aunt Helene. I didn't know you were here. I didn't know you were coming today."

"It was a surprise. How are you, Annie darlin'?" Helene said, getting up and moving to give Annie a hug. "Besides very, very pregnant."

"I think I'm in labor."

"What?" I said. "You are?" *Oh, no! It's too soon!* And in some far corner of my mind, *I've got spanakopita spread all over the counter. We've got a wedding next Saturday!*

Helene steered Annie to a stool at the counter. "Here. Sit down. Take a load off."

Yes, by all means sit, don't be walking around and speeding things up!

"Yeah. I've been having contractions for about an hour. They're still twelve or thirteen minutes apart, but I called Dr. Tsarnaokva and she said to come to the hospital now."

"Maybe we should just go to the Langston Hospital?"

"I'm monitoring my blood pressure, Mom, and it's within normal range. It should be okay to go to Pittsburgh, if the contractions are still that far apart and my blood pressure behaves. I'd feel a lot better, Mom, going there. It's not an emergency now, for me or the baby, but if it turns into one, my NICU is there. I know everyone. It's hands-down the best place for babies who need intervention."

"Oh, Annie—" I said, my mind still processing.

"I have every hospital between here and AWAC programmed into my phone." She pronounced it A-Wack. "If my blood pressure spikes, or if anything else goes south, we can stop at any one of them. They're all small-town hospitals, like Langston. They'll have that same level of care."

"Do you think we should call an ambulance? You'd have experienced medical assistance if you need it."

"We don't need an ambulance, Mom. It's only a little over an hour. And I can monitor my blood pressure just as well as an EMT."

The expression on my daughter's face was a combination of the fierce determination that I knew only too well, and something else, something vulnerable. I gave in. "Okay. If you're sure. If your doctor is sure."

This morning I'd been starting to feel...not exactly panicked, but definitely aware of the clock ticking on the wedding. In eight days. Seventy-five people. In my backyard. I had not figured on Annie's baby making an appearance before next Saturday. Though I should have.

I grabbed a clean dish towel out of the drawer and threw it over the baking sheet with the spinach, made sure the burner under the pan of melted butter was off, turned off the oven, untied my apron— Got Pierogies?—and tossed it on the counter. "Let's go then. I'll make spanakopita later." I shrugged. "Or I won't."

Annie's having her baby! I'm going to be a grandmother!

"Corey's not answering his phone." Now I heard a note of something in Annie's voice that caught my attention. "He left for West Virginia today, for work. He was supposed to be gone for a couple of days. I left him three messages—"

"I'm sure he'll be checking—"

"I don't know. There's shitty cell service where he is. There's always shitty service in the places he goes." It was the first time I had ever heard Annie offer even a whiff of criticism of Corey.

Helene said. "He's probably on his way right now."

"If you left him messages, he'll get them at some point. But we should go. I'll grab your bag and I'll call Dad. He'll want to come, I have no doubt. We can pick him up on the way."

"He's at the dentist," Jeri Ann told me when I called the office line when Joe's cell went right to voice mail. "He broke a tooth this morning and Dr. Farnsworth told him to come right over. He doesn't have his phone. Left it on his desk. I can see it from here."

Of course he did. He always forgot his phone. "Well, shit."

"Is something wrong? You can call Dr. Farnsworth, or I can?"

"Could you? Tell Joe to meet us at Allegheny Women's and Children's Hospital in Pittsburgh. Annie's in labor."

Annie was in the bathroom, peeing one more time. After breathing through another contraction that had made sweat break out on her upper lip. I felt like it broke out on my own lip, just watching the way pain had seemed to flow over Annie, from her abdomen up to her scalp.

"He's at the dentist."

"We need to get this show on the road," Helene said. "And I can drive so when Joe gets there, you won't have to deal with two cars."

"All right. Let me go tell my dad. He's out in the garage fixing chairs. He can fill in my mother and Lillian."

Minutes later, we were in Helene's car heading to Pittsburgh. I kept checking Annie, sitting in the backseat. She had her head back on the headrest and I could tell when a contraction hit because she would close her eyes, the expression on her face would tighten, and her breathing would change.

"You okay?" I asked at one point.

"Yes," Annie answered without opening her eyes. The blood pressure cuff was loose on her upper left arm; she pumped it up and read the gauge after every contraction. So far, so good.

"They're eleven minutes apart," I said once the most recent contraction passed. "We're about forty minutes out."

Annie nodded then, opening her eyes and sitting up, taking a deep breath. The muscles of her face seemed loose under the skin which was flushed, her hairline along her face damp. Glancing at her phone, clutched in her hand. "Still no word from Corey," she said.

"Maybe Helene was right. He got your message and he's on his way back to Pittsburgh and can't text because he's driving."

"He would have called."

Of course he would have. "I know you want him to be with you; I'm sure he wants that, too. But you have to put him out of your mind now. I mean, you can't worry about him."

"Your mom is right," Helene said, glancing at Annie in the rearview mirror. "Labor is all-consuming. Until you get the drugs."

My phone buzzed then. Joe. "Hey," I answered. "You got my message?"

"Yeah. I broke a molar. Hurt like a bitch. Doc Farnsworth thinks he can put a crown on it. Annie's in labor?"

"Yes. And we're on our way to the hospital. Helene's driving."

"Helene? What's she doing here?" I could picture him trying to make sense of what was happening.

"She was in State College...with a friend. She just came up to Langston to surprise me. She offered to drive when we found out you were at the dentist. I figured you'd come as soon as you got finished with your tooth."

"Why are you going to Pittsburgh? Why didn't you just go to Langston Hospital?"

"Because Annie wanted to come to Allegheny Women's and Children's, and her doctor said it would be fine." I spoke slowly, at least sort-of patiently. This was so Joe. Things had to be spelled out. "We're about thirty minutes out. Annie's monitoring her blood pressure and she's okay. Can you just get in the truck and come meet us as soon as your tooth is fixed?"

"Well. I guess if her doctor said it's okay... But Langston Hospital is just across town—"

I wanted to yell, but I restrained myself. "It's what Annie wants." I ignored the mention of Langston Hospital. That ship had sailed. Literally. In this case the Lexus had sailed. "She's hoping Corey will meet us there, too."

"Where's he?"

I glanced into the back seat to see Annie resting, head back on the headrest, eyes closed, breathing slow and relaxed. "He had to go out of town for a couple of days for work. Annie's left him messages but she's not sure if he would have gotten them yet. I'm sure he'll be checking and will come as soon as he can," I said for Annie's benefit.

"I'm not a candidate for an epi," Annie said in answer to Helene's earlier comment about *the drugs.* "My complications make me high risk. But Corey and I talked about it. He's done birth twice already."

He's maybe observed birth twice already. He hasn't done birth.

He's going to coach me through it. If he gets there. If he answers his fucking phone." Her voice caught as another contraction bore down on her. I watched as Annie's eyes closed and her head fell back against the seat again.

"That's it. Steady. Relax. Breathe in. Breathe out." I blew through my lips in concert with her.

"Oh ohohoh ohhh," Annie exhaled when the contraction eased, leaning forward like she'd just run a race. I felt as if every muscle in my own body was clenched.

It was a good thing Annie had the address of the hospital in her phone, which at some point she'd handed to me, because by the time we got close, her contractions were stronger, strong enough so that one of her hands clenched the door handle and the other the strap of her bag beside her on the seat. The hair all around her face was now damp with perspiration, her cheekbones looked too prominent, her lips bloodless. Her eyes stayed closed and she rocked rhythmically in her seat during each contraction, like a metronome, or as much as she could strapped in behind a seatbelt.

The contractions still seemed to be ten or eleven minutes apart. Not much closer, but they definitely seemed stronger. I worried about her blood pressure. Annie still checked it following each contraction, but she hadn't said what it was since the first time. Was it okay? Was the baby okay?

It felt like a lot of merging and changing lanes, turns and red lights, the buffeting of city traffic, before Helene pulled into the entrance that was marked AWAC Emergency.

"Thank God!" I felt nearly lightheaded with relief at the sight of a nurse in blue scrubs pushing an empty wheelchair though the automatic doors.

"Fifth floor," Annie said, pushing open the door and climbing awkwardly out.

"I'll park, then I'll find you. I'll bring the bag. Good luck sweetie! I love you."

"Thanks, Aunt Hel," Annie said automatically, without looking back, moving slowly and sinking clumsily into the wheelchair. I could see her mouth pursed as she began blowing again. Another contraction. I checked my watch. Ten minutes. Still about ten minutes. The contractions seemed to be a lot more intense than when Annie had appeared in the kitchen doorway earlier, but they were not that much closer together.

I followed the nurse and wheelchair into the elevator in time to hear Annie say, "I think I'm going to throw up."

I looked at the nurse who met my eyes with an, *oh, no*, expression. I had my purse, Annie's phone and the sweater I'd grabbed just before leaving the house, a black cotton cardigan. Now, I yanked out the sweater out of my purse where I'd shoved it and opened it on Annie's lap.

"Oh, God," Annie said again, just before she vomited. Again and again she heaved.

"Oh, Annie, sweetie," I said, watching helplessly, at a loss for what to do, knowing that this was part of it, this loss of any semblance of control. No matter how prepared you thought you were, no matter how much you thought you knew, or how determined, childbirth was a humbling, leveling-the-playing-field kind of lesson in the power of nature, and all of the women who were blessed enough to experience it learned that their control over the other facets of their life were nothing in the face of it.

This wasn't just labor, this was the relationship between Annie and me changing forever. After today, we would still always be mother and daughter, but we would both be mothers, too.

Her hands grasped the arms of the wheelchair until her knuckles were white. "Oh, Mom, I'm sorry," Annie said after the contraction had passed and she had come back to herself somewhat, wiping her mouth with the side of her arm, her voice shaky.

"Don't worry about it. I've never liked that sweater."

"Ha. Good thing," Annie said, her voice raw.

The elevator whisked us up and when the doors opened, we were in front of a tall desk where a thin, elegant woman in a long white lab coat stood, writing something in a folder. Two nurses stood behind the counter.

"Annie!" one of them said.

"Girlfriend!" the other said, coming around the counter.

The nurse from the emergency room carefully picked up the vomit-filled cardigan by the corners and went off to dispose of it somewhere.

"Annie love. You made it." The woman in the lab coat spoke, her accent London or Ireland, somewhere in Great Britain. This must be Dr. Tsarnakova. "How are the contractions?"

"About—" and then she just seemed to lose her words. Her eyes drifted closed, and the bones in her face appeared to shift, and she began the rocking again. "Here comes another one. Ohh!"

"Let's get you into an exam room and see what's happening."

"We're ready for her," the nurse said, wheeling Annie down the hall. Another nurse appeared from somewhere and followed them, an electronic tablet in one hand.

Dr. Tsarnakova smiled at me. "I assume you're Mom?"

"I am," I said.

"Well. We'll do an exam and get her admitted. Do you want to come? Will anyone else be joining us?"

"My friend and Annie's dad are coming. The baby's dad, too, we think. We hope. He's out of town on business and Annie's left him messages—"

"Well, come along, then. The nurse here at the desk can let the others know what's happening and where we are when they arrive."

And then we were in a regular exam room where a nurse was helping Annie out of her clothes and into a hospital gown. I caught a glimpse of her belly and was struck, almost heart wrenchingly so, at the sight. Its ripeness and vulnerability, marked with lines of veins and, lower, the pale maroon streaks of stretch marks.

One of the nurses deftly started an IV. There were fetal monitors, little clear squares of plastic tape with wires someone stuck to Annie's belly and chest. Screens came to life, making soft beeps, flashing numbers and squiggly lines, a whirlwind of activity that seemed to center around each contraction, like planets around a sun. I watched, tried to stand where I was out of the way, and wished for Joe. And Corey.

"I'm freezing," Annie said, her teeth nearly rattling in her mouth, her arms shaking noticeably, in contrast to the sweat that dampened her hair and beaded on her upper lip.

One of the nurses brought a warm cotton blanket. I stood at Annie's side and held her hand, exceedingly relieved to be here, where there was every kind of state-of-the-art equipment and doctors and nurses and resources I probably couldn't begin to even imagine at the ready.

"Mom," she said. And I realized Annie was looking at me.

"Yeah, baby." I reached out and brushed the hair back from her face.

"I knew it would be hard, that it wouldn't be perfect." I knew somehow that Annie wasn't talking about labor. "Corey has the boys. He has Danielle. He's always going to have them. But I thought he would be here. It never occurred to me that we would not be together when our baby was born."

"Oh, honey. I'm sorry there's only me here. But women have babies without their significant others all the time. Every day. You can do this."

"Shit happens."

The cynicism in Annie's voice broke my heart. "It does."

And then her eyes closed and she began the rocking that presaged another contraction, seemingly oblivious to one of the machines that began to beep alarmingly.

"What is it?" I asked the nurse who materialized in the doorway.

Dr. Tsarnakova appeared, as well, both of them checking monitors, Dr. Tsarnakova opening Annie's gown and laying both hands on the swell of Annie's belly as she watched the numbers flash and lines crossing the screens. When it was over, Annie seemed to collapse on the bed, though she hadn't moved, not really.

"Okay, that's it," Dr. Tsarnakova said. "Annie, love. We need to C-section your baby now. We talked about this. That it was a possibility."

"Is the baby okay?" Annie asked. She looked pale, her lips pinched, her skin like tissue over the bones of her face, her gray eyes fixing on the doctor. "Is she okay?"

She? I looked from Dr. Tsarnakova to Annie. The baby was a girl? A granddaughter.

There was more talking, the nurses saying things about the OR, and Dr. Tsarnakova saying she'd get scrubbed and see them in there, the nurses flipping up the side rails on the bed and efficiently gathering the paraphernalia of IV and wires and machines and then Annie was gone, out the door and down the hall.

And I was alone in the room. That's when I began to cry. Rooting round in my purse, I found my phone and called Joe.

Chapter 19

I cried a little, again, when I first found Helene sitting in the family waiting room, more a surfeit of emotion and adrenaline than outright fear. Though there was some fear. There were complications; Annie did have risk factors. Now we waited. Joe had called, was trying to find parking: cursing the city, other drivers, the need to use a credit card, which he couldn't find.

"She's going to be okay. The baby will be okay," Helene said, squeezing my hand the same way I'd squeezed Annie's, the reassurance the same.

"I hope so. I love her so much."

"Of course you do. But she's young and healthy and she's getting the best care possible right now. You're going to be a grandmother."

"I can't wrap my mind around that. Sometimes it feels so normal, so...ordinary. And other times it hits me like a ton of bricks: My baby is having a baby. Our baby—"

There was a muted ding of the elevator at the other end of the hall and then voices and I realized that one of them belonged to Joe; the other was Doug. I could see the two of them stopping at the desk before heading toward the waiting room where Helene and I sat.

"And sometimes a good man is good enough," Helene said, and she was looking down the hall, too.

"Is it?"

"Yep. Yep it is."

About an hour after Joe and Doug had shown up, Dr. Tsarnakova came into the little waiting room which was now full of Annie's fan club since my mom and dad and Lillian had also appeared soon after Joe and Doug. At some point, Mom had gone off and apparently found a vending machine, coming back with bottles of water, Gatorade, Lipton tea and an assortment of packaged cheese and peanut butter crackers. Now the detritus of cracker crumbs and plastic bottles littered the little coffee table in the waiting room.

I had Annie's phone and repeatedly checked for text or voice messages but there was no sign or word of Corey. I'd tried calling him twice, as well, but each call was routed immediately to voice mail.

Everyone in the room stood when Dr. Tsarnakova came in wearing a pair of blue scrubs, a smile on her face that showed a gold incisor tooth I hadn't noticed before.

"Everything went very well. Annie's fine. She's in recovery. Her baby is small, just under five pounds, but her APGAR was good, considering. She's doing well for a baby of that size. As soon as Annie is able to return to a patient room, someone will come and let you know." She smiled at us again, flashing the gold tooth and I couldn't believe I hadn't notice that earlier.

"She said to tell you the baby's name is Nora Daley."

———

On Saturday, the first whole day of my granddaughter's life, I woke early, made a cup of tea and went out to sit on the step on the back porch. Thoughts of my first born, the baby who had died before she'd lived a full life, the grief of losing a child tangled inside me with the joy and happiness of knowing that Annie had a daughter now. Another Nora.

And this quiet time, this morning just after dawn, when there was still dew on the grass, and the air smelled of lilac and something else sweet, this was the lull before the storm. Exactly one week 'til Jamie's wedding. I finished my tea when I heard a door bang, and water in the kitchen sink, and then voices. I got up and went inside.

"Hey. There you are!" Joe said when he saw me, as he poured water into the carafe of the coffee maker.

Laura was perched on one of the stools at the island. "Hey!" she said, jumping up and coming over to give me a hug. I was surprised to see her, here, now. I hadn't known she'd gotten to town. "Congratulations! A new grandbaby!"

"Yes," I answered. "We're grandparents."

"I can't wait to meet her! They're doing okay? Annie and the baby?"

"Haven't talked to her yet this morning, thought I'd call in a while. But as far as we know...everyone is good. Annie will be sore, she'll have a bit of a recovery."

"How special that Annie named the baby Nora."

"Yeah," I said. "It is." Laura couldn't know, not really, how that made me feel.

"We're going to Pittsburgh later?" Joe was still glowing this morning, practically beaming with happiness, his head in the clouds. Clearly being a grandpa agreed with him. It was kind of funny.

"I assume we will. But I should talk to Annie, see how she's feeling. Maybe we need to come up with a schedule. There's a lot of us. We don't want to overwhelm her. And Corey will no doubt be there, too."

He had not gotten to the hospital last night, at least not before Joe and I left. He had called, though, at some point getting Annie's messages.

"You can check ice off your list. I have a dozen bags I need to go put in the freezer."

Joe had been up and gone when I came downstairs this morning.

I'd assumed he was at the warehouse, but apparently he'd been on an ice run.

"You want some coffee?" I asked Laura as he headed out to the garage to rescue the ice. "Did you just come up this morning?"

"No, last night, late. I brought stuff so I can work remotely from Mom's all week. I can help out, with wedding prep, too, if you need anything. Coffee would be great."

"Thanks. But I think we're in good shape. The tent comes Wednesday, the guys are going to get the tables and chairs Thursday morning. Dinner here Thursday night with Molly's parents and any Daleys that are around."

After that, the conversation seemed to lag, and I wondered if Laura felt the awkwardness. "I haven't seen you in a while," she said.

"Not since Thanksgiving."

"How's your cookbook? Was Charleston relaxing and less distracting? Joe said it was a good break."

Is that what he said?

Laura smiled, and the awkwardness was definitely there. "I'm glad the trip was productive, and that you could work in such a gorgeous place. I've been there a couple of times. It's awesome. As retreats go, it would be five stars in my book."

Was it me, or was that a lame attempt by Laura to justify or excuse the extravagance of the "family only" cruise? To remind me that I had had a luxurious experience, as well?

"I should have called you. Or texted at least. I meant to. Wasn't sure what to say? If Mom's cruise had anything to do with you going..."

I paused, a mug from the cupboard in my hand. "Is that what Joe said?"

Laura shook her head. "No. Just reading between the lines. But if that's the reason, I'm really sorry."

As I looked at my sister-in-law, all the years, all the miles of shared family history flashed before me, like a highway through the last three-plus decades of my life. I thought of the people I knew—three? four? just off the top of my head—who were estranged from other family members. My mother had a brother she hadn't spoken to in more than forty years. One of the "Got Pierogies?" team members had a father she hadn't seen since she was ten. Pat had a sister in Colorado or somewhere he never saw, never spoke to. My relationships with Joe's family were never going to be the same. My relationship with Joe was never going to be the same. But maybe in the end, was that a bad thing? Different wasn't necessarily bad.

Something had changed inside me while I was in that achingly beautiful city, where lifetimes of history not my own filled every corner. There had been something comforting about that. Memories of that southern city pulled at me like nothing I had ever known or experienced before. I would go back. I knew that with a certainty.

When I realized Laura was waiting, watching me, it took me a moment to remember what my sister-in-law had said. She was really sorry if the cruise had been the reason I had gone to Charleston.

You can't change that you conceived that "family only" cruise. You can't unring that bell. No matter how "sorry" you are. And nothing I say now will change that. How did Laura not understand that? Was it a cop out? That I didn't tell her how I felt?

I preferred to think it was a deliberate choice. Besides, telling her wasn't going to change anything, not how I felt, not the fact that The Cruise had been conceived, and taken. I noticed again how much Laura looked like Joe. Those Daley genes. I wondered if Nora would have that nose, those freckles, the thick hair.

Your actions are you. My actions are me. For me.

"Oh, no doubt your mom's cruise was the inspiration," I said finally. "But Charleston was something I did for me."

On Thursday morning, it rained. Not a torrential downpour, but a summer shower, and by noon, the sun was out making everything sparkle. By 2:00, it was starting to feel steamy, a prelude to the summer to come. Under the tent, which sat square in the backyard, behind the summer kitchen, it smelled like summer camp. Musty canvas, and sunshine, a smell that actually made me smile. I checked the weather app on my phone and decided the rain was over for the day, for the weekend—yay!—so dinner tonight, the casual, family dinner that Jamie and Molly had requested, could be on the patio. It wouldn't have to be in the dining room or under the tent.

Everyone was busy: Joe and Doug were at the warehouse dealing with a minor crisis that had to do with a truck breakdown, then they were going to pick up the tables and chairs on their way home. My mom and dad had taken Lillian and Laura and gone to visit Annie, and Jamie was running errands, though he'd been gone for several hours now. Likely checking in on Molly and her parents who had rooms at the Holiday Inn, the only—hotel—game in town.

I'd just taken a shortcake out of the oven, five pints of strawberries were sliced and lightly sugared. I had some heavy cream to whip for on top but wouldn't do that until this evening.

I was surprised when someone rang the doorbell. I knew immediately this was Molly's mother. She had Molly's thick, dark hair, or rather Molly clearly had her mother's hair, though her mother wore it in a style Helene and I had always called Tri Delt hair, the style Jackie O had: chin length and swingy, and there were streaks of gray in it. Molly had her mother's dark brown eyes, too. And the same clear, creamy complexion, the same smile.

"Cathleen!" she said. "I'm Mina. Molly's mom."

"Oh, Mina! It's so lovely to meet you in person!" I pulled her into an awkward hug, awkward because the woman was carrying a big shopping bag in each hand, and we were standing in the doorway. I glanced toward the driveway, to see if Molly's dad was here, too, but the car, some kind of gray generic sedan, a typical rental, was empty of other people.

"I'm sorry to intrude. I couldn't wait until tonight to meet you, and I wanted to drop these off," she motioned with the shopping bags, "so I left Danny at the Holiday Inn. I hope this isn't a bad time."

"Come in! I'm glad to meet you finally. And it's not a bad time, at all. You're welcome anytime. But you didn't have to bring anything. My goodness, you just flew halfway across the country. Anyway, dinner is going to be easy." I glanced at Mina while leading the way to the kitchen, and rolled my eyes. "As you know, that's the buzz word for this weekend. Easy."

"Oh, believe me, I know. I've been told countless times."

She settled on one of the stools at the island, parking the two shopping bags on the floor beside her. "Our children are getting married. In two days. Can you believe it?" she said. "The hell with easy. Watching my baby get married is going to be damn hard. Hard and good at the same time. Does that make sense? Oh, and nothing against Jamie. We love Jamie. He's good for her. She could be marrying a crown prince or Tom Hanks and I'd feel the same way."

It took a moment for that to register, and then I laughed. "I love Tom Hanks. He's just the kind of guy I'd want my daughter to bring home. Actually, I'd be happy if her choice wasn't married. And seventeen years older." I had no idea why I'd revealed that.

Molly's mom looked at me and I saw empathy in her dark eyes. "I hear you have a new granddaughter. Congratulations. *Mazel tov*. Very exciting. You're a bleepin' saint, in my book. Hosting a wedding with everything else you have going on."

I smiled, waved a hand. "This weekend is just for Jamie and Molly."

"I'm going to cry a river on Saturday, I just know it. The kids say that when they're being snide: Cry me a river. Well, on Saturday, I'm going to. I won't be able to help it. Are you ready for this? The wedding? You've had to do so much. I feel bad about that. It's because I'm so pushy." I opened my mouth to protest, but before I could say anything, Mina waved a hand dismissively, and went on. "Oh, I am. No doubt about it. It's in my genes. I had the typical pushy Jewish mother. I tell Molly just wait. She's got the same genes. That's why they want a civil ceremony. I understand. Molly wasn't even raised Jewish. Much. Danny's family is Lutheran. But there are some things—I mean, I wanted them to have the option. You got the chuppah? And I brought yarmulkes. They may not require them for their male guests, but maybe there will be some nice Jewish boy who forgot to bring one. I mean, be prepared. That's my motto. What can I help with?"

And after less than five minutes, I could see what Jamie meant. Mina McDonald was *a lot*. But she was candid and funny and I could sense her vulnerability, no matter how chatty. I also sensed a core of strength that I understood, that somehow bonded us.

"I'll cry, too. I cry at the weddings of people I don't really know. But I have plenty of tissues. I bought two boxes just for Saturday. The kind with lotion. And for tonight, I have a couple of special bottles of chardonnay. For the mothers of the bride and the groom."

"A woman after my own heart. I knew I'd like you." Mina blinked a couple of times and I realized she was trying not to cry now.

"Can I get you a cup of coffee or tea? Iced tea? Or something stronger? We could open one of those bottles of chardonnay now? It's barely 11:00, but hey, it's a special occasion!" I'd felt torn about buying and having liquor around, because of Doug, but it was Jamie's wedding weekend. There was going to be drinking. I'd have to pray, and trust in a higher power, that Doug could manage the temptation. And I felt suddenly like having a drink. Like maybe even getting a little buzzed. Right now. With Mina.

"I'd love a drink. I had one teeny, tiny glass before I came over. 'What if she's cold and intimidating,' I said to Danny. I should have known you'd be lovely. Jamie is wonderful. So polite. So mature. I knew we'd hit it off. Both of us giving up our first born... Well, for me, first born daughter; Molly's brother, Asa, is older, but he'll never get married. Well not to a woman. He's gay."

After a bit, Mina seemed to remember the shopping bags. "I brought some pictures. I thought it might be nice to have some of the wedding pictures of family. You know, displayed here and there. On Saturday. My parents and Danny's. Our grandparents. Us." She made a face. "I didn't say anything to Molly. I thought it could be a surprise. You think it's a good idea, right?"

I could feel my mind working. Would Molly and Jamie like that? It wasn't something that had been planned for, but it wasn't too forward or pushy. It seemed like a thoughtful gesture. And I could tell, by looking at Mina's face, that the woman was just desperate to have a role, to make a contribution to the day her daughter got married. Her only daughter. I could so understand that.

"I think it's a lovely idea. I have photos of our wedding. And Joe's mom will have some of hers. We might have to scramble to find some of my parents', but we'll manage something."

"Oh, God," Mina said, her dark eyes brimming with tears suddenly, once more. "I was worried I'd overstepped. Again. Like the chuppah." She paused, as if she couldn't find the right words then finally she shook her head and said, "I'm getting old. I *am* old. I'm eleven years older than my mother was when I got married."

It took me a moment to follow that math.

"I have hot flashes that require a change of clothes."

"Ha. No one ever told me about night sweats and periods that give new meaning to Red Sea."

I couldn't help it, I laughed.

"I want to ask my mother, did you feel like this when I married Danny? But she died fourteen years ago. Am I crazy?" Mina sniffed.

I blinked, feeling tears burning suddenly under the laughter, and impulsively pulled this woman who was going to be part of my family going forward into a hug. No matter what happened, we would have this time, this moment when two mothers came to terms with growing old, with watching children grow up, and away.

"If you are, you're in good company. Let me go get that wine before everyone gets home and wonders who are those crazy women crying in the kitchen."

———

"GREAT DINNER, BABE," Joe said, coming through the screen door behind me into the pantry. I'd come in to make some coffee. Lillian had jumped up when Mina had asked for a cup, but Joe had trumped her offer. "They really liked your salad dressing. You should have told Mina the recipe is in your cookbook. If you keep giving out recipes whenever someone asks, no one will buy your books." He pinched my butt as I reached up in the cupboard for the coffee cups.

"What are you now, my agent?" I asked, but I smiled when I said it. He was in such a good mood, still glowing about baby Nora.

"Someone looking out for your best interests," he whispered, leaning close to my ear. "And holy moley, does she talk! A lot. Good God."

"She's chatty. But I like her."

"Chatty? She'd eat chatty and spit out won't shut up for breakfast."

Despite myself, I laughed. It was one of those things that Joe said about people who talked a lot that he totally made up and that made no sense. Joe had a whole assortment of sayings like that, and he seemed to make up new ones whenever the urge struck.

Joe went on. "I like her, too. I'd just smother her with a pillow if I had to spend a week with her."

"Shhh," I hissed, fighting a smile, and reaching for the cream in the fridge. "Be nice."

"I'm the nicest guy I know. Or you know," he pinched my butt again.

It was like someone had pumped him up with helium. On Friday, after Annie had been settled in a patient room at AWAC, a nurse had allowed us all in to see Annie, two at a time, and then we could stop at the window in the hallway that looked into the nursery at the special isolette where Nora lay. She was tiny, scary tiny, I thought, though she was not wired up to any of the even more scary-looking machines in that room. She'd been swaddled, and at the moment was sleeping, her eyes squinched shut.

I glanced at Joe and the look of awe, of wonder, on his face stirred some melancholy inside me, so deeply I could barely swallow against it. and we'd been allowed in to see her. What was already a joyous, ecstatic event became something else. Something more. The love I could see in his eyes moved me so.

Joe had been over the moon since. It made me feel tender toward him, more than I could ever remember feeling before, really. I didn't recall feeling this way when our own children were born. I'd been too worried he would drop them.

Annie had told me that Corey came to the hospital every day, though he didn't stay all the time because of his job, because of his other children, because of his wife. I didn't want to think about it, it made me too angry. Joe wouldn't talk about Corey, and I knew he was trying to come to terms with the situation in his own way. But ever since the night Nora was born, I thought I could hear something in Annie's voice that was different, harder, and not just when Corey's name came up. That made me sad. I wanted to ask her about it, but at the right time, not while she was in the hospital recovering.

She was supposed to be discharged tomorrow. A week after her surgery and Nora's birth. For a preemie, Nora was doing well and slowly gaining weight. Most importantly, she was maintaining her body temp.

We hadn't heard what Annie's plans were after leaving the hospital. I had offered to stay at Annie's apartment for as long as she wanted or needed once the wedding weekend was over; I had suggested she could come here, until she was recovered and ready to manage on her own. I hadn't pushed; Annie had been noncommittal. Joe and I had agreed that we needed to support Annie whatever she decided, but it had to be her decision. In the meantime, Joe and I had a wedding to host in two days. That was priority number one for now.

The coffee was ready and I carried the pot over to the island where Joe had gotten spoons out of the drawer, and had even found an old wicker tray in the dining room. Since when did Joe know where things like wicker trays were in this house? I was just reaching for the creamer in the cupboard when the sound of the squeaky hinge of the kitchen door made me and Joe both look up.

"Hi," Annie said, appearing in the doorway. She looked a little bit wan, thinner in the face, and the midsection, a little stooped.

"Annie!" I said. "Sweetheart! How did you get here?"

"Princess!" Joe said.

Behind Annie appeared Father J, carrying a car seat. "We caught a ride home with Father J."

Home. That word didn't escape my notice.

"I try to visit all my parishioners in the hospital. Especially the beautiful ones with beautiful babies. It's just my good fortune that this time, I got to take them home." He was smiling like he'd won a trip to the NCAAs. And the car seat looked practically miniscule in his big freckled hand.

On the wings of angels, I had the random thought.

"I got them to discharge me today. Saved someone a trip to Pittsburgh tomorrow to pick me up. And with all the wedding stuff, I knew everyone would be busy."

"It wasn't going to be a problem to come pick up our baby girls," Joe said.

"But that's great," I said. "Oh, I'm so happy you're here!"

Just then Nora gave a little cry, no more than a whimper, really. "She's hungry. And she needs changed," Annie said, holding in her hand a disposable diaper that was about half the size of a cocktail napkin.

"Let me," Joe said, moving to take the car seat from Father J. And I couldn't help it, I broke into a grin.

"Really? "Annie said.

"Don't look like you've swallowed a diaper pin, Sweetpea. I can change a diaper. You sit down, and as soon as she's changed, you can feed her."

"Nobody uses diaper pins anymore, Dad."

"I know that."

"Speaking of diapers, I brought some." She waved the one in her hand. "But we're going to have to make a run to the store to get more."

"I can do that," Joe said.

"Or, I can," Father J said. "If that would be helpful. I feel invested in the lives of all my parishioners, but Nora is special. I gave her her first car ride. I flashed to the image of Father J's car, an older model white Lincoln Town Car, as long, practically, as the Queen Mary, with bench seats and velour upholstery the color of red wine. A little statue of the Virgin Mother perched on the center of the dashboard. When I'd commented about it once, Father J had grinned, then sung a song about "plastic Jesus." When I'd stared, no doubt open-mouthed—Father J had a rich, smooth baritone, perfectly suited to Latin and hymns—he'd grinned and confessed: Cool Hand Luke. At the time, it had struck me that he was like a male version of that woman who sang on the British Talent Show. He didn't look like a singer. He looked like a little boy in priest clothes. A very tall, very large, red-haired, very freckled boy. Tonight he was wearing a black shirt and his priest collar and a tweedy sport coat.

"I'll go get Annie's bag out of the car," he said.

"Everyone is going to be so surprised to see you. And Nora!" I said, smiling and moving to give Annie a hug, carefully, conscious of the deflated bulge of her belly, and the incision there. Annie smelled like Annie, and foreign at the same time, sharp and medicinal, like hospital smell, though maybe that was only my imagination.

"Mom, if it's okay, I'd just like to change and feed Nora, then head to bed early, and save the welcome home for tomorrow? I don't feel up to a party. I'm wiped out. Besides, I don't want to be the center of attention. It's Jamie and Molly's weekend."

"Well, sure, honey. Dad and I were just getting coffee ready to take out to the patio. If that's what you want..."

"It is." Annie did look tired. But there was also something else in her eyes, a kind of tired that was more than childbirth and major surgery. Something that had to do with Corey? I hugged my daughter again and kissed the top of her head. I could hear Nora begin to cry in the family room.

"We played another game of musical beds after you went to the hospital. Doug moved back to his room, and Jamie's there, now, too, of course. Grammie and Poppy moved to the guest room, and Dad and I moved back down to our room. Your bed has clean sheets and Grammie got it all ready for your next visit. We just weren't sure when that would be...." Joe and I had spent almost a week sharing a bed. So far, the most intimacy that had happened was Joe reaching to hold my hand the first night, and even in the dark, I could feel the uncertainty in it. It had been odd, familiar, and somehow strange at the same time. The next couple of nights, he'd done the same thing. I'd awakened in the mornings facing the wall, my hands unencumbered and no memory of falling asleep, or of any other touching.

Last night, though, Joe had rubbed my back, on top of my paja-mas, while I had been reading before turning out the light. That backrub had been full of portent but he'd never pushed aside my nightshirt, never touched my bare skin, as if he knew that would be too much.

Now, I told Annie, "We can move up to your room tonight, and you can have ours, so you don't have to do the stairs. At least until your incision heals."

"That's okay. I'm supposed to walk. I probably can't carry Nora up or down, at least for a couple of days. But we can stay up there. In my room. If you and Dad don't mind being the baby carrier for a bit."

"Of course we don't mind that! I got the bassinet out of the attic the other day," I smiled at Annie. "You all used that. I cleaned it up and it's in the living room. So we'd be ready for Nora to visit. Dad can take it up to your room."

"Thanks, Mom." Nora had started to squall in earnest now. "I'd better go feed her."

"Okay." I kissed my daughter on the forehead again, feeling like I couldn't touch Annie enough. "I'll come up and check on you before bed. Just text me if you need something before then."

Father J appeared then in the door carrying Annie's overnight bag and another plastic shopping bag full of what appeared to be supplies provided by the hospital. "Father, come in. Joe will take all that stuff upstairs in a bit. What a wonderful surprise! Thank you for bringing our girls home. We weren't sure where Annie was going to go when she left the hospital."

"I gather she's still working out what her life will look like now. Now that Nora is here," Father said, and I understood that he was trying to alleviate my worries, without violating Annie's trust, or breaking her confidence. "I think there's a tentative plan for Doug to move down to the city and stay with her for a while."

"What? Seriously? He hasn't said anything about that!" Just then, there was a burst of laughter from the patio where family and our guests, who would technically be family, too, after Saturday, were waiting for coffee.

"Plans are still *fluid*," he said. "But don't worry. It's going to work out." He winked at me, also whispering. "Have faith."

"Oh. My. Okay. I'm glad she had the chance to spend some time with you, to talk. I have been worried. So thank you, Father. For bringing them home...and everything."

He smiled at me, the kind of smile that was patient and indulgent. I noticed, suddenly, the wrinkles at the corners of his eyes, and was reminded that he was older than he looked. He was going to be one of those men who looked forty for about thirty years. "She's a good kid. You did a good job raising her. Now you have to trust. In her and in Our Father. I know that's not easy."

"She *is* a good kid. Who now has a kid. And the baby's father has...other commitments."

"A family. I know, I know." He smiled again, sadly this time. "She's working it out. Like I said. It's not easy. But pray, Cathleen. Pray and trust."

"Your go-to advice, Father. You should have that on a T-shirt."

He cocked his head. "Hm. That's a great idea. Maybe we can put it on the summer softball league shirts. Our Lady of the Angels on the front, Pray and Trust on the back."

I laughed, suddenly filled with joy. Knowing Annie was in the house, that baby Nora was here, created a warm glow inside me. A kind of happiness that cast its light over everything else. All of my children were home, and my granddaughter, as well.

Chapter 20

"Thanks, Mom! This was perfect." Jamie pulled me into a hug and kissed my cheek.

I could smell alcohol on his breath. There had been beer and other alcohol available all evening. Part of me was worrying about Doug, and watching him like a hawk while trying not to be noticed watching him like a hawk, the other part of me was upstairs helping Annie and Nora get settled. I'd come in to make another pot of decaf. I opened the cupboard to get out a paper filter.

"This is just what Molly and I imagined when we decided to get married here. Having our families hanging out, grilling, playing cornhole. Everything easy and low-key."

"It's been nice having a chance to sit and visit and get to know Molly's family."

"This will make Saturday even nicer because everyone will have met already and won't be all weird. We didn't need a rehearsal dinner. We aren't having a rehearsal. Tonight is just perfect."

I laughed. "No problem. It was my pleasure. Though hopefully we wouldn't have been 'all weird' even if we didn't get to have an evening like this before the actual wedding."

"You know what I mean. Molly's mom is wrapped pretty tight. It's good for her to come here, see how laid back you are, how cool."

"You think I'm cool? No! Don't answer that. I'm just going to pretend you do and call it a win."

"You are cool." He hugged me again. "Love you." He opened the fridge and stood looking inside. "Glad you and Dad worked out whatever was wrong. How sad would that have been if you were getting divorced while your son was getting married?"

I opened my mouth to say something, but I didn't know what to say, so I shut it. Had Joe and I worked out whatever was wrong?

"I mean, I know lots of people are. Split up. Most of my friends' parents are, probably, if I think about it. But not my parents. You and Dad are, like, the poster child for marriage. Poster children?" He looked at me, still hanging on the open fridge door. He was more lubricated than I'd thought.

"What are you looking for?"

"Do we have any pickles?"

"On the door. Have you noticed if your brother is drinking?"

He shrugged. "Iced tea. He's the poster child for iced tea."

"Just iced tea? Are you sure?"

Jamie was still looking for the pickles, moving things around on the shelves and clanking glass jars. He loved dill pickles, especially when he was drinking. "On the door."

"Yeah, I'm sure."

Later, after everyone had left, after the dishwasher was loaded and running quietly, I poured myself the last of the white wine (no point leaving it in the fridge to tempt anyone), and went out the pantry room door to the back yard. I sat for a while on the top step, my usual spot. The night was pleasantly warm.

From here, I couldn't see much but tent, glowing white in the dark, and still smelling faintly of musty canvas, so I moved out to one of the two lounge chairs someone had pulled over to the space between the summer kitchen and the garden. From here, now, I could see the whole of the sky, could see where the darker-than-night tree line of the woods beyond the yard blocked the starlight, could hear crickets and the peepers and the occasional night bird somewhere off in the field.

One of my babies was getting married. Another had spent a couple of hours this afternoon hitting golf balls into the scrub, thinking, I supposed, of the toast he would give in his brother's and his new sister-in-law's honor. It would touch my heart in one of its most secret places, hearing Doug, whatever he devised to say, pay tribute to Jamie, and their relationship, their lives as brothers first, and maybe, maybe, friends, now.

One of my babies—my baby!—had a baby. Upstairs in the room where she'd grown up, where she'd slept for a good part of her life. Now, my grandchild slept there, too. The thought filled me with happiness. Nora. For now, I couldn't think the name without feeling an ache in my chest, without remembering my own Nora. Tears burned at the back of my eyes. No doubt that bearable ache would become something else, another, different emotion. But for now, it was there.

The ticking of the clock of my lifetime seemed suddenly so clear, so unmistakable. This was my life. My children, this place, and now Nora. Could I live somewhere else? Without Joe?

As if I'd conjured him, he appeared. "There you are. What are you doing out here?"

"Drinking the last of the wine. Thinking."

"I was a little worried when I couldn't find you."

"Sorry."

He pulled the other lounge chair close, and arranged himself with a grunt. He sighed and the moonlight reflected off the planes of his face as he looked up. The sky was filled with a million stars. The moon was just a pale sliver, a pinky nail sliver.

"Do you think you'll always be wondering if I'll leave again?"

He rolled his head toward me. I couldn't see his face, or the expression on it, but I could tell he was no longer looking up at the sky. "Will you?"

I took a deep breath, then I looked up at the sky. It was such an incredible thought to know this was the same sky, the same stars, the same moon that people in Charleston were looking at. I closed my eyes. The calm, the peace I'd known there pulled at me, but it was a gentle pull.

"Isn't it crazy to think people in Charleston are looking at these same stars?"

"Yep. And Pittsburgh and Miami and Nova Scotia."

"I loved Charleston." I closed my eyes and remembered the smell of the air there: full of the sea, boxwoods, old brick, sunshine. "It gave me something I needed, that I didn't even know I needed. It fixed me. Or rather, it gave me what I needed so I could fix myself."

"And that was...?"

"I don't know. Maybe just time? Just space? I really don't understand it, not enough to be able to say definitively. I'm sorry."

"I'm sorry that you felt broken. That I broke you."

I wanted to say *I wasn't* broken. *You didn't* break *me*, but that wasn't true. Joe's response, or his lack of response, about Lillian's Cruise when it was first introduced, was the reason I had been so angry. At least it was what had unleashed the anger.

"I know," I said. It struck me suddenly that it truly wasn't Joe's fault: the anger. He hadn't felt the way I'd thought he should feel about the "family only" cruise, but wasn't that on me, not on him? For the same reason I didn't want to tell my in-laws what I thought about them or the cruise—they couldn't "un-ring that bell"—wasn't that true for Joe, too? Was part of the anger I'd felt me having to come to terms with my disappointment in Joe?

"Are you going to leave again?"

The pull of that magic city was like a low-grade thirst. "No. Not like I did. I promise you. I won't leave without telling you ahead of time. Without giving you notice. I promise."

"But you might still leave."

"I want to go back. I know I will go back. I left stuff in the apartment there. I'll have to retrieve that, at least. The lounge cushion rustled as Joe turned his head and again I could see the planes and shadows of his face, could almost feel his reaction.

"You can come with me. We can go together."

Eventually, I saw his head nod. "This is coming up on my busy season. It'll be tough getting away—"

Whatever, I wanted to say. *Your decision.*

"But I'd like that," he said. "Though we have a granddaughter now. You won't want to be too far from her. Not for long, anyway."

"Are you asking or telling me that?"

"Both." I could hear the smile in his voice.

"I know. Another Nora," I said.

We both just watched the sky for a while.

"Why didn't you tell me you bought the cemetery?"

He didn't answer for so long I thought he'd fallen asleep. "I don't know. I didn't want to hurt you. I was afraid it would. I always feel like even mentioning her name causes you pain. It was so awful. When she died. The grief. I thought I might lose you then."

"Lose me?"

"Your grief was so big, it didn't leave any room for me. I wasn't sure there would ever be room for love for me again."

"That was a long time ago. We've had three more children. We have a family. Clearly there was room for you again...."

"Yeah, but I always feel like that pain is still there, just waiting. I didn't know if buying the cemetery would resurrect it. I didn't want to take the chance, so I didn't tell you. I figured I would tell you sometime. When the time was right."

"And you replaced the old fence there."

"Yep. That, too. I did that before I bought it, though. It just seemed like the right thing. The old fence was falling down. More rust than fence."

"I wish you'd told me. I always feel like you've forgotten her. You never mention her; you never go to the cemetery."

I was looking at him, but couldn't see his face now, not the planes or shadows of it. A cloud had obscured the stars momentarily. But I could tell he shrugged. "That's your thing. Yours and Annie's. But I've never forgotten her. I couldn't. She was my daughter, too."

"I wish you would talk about her."

"I wouldn't know what to say."

I sniffed, disappointed, and turned back to watch the cloud sweep past so the stars were visible again. *Say anything! Say everything!* I could feel tears in my eyes but didn't bother to brush them away. Who was there to see in the dark?

After a bit Joe spoke. "I worried that it might cause you pain, that Annie named her baby Nora."

"Not at all. I want to remember her. I need to remember her. I want everyone to remember her."

"I'm sorry. That I didn't tell you about the cemetery."

"Do me a favor? Talk about her?"

"I'd been positive that she was going to be a boy. When you were pregnant? And when you were pregnant with Jamie, I was sure he was going to be a girl."

"You never told me that."

"Telling you now."

Despite myself, I smiled into the dark. I could feel the air on my cheeks where the tears had tracked. "What about Doug?"

"Knew he was a boy."

We were both silent then for a while.

"My knees are killing me," Joe said.

"Arthritis?"

"I suppose. Too much squatting behind home plate."

He'd caught on baseball teams for all the years of his youth. Even intramurals at Penn State. I'd loved to watch him then. He'd played with so much passion. Where Joe was normally so laid back (site him with a post, the boys always said), he'd played baseball as if he was possessed.

"It doesn't seem like that long since we were getting married."

"A banner day."

"Very different from what Saturday promises to be."

"Whaddaya mean?" Joe said.

"Are you kidding? Parents on both sides who are happy and supportive and a bride and groom who are taking vows because they want to, not because one of them is two months along."

"That's not why we got married."

"Who are you and what have you done with the real Joe Daley?"

He ignored that. "We loved each other. We got married because we wanted to be married. Not because you had a bun in the oven."

"Do you really think that?"

"Of course. Don't you?"

"No. I never have. I mean I knew *I* loved *you*. But you were so commitment averse. Before I got pregnant, I wasn't sure you'd ever settle down. With me."

"Oh, babe." Joe's hand snaked over the distance between our chairs and reached around until it found mine. "I wasn't sure about getting married. It scared the shit out of me. Holy God. The responsibility! I was terrified. You, on the other hand, were so confident, so certain, so solid."

"Solid? You thought I was solid?"

"A rock."

"Oh, my God. You really are clueless. I was terrified. And ashamed. And humiliated. My parents made it clear that I'd erred. Your mother..."

"Oooh, my mother. She was terrified about losing me."

"Well that didn't happen. She didn't lose a son. I gained a mother-in-law."

"I was the first to go. That's just gotta be hard for every mother. Don't you have mixed emotions about Jamie and Molly?"

"I feel sad, melancholy really, about what his marriage means in terms of me growing old. But I don't think I feel quite as grasping as your mother has always seemed. I suppose Jamie living a thousand miles away and having a life of his own is a big part of that."

"Well, hell, yes. After we got married, we lived two miles up the road."

"You never really left home."

"Four years at Penn State."

"That's an hour and a half down the road."

"I guess not," he conceded. "Not like Jamie. Or Doug."

"Annie is two hours away."

"Yeah. But she's Annie. Sweetpea. The Princess. She could live on the fucking moon and she'll never not be the Princess.vSeriously. I can't believe you think we wouldn't have gotten married if you weren't pregnant. You never told me that."

"I just assumed you thought that, too."

There was a long moment when neither of us spoke. "You're my life, Cath. I don't know what I'd do without you. Well...actually I do. It sucked. It was fucking awful. You know how Father J is always saying life's a journey? Well you're the only one I want riding shotgun."

I snorted again. My husband was such a romantic.

"I love you. I'm sorry if I don't show it enough. I'm sorry that you didn't know that the day we got married. Which was the best day of my life. Next to the days our kids were born. By that measure, marrying you when you were pregnant made our wedding day a two-fer."

I thought—knew—he was full of shit, but I needed that, needed to hear those words. For some reason, my throat filled with words of my own, so many that I couldn't sort them into language, at least none that he would understand. I squeezed his hand.

"Nice to have Annie and the baby here," he said eventually, filling the silence that was now curiously bright and almost buoyant. His hand was warm and calloused against mine, holding not tightly but not letting go, either. "I still can't believe we're grandparents."

"I'm so glad she came home. I was really worried about her being in her apartment without help."

"She said she told Corey not to come to the wedding."

"What?"

"Yeah. Earlier. When she was feeding the baby. I could tell there was more to the story, but you know how she is. She gets that look on her face..."

"I know the look you mean."

"I figured we'd find out what was going on soon enough. She'll tell us when she's ready. You can lead a horse to water but you can't make Annie do what she's not ready to do. Or tell what she's not ready to tell."

I laughed. "No you can't. Do you think it's over between them? Would we be happy about that?"

"What do you think?"

"I don't know. He's always going to be Nora's father. Even if he and Annie are not together. We want what Annie wants. I want Annie to be happy. To have a man who loves her, who is free to love her. And be with her."

"I know. I want the same thing."

"Father J mentioned that Doug may be moving down to the city, with Annie, to help out. But don't say anything. 'Plans are fluid,' Father said."

"Hmm." Joe said finally, and there was a note of satisfaction in his voice.

"You're glad about that? I thought he was really helping out at the warehouse?"

"He is. But the other day, he was explaining how a lot of what he's been doing, the office side of the business, IT stuff, could be done from anywhere."

"Hmm." I said. "Like from Pittsburgh?"

I felt Joe's shrug though our clasped hands.

"Maybe being needed by his sister and his niece would be a good thing. Maybe he wouldn't drink if he knew he was being depended on."

"Uhhh. Maybe. But we'll figure it out. You think about what grandma name you want to be called?" Joe asked after a while.

"What?" I said. It was so not something Joe would ever give any thought to. It would be months, realistically, before baby Nora would be calling us anything.

"Yeah. You know. Nana. Grammie."

His mother, my mother.

"Those names are taken."

"I know. That's why I asked."

"I can't believe you're thinking about that."

"Why?"

I shrugged. "I don't know. It's just not the kind of thing I think you think about."

"I think about lots of stuff."

Despite myself, I laughed. He was still goofy Joe. The joy at being a grandfather, a grandpa, or a grampie, whatever he decided he wanted to be called, was in his voice. It was kind of surprising, and amusing, that he was so jubilant at having a grandchild. I smiled again, in the dark. He could still make me do that. Make me laugh, or smile. "I'm sure you do," I said.

"Well? What do you want to be? You're too young, and hot, to be a *grandma*. How about Mimi?"

"Mimi?"

"Yeah. I googled grandma names."

"Mimi." I said it again, thinking about hearing it from little mouths, chubby cheeks, big blue eyes looking up at me. "Maybe. I'll think about it."

We sat in silence until someone turned on the light in one of the upstairs bedrooms. One of the boys. At least one of them must be home. I glanced over my shoulder and looked to see if I could glimpse who it was in the bedroom. What time was it? I couldn't see anyone, just the shadow of movement inside.

"He's fine," Joe said, knowing somehow I was thinking about Doug. "And if he's not, we'll deal with it."

I glanced at Joe, though I couldn't see his features, just the paler-than-night shape of his face.

"We can deal with anything." He snorted. "That's all we can do."

I could feel the warmth of Joe's fingers, his thumb rubbing against my hand. He held firmly and there was the sense that he wasn't going to let go, that he was telling me something more than his words were. He was ignoring the fact that I had just spent almost five months in Charleston, without him. That I had left him. In the middle of preparations for the company Christmas party. That was so Joe. *So* Joe. He had moved on, in Joe fashion, and there was something in his voice, in the way he was holding my hand, something uncharacteristically strong. Assertive. It was the way he was, the way he used to be, when he wanted sex. We hadn't had sex since I'd returned from South Carolina. It was the elephant in the room. At least it felt that way to me.

"Not much choice about it, is there?" I said, referring to his comment about Doug.

"That's life, baby doll. Even the things we don't like."

I sniffed, smiled into the dark.

"Are we good?"

The shadow of whoever was in the bedroom upstairs moved across the square of light.

I knew what he was talking about. "We're good. But we're different."

"I love you."

Jamie yelled from the back door then. "Mom? Do we have more pickles?"

www.ingramcontent.com/pod-product-compliance
Lightning Source LLC
Chambersburg PA
CBHW020416030726
47495CB00006B/1536